With This R

D0051448

SUZANNE ENOCH

"Indulge and
be delighted!"
Stephanie Laurens,
author of
All About Love

A Matter
of Scandal

*The Delightfully Romantic
Road to "I Do"*—
SUZANNE ENOCH's
WITH THIS RING Series:

"LIVELY, WITTY,
AND WONDERFULLY
ENTERTAINING."
Stephanie Laurens

"THIS SPARKLING
DUEL OF HEARTS IS A
READER'S DELIGHT."
Romantic Times

EAN

ISBN 0-380-81850-7

9 780380 818501

50599

"IF YOU DON'T
FALL IN LOVE WITH
RAFE BANCROFT,
YOU'RE NOT BREATHING."
Julia Quinn

"You know as well as I that all that nonsense you teach is just to enable your students to marry.

"You, Miss Emma, are a paid matchmaker. And in less polite circles, you would be called worse," Greydon said, torn between irritation and the desire to pull off her ridiculously straitlaced bonnet. "So if you don't wish to pay the increased rent, you can find another location for your school."

Emma lifted her chin. "Are you threatening me?"

"I'm stating facts."

"The *fact*, Your Grace, is that you obviously don't approve of the education of women." With a flounce of her skirt, Emma stalked off down the road.

Greydon watched, admiring the angry sway of her hips. After her bonnet, that dress would be the second thing he removed. Since she was a girls' school headmistress, she probably starched her shift.

The thought was unexpectedly arousing, and he followed her.

"Wickedly funny!
One of my very favorite authors."
Julia Quinn,
An Offer From a Gentleman

SUZANNE ENOCH

A Matter of Scandal

With This Ring

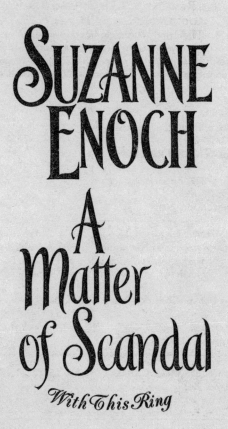

AVON BOOKS

An Imprint of HarperCollinsPublishers

AVON BOOKS
An Imprint of HarperCollins*Publishers*
10 East 53rd Street
New York, New York 10022-5299

Copyright © 2001 by Suzanne Enoch
ISBN: 0-380-81850-7
www.avonromance.com

First Avon Books paperback printing: August 2001

Avon Trademark Reg. U.S. Pat. Off. and in Other Countries, Marca Registrada, Hecho en U.S.A.
HarperCollins ® is a trademark of HarperCollins Publishers Inc.

Printed in the U.S.A.

10 9 8 7 6 5 4 3 2 1

For my cousin, Lennie Scott,
who also likes to quote lines from
The Princess Bride.

I'm so proud of you.

Chapter 1

◦◦◦∞◦◦◦

Visitors never came to west Hampshire during the Season. Not on purpose, anyway.

Thus the three massive coaches bumping down the rutted lane that ran from Westminster to the main road had to be lost. Very lost.

Hiking her brown muslin skirt up a little because of the mud, Emma Grenville hurried into the field at the edge of the road. Expensive-looking vehicles like that weren't liable to turn aside for the headmistress of a girls' school. And they *were* a magnificent sight. Elizabeth and Jane would wish they'd gone walking with her this morning, as she'd encouraged. Three grand coaches gracing west Hampshire in the summertime—who would have thought?

The first vehicle rocked by her without pause, a

1

red dragon and sword emblazoned on the door and the flimsy curtains drawn. *Nobility,* she thought, her curiosity deepening. As the second coach neared, the small, balding driver tipped his hat at her and grinned.

For heaven's sake—she was staring like a milk-maid on her first trip to market. One of the most basic lessons she taught her students was not to stare; she needed to practice following her own teachings. Flushing, Emma continued toward the Academy at a faster pace.

A thunderous crack made her jump and turn around. The second coach lurched with a crooked twist into the air, careening off one of the numerous boulders that had risen after the spring rains. It slammed back onto the road again with an even louder crunch. The near wheel snapped off the axle, hitting the ground a foot from Emma and rolling past her into the tall grass. The vehicle pitched forward and came to a grinding halt in the mud.

"My goodness!" Emma gasped, putting her hand to her heart.

The horses were stomping and snorting, and the driver cursing, as she hurried back to the coach. The flimsy door swung open just as she reached it.

"Damnation, Wycliffe! You and your stupid expeditions!" The well-dressed young man tottered in the doorway, then slipped and fell face first into the muddy road. He very nearly landed on her foot, and Emma hastily stepped backward—and collided with a brick wall.

Not a brick wall, she amended as it grabbed her elbow when she stumbled. "Steady," it said in a deep voice that resonated down her spine, and lifted her upright again.

Emma's surprised shriek caught in her throat as she whipped around. The brick wall was a giant of a man, tall and broad-shouldered and solid. The giant had light green eyes, and they gazed at her from beneath curved aristocratic eyebrows. One of them arched in obvious jaded amusement.

"Perhaps you could move aside."

"Oh." She stumbled sideways, her words catching as her feet slipped again. "Beg pardon." She couldn't recall ever seeing anyone, much less a nobleman, put together in quite so . . . magnificent a fashion.

The devilish handsome giant brushed past her and with one arm heaved the fallen fellow back to his feet. "Injured, Blumton?" he asked.

"No, I'm not injured, but look at me! I'm a bloody mess!"

"So you are. Get away before you fling mud on me." The giant gestured at the edge of the road.

"But—"

"Oh, Grey!"

A woman appeared in the coach's doorway and collapsed artfully into her rescuer's arms. Long blond tresses, several shades lighter than the giant's wind-ruffled, honey-colored hair, had come loose from their clips. Her curls spilled over his arm in a golden cascade as he held her close against his chest.

"Excellent aim, Alice." Apparently unmoved by her unconscious state, he made as though to drop his burden in the muddy road.

Emma stepped forward. "Sir, you cannot mean to—"

Alice recovered instantly and flung her arms around his neck. "Don't you dare, Wycliffe! It's filthy!"

"That's not likely to convince me to continue hauling you about. I'm standing in it, and so is this chatty female."

"Chatty?" Emma repeated, scowling. Handsome or not, his manners were obviously lacking, and as she taught her students, manners were the first measure of a gentleman.

A second female pulled herself up to the door of the coach. "Oh, let him go, Alice, and give someone else a chance."

"I'll rescue you, Sylvia," the muddy gentleman stated, slogging back toward the coach and lifting his arms.

"After you've been wallowing in the mud? Don't be absurd, Charles. Grey, if you please?"

Emma started to say that if they would all just relocate to the edge of the road, they would find the ground much drier, but as they were nobles and nobles seemed to thrive on such silliness, she folded her arms and watched. *Chatty female—ha.*

Grey, as the ladies were calling him, seemed an odd nickname for such a powerful-looking, golden male. "Lion," or something equally dangerous sounding, would have been a better fit.

He scowled at the other female. "I can't carry everyone."

"Well, I refuse to be rescued by Cousin Charles."

A low-pitched sigh sounded several feet behind Emma. At the edge of the road, on the one nice, dry strip of soil, another nobleman stood gazing at the scene. His hands were in his pockets, and his light blue eyes twinkled despite the look of horrified affront on his lean, handsome face.

"Gads, I suppose that leaves me," he drawled, eyeing the sodden roadway with distaste.

Sylvia's lips tightened. "I would prefer n—"

"Yes, it does, Tristan," the larger man snapped. "Quit tiptoeing about and get over here."

"I will expect you to purchase me a new pair of boots, Wycliffe."

As the dark-haired Tristan trod toward them, Emma gazed at the giant again. The name Wycliffe tickled at the back of her mind, but she couldn't quite place it.

She had friends who had left the Academy in years past and married well, and she supposed one of them might have mentioned the name. Certainly she'd never set eyes on him before. Contented spinster and firmly on the shelf though she was, he was handsome enough that she would have felt herself remiss not to notice. Splendid gentlemen hardly ever came driving along this road.

As though remembering her presence, he faced her again, and Emma couldn't help blushing at her unscholarly thoughts.

"If you're intent on witnessing this idiocy, girl," he rumbled, "at least make yourself useful. Go watch the horses while Simmons has the other coaches brought up."

No man spoke to the headmistress of a reputable girls' school in that tone. "I am hardly a girl, sir," she said crisply, "and since no one appears to be injured, which was my reason for approaching, I have better things to do than wade through mud you people are too silly to get out of." She turned around and picked her way back to the edge of the road. "Good day."

"What cheek," the mud-covered Charles sniffed.

"Serves you right, Wycliffe," Tristan's deeper voice said. "You can't bully everyone into doing your bidding."

"I suppose we can't expect the peasantry to recognize their betters," Sylvia added from her precarious perch in the coach's doorway.

Although Emma wanted to point out that "peasantry" was an archaic term, given the current state of economic growth and industrial advances, she kept walking. They could deuced well wallow in their own ignorance and in the thick Hampshire mud, for all she cared.

By the time they sorted out who would continue on to Haverly Manor in which carriages, Greydon Brakenridge, the Duke of Wycliffe, was beginning to wish he'd simply walked down the road with that odd chit. On foot, he would already have been at his uncle's estate and tilting a blessedly strong glass of whiskey down his throat.

"They grow the girls pretty in Hampshire," mused Tristan Carroway, Viscount Dare, as he took his seat in the lead coach.

Greydon glanced at him. "She was soft-headed."

"You think everyone is soft-headed. She told you off well enough."

"She was rude." Alice sat as close to Wycliffe as she could, ostensibly so he could catch her if she happened to faint again. In the closed, stuffy coach, it was nearly suffocating. Thank God Sylvia had opted to ride with her maid. "I suspect everyone in this godforsaken wilderness will be quite as barbaric." She shuddered.

Tristan snorted. "This is Hampshire—not Africa."

"As if one could tell from that encounter."

Ignoring the argument, Grey pulled back the curtain on his side of the coach, hoping for a breeze as he slouched to gaze out the small window. That girl on the road had been an odd little thing, more well spoken than he'd expected, with large, hazel eyes in a pert oval face, capped by an absurdly proper bonnet. He would have to ask Uncle Dennis or Aunt Regina if they knew who she was.

Greydon sighed. He'd seen Dennis and Regina Hawthorne, the Earl and Countess of Haverly, less often than he should have over the years, and even more infrequently in the last few since he'd inherited the dukedom. The unexpected invitation to Hampshire had been well timed for several reasons, yet it was troubling. He couldn't think of many reasons why Dennis would want him at Haverly in the middle of the London Season, but the most likely one would seem to be money.

"What did you say the nearest town was, Grey?" Tristan asked, fanning himself with his hat as he viewed the green countryside through the window.

"Basingstoke."

"Basingstoke. I'll have to visit."

Grey eyed him. "Why?"

The viscount flashed him a grin. "If you didn't notice, don't expect me to point out the details."

He *had* noticed, which bothered him. If there was one thing he didn't need more of, it was female entanglements. "Have at it, Tris, if it'll keep you from annoying me."

"A fine thing to say to a guest."

"You aren't my guest. In fact, I don't recall inviting any of you."

Alice laughed. "London would have been a hopeless bore without you there, Your Grace." She leaned closer. If he'd been a more moveable object, her attentions would have pushed him out the door of the carriage. "And I promise to keep you entertained here."

Tristan sat forward, placing a hand on Greydon's knee. "And so do I, Your Grace."

"Oh, get off."

"Get away, Dare," Alice complained. "You'll ruin everything."

"Don't forget, *I* was the one in the coach with Grey. You were behind us, with Sylvia and Blum—"

"Try arguing in pantomime for a bit, please." Grey folded his arms over his chest and closed his eyes. He really didn't mind having Tristan about. Besides owing the viscount a large favor for rescuing him from the claws of a particularly predatory female, he'd known Tris since before university—and Hampshire during the Season didn't have much native entertainment to offer.

Alice would have been tolerable as well, if she hadn't decided to view him as marriage material—as if he had any intention of marrying anyone after his narrow escape from Lady Caroline Sheffield. Alice apparently didn't believe the depth of his convictions, though, because every time she'd ended up in his bed over the past few weeks, she seemed to want to talk about jewelry—rings, in particular. And Alice wasn't the only female hunting him, so fleeing to Hampshire for a week or two had been an irresistible opportunity.

"Isn't that Haverly?" Tristan asked.

Grey opened his eyes. "That's it."

He'd always been fond of his uncle's old estate. A profusion of green vines crept up toward the windows, which reflected onto the glassy surface of the pond that nestled at the foot of the long, sloping hill. Swans and ducks swam at the edge of the water, while grazing sheep dotted the park on either side of the wide, curving front drive, lending the whole scene a sense of pastoral paradise, the very model for a Gainsborough painting.

"Everything looks well," he mused.

"You were expecting something ill?" Tristan sat forward to get a better look.

Cursing at himself for whetting Dare's bottomless curiosity, Grey assumed a relaxed pose. "I wasn't expecting anything. The invitation to visit surprised me, is all, and I'm relieved everything looks to be in order."

"I think it's quaint." Alice leaned across his arm, pressing her ample bosom against him. "How far is Basingstoke, did you say?"

"I didn't. Two miles or so."

"And the nearest neighbors?"

"Are you planning to be social?" Tristan gave a slight grin. "Or are you scouting out the nearest female competition?"

"I am being social, something you obviously need to practice," she complained.

"That's what I'm attempting at this very moment, my dear."

Grey shut his eyes again, his temple throbbing, as the two of them resumed their sparring. The trip to Haverly should have been a pleasant and peaceful diversion. He hadn't counted on his troubles accompanying him to Hampshire.

Once Alice had discovered his plans, though, she had promptly told everyone occupying his box at Vauxhall Gardens. Short of killing them, the only viable alternative had been swearing them all to secrecy and suggesting they come along.

"Grey, aren't you going to defend me?" Alice demanded.

He opened one eye. "It was your idea to come to Hampshire. Fend for yourself."

Usually he liked a good argument as well as anyone, and a good challenge even more. The former, however, had begun to seem pointless, and the latter nonexistent. He was the bloody Duke of Wycliffe: anything he wanted was within easy grasp, and *more* than he wanted was pushed at him relentlessly. Lately he seemed to spend more time evading trouble than seeking it out. So much for the excitement of one's reckless youth.

The coach rolled to a stop. Quelling the urge to leap out and escape into the beech forest, Greydon waited until Hobbes, Haverly's butler, pulled open the carriage door.

"Your Grace," he said in his worn, gravel-rough voice. "Welcome back to Haverly."

"Thank you, Hobbes." He stepped down, turning to offer Alice his hand. "We lost a coach about a mile back. You'll need to send a smith and probably a new wheel. I left Simmons and half the servants behind with the horses."

"I'll see to it at once, Your Grace. I trust there were no injuries?"

"My clothes will have to be put down," Blumton said, as he climbed down from beside the driver. "Thank you so much for making me bake out in the sun. I feel like a brick."

"You look like one," Tristan said helpfully. "There's always the pond."

A look of horror crossing his face, the dandy backed toward the manor. "Just keep your distance, Dare."

"Oh, shut up, Charles." Lady Sylvia swished up from the rear coach. "You prattle more than anyone I know, Cousin. You should have heard him all morning. Prattle, prattle, prattle."

"Hm." Grey turned to lead the way to the wide oak front doors of Haverly. "You weren't recommending that Parliament be disbanded again, were you, Blumton?"

"Of course not. I only pointed out that limiting the power of the king limits the power of the country."

Tristan opened his mouth, but Sylvia put her dainty hand over it. "No. You will not encourage him. I've been listening to it since we left London. Next time, I get to ride with Gr—"

"Greydon!"

Dennis Hawthorne, the Earl of Haverly, strode around the side of the house. His round face bore a wide grin, and he clapped his hands as he approached. Yet even as he was smiling, lines of worry creased his forehead, and his eyes seemed disturbingly somber. Grey went forward to meet him, revising his earlier assessment. Something was definitely wrong.

"Uncle Dennis," he said, allowing the shorter man to pull him into a sound embrace. "You look well."

"As do you, my boy. Introduce me to your friends. I know Dare, of course."

Tristan stuck out his hand. "Thank you for the invitation, Haverly. His Grace was wasting away in London."

"Eh?" Dennis looked up at his nephew, his brow furrowed. "Not taken ill, are you, lad?"

Only Uncle Dennis called him "lad" any longer. "Hardly," he said dryly, sending Tristan a warning glance. "Just getting older. Uncle, allow me to present Lady Sylvia Kincaid and Miss Boswell. And the mud hen is Sylvia's cousin, Lord Charles Blumton."

"Welcome to all of you," the earl said, bowing and shaking hands. "I hope you don't find Hampshire too rustic. We're not London, but we do have our diversions."

"Like what?" Alice asked, eyeing Greydon from beneath her lashes.

"Well, Haverly is host to a picnic, almost a fair, every August. And Thursday, the Academy will be presenting *Romeo and Juliet.*"

Charles's expression brightened. "Academy? Which Academy?"

Greydon scowled as he realized he'd landed squarely in the middle of enemy territory. "Good God. The damned Academy. I'd nearly forgotten about that blight on the landscape."

"That's hardly fair," his uncle returned, gesturing them toward the front entry. "Miss Grenville's Academy is a finishing school for young ladies of breeding, Lord Charles. It stands on Haverly land."

"A girls' school?" Charles looked as though he'd swallowed something bitter. "I take it then, Wycliffe, that you also disapprove of the education of females?"

Grey sidestepped his muddy companion and strolled into the manor. "I have no problem with the education of women," he said over his shoulder. "I've just never seen it done properly."

"Don't be a beast, Wycliffe," Lady Sylvia cooed. "I attended a finishing school."

"And what did you learn?" he asked, scowling as Dare mumbled a curse. They should have known better than to bring it up. "Oh, yes. You learned to say whatever I want to hear. And to follow the tradition of becoming clinging, helpless—"

"So I suppose we're not going to be attending the performance?" Tristan interrupted, following him inside.

"Only if you kill me first and drag my rotting carcass along with you."

Chapter 2

Aunt Regina took charge of assigning the guests their various bed chambers and of having a bath drawn for Blumton. If she had any suspicions regarding Alice or Sylvia's presence, she didn't voice them. The entire family was familiar with his late father's proclivity for carting mistresses about with him, so she probably expected it of his son, as well.

But Greydon had more significant things to worry about than his aunt's reaction to his companions. He dropped into Dennis's padded desk chair, noting that the stitching was beginning to come loose on one side. "All right. What is it, Uncle?"

Dennis Hawthorne circled the small room a few times and ended up leaning on the back of the opposite chair. "You might at least do me the courtesy of thinking we—I—invited you to Haverly because I haven't seen you in four years."

"Has it been that long?"

"Yes, it has been. And I do miss you, lad. I'm glad you brought friends along. I presume that means you intend to stay awhile this time?"

"That depends on you, I suppose." And on how long he could hide out from the London hounds. "Why am I here?"

With a heavy sigh, the earl sat. "Money."

Sometimes, it would be pleasant to be wrong, Grey thought. "How much?"

Dennis gestured at the tattered ledger book beneath Grey's left elbow. "It's . . . not good. I should have sent for assistance sooner, but until the spring crop came in, I thought . . . well, you'd best take a look."

Unpaid invoices marked the page of the most recent entries. Grey owned and managed several sizable properties and the two town houses in London, and it took only a moment of perusal to realize that Uncle Dennis was correct. "Good God," he muttered. "It's a wonder you haven't been dragged off to Old Bailey for unpaid debts."

"I know, I know. I didn't—"

"How could you let this happen?"

Dennis's ruddy cheeks darkened further. "It didn't happen overnight, you know. It just seemed to . . . creep up on me. Prentiss—you know him—took ill last year. Rather than replace the old fellow, I started doing the books myself. That's when I began to realize that my manager might not have been entirely . . . diligent in apprising me about the state of things."

"Prentiss should be shot for negligence," Grey snarled, flipping backward through the pages. "And so should you be, for trusting that doddering old—"

"That's enough of that, boy."

Grey looked up at him. "I am four and thirty, Uncle. Please do not call me 'boy.'"

"Seems to me by that age you might have learned to spare a body's feelings."

With a sigh of his own, Grey closed the ledger. "I don't suffer fools gladly, if that's what you mean."

"You can't help being your father's son, I suppose."

Anger began curling up Grey's spine. "I've been hearing that a lot, lately. I'll take it as a compliment, since I'm sure that's how you meant it. Now. Once again, why am I here?"

Dennis cleared his throat. "Right. Best not to annoy the lion when you're about to stick your hand in its jaws, I suppose."

Grey sat looking at him.

"Oh, all right. I know you could afford to buy Haverly, or to pay off every debt I have hanging over my head."

"Yes, I cou—"

"But I don't want you to do that. I've owned this estate for thirty years, and it's been in the Hawthorne family for the last three hundred. I've only had trouble over the last season or two."

"At least," Grey muttered.

"Help me get Haverly back on its feet. I need a plan."

"You need a miracle."

"Greydon!"

Taking a deep breath, Grey stifled his annoyance at the shoddy accounting and carelessness which had led up to the present disaster, and at the realization that his escape from his responsibilities was going to be mired in invoices and numbers and too damned much time behind a desk. "I'll need to look at everything."

His uncle relaxed a little. "Of course. I must have the final say, but I shall put Haverly into your capable hands." He stood and began pacing again. "I'm sorry to drag you out of London, but I really didn't know what else to do."

"That's all right." He shifted in the chair, hearing it squeak in protest. "London was becoming a bit crowded for me, anyway."

Dennis grinned for the first time since they'd begun their meeting. "Your mother, eh?"

"Among other things." *Mostly of the female persuasion.* "How did you manage to grow up with her and avoid having her marry you off?"

"Believe me, she tried. Practically had me engaged to the local parson's daughter when I was eight. I daresay if I hadn't offered for Regina when I did, Frederica would have set the hounds on me."

"Well, my heels are chewed bloody this Season." His uncle's expression grew curious, but Grey had no intention of providing any further details. He opened the accounts book again. "Are these your current tenants?"

"Yes."

"And where are the rental amounts you charge?"

Dennis pointed at the notations. "Right there."

Grey blinked, not certain he was seeing

straight. "These are the rents you're charging now. Today." At his uncle's nod, he looked at them again. "When was the last time you raised the rent? At the turn of the century?"

"I thought Haverly was in good condition, remember?" the earl answered, his tone defensive.

"The first thing you're going to do is dismiss Prentiss."

"But—"

"Provide him with a pension if you want, but he is *not* to set foot on Haverly land again. And the second thing you're going to do is raise the damned rents."

"The tenants won't like it."

"And you won't like debtors' prison, Uncle Dennis. Raise the rent."

"But it's tradition!"

"Jane, if we went by tradition, *all* the roles would be played by men." Emma Grenville folded her hands in her lap, torn between pulling out her hair and laughing. "Being that this is a girls' school, that would leave the stage rather bare of performers."

"But I don't want to kiss Mary Mawgry! She giggles!"

Emma glanced at the group of young ladies standing at the far end of the stage, practicing their swordplay and wisely keeping their distance from Lady Jane Wydon's rare bout of foul temper. "Then perhaps we should find you a part that doesn't require kissing," she said in the cool, logical tone all of her students had quickly learned to dread.

"Jane could play the fat old nurse," Elizabeth

Newcombe, the youngest of her pupils, suggested from the edge of the crowd. "Nurse doesn't have to kiss anybody."

"Lizzy Newcombe, you be quiet! I am *not*—"

"*I* am playing the fat old nurse," Emma interrupted, stifling a grin, "so none of you will have to do it."

"But I know Freddie Mayburne would do a bang-up job as Romeo," Jane persisted.

That didn't bode well. Emma hoped Jane didn't speak from firsthand experience, or she was going to have to start double-locking the front gate and posting guards at each entrance. "First of all, Lady Jane Wydon," Emma said in her firmest tone, "we do not use slang or vulgarisms at the Academy. You know that. Please revise your statement."

Jane flushed to the roots of her raven black hair, even her blush becoming. "Freddie Mayburne would be splendid as Romeo," she amended.

"Yes, I'm sure he would be. But this school is for young ladies, not for Freddie Mayburne. And my task with this play is to teach you poise, confidence, and diction. Not him."

"Besides," Elizabeth chimed in again, "Mary Mawgry's been practicing for weeks, and so have I. And I don't want to play Mercutio if Freddie Mayburne is going to be Romeo. He smells funny."

"He does not! It's a very fashionable French cologne."

They all seemed far too familiar with Freddie Mayburne. Clapping her hands together for attention, Emma rose. "No one is changing roles. Jane, if you wish to earn Mr. Mayburne's—or anyone else's—admiration, you would best do so by excelling at the task at hand."

Jane's shoulders sagged. "Yes, Miss Emma."

"All right. Why don't we go through the Capulet party, Act 1, Scene V, once more, and then we'll go to luncheon."

"At least I don't have to kiss Mary in that scene," Jane muttered, and with a flounce of her skirts, she returned to the stage.

Emma seated herself in the second pew of the old monastery's church. Once they'd removed the rather oppressive-looking apostles lining one wall, the large room had converted quite nicely into a lecture hall and theater.

The girls not attending the Capulet ball took seats around her. "Begin," she called, gesturing at Miss Perchase, who was in charge of the stage curtains, as well as Latin and crochet.

"Miss Emma," Elizabeth Newcombe whispered, turning around on the front pew to face her, "tell us about the carriages."

"Not during a rehearsal. Face front, bottom on the seat, miss. Show courtesy and respect for your fellow students, and they will do the same for you."

Elizabeth rolled her eyes, but complied. "You'll never tell us anything, anyway," she muttered.

"Proper ladies don't gossip," Emma returned.

"At least tell us if they were handsome," Julia Potwin urged from the seat behind her.

Cynical green eyes glittered in her mind. "I didn't notice," she hedged. "And what is more important than outward appearance, anyway?"

"Money," Henrietta Brendale said, eliciting a chorus of hushed giggles.

"Henrietta."

The pretty brunette sighed and resumed playing with a strand of her long hair. "Inward integrity."

"But isn't—"

"No, Mary," Emma called toward the stage, standing. "It's 'as a rich jewel in an *Ethiop's* ear'—not an 'antelope's ear.' "

" 'Antelope' sounds more poetical."

"Yes, my dear, but Mr. Shakespeare decided to use 'Ethiop.' "

"All right."

Mary repeated the line correctly, and Emma sat again. Since yesterday, those green eyes had taken up a preposterous amount of time better spent on rehearsals and budgets and organizing summer curriculums. No one in the area had heard a whisper about Haverly's guests, or about the golden lion in particular, and she hadn't been successful in conjuring a reason to go visit Lord and Lady Haverly and find out about them. It was too silly, anyway—she'd never indulged in such delicious, shivery daydreams even as a young girl. Hopefully she wasn't going to become soft-headed before she turned twenty-six.

A tap on her shoulder made her jump. "Yes, Molly?" she asked, turning in her seat.

The maid handed her a note. "Tobias said Lord Haverly sent this."

Emma took the paper, that same ridiculous feeling of anticipation running through her again. Trying not to appear as though she was hurrying, she opened the missive and read it—and her heart began thumping even faster. "Hm. It seems Lord Haverly would like to see me as soon as possible."

"Ooh! Maybe you're to meet his guests!" Elizabeth popped up over the back of the seat again.

"Lord Haverly and I often converse on various matters concerning the Academy. I shan't speculate." She rose again. "Miss Perchase?"

"Yes, Miss Emma?" The Latin instructor poked her head around the edge of the curtains.

"Please take Nurse's lines for me, through the end of the Act."

"Me?"

Emma made her way to the back of the small auditorium. "Yes. I need to call on Haverly. Molly, have Tobias saddle Pimpernel."

"Yes, Miss Emma."

As she went upstairs to change into her riding habit, Emma's heady excitement continued to grow, and she tried to combat the giddiness with logic. He—*they*—probably wouldn't even be at the manor house. On a day this fine, she certainly wouldn't stay cooped up inside if duty didn't require it.

Out in the yard, Tobias Foster, the Academy's stable hand and jack-of-all-trades, handed her up into the saddle. With a cluck to the sorrel mare, Emma set off down the road toward Haverly.

Even before the earl's visitors had arrived, she'd intended to call at Haverly. The Academy's stable roof needed mending, and so did the ivy-covered wall bordering the north end of the property. The school could afford the repairs, but she would rather use the funds elsewhere. As landlord, Lord Haverly had offered to help her with such costs in the past, and she wanted to ask if he would at least stable the school's five horses until the roof work could be completed.

When she reached the manor she left Pimpernel with a groom and went around the front of the house, climbing the shallow steps of the main entry. The butler opened the door before she reached it, and she smiled at him.

"How do you do that, Hobbes?"

He stepped aside so she could enter the cool, high-ceilinged foyer. "I have very sharp hearing, Miss Emma."

"I see."

His stern face cracked into a half smile. "And you were expected."

Except for a few servants passing through the hallway, Haverly seemed quiet and deserted. A small, guilty twinge of disappointment soured Emma's mood as she followed Hobbes to the earl's small office. She always enjoyed chatting with both Lord and Lady Haverly, she reminded herself. The guests and their whereabouts didn't matter. While the butler went to find the earl, she wandered over to the window.

The white pieces of the chess set on the table there had advanced by one, and after a moment's study she shifted her black bishop. She and the earl had been playing the same game for almost two months, another indication that she needed to visit more often.

"Emma."

She turned as the earl hurried into the room to take her hand. His color seemed high, and she abruptly wondered why he had needed to see her so urgently. "My lord. I hope all is well with you and Lady Haverly?"

"Oh, yes. Fine, fine. I didn't mean to take you away from your students."

"We were rehearsing *Romeo and Juliet*. I don't think anyone will miss me."

His smile, before always warm and open, seemed to have developed a tic. "I find that difficult to believe. But take a seat, if you please. I . . . need to discuss something with you."

Emma seated herself before the desk and folded her hands in her lap. "I was glad you sent for me, actually. It's been too long since we've chatted, and I wanted your opinion on something."

The earl cleared his throat. "Well. Ladies first, then."

Something was definitely going on. As she'd taught her students, though, one didn't pry. "All right. You know my aunt began restoration and repairs on the various parts of the Academy that were beginning to show their age. In the two years since Aunt Penelope passed away, though, I'm afraid I haven't kept up the project as I should have."

"You can't blame yourself for that. I know how busy you've been, my dear. Taking on the running of the Academy at the age of three and twenty wasn't easy on you, and you can't convince me otherwise."

She smiled. "Thank you. Even so, it would be decidedly unwise to wait much longer. The stable roof is a sieve, and I'm afraid the north wall might collapse in the next strong wind. So, I was wondering whether you were still willing to consid—"

He stood, the speed of the movement startling her. "Speaking of your aunt," Haverly rushed, striding around the desk and sitting again, "I'm— I'm going to have to raise the Academy's rent."

He pushed a paper toward her. "Here are the calculations and the terms. If you'll sign at the bottom, we can conclude this as painlessly as possible, and then we can have some apple tarts in the garden. I know you like apple tarts. Regina had Mrs. Muldoon bake them especially for you."

Emma looked at him. The earl seemed utterly serious, and yet . . . she forced a laugh. "My goodness. If you keep this silliness up, I shall have to make you pay a shilling to see our play."

"It's . . . well, it's not silliness, Emma. I hate to do it, but it's become unavoidable."

Emma glanced down at the paper he'd placed in front of her. Her heart skipped a beat as she read through the figures and the precise, legal-sounding terms. "This is *triple* what the Academy's been paying."

"Yes, I know, but I haven't increased the rent in . . . in a very long time."

She shot to her feet. "That is certainly not my fault!"

His ruddy complexion darkened. "Now, now," he said, patting the top of the desk, "I know that. Calm yourself, Emma. Please."

Emma forced herself to sit again, despite an unladylike urge to throw something. "You and my aunt, and you and I, have had a very cordial relationship. I consider you a dear friend, Lord Haverly."

"And I you," he returned in a soothing tone. "This is not personal, I assure you. If it makes you feel any better, Wycliffe has had me increase the rent of all my tenants. Everyone's been quite understanding."

So this was that Wycliffe person's idea. Handsome

or not, Emma decided that she didn't like the golden lion at all. Not one whit. "If your other tenants are paying you more, there's very little reason for the Academy to do so," she said, trying for her calmest tone. She was very logical; everyone always told her that was her strongest suit. "We are an institution of learning. Surely for that reason alone the Academy deserves special consideration."

A muscle in his round cheek twitched again. "Well, I—"

"And Miss Grenville's Academy has earned a fine reputation for itself in London," she continued quickly. Overwhelming him with facts seemed her best chance. "Just in the last two years, we've seen our graduates marry a marquis, two earls, and a baron. That can only reflect well on you, as our landlord. We could never have fared so well under some harsh dictator's hand."

"I'm hardly a dictator, Emma."

She smiled, squeezing his hand. "No, you aren't. You are very kind, and helpful, and understanding. Which is why I won't press you any further than to ask that Haverly take in the Academy's horses while we repair the stable roof. I hope that is agreeable—and I won't ask you for anything more."

"I—no, that's—that's not a problem. Of course."

The earl looked befuddled, which Emma took as her cue to retreat with as much speed as she could manage. She needed to think up a strategy before Haverly's new rent ruined her plans for the Academy. She stood, nodding. "Thank you, my lord. I trust I'll see you and Lady Haverly on Thursday evening, for *Romeo and Juliet?*"

"Ah, yes. Yes."

Hardly daring to breathe, Emma escaped out of the office, down the hall, and through the front door with no one calling her back to empty all of the change out of her pockets. This was a disaster. Worse than a disaster. The groom was nowhere in sight to help her into the saddle, so she grabbed Pimpernel from a pen and led the mare back toward the Academy as swiftly as she could. Her tactics, though not the most scrupulous, would at least give her until Thursday to come up with a way of countering this Wycliffe person's idiocy.

At the sound of the front door closing, Greydon set aside the Hampshire planting almanac he'd been reading and rose. He could sympathize with his uncle's reluctance to increase the rent of Haverly's tenants, in all instances but one. A finishing school for females—bah. They might as well have named it the *How to Trap a Husband* Academy. He could vouch for how successful the damned establishment was; Caroline had attended it, and she'd nearly gotten the wedding shackles locked around his neck.

He'd left the library door open, hoping to hear the exchange between Miss Grenville and Uncle Dennis, but they'd managed to keep it fairly civilized, and he'd only discerned an occasional murmur of raised voices.

Dare and the others had deserted Haverly for the day, ostensibly to tour Basingstoke and the surrounding countryside. He knew better, though; Tristan had gone looking for the pert miss from the roadside. He wouldn't have minded running across her himself, and he added the lost opportunity to his list of Miss Grenville's faults. Crossing the hallway, he rapped on the office door and strolled inside. "I assume your news displeased the old spinster?" he asked, unable to keep the satisfaction out of his voice.

The earl stood by the window, gazing into the garden. "You don't need to enjoy it so much," he grumbled.

"You're a better man than I am." Grey joined him, shifting a white pawn on the chess board to counter his uncle's move. "Nevertheless, being compassionate won't save Haverly. Did you schedule the payments?"

Dennis frowned. "No. I—" He stopped, and to Greydon's surprise, chuckled. "Outmaneuvered me, she did. Outsmarted me, really."

"What are you talking about?" With a scowl of his own, Grey strode to the desk and grabbed the agreement he'd painstakingly drafted last evening. "She didn't sign," he said unnecessarily. He glared at his uncle. "Why didn't she sign?"

"I believe it was because she was more concerned with having me board the Academy's horses while she repairs the stable roof."

"Damnation! Haverly's not entailed, Uncle. And I doubt the rich merchant you end up having to sell to will be as generous with his tenants as you've been," Greydon growled.

"She makes a good argument."

"I don't care. You would allow a *female* to bring your estate to ruin?"

"It's not as desperate as—"

"It will be, if you allow this to continue!" Folding the paperwork, he jammed it into his pocket. "*I* won't allow this to continue."

He strode out of the office. A barked inquiry to Hobbes informed him that the headmistress had arrived on horseback, so he commandeered one of his uncle's mounts and went after her.

She had apparently decided to take the morning to savor her victory, because he caught up to her less than a mile from the manor, on foot and leading a small sorrel mare.

"Miss Grenville!" he bellowed, charging up behind her on his uncle's big bay gelding, Cornwall.

She jumped, spinning around to face him with one hand to her breast. And Greydon forgot what he'd been about to say.

Large hazel eyes, wide and startled, gazed up at him, and her soft, full lips formed a perfect, soundless *oh*. The chit from the roadside. The one he hadn't been able to get out of his thoughts. The one Tristan had gone into Basingstoke this morning to find.

"*You're* Miss Grenville?"

The *oh* snapped into an annoyed line. "I am Miss Emma Grenville. Miss Grenville was my aunt."

Was. "You're the headmistress of that blasted Academy."

It wasn't a question, but she nodded anyway. "Yes. And thank you for your condolences about Aunt Patricia."

Grey narrowed his eyes. He had no damned intention of being chastised by a chit who looked barely out of the schoolroom. "You're just . . . a girl. You can't be old enough to—"

One fine eyebrow lifted, mocking him. "I am

five and twenty—a grown woman, by any definition. I suppose, though, that you didn't charge
out here to inquire after my age. Or did you, sir?"

"Your Grace," he corrected.

The surprised look came into her eyes again.
She should never play cards, he thought abruptly.
He could read her from a mile away.

"You're a duke," she said dubiously.

He nodded. "Wycliffe."

Miss Emma Grenville stared up at him for another moment, while an absurd feeling of triumph ran through Grey. He'd found her, and
Tristan hadn't. She was his. As he had the first
time he'd set eyes on her, he knew precisely what
he wanted to do with her. And it would involve
silk sheets and naked skin.

"Wycliffe," she mused. "Greydon Brakenridge.
One of my friends spoke of you."

"Which friend?" He doubted any of a glorified
governess's friends would be acquainted with
him.

"Lady Victoria Fontaine." She revised that. "I
mean Victoria, Lady Althorpe."

"The Vixen?"

She must have heard the disbelief in his voice,
because she put her hands on her hips. "Yes,
Vixen."

"And what did the Vixen say about me?"

A touch of amusement entered her eyes. "She
said you were arrogant. Now, I'm pleased to have
made your acquaintance, Your Grace, but I do
have a class waiting for me. Good day." She
walked on.

"You didn't sign my uncle's rental agreement."

She stopped, then looked up at him again from

beneath the brim of her prim green bonnet. "That matter, Your Grace, is between Lord Haverly and myself."

His towering over her didn't seem to be intimidating her in the least, but it was making him feel like a bully. Grey swung out of the saddle. "If you don't wish to pay the increased rent," he continued, torn between irritation at her statement about his arrogance and the desire to untie the green bow under her chin and pull off that ridiculously strait-laced bonnet, "you can find another location for your school."

The petite headmistress lifted her chin. "Did Lord Haverly ask you to ride me down and threaten me?"

Somehow this wasn't going quite the way he'd envisioned. "I'm stating facts."

"Hm. The *fact*, Your Grace, is that you obviously don't approve of the education of women. The *fact* is, Haverly belongs to Dennis Hawthorne, and I will conduct any and all negotiations with him. If you'll excuse me."

With a flounce of her green riding skirt, she stalked off down the road again. Grey watched for a moment, admiring the angry sway of her hips. After her bonnet, her dress would be the second thing he removed. A girls' school headmistress. She probably starched her shift. The thought had the unexpected result of arousing him, and he tugged on Cornwall's reins to follow her.

"For your information, I *do* approve of educating females."

She kept walking. "How wonderfully condescending, Your Grace."

Greydon swore under his breath. "Your

Academy," he continued, trying to maintain a grip on his temper and his damned unexpected lust, "doesn't educate females."

That got her attention. She faced him, folding her arms across her small, pert bosom. "I beg your pardon?"

Her breasts were just the right size to fit a man's hands. His hands. "Correct me if I'm wrong, but—"

"Oh, I intend to."

"—But you instruct your students in etiquette, do you not?" He didn't wait for an answer. "And dance? And polite conversation? And dress?"

"Yes."

"Aha. You know as well as I that all that nonsense is for the ultimate purpose of enabling your students to marry—and to marry well. You, Miss Emma, are a paid matchmaker. And in less polite circles, you would be called worse."

Her face went white. He hadn't meant to be so biting, but she kept making him lose his train of thought—he had no idea why he was lusting after a prim headmistress. Now, he supposed, she would swoon and expect him to catch her. Grey sighed, taking a step closer in anticipation.

Instead, she laughed. It wasn't an amused laugh, by any stretch of the imagination, but it was the last thing he expected to hear. Women, as a rule, didn't laugh at him.

"So, Your Grace, if I might reiterate," she said, her voice clipped, "you disapprove of women who feel they need a husband to make their way in the world, despite the fact that this is exactly what society has dictated since before the Norman Conquest."

"I—"

She jabbed a finger in his direction. "And at the same time, you deride me for taking up a career which leaves me completely independent from the male of the species." She stalked closer, glaring up at him. "What I think, Your Grace, is that you like to hear yourself talk. Thankfully, that does not require my presence. Good day."

He suddenly realized they had reached the Academy grounds, and swiftly stepped back as the heavy wrought-iron gate banged shut with a clank Miss Emma Grenville must have found utterly satisfying. A moment later she and her horse vanished behind the high, ivy-covered walls.

Grey stood where he was for a moment, then turned and swung into the saddle to head back to Haverly. He couldn't remember ever having been shut down so efficiently, even by his mother—who was renowned for her razor-sharp tongue. And surprisingly enough, he was as amused as he was infuriated and aroused.

One thing was for damned certain. He was going to see *Romeo and Juliet* on Thursday. Miss Emma Grenville was not going to escape that easily.

Chapter 3

"Men perform only one necessary function in the world," Emma growled. "I have no idea how they managed to convince themselves of their superiority in every other aspect of creation, just because of a stupid accident of biology."

"I assume your conversation with Lord Haverly did not go well, then?"

Glaring toward Haverly didn't seem to be causing the estate to burst into flames, so Emma stalked away from the office window and plunked herself down at her desk. "They want to triple our rent, Isabelle."

The French instructor's pencil tip snapped off. *"Zut!"*

The curse startled Emma out of her black ruminations. "Isabelle!"

"Beg pardon. But triple? How can the Academy afford that?"

"We can't. And we won't pay it."

Isabelle set down her examination papers. "Did Lord Haverly give a *raison?* He and the countess have always supported the school."

"It wasn't he, I'm sure."

"I do not understand. Who else—"

"Someone I hope you never have the displeasure of meeting." Miss Santerre was beginning to look at Emma as though she'd become rabid, but she couldn't keep the scowl from her face. That arrogant lion of a man was impossible. She had been trying to have a civil discussion with him, and he kept looking as though he wanted to leap on her and devour her for luncheon. For some reason, the thought made her blush. "Lord Haverly's nephew. The glorious Duke of Wycliffe," she sniffed.

"A duke? A duke is making us pay more rent?"

Emma clenched her hands together. "He is not doing any such thing." In the two years since she'd become headmistress, she'd managed irate parents, lovestruck young ladies and their beaux, storms, influenza, and innumerable calamities without ever being this . . . annoyed. "Do you know what he called me? A matchmaker! A *paid* matchmaker! He practically accused me of being a . . . a . . . procurer of flesh!"

"*What?*"

"Yes. He obviously has no idea what we do here." That sparked an idea, and she gave a grim smile. "I shall have to enlighten him."

She yanked open a drawer and pulled out several sheets of paper. Stacking them neatly on the

•

desk, she dipped her pen in the inkwell. " 'Your Grace,' " she said aloud as she wrote, " 'Our recent conversation has made it clear to me that you have several . . . misconceptions concerning the curriculum of Miss Grenville's Academy.' "

Isabelle stood, gathering up her papers and books. "I shall leave you and your correspondence in peace," she said, her tone amused.

"Laugh if you want, but I will not tolerate any abuse—verbal or otherwise—directed at this Academy."

"I'm not laughing at you, Em. I am only wondering if His Grace has any idea what he is in for."

Emma dipped her pen again, ignoring as best she could the anticipation that coursed through her at the French instructor's words. "Oh, he will—soon enough."

Grey glanced up as the office door opened, then went back to his calculations. "How was Basingstoke?"

Tristan dropped into the opposite seat. "Dull as wet sheep."

A small breath of satisfaction went through the duke. "You didn't find anyone interesting to chat with, then?"

"I'm beginning to think we imagined her. There aren't that many places in west Hampshire she could be hiding. Winchester Cathedral's too far a walk, so she can't be a nun, thank God. I'd ask your aunt, but I think she's been corresponding with your mother. Your entire family hates me, you know."

"I know. And I'm sure you'll run across your

mystery woman sooner or later." Grey wasn't certain whether he was simply torturing Tristan, or whether he just wanted to keep the knowledge of Emma Grenville's whereabouts to himself. Either way, the idea of extending his stay had become much more tolerable.

"Is that what you're going to be doing the entire time we're here?" the viscount asked, gesturing at the mounds of paperwork on the desk Grey had commandeered from his uncle.

"Probably."

"Ooh, fun. We might have stayed in London."

Grey felt his jaw clench. "No, thank you."

Tristan lifted an almanac, then with a grimace replaced it on the desk. "You escaped her, you know. It's not likely that she'll confront you again."

No one but Tristan would dare even speak to him about Caroline, and he wished the viscount had chosen a different topic of conversation. "I knew she wanted to marry me," he said slowly, "but for God's sake—disrobing in the coatroom of Almack's?"

"How do you think I felt? I was just looking for my hat."

Grey scowled. "If it had been someone besides you coming through that door, that damned female would—"

"—Would be Her Grace, the Duchess of Wycliffe, by now. But she's not the only female you've seen naked, or the only one who's tried to seduce you into marriage."

"It's not that. It's the being trapped, and it's that bloody finishing school education. They're trained from birth to hound us and hunt us down. Thank God for fast horses and Haverly."

"They're not all like that, I'm sure. The Academy here has a fine reputation."

"Caroline attended it."

The viscount sat straighter. "Damn. Well, just because you're jaded beyond redemption doesn't mean I'm becoming a monk—even for a short stay in Hampshire. Why don't—"

"No females," Grey stated, as annoyed hazel eyes flitted across his vision. "There're too many here already."

"Humph. You might at least thaw enough to go see that play. Maybe you'll realize females aren't all feather-brains and lavender-scented snares."

Grey lifted an eyebrow. "Which play?"

"I don't remember which one it was. The one at the girls' school."

Grey leaned back, feigning resignation. This was going to be even easier than he'd anticipated. "If it'll stop you from complaining, I suppose I could manage to attend," he grumbled.

"Good. Another evening playing whist with Alice, and I'd be ready for the priesthood."

The duke glanced at his friend again. "There's no reason you can't go back to London, Tris. I told you Hampshire didn't have much to offer in the way of excitement."

Tristan lifted a duck-shaped, bronze paper-weight from the desk. "I just hate to admit when you're right about something."

Greydon grinned. "You should be used to it by now."

The butler scratched at the half-open door. "A letter has arrived for you, Your Grace."

Curiosity stirring, he gestured for Hobbes to bring it in. "Who knows I'm here?"

"Your mother?" Tristan suggested dryly.

"Good God, I hope not. I'm not ready to be discovered yet." Suppressing a shudder, he removed the missive from the butler's tray and flipped it over to see the address.

"Miss Grenville's Academy?" Tristan read, leaning over the desk. "Who in the world do you know there?"

Grey knew precisely who must have written it. His pulse heated, and he had to stifle the urge to smile. "Hm? Oh, I'm attempting to settle a rental dispute for Uncle Dennis." He broke the plain wax seal and unfolded the missive. "This is undoubtedly the headmistress's reply to my query."

"Your uncle's letting you deal with a girls' school?" the viscount asked skeptically. "*That* girls' school?"

"I think I'm qualified."

Tristan watched as three pages of closely spaced writing unfolded. "That's quite a reply."

"Rental dispute, indeed." Alice swept into the room, an arch smile on her face. "I've figured you out, Wycliffe. You've led us all here so you can carry on some clandestine affair with one of the pretty young schoolgirls at the Academy." She snatched the letter from his fingers before he could even read the salutation. "Let's just see, shall we?"

In London, she would never have attempted such a stunt. Obviously desperation had outweighed her scanty common sense. "Miss Boswell," Grey said, anger dropping his tone by half an octave, "I don't recall asking you to view my private correspondence. There are several fine volumes of poetry in the library if you want something to read."

"I'm only bored, Grey," she tittered, but with a swish of her skirts she returned the missive to the desk. "Beast."

"Hm. He seems terribly sensitive about something," Lady Sylvia said silkily from the doorway. "Wouldn't you agree, Cousin?"

Grey cursed under his breath as Charles Blumton strolled into the office behind Sylvia. Now Tristan was eyeing him, as well. Damnation, all he wanted to do was read a blasted letter in private. With a heavy sigh, he folded the missive and dropped it beside the stack of ledgers. "You lot are pitiful." He pushed away from the desk and stood. "I'm going fishing. Anyone care to join me?"

"Fishing? I say, that's splendid, eh, Sylvia?" Blumton took her hand and squeezed it.

"You'll have to teach me, Grey," Alice said, all charm again. "Viscountess Leeds fishes. She says it's an elegant sport."

Blumton's brow furrowed. "Well, I don't know about—"

" 'Your Grace,' " Tristan's low drawl began, " 'our recent conversation has made it clear to me that you have several misconceptions concerning the curriculum of Miss Grenville's Academy. It is my pleasure, then, to correct any misapprehensions.' "

Greydon stopped dead, a dozen curses at Tristan Carroway and all of his inbred ancestors springing to mind. Of course the letter was going to be insulting; that was why he'd wanted to read it—to savor it—with no one around to interrupt him. "That's enough, Tristan," he growled.

"It sounds very interesting," Sylvia countered, taking a seat. "Please do continue, Lord Dare."

Tristan cleared his throat, glancing up at Grey, then lowered his gaze to the letter again, his penchant for causing trouble clearly stronger than any concern over reprisals. " 'You were correct in your assertion that the Academy teaches what we have termed "the Graces"—elegance, modesty, manners, politeness, and fashion. An accomplished lady is expected to have mastered these Graces, and so we would be foolhardy to neglect including them in our students' studies.' "

"Miss Grenville is a bluestocking," Alice said.

"Apparently," Grey grumbled. "Tris—"

"It's just getting good. 'Your opinion, as I recall, was that the sole function of the Academy is to produce wives.' She's underlined 'wives' several times here," Tristan added.

"A splendid argument, Wycliffe," Blumton interjected.

"Stay off my side."

" 'The goal of this Academy under both my aunt's and my direction is to produce competent women.' More underlines here, by the way. 'To that end, in addition to the Graces, we offer instruction in literature, mathematics, language, politics, history, music, and the arts, as I have detailed below.' "

"Ye gads," Alice muttered, shuddering. "That's horrifying."

Tristan flipped through the rest of the letter.

"The next pages are a detailed curriculum." He glanced at Greydon. "I won't read that part."

"Thank you," Grey murmured.

"There is another bit at the end, though. 'As you see, Your Grace, I make every effort to see that my students receive a complete, well-rounded education. Your behavior, on the other hand, suggests to me a severe deficiency of instruction in the Graces. If you wish, I can recommend several books on the subjects of politeness, modesty, and manners for you to peruse at your leisure. Yours in sincere concern, Miss Emma Grenville.' "

After a lengthening moment of silence, Lady Sylvia burst into laughter. "Poor Grey. You've failed to impress the headmistress of a girls' school."

"Well, I don't know about that. She only says she's sincerely concerned." Tristan returned the letter to the desk.

Grey let them have their amusement. In fact, he barely heard what they said. He was imagining a very satisfying manner of closing the mouth of that hazel-eyed sprite. Miss Emma Grenville obviously had no idea with whom she was dealing, but she was about to find out.

Miss Elizabeth Newcombe fell back against the empty whiskey barrel that represented the central well in the fair city of Verona. " 'Ask for me tomorrow, and you shall find me a grave man,' " she croaked, clutching her side.

Shifting the padding which bulked her up for the part of Juliet's nurse, Emma smiled. No one could fault Elizabeth for shyness. In fact, in another year or so, she would have to begin work in earnest to mold her youngest student's wild humor into wit. They'd already come a far way with it, yet the last thing she wanted to do was stifle Lizzy's natural openness and charm.

"Miss Emma," her nearly deceased Mercutio called, straightening, "can't I use just a little berry juice for blood?"

"Eeewww. If you do, I shall faint," Mary Mawgry said, using the tip of her sword to clean one fingernail.

"No, you may not." Emma entered Verona from the backstage area. "That's what the red scarf symbolizes. You all worked very hard on your splendid costumes, and I won't see them ruined, even for the sake of drama. Now please continue; this is our last dress rehearsal. We debut in six hours."

She retreated backstage again as Elizabeth finally succumbed to her wound, and Romeo and Tybalt began their duel. Despite Mary's frequent threats to faint, the shy miss had improved so much as Romeo that Emma wanted to cheer. Miss Mawgry's parents would be amazed at the change the next time they saw their "mumbling" daughter, as they'd referred to Mary on far too many occasions.

"Em," Isabelle whispered, waving a letter at her as she made her way through the wardrobe area, "I think you've received an answer."

Finally. She'd waited over a day for it. The sudden fluttering in her stomach had nothing to do with concern over her students' performance. She wasn't certain why she'd felt the need to write Wycliffe when he so obviously didn't give a hang about the Academy, but knowing he had her letter had kept her restless and awake all night.

Emma took the missive from her French instructor and unfolded it. The sight of the dark, masculine scrawl made her pulse skip—until she read it. " 'Madame,' " it began, " 'I am in receipt of your recent overblown correspondence.' " She shook the letter at Isabelle, annoyance flooding in.

"*Overblown*? He says my letter was overblown!"

"Shh, Emma. The rehearsal."

Snapping her jaw shut, she continued reading to herself. " 'While a sentence or two was of passing interest, it unfortunately did not address the matter lying between your Academy and Haverly. I have enclosed the rental agreement for your signature. I shall collect it this evening after your play, which my friends and I have been persuaded to attend.' " There was no long list of titles and honors at the end of the letter; just the word "Wycliffe," scrawled across the bottom of the page.

Emma blanched. He was coming to see the play.

"Are you well?" Isabelle asked, clutching her elbow as she abruptly took a seat.

"Yes, quite." She couldn't tell her students, of course; their confidence and concentration would be ruined as soon as they learned a duke—especially a large, golden lion of a duke— would be in attendance.

She scowled. That was probably why he had informed her—so her girls would be nervous and make a bad showing. Her first instinct was to tear up the letter, tromp on the pieces, and set the remaining bits on fire. While that would be immensely satisfying, though, it wouldn't take care of her problem.

"Isabelle, Sir John will be in attendance tonight, won't he?"

"*Oui*. He said he would come early, to help Tobias secure Juliet's balcony and the ladder."

"Good." Basingstoke's resident solicitor, Sir John, had always been a staunch supporter of the Academy. She refolded the letter and the agreement and stuffed them into her Nurse padding. The Duke of Wycliffe might think he could bully her into doing what he wanted, but she had no intention of giving in without a fight—or a war.

A chorus of giggles from the stage caught her attention. Lady Jane leaned behind the curtain and grimaced at her. " 'O, here comes my nurse,' " she said loudly, " 'and she brings news.' "

"Oops." Emma jumped to her feet and hobbled onto the stage. Now that dratted Wycliffe was interfering with her instruction—another black mark against him. " 'Ah, weraday, he's dead, he's dead, he's dead!' "

Or he would wish he were, when she was finished with him.

Chapter 4

Miss Grenville's Academy looked more like a military camp than a girls' school as Lord and Lady Haverly and their guests made their way through the long, rambling building to the old converted church at the far end. Stout women stood guard at every hallway juncture and staircase, no doubt to prevent any males from wandering into the bed chambers and interfering with the marriageability of the students.

Or perhaps Miss Emma feared that Grey meant to collect the rent from the pockets of the infants. If she suspected how little contact he wanted with marriageable young ladies, she might have realized that a better strategy for protecting the school would be to send the chits charging at him.

"I had no idea this was a finishing school for

grandmothers," Tristan murmured as they passed another of the gray-haired sentries. "I am supremely disillusioned."

"I have no idea why you wanted to come, Grey," Alice put in from his other side, her voice plaintive. "In London, we could be at the opera with Prince George."

"I know why we're here," Lady Sylvia said smoothly. "Our duke has been wanting to throttle the school's headmistress since he received her letter yesterday."

Sylvia was right; he *did* want to see Miss Emma, to learn of her reaction to this morning's letter. Throttling her, though, wasn't as high on his agenda as simply getting his hands on her. All over her.

"Even so," Blumton grumbled from the rear, "a gaggle of females playing at Shakespeare? Edmund Keene is performing *Hamlet* in London. I've gone to view it twice. Magnificent. Nothing resembling this insult to the bard, I'm sure."

"I doubt the Academy's insulting anyone," Uncle Dennis countered with a patient smile. "Their production of *As You Like It* last year was quite impressive."

"By Hampshire standards, perhaps."

Alice rubbed her bosom against Grey's arm. "You're being quiet tonight."

"I'm enjoying the sights."

In truth, he was a little nonplussed. The interior of a girls' school, in his infrequent imaginings of such a thing, had a great deal more lace in the windows. Though crocheted pillows and throws did cover the couches and chairs in the common rooms, they were the only feminine trappings in

sight. Most surprising of all, hordes of young females about to make their debuts in Society
hadn't appeared to gawk at and giggle and flirt
with every male present.

"Lord Haverly, Lady Haverly, good evening,"
a female voice said from the dim depths of the
hallway in front of them.

Grey's pulse jumped, then steadied again as a
tall, dark-haired young woman appeared. It
wasn't *her*.

"Miss Santerre," his aunt replied, more
warmth in her voice than Grey had heard since
his arrival. "A good evening to you."

"I am pleased you and your guests could attend," Miss Santerre continued in a light French
accent.

"We're pleased to be here."

"Emma would have greeted you herself, but
the students have recruited her to perform this
evening."

"Which part?" Tristan asked, before Greydon
could.

The woman smiled. "The Nurse. If you will follow me, I shall show you to your seats."

"I will require a word with Miss Emma sometime this evening," Grey said, falling in behind
the female, a determined Alice still attached to
his arm.

"I shall inform her of your request," Miss Santerre answered, "though she will be quite busy
tonight."

"You're being avoided, Wycliffe," Charles supplied. "I know all about that."

"I'm sure you do." Tristan grinned at Sylvia,
who gave him an arch smile.

At the mention of his name, the French-woman's gaze sharpened for just a second before her face resumed its placid expression. The Academy females seemed to have been gossiping about him. Females were always gossiping about something. So be it. He didn't want much to do with any of them, anyway—with one exception.

He definitely wanted to do something with Miss Emma Grenville, to the point that he was actively avoiding Alice. He'd even taken to locking his bed chamber door the last few nights against her. And he did not, under any circumstances, enjoy being chaste.

When Miss Santerre showed them to the back pew, Grey was sure his party was being singled out for persecution. Neither his aunt nor his uncle, though, looked the least bit surprised, and they slid onto the bench without protest.

"Not entirely proper etiquette, I know," Dennis said, as Blumton gave the French woman an insulted glare, "but I always insist on sitting in the back so as not to rattle the girls."

"That's generous of you, Lord Haverly," Lady Sylvia said, seating herself beside him.

The remaining pews of the old church were occupied, anyway, with what looked to be the entire population of Basingstoke and the surrounding countryside. From their clothing, a few other gentry were present as well, no doubt landowners from neighboring estates who'd forgone London this Season. That perked up Alice, and she made a show of taking the seat beside him.

A half dozen girls, dressed in simple dark robes, emerged from the rear doors and one by one snuffed the candles in the wall sconces. Tristan leaned across Alice as the audience quieted. "I still haven't seen that blasted chit from the road. You would think she would be here."

"Perhaps you'll glimpse her later," Grey replied in a low voice. "Now shut up; the curtains are parting."

The viscount straightened, offering a mock salute. "Yes, Your Grace."

Unlike the audiences in London's Mayfair theaters, tonight's attendees actually seemed interested in watching the play. Many had turned to view the Haverly party as they entered, but once the curtains parted, the only things in view were the backs of a hundred heads. Grey settled back on the hard oak bench to watch, as well.

The major characters seemed to be acted by older students, though even girls barely in their teens swarmed onto the stage for the initial Montague–Capulet brawl, swords swinging enthusiastically. "Good God, they're ferocious," Tristan murmured. "I'm terrified."

Finally the Montagues exited the second scene, and Grey straightened as Lady Capulet and Nurse took the stage. There she was. It seemed longer than two days ago that he'd last seen her, and the view from the rear pew didn't do anything to quell his impatience over that fact.

"*That's* your unrelenting foe?" Tristan chuckled.

"That plump, white-haired old bat?" Alice elbowed Grey in the ribs. "She looks ninety."

"Shh. I'm watching." He couldn't quell his abrupt satisfaction; Tristan had no idea of whom he was making fun. Grey, though, had no trouble at all recognizing her despite the wig and the con-

siderable padding and the god-awful fishwife's
tone she'd adopted.

" 'Where's this girl?' " she called, and he
grinned in the darkness. " 'What, Juliet?' "

Juliet, a lovely young lady with long, coal-
black hair, glided onto the stage. " 'How now,
who calls?' "

"Now, that's more like it," the viscount muttered, sighing happily.

Several rows in front of them, a slim young
man stood and began applauding. He continued
until the actress on the stage looked in his direction, blushing. Ignoring the annoyed looks of his
fellows in the audience, he slowly seated himself
again.

"Apparently you're not Juliet's only admirer,"
Grey whispered.

Frowning, Uncle Dennis leaned across Sylvia
and Blumton. "That's Freddie Mayburne," he
whispered, gesturing. "He's been in pursuit of
Lady Jane all year."

"Poor fellow," Grey muttered, his eyes on
Emma.

The rest of the play proceeded without further
interruption and nearly without flaw, and Grey
joined the rest of the audience on their feet as the
curtains closed and then opened again to reveal a
stage full of beaming young actresses taking their
bows.

"You see, Mr. Blumton?" Uncle Dennis said
proudly, applauding. "They were splendid. Brava,
ladies! Brava!"

"Very passable, for females," Blumton said
grudgingly.

"That pint-sized Mercutio could give Edmund

Keene a run for his money," Tristan said, chuckling, as the curtains closed again.

"Might we go now?" Alice asked, putting her shawl across her shoulders and exiting the pew behind Lord Dare. "I have no wish to be accosted by half the farmers of Hampshire."

Grey could sympathize. Now that the play was over with, Lord Haverly's party seemed to have become the center of everyone's notice. All that lacked was for eligible young females to begin throwing monogrammed handkerchiefs in his direction, and he could imagine himself back in London with his mother and the unwed hordes hounding him.

He was daft to enter a girls' school, he decided belatedly. Lusting after the damned headmistress was affecting his brain.

"All right, we'll leave . . ." he began, trailing off as he spied a short, rotund form making its way through the admiring crowd toward them. "In a moment."

"Grey, do you have to talk with that old witch tonight?"

"Yes." He stepped forward as she reached them. "Miss Emma."

"Your Grace."

She curtsied, the motion elegant despite the enormous amount of padding beneath her frocks. Grey's fingers twitched with the desire to begin unstuffing her. He shook himself. That could wait until after they settled the damned rent issue. "Do you—"

"Please excuse me, Your Grace," she interrupted, turning her attention to his uncle, "but Lord and Lady Haverly traditionally join the cast for punch and cake after the performance. I wanted you and your guests to know you're all welcome tonight."

"We would be delighted," the earl returned warmly. "We shall meet you in the dining hall."

"Oh, lucky us," Alice muttered, offering her arm to Grey.

He evaded capture, placing her hand over a surprised Tristan's elbow and striding off after the headmistress before she could vanish into the crowd. "You received my letter, I presume?" he asked as he caught up to her.

She slowed, glancing over her shoulder at him. "Yes, I did. It was remarkably rude."

"Just carrying on the tradition your letter began," he said amiably.

"I was not r—"

"Oh, Miss Emma." Another female, taller and nearly as rotund as the padded headmistress, swept up to clasp both of Emma's hands. "I nearly fainted when Juliet woke up, looking for her Romeo, and him already dead beside her. It was even better than last year's play."

"Thank you, Mrs. Jones. I'm so glad you could attend. And I see even Mr. Jones came this year."

The large woman chuckled. "He said it would be nonsense, but I saw him wiping away a tear at the end." She leaned closer, lowering her voice. "Not that he'd ever admit to it, of course."

"It'll be our secret," Emma whispered, smiling. "Now, if you'll excuse me." Adjusting her padding, she waddled off again.

Grey wasn't about to let her escape that easily. "Parents won't appreciate your turning their well-bred daughters into actresses, you know."

"That wasn't the purpose of this exercise, though I don't expect you to understand."

As she continued down the long hallway, turned another corner, climbed a flight of stairs, and entered a small office, he abruptly wondered whether she hadn't led him into some sort of ambush. A tall, silver-templed gentleman stood at one window, gazing in the direction of Haverly.

"Your Grace, this is Sir John Blakely, my solicitor," Emma said, moving to the far side of an old oak desk. "Sir John, His Grace, the Duke of Wycliffe."

"Your Grace," Sir John said, coming forward and offering his hand, "it is a pleasure to meet you."

Grey shook it, his attention on the headmistress. "Why am I meeting your solicitor?"

"Because I thought you might listen if a man explained to you that you cannot order me to do anything. My telling you obviously has had no effect."

"I beg your pardon, but . . ."

He trailed off as she removed her wig and dropped it onto the desk. Disheveled auburn hair cascaded down past her shoulders in a riot of red-tinted curls.

She looked up at him. "But what?"

Grey tried to concentrate his attention on the solicitor. "My uncle has approached me to make certain changes in the management style of Haverly. Increasing his tenants' rent is but one of them."

"And do you have this transfer of authority in writing, then, Your Grace?"

Emma rose and walked through a door on one

side of the office, then returned with a wash basin. She dipped a cloth in the water and began wiping at the heavy makeup on her face. Slowly the white and grey mask faded, replaced by the soft, lustrous cream of her skin. Usually Grey had no difficulty at all separating business from pleasure, but Miss Emma Grenville was distracting the hell out of him. "I can get it in writing, if that is what you require," he said shortly.

"That would be helpful," Sir John continued. "And of course, the document would have to be notarized by a solicitor."

The headmistress reached around her back for one of the ties that held her bulky frock on, presumably over some other garment. Whatever he might like to imagine, he didn't think she intended to render herself naked in front of two men.

"Fine. Please direct me to the nearest solicitor," he said curtly.

"Ah. That is a difficulty. I am the only solicitor residing in Basingstoke at the moment, and as you see, I am representing Miss Grenville's Academy. It would be a conflict of interest for me to—"

"Here, let me get that," Grey interrupted, closing the distance between himself and the headmistress. Before she could do more than squeak, he had untied the four fastenings at her back. Slipping the heavy garment down her arms, he let it slide past her hips to the floor. Her hair smelled of lemon and honey, and he was seized with the sudden desire to run his fingers through the soft auburn tangles.

She moved away from him at high speed before he could act on his impulse. "So you see,

Your Grace," she stammered, her fresh-scrubbed cheeks flushing prettily, "you will have to return to London or somewhere and employ a solicitor."

"I employ a dozen solicitors already," he said, stifling a scowl. "And I don't need a notarized document; all I need is for my uncle to repeat his request in front of witnesses." He pinned the solicitor with a glare. "Isn't that correct, Sir John?"

"Ah, yes."

"And when I do that, we will be back in the same exact situation we are now—except that you, Miss Emma, will have no legal recourse but to pay your rent."

"I'm not as certain of that as you seem to be. I've been thinking of having Sir John draft a petition for presentation to Parliament," she said, still backing away from him, "with the goal of having the Academy declared an historical building. This will give me special dispensation in paying—"

"Why, you little—"

"Your Grace!" the solicitor protested.

"So you would rather see Haverly bankrupted than pay another shilling," he snapped, clamping a fist over his temper. No one outmaneuvered him. And certainly not this sprite of a headmistress. "Just to keep this trivial pretty-house open."

She lifted her chin. "You're rich; you pay to keep Haverly solvent. And this is a place of learning, not a 'pretty-house,' as you so inaccurately term it."

" 'Inaccurately?' I hardly think—"

"No, you don't, do you?"

Women never argued with him. They sighed and agreed and tittered and talked of inane nonsense until his head was ready to explode. This was exceedingly . . . invigorating. "What would you have me call it, then? You refuse to pay rent to Haverly, all the while playing dress-up and looking for rich husbands for your so-called students."

She advanced on him, looking angry enough to spit nails. "That is *not* the function of this Academy, and I will *not* tolerate your insulting these young ladies when they have worked so hard to—"

"—to learn how to discuss the weather?" Grey suggested, folding his arms across his chest. "Name one *practical* piece of knowledge your girls acquire."

"As if you know how to do anything but bellow and order everyone else around. Ha! Who shaved you this morning, Your Grace?"

"I shave myself, Miss Emma."

"Good for you. How many people helped you dress, excluding the servants who polish your boots?"

Grey narrowed his eyes. "I believe we were discussing the uselessness of this school, not your fascination with my morning toilette."

"Your Gr—"

"Quiet," Grey snapped at the solicitor, not bothering to glance in Sir John's direction.

"You do not fascinate me in the least," Emma stated in a loud voice. "I am making a point."

The idea that he didn't affect her was even more annoying than her absurd stance in defense of females. "And just what do your students learn here that is more significant than the knowledge they could acquire from a fortnight in Whitechapel or Covent Garden? All you do is provide a stamp of respectability for their seductions."

The solicitor stepped forward. "Your Grace, I must warn you—"

"Get out," Grey growled.

"I will n—"

"Please, Sir John," the headmistress said unexpectedly, her voice tight. "I am quite capable of fighting my own battles." To Grey's surprise, she escorted the solicitor to the office door and ushered him out.

"Close it."

"I intend to," she said, complying. "I really didn't think you wanted anyone else to overhear your ignorant prattling."

Despite the bold words and the closed door, Emma was white-faced. If not for the unmistakable fire and fury flashing in her eyes, Grey would have ceased his attack. That realization surprised him. The imminent collapse of his opponent was generally his signal to go in for the kill. "We were discussing the difference between graduates of a finishing school and . . . actresses, we'll call them."

"Why not say what you think? I find innuendo tedious and the forte of simple minds."

So now he was a halfwit. Grey crossed the room toward her. "Whores, then," he said distinctly.

"Ha." Though her cheeks flooded with color, she stood her ground. "You've destroyed your own argument again. Obviously, Your Grace, you don't have enough people around you informing you when you're not making any sense."

Grey couldn't remember the last time anyone had dared insult him so directly. Anger coursed through his veins, accompanied by a darker, equally heated sensation. Good God, he wanted her beneath him. "Pray explain," he ground out, wondering if she realized just how much peril she was in.

"Gladly. You have several times insisted that the Academy's only *raison d'être* is to produce wives, presumably for you and your peers. Men of your station, to be blunt, don't marry whores. Ergo, my school does not produce whores."

"A flower, sweetly perfumed or rotting on a trash heap, is still a flower."

"I pity you if you can't tell one from the other. A stinking bog and a fertile field are both pieces of dirt, yet I would think you, as a landowner, would find them more different than similar."

"As if a female would know the difference between mud and cow dung, if not for the smell."

Emma wrinkled her nose, though he couldn't be sure whether the expression was for him or for his allusion. "Better than you could tell a whore from a lady, obviously." She put her hands on her hips.

Grey studied her for a moment, his lust for this assertive woman warring with his exasperation at her for daring to think she could stand toe to toe with the Duke of Wycliffe—though she was making a damned fine show of it. "Care to wager on that?" he asked.

She blinked. "What?"

It was ingenious. The impertinent chit—he'd prove to everyone that she didn't have the dimmest idea what she was talking about. "I'm talking about making a wager, Miss Emma."

Her hazel eyes narrowed. "A wager over what?"

"Rent," he said promptly. The more he thought about it, the more brilliant it seemed. If she thought she had all the answers, she could damned well try to prove it. "If you lose, you pay the new rent. No more arguments."

"You're mad," she said, looking at him warily. "What are you proposing we wager over? I have better things to do than sniff manure."

He shook his head. "No. Much better than that." This would need to be official, or she'd find a way to slip out of his grasp before he could make his point. He strode past her to the door and yanked it open. "You—Sir John. Get in here."

The solicitor practically fell into the room; obviously their conversation had been overheard. Well, that would leave him less explaining to do.

"Humph," the headmistress snorted, her color still high. "What in the world are you talking about, Your Grace?"

He gestured at the solicitor. "Sit down and take notes."

"Please stop ordering my solici—"

"Excuse us," Tristan's voice came from the doorway, "but I don't believe we've been properly introduced."

Barely sparing a glance at the Haverly party as they crowded into the room, Grey nudged the solicitor toward the tiny desk's chair. "Glad you're here. We're making a wager."

"We are *not* making a wager!"

He lifted an eyebrow. "Why, because you can't support your silly claims of superiority?"

"Not superiority." She hesitated, the first time he had seen her struggle to find the right word. "Equality."

"Excuse us, Grey," Lady Sylvia said in her silky voice, "but whose equality are we discussing?"

"Miss Emma's to mine, obviously." He circled the headmistress, his plans falling into order.

"Surely not." Alice tittered behind her fan, the expression of innocence on her face ridiculous. He didn't know why she bothered with it any longer, unless she hoped to fool some unsuspecting halfwit. "Everyone knows a duke outranks a headmistress."

"Not that kind of equality," Emma snapped, obviously so out of patience that she was neglecting her own rules of politeness. "*Mental* equality."

And the trap clicked shut. "Then prove it," Grey murmured, stopping directly before her and holding her hazel gaze.

"How?"

"As I mentioned," he began, "I'm looking for a more efficient and profitable way to manage Haverly. I propose that you attempt to come up with a better plan than mine."

"An estate plan," she said dubiously.

If he didn't secure her agreement quickly, she would realize he was trying to bully her into a corner, and she would escape. "If you can do it, *I'll* pay your damned Academy's rent, *ad infinitum.*"

Emma pursed her lips, which made Grey want to kiss them. "All right," she said slowly, "but I don't see why I should be the only one to have to prove anything. Otherwise, when I *do* come up with a better plan than yours, we will simply have to assume that I am more intelligent than you are."

Uncle Dennis drew in a breath. "Sweet Mary," he muttered, and Grey distinctly heard Tristan snicker.

Accepting his challenge was one thing; insulting him while doing it was something else. "I don't think you have a prayer of devising a better plan than mine," he said.

"Yes, but you're wrong, Your Grace."

"I see. What do you suggest, then?"

She looked at him speculatively. "As it happens, I take personal responsibility for a small group of students at this time each year. The topic of this special class is London Social Graces. You seem to have very definite ideas of what makes a young lady successful in London."

Grey's chest began to tighten. "And?" he ground out.

"I suggest you attempt to pass on your expertise to my students. Perhaps in ballroom decorum, as that discussion is to begin on Monday, anyway."

"Excuse me for interrupting," Tristan said in a choked voice, "but wouldn't that be rather like putting a fox in charge of a hen house?"

Emma blushed prettily. "His Grace and my students would be well chaperoned, of course."

"That's ridiculous." *Socialize with schoolroom chits?*

"If you back down," she returned, "I will consider myself removed from any obligation to pay your absurd rent."

Damn. She'd certainly managed to raise the

stakes easily enough. "And just who would judge this?"

"I imagine you and your male friends will be assessing my estate plan," she said airily, waving her hand in his companions' direction. "I think it's only fair that the students involved should judge your abilities as a teacher—in comparison with mine."

"Schoolroom girls?" Sylvia cooed, while Alice stifled another bout of grating giggles. "That should be simple for you, Grey. Just charm them into voting for you."

"My students are more sensible than that, I assure you."

His amusing little plan suddenly didn't seem so amusing. He faced the headmistress again. "If you lose—*when* you lose—you will agree to pay the new rent, retroactive for the past ... two years."

She looked as though she couldn't decide whether to be angry, horrified, or amused. "Then you should have an additional penalty, as well."

"We already discussed that. If I lose, I will pay your rent every year."

Emma shook her head. "That's not good enough."

He tilted his head at her, surprised she hadn't immediately backed down, and in fact was still negotiating with him. "What do you propose, then?"

"If you lose, Your Grace, you will establish a fund to sponsor three young ladies to attend the Academy for the entire period of their enrollment."

She was setting him up to be humiliated. Everyone knew what he thought of finishing schools, and of this one in particular. To pay the rent *and* to sponsor chits to attend Miss Grenville's Academy . . .

A ridiculous prospect. She would lose and he would win. Besides, this was beginning to sound much more interesting than he'd anticipated. Perhaps he could even persuade her to make a small personal wager on the side, just between the two of them. He knew precisely what it would entail. "Done," he said.

"Emma," Sir John murmured, his expression grave and worried.

She lifted her chin. "Done."

Chapter 5

❦

"Emma, you have to call off this wager. Immediately."

Emma sighed. She had spent the entire night pacing up and down her small bed chamber telling herself the same thing. Every time she decided to back down, though, cynical green eyes laughed at her for being a coward. The dratted Duke of Wycliffe thought that she—and her students— were stupid and useless, and he didn't make any secret of that fact.

A great many men thought that way; she knew that. And convincing one out of thousands would hardly make a dent in their thick, ignorant skulls. At the moment, however, logic could go hang itself. She was deuced well going to convince this one, and bring three more students to the

Academy. More than that, if he truly paid her rent as he'd said he would.

"I am not here for advice, Sir John," she said with as much bravado as she could muster, pulling another book off his crowded office shelves. "Tax research." She held it up for his inspection. "Estate taxation?"

"Goods and property. Emma—"

"You don't think I can win." She placed the book on her rapidly growing pile of research materials.

"You've never attempted anything like this before. Wycliffe was practically bred to it. Pay the new rent. It's high, but you can manage it."

She flipped through another book and replaced it on the shelf. "No. That money is needed elsewhere. Some things simply cannot be compromised, no matter what."

"And if you lose the wager?"

"I won't. You know I rarely fail at things when I set my mind to them, and believe me, this wager has my complete attention."

She dusted her hands off on her skirt. Despite her bold proclamations, her confidence felt ready to crumble. Ignoring Sir John's advice was difficult, especially since she had invited herself into his Basingstoke office to look through his research books. Another warning from him would probably cause her to burst into tears, and she couldn't afford to show weakness now.

"I know nothing about estate management," he continued. "I can't give you any more assistance than the loan of these books—and my advice, which you obviously aren't going to take."

Emma forced a smile. "Would it compromise

your principles if I asked you to help me carry the books to my cart?"

"Allow me," a low, masculine voice drawled.

She jumped. For a mountain of a man, the Duke of Wycliffe seemed able to sneak up behind her without any noticeable effort. "Your Grace," she said, running her conversation with Sir John through her mind and deciding she hadn't given him anything to use against her, thank goodness. "What are you doing in Basingstoke?"

Wycliffe leaned in the office doorway, his broad shoulders nearly filling the opening. His tight-fitting buckskin breeches and rust-colored riding coat made him look even more like a great African lion, golden, powerful, and confident—and looking for a gazelle to snack on. Emma swallowed.

"I was looking for you, Miss Emma."

Gazelle or not, she had no intention of giving up without a fight. Or of showing this lion anything but her horns. She had an entire herd of little gazelles to protect. "Oh? And why is that? To apologize?"

The duke pushed away from the door frame. "Not me. I will, however, still accept an apology—and payment—from you. There is no need to involve Sir John."

"I'm not involving Sir John; *you* did that. *I* came here," she said, gathering an armload of books, "for research materials. Nothing more." Brushing past him, she went outside and placed the books on the floor of the Academy's small horse-pulled cart, usually used for transporting students into the village or out to Haverly's pond for flora and fauna lessons.

As she turned around to collect the rest of the heavy tomes, she nearly collided with Wycliffe. Leaning past her, he took one of the books from the cart.

" 'Entailment Laws'? This isn't going to help you."

Emma snatched the book back. "That really isn't any of your business, Your Grace."

She stalked back inside the office. Without looking, she knew he followed her. Goose bumps prickled up her arms. The sensation, and the heady anticipation which accompanied it, were so odd; she didn't even like him. Despite that, his physical presence was . . . exhilarating.

"You might ask *me* your estate questions," he continued. "I do have some experience in this area, after all."

Emma glared up at him. "As if I would trust anything you told me—we both know you have no intention of losing to me. You're only prattling on to hear yourself speak, again."

Emma gathered another armful of books, but he pushed them back down against the tabletop. The duke's hand fascinated her. Since he was large, she had expected him to have thick, heavy hands; instead, Wycliffe possessed the hands of an artist, long-fingered and elegant and graceful.

"I do not prattle," he murmured, "and I said *I* would carry your books. Besides, it wouldn't matter if I gave you every piece of knowledge and advice I possess. You would still lose."

She met his light green eyes, shivers running all the way down her spine. "Fine. You may carry my books." Tearing her gaze from his, she made her way around the clutter to shake the solicitor's hand. "Thank you for the loan, Sir John. I will return them shortly."

"No hurry." He looked from her to Wycliffe. "Your Mr. Blumton and I are setting down the rules and stipulations of the wager this afternoon. When is this business to conclude?"

"Four weeks—if that is sufficient, Miss Emma. If you requi—"

"Four weeks is fine."

"Fine."

Sir John cleared his throat. "I was about to suggest that you might wish to settle your disagreement now, rather than later."

"I've already offered." The duke hefted the heavy, cumbersome tomes effortlessly. "The decision, I believe, belongs to Miss Emma."

Now he was just goading her. "I have no intention of backing down from a wager I cannot possibly lose. Good day, Sir John."

"Sir John."

As the duke followed her out to the cart again, that damned humming resumed in her veins. "Don't you have things to do, Your Grace?" she said in her most flip, uncaring voice. "Tenants to evict from their homes, or cattle to count?"

He dumped the books onto the floor of the cart. "I counted this morning, just to stay in practice. With my uncle's permission, of course."

The duke had a sense of humor. If she didn't have such a strong desire to kick him, she might have appreciated it. "What are you doing here, really? You can't have expected an apology."

"Walk with me," he said, and offered her his arm.

The blasted shivers started all over again. "I don't want to walk with you," she forced out.

"You will when I've told you why I'm here."

With a sigh to cover her perturbation, Emma set down the last book and folded her arms. "Then perhaps you should tell me, first. Otherwise, I must decline."

He studied her face for a moment, while Emma did her best to think glacial thoughts and avoid another blush. She never had this problem with Sir John or Lord Haverly or any other man she dealt with in running the Academy. If she was acting so silly because of Wycliffe's handsome face, then she was a fool. If it was because of some odd, deeper attraction, then she was worse than a fool. He meant her no good, and he'd made no secret of that fact.

"I thought we should begin the contest on an even footing," he said. "With my uncle's permission, I have copied down all the information regarding Haverly I thought might be pertinent."

Surprise made her blink. "Such as?"

"Current crop acreage, head of sheep, cattle, pigs, etc."

"Well." Emma cleared her throat. "That's very generous of you, I suppose."

His lips curved into a wicked, sensuous smile. "I've also outlined my plans to date for improving Haverly's finances. But I won't give any of it to you unless you walk with me."

"Isn't that blackmail?"

"No. It's bribery. Yes or no, Miss Emma?"

Emma hated being manipulated, even when it was as obvious as this. On the other hand, that information could save her a great deal of time in organizing her strategy. If not for that little fact, she would have driven back to the Academy as fast as Old Joe could take her.

"Yes—if it's a *brief* walk." She folded her hands behind her back and started off along the cobblestoned street at a crisp pace.

A moment later he caught up to her. "I offered you my arm."

"As we are not related or on equal social footing, and we are certainly not chaperoned, I must decline it."

His lips twitched. "Is that one of your lessons?"

She slowed, irritated that he found her humorous. "My goodness. I had no idea you were so ill prepared to instruct my students. Are you certain you don't wish to concede?"

He still looked amused, blast him. "I don't believe in your topics of instruction, if you'll recall."

Suddenly she wasn't so certain that giving him a class was a good idea. "Just remember, Your Grace, that your task is to enable your students to become successful *ladies*. If you stray one inch from that, I will consider you to have lost."

"Thank you for your confidence in my lack of morality, but I do know the rules."

"Good." Even so, she would be keeping a close eye on him. "I instruct some of the more remedial young ladies in basic, common-sense etiquette, Your Grace. Perhaps you might wish to sit in on a class or two."

"I'll consider it," he said dryly. "Perhaps you might wish to attend a class or two of mine."

"Oh, I intend to."

"Good. I may conduct private classes, as well."

Emma stopped. His lascivious tone and what it

might portend were precisely what she'd been worried about. "Not with my students, you won't."

The duke halted directly in front of her, so she had no choice but to look at him. Her eyes were level with his broad chest, and with a sigh she barely remembered to stifle, she lifted her gaze to meet his.

"I wasn't talking about your students."

Emma swallowed again. "Oh." She reminded herself that he was a practiced rake and probably flirted with every sentence he uttered in that deliciously low voice, so she'd have to be on her toes every moment he was near her students and herself, just in case. "Private classes are very well, I suppose, but what do they have to do with the number of pigs at Haverly?"

Wycliffe shrugged. "Just seeing how willing you are to be distracted."

"I'm not." Emma glanced through the window of William Smalling's bakery and saw Mr. Smalling, Mrs. Tate, and Mrs. Beltrand staring back out at her. *Drat.* Mr. Smalling was such a gossip. "For your information, I teach an entire course about men like you. You aren't likely to trip me up, at all."

His teeth flashed in a wicked smile. "By that I assume you mean handsome, charming men?"

Her pulse sped up. "Yes. Precisely."

"Then why do I still make you blush?"

Emma felt an even deeper flush creeping up her cheeks. "I may not be able to keep myself from blushing in sympathetic embarrassment at your exceeding arrogance, Your Grace, but don't think that means I intend to turn tail and run."

Wycliffe lifted an eyebrow. "But I don't want you to run," he said softly. "Where would the fun be in that?"

Oh, goodness. She needed to attend her own class on rake avoidance again. Immediately. "F—fun? That is precisely why you are going to lose this wager, Your Grace: it's a game to you. Allow me to assure you, though, that it is much more serious to me."

The duke reached one hand toward her, and Emma froze. But instead of caressing her cheek as she'd expected, he merely lifted her slipping shawl back onto her shoulder. "Pity," he murmured.

And she was even *leaning* toward the blackguard. "As I said, this is not a game to me," she continued stoutly. "You, however, seem to be playing several, and none of them very well. I am unmoved by your seductions, and unimpressed with your . . . delivery." With a sniff she turned around and strode back to her cart.

Grey watched her recede into the distance and wondered when, precisely, he'd lost his mind. This wasn't the first time he'd dealt with a defiant tenant, for God's sake. Bellowing ultimatums without listening to opposing arguments, though, and making wagers with them—that was new. And tenants—even impertinent hazel-eyed ones—did not boldly face him and inform him that he was rude and unimpressive.

"I'm not finished playing yet, Emma Grenville," he murmured, as her cart bumped down the lane toward the small stone bridge which marked the east border of Basingstoke. "And neither are you."

With a slight grin, he returned to his horse to go after her. She'd stalked off before he could give her the notes about Haverly. And she wouldn't have the last word this morning, if he had any say in this little farce—which he did.

As he rounded the curve in the road, though, he reined in the gelding. Emma's cart sat in the middle of the track, a mounted figure beside her.

At first glance he thought it was Tristan, but the rider didn't have the viscount's easy line. Viscount Dare had practically been born on horseback. This fellow looked as though he'd be much more comfortable with both feet on the ground. Seeing the way he was leaning over the headmistress, one hand gripping the back of Emma's seat, Grey abruptly wanted to set his backside in the dirt.

Narrowing his eyes, he urged Cornwall forward. "Emma, what a coincidence," he said in a carrying voice.

The other rider straightened and turned. As he did so, Grey recognized him—the dandy from the theatrical audience. He clenched his fist. No upstart was going to ruin his plans for the headmistress.

"It's hardly a coincidence," Emma said, not looking at all pleased to see him again. "I only drove away from you two minutes ago."

"I say, you're Wycliffe," the youth drawled.

"And you're . . ." He scoured his memory for the name Uncle Dennis had mumbled at him last night. ". . . Freddie Mayburne." Whoever he was, Grey wished he would take the hint and go away. He had a conversation with Emma to finish.

"You've heard of me, eh?" Far from being discouraged at the cool reception, Freddie smiled. "I told Jane I'd made something of a name for myself in London, but I had no idea even the likes of the Duke of Wycliffe knew of me."

Grey sent him a dismissive glance. "Actually, I saw your performance last night at the Academy."

Freddie's confident smile twitched. "Oh."

"For your future reference, Mr. Mayburne," he informed the pompous oaf, "the trick is never to let a chit know you're the least bit interested."

"Hmph." Emma sniffed, and clucked to her horse. "Tricks. I would suggest sincerity." With a lurch the cart began rolling down the road again.

Freddie urged his mount closer to Cornwall. "Actually, Your Grace, I'd been hoping to have a word with—"

"Excuse me," Grey interrupted. Leaving Mr. Mayburne in the middle of the road, he set off after Emma again. Following her around while she stampeded across Hampshire was *not* going to become a habit. Women pursued *him*, not the other way around. "You forgot something," he said as he rounded a turn and drew even with her.

"Yes, I know, but I had already stormed off."

"So you admit that you turned tail?" he asked, surprised.

"I departed your conversation, in which I had little interest. So, do you intend to insult me further before you hand over your notes, or do you intend to be honorable?"

She looked sideways at him from beneath the brim of her straw bonnet, the closest he'd yet seen her come to actual flirtation. Lust hit him again like a hot breeze. Burningly aware of Emma

Grenville's upturned face, and her full, slightly parted lips, he leaned down and touched his mouth to hers.

At the feather-light contact, lightning shot down his spine. He straightened, startled. Emma's eyes were closed, and he was abruptly torn between the desire to join her in the cart and see how well sprung the vehicle was, and the gut-wrenching need to flee. Grey blinked. He didn't react like that to a kiss. He liked kissing, and had been told he excelled at it, but a simple touching of lips did not turn him addle-brained.

Her eyes fluttered open, startled and wide. "What . . . what in the world do you think you're doing?"

Using every ounce of hard-earned self-control that he possessed, Greydon shrugged. "You said you gave lessons about men like me," he drawled. "What do you think I was doing?"

A delicious blush crept up her cheeks. Grey followed her flushed skin down to the prim neckline of her gown and shifted uncomfortably in the saddle.

"I will not . . . dignify that with a response," she stammered. "If you will please give me those papers, Your Grace."

Wordlessly he reached into his coat pocket and handed the bundle over, brushing her fingers as she took it from him. Not even sparing it a look, she set it on the seat beside her. Then Emma cleared her throat, her eyes on the road in front of her, and scarlet still staining her cheeks.

"Thank you." With a weak cluck she flicked the reins and the dilapidated cart and horse lurched into motion again.

Grinning, Grey fell in beside her. However much the kiss had startled him, she'd obviously been even more affected. She probably was unused to having males about. Now that she'd begun to figure out what benefits his masculine presence could provide, this was going to be the easiest seduction—and thereby the most satisfying wager—he'd ever won. He'd be surprised if she managed a mile before she threw herself on him.

They'd only gone half that distance when she looked over at him. "Why are you still here?"

That was unexpected. "You've begun work on your part of the wager," he improvised. "I would like to begin on mine, as well."

The cart jerked to a halt. "What?"

"I would like to meet my students, Miss Emma. If you don't mind."

From the look in her eyes she clearly did mind, but he had little sympathy for her. Emma pressed her lips together, then nodded. "We do not allow men on Academy grounds, but I suppose I will have to make an exception this one time."

"At least this once," he agreed.

"You will be supervised—at all times."

He gave a slow smile. "By you?"

She faced forward again. "I am the headmistress. Competent instructors staff the Academy, Your Grace. I will look in on your progress when I can, but winning this wager will occupy most of my time."

Grey scowled at her profile. Perhaps she hadn't been as affected by the kiss as he'd thought. He would put more effort into the next one. "You may be occupied, but you won't be winning anything."

"Well, one of us is wrong, and I'm fairly certain it's not me."

They could continue their little disagreement all day, but in truth, Grey was curious to meet the small females who were going to help him triumph over Miss Emma. Training girls to enter Society successfully would have been at the top of the list of things he'd thought never to do, but teaching a few chits to flirt and twirl would be a small price to pay for bringing the Academy—and Emma Grenville—to her knees.

A troll stood guard at the front gate. At least he looked like a troll, old and gnarled and seated on a stool which leaned against one side of the old wrought iron. All he needed was a pipe to complete the image. As they approached, the troll unfolded surprisingly long legs and stood, doffing his malformed hat.

"Morning, Miss Emma."

"Tobias."

As the cart passed him, the troll moved into the center of the carriage path, blocking Grey. "Sorry, yer lordship. No men allowed."

Grey lifted an eyebrow as Cornwall snorted beneath him. "What are you, then?"

The troll grinned. "Employed. An' I intend to keep it that way."

"It's all right, Tobias," Emma called. "His Grace may enter—today. I will give you a written schedule detailing when he will be at the Academy."

Doffing his hat again, the troll moved out of the

roadway. "You must be the duke of all dukes, Your Grace, t'be allowed beyond these gates when it ain't visiting day."

Glancing ahead at Emma's disappearing figure, Grey leaned down. "Is she always this strict?"

"Where outsiders and rules 're concerned, aye. She'll do anything for those girls, though. Miss Emma's tough on the outside, but she's got a heart bigger than west Hampshire."

Somehow, knowing that Emma was so well regarded didn't leave him feeling particularly masterful. He wasn't necessarily putting her out of business, though, he decided as he tapped Cornwall in the ribs. He was teaching her a lesson about a chit's proper place in Society. And, hopefully, in his bed.

"Are you coming, Your Grace?"

Emma had hopped down from the cart and stood, arms folded, waiting for him at the main building's front entrance. Behind him the gate clanged shut. Grey stifled a scowl as he swung down from Cornwall. Here he was, locked in a girls' school. If his mother knew, she would be faint with laughter. Lady Caroline and the hounds, on the other hand, would probably be suffering a collective apoplexy. That particular thought made him smile. In some ways, this wasn't such a bad way to spend his time, after all.

Chapter 6

Emma smoothed her skirt and tried to keep to a normal pace as she led the duke into the depths of Miss Grenville's Academy. Her London Social Graces students would be waiting for her already, probably wondering why in the world Miss Emma was late. And she had no idea what to tell them.

She couldn't blame it on Freddie Mayburne, that blasted rakehell. As if she would ever permit him to call on Jane. No, annoying as Freddie was, today she barely spared him a second thought. Today, her problem was much larger. Several inches over six feet larger.

The Duke of Wycliffe had *kissed* her. Why in heavens would he want to do such a thing? Greydon Brakenridge might indeed be a rake, but he

was a wealthy and exceedingly handsome one.
The most lovely ladies in London probably surrounded him at every soirée, and he could kiss
anyone he wanted.

Now, as his gleaming black Hessian boots
stalked down the hallway behind her, all she
could think of was how good it had felt when he
kissed *her*. Her first kiss, given by a duke. She
wondered whether he intended to do it again.
The next time she would pay more attention to
the warmth and the firm yet soft feel of his lips,
and how she had wanted to melt like warm but-
ter into his arms.

She suddenly realized they had reached her
classroom, and stopped so quickly he nearly ran
into her from behind. Not daring to look at him in
case her befuddlement showed on her face, she
marched to the front of the room as her five hand-
picked students stopped chattering and turned
nearly as one to look at the large golden lion behind her. She'd meant to meet with them first and
explain the situation, but the duke had outmaneuvered her.

"Ladies," she said, in her most matter-of-fact
tone, "allow me to introduce His Grace, the Duke
of Wycliffe. He will be taking over this class for a
short time."

"Gadzooks," Jane whispered, sinking into her
chair.

Emma should have made Lady Jane amend the
vulgarism, but given the circumstances, it
seemed appropriate. "Please stand and introduce
yourselves."

Jane shot to her feet again. "Lady Jane

Wydon," she said, curtsying. Her voice shook only a little, and Emma relaxed a fraction. They were her best and her brightest; whatever the outcome of the wager, they would do themselves proud.

"Lady Jane," the duke repeated, his tone tight.

Emma risked a sideways glance at him. His stance was easy and relaxed, but she could have sworn that his tanned face had grown several shades paler. His jaw also seemed to be closed rather firmly. In fact, he almost looked as though he wanted to flee.

Mary Mawgry managed to utter her name without fainting, and neither Henrietta Brendale nor Julia Potwin so much as giggled during their introductions. So far, so good.

The petite, freckled figure sitting to Jane's right climbed to her feet and curtsied in distinct military fashion. "Miss Elizabeth Newcombe," Lizzy enunciated. "Did you lose your land?"

"Elizabeth!" Emma chastised, unsurprised that the Academy's young imp was underwhelmed by the golden nobility in their midst.

Wycliffe straightened almost imperceptibly. "No. Why do you ask?"

"I'm trying to discover why Your Grace would want to teach at Miss Grenville's Academy."

"Ah." He rocked back on his heels. "Miss Emma and I made a wager."

Emma winced. Obviously Greydon Braken-ridge didn't have the slightest idea how to handle young, curious females—which boded well for her, but certainly not for him.

Lizzy nodded. "What did you wager over?"

Folding her arms across her chest, Emma sank back against the edge of the small desk at the front of the room. "Yes, Your Grace, what did we wager over?"

The glance he sent in her direction was full of annoyance. She hadn't been the one to call half of the human species stupid and useless, though, so he could just fend for himself.

"Miss Emma wagered that she could manage my uncle's estate better than I could," he said in an over-loud, patronizing voice, "and I wagered that I could instruct you in ballroom decorum better than she could."

"Well, that's silly." Elizabeth snorted. "No one can do anything better than Miss Emma. You're going to lose."

"I am certain your headmistress is quite competent in the instruction of embroidery and etiquette. However, my—"

"Actually, Your Grace, Miss Perchase teaches embroidery." Mary bobbed another curtsy, her gaze on the hardwood floor.

He cleared his throat. "Yes, thank you Miss . . . Mawgry, but my point is that my instruction will be more practical-minded."

The girls looked baffled, and Emma allowed herself a small smile at Wycliffe's broad back. All she had to do was estimate the market value of a few acres of barley and some cattle, and recommend their sale in the correct proportions. The duke's task involved both communicating information to headstrong young ladies who weren't nearly as dim as he seemed to think, and gaining enough of their respect that they would be willing to put into practice what he preached. Asking them to declare that he was better at it than she was—well, he hadn't a chance in Hades.

A movement in the doorway caught her attention. Students and instructors filled the hallway beyond, straining to catch a glimpse of the Academy's unusual visitor. Emma straightened, walking to the door. "Back to your studies, ladies," she told them, closing it firmly.

She could hardly blame them for their interest; other than fathers, brothers, and the visitors on performance nights, men did not set foot on Academy grounds. Having this particular magnificent, virile specimen in the midst of five dozen curious girls was rather like bringing a torch into a room filled with dry kindling. Heavens, even *she'd* allowed him to kiss her, and she knew better.

The classroom seemed very quiet, and Emma yanked her thoughts back to the present. The instructor and his students were clearly sizing one another up, and she knew from past experience that Lizzy, at least, was probably girding her loins for battle. Emma moved back into the room.

"I know this is odd, ladies," she said, "but think of it as an experiment. His Grace has a great deal of . . . familiarity with the London Season and its regimens, and he wishes to pass some of that knowledge on to you." Emma gestured at the duke. "His instruction could very well be helpful for those of you nearing your own debuts, Jane and Mary."

There. That made them even for the notes he'd given her. He met her gaze for a moment, light green eyes assessing her. Then he took a slow step closer. For a heart-stopping moment she thought he meant to kiss her again. Emma took an unsteady breath. His back was to the young ladies, so they couldn't see the slow, wicked smile that touched his mouth.

She belatedly backed away a step. "Not in front of my students," she whispered.

The humor in his eyes deepened. "Later, then," he said in the same low tone, and reached past her for the pointer resting across the desk.

"Miss Emma, does this mean we don't have to do our French?" Julia asked.

She tried to ignore the warmth creeping up her cheeks, and hoped the girls wouldn't notice it. "You will have to keep up with the rest of your studies, just as you would if I were instructing this class."

"Do you all take French?" Wycliffe asked unexpectedly.

"Henrietta and Julia and I do," Elizabeth answered. "Jane tutors me, but she can never remember the imperfect tenses."

"Lizzy!" Jane blushed. "I do so remember them. You just never want to look them up for yourself."

Elizabeth sighed. "I wouldn't have to, if you would tell me what they—"

Emma returned to the door. This had deteriorated nicely—a good first lesson for the Duke of Wycliffe, if not for the girls. "If you'll excuse me, I have some papers to look over." She leaned out the door. As she'd already instructed in case of the duke's appearance, Miss Perchase waited in the hallway, though the poor woman looked ready to faint.

"Miss Perchase will oversee your instruction today," she said, pulling the gray-haired woman into the classroom.

"Ah. The embroidery instructor."

"She teaches Latin, as well, Your Grace. I'll return to escort you off the grounds at the luncheon break. You have ..." She glanced at the small clock resting on a bookshelf, ". . . forty-two minutes. Good luck to you, Your Grace." She gestured at a small bell sitting beside the clock. "Just for your information, that is there in case of emergency. Ring it if you need to be rescued."

"Thank you, but I won't be needing it."

"We'll see."

Tristan waited for Greydon outside the Academy's guarded gates as he made his exit precisely forty-two minutes later. "Thank God you're still alive," the viscount exclaimed, looking toward the school with eyes narrowed against the bright noonday sun.

"And why wouldn't I be?" Grey asked, as the gates clanged shut behind him. The dull headache he'd acquired thudded in response.

"Good day, Your Grace," the troll called from behind the fortress walls.

"Tobias."

The viscount's gray gelding fell into a canter beside Cornwall. "The first time you mentioned Miss Grenville's Academy, you said something about becoming a rotting carcass before you'd go through those gates. When your valet said you'd headed in this direction for the second time in two days, naturally I feared the worst. I had no idea, of course, that you were on a first-name basis with the gatekeeper."

The country air had apparently loosened his valet's tongue. He and Bundle were going to have to have a little chat. "Since when do you interrogate my valet over my whereabouts?"

"Since you've begun making wagers with pretty headmistresses and concealing their whereabouts from your closest friends."

Grey glared at Dare, that odd, heated sensation running through him again at the mention of Emma. This was becoming bothersome. "You know where she is now," he said stiffly. "Have at her."

"*I* can't get through the gates. That seems to be a privilege reserved for you, Your Grace. Have you charmed all of your students into voting for you, yet? If the wager's over, you might at least have invited me in to view the resolution."

He wouldn't exactly say he'd charmed the chits; a more accurate description would be that he'd survived the first meeting with them—barely. "If you followed me here to complain, I'm really not in the mood, Tris."

"Then you probably don't want to go back to Haverly right now, either," the viscount replied, undaunted. "Your Alice is convinced you've come to Hampshire to find a replacement for her, since you've apparently been celibate since we arrived. The entire scenario's dissolved into something of a tantrum by now, I would think."

Grey closed his eyes for a moment. "First of all, she's not *my* Alice, thank you very much. She's more like a . . . leech that keeps attaching itself to my nether regions."

"Yuck." Tristan grimaced, then took on a more thoughtful expression. "Or maybe not."

"And secondly, I am not looking for a replacement anything—much less if it's female. As far as I'm concerned, cousin William can have the dukedom when I've hopped the twig."

"Then—"

"I am attempting to win a wager which will hopefully result in shutting down that damned Academy."

"That's exactly what I told Alice." They made the turn up the road toward Haverly. "That does leave me with a question, though."

He'd clenched his jaw so much today, it was beginning to ache more than his throbbing skull. "What question?"

"Why didn't you tell me about Emma Grenville's whereabouts?"

Sometimes Viscount Dare's enjoyment of pandemonium could be very tiresome. "I had more pressing things on my mind. You know where she is now. Leave off."

"Fine. I only came out here to find you because I was concerned."

"You came out to see how much trouble you could cause. What's going on with you and Sylvia?"

A rare sneer appeared on Dare's face. "Before she realized how limited my finances were, she thought she might wish to become my viscountess."

"And when did she realize otherwise?"

"I told her the morning we left to come to Hampshire. Why do you think she wanted to ride with Blumton and your cast-off?"

"Hm. I thought Sylvia would know better than

to associate with you under any circumstances, anyway."

Tristan put a hand to his breast. "Now I'm wounded. Direct me to the nearest inn and lend me a quid so I can drown my sorrows."

Grey rubbed his knuckles against his aching temple. "If my finances were as limited as yours, I would be spending my time going over the new estate plans for Haverly and figuring out how to adapt some of them to Dare."

The viscount rode in silence for a long moment. "Well," he said finally, pulling his horse back around to face toward Basingstoke, "since we're giving unsolicited advice, allow me to inform you that if you keep heading down this particularly obnoxious path, Your Grace, you may find the rest of yourself resembling the rotting carcass your insides have already become."

As Dare disappeared back around the curve in the road, Grey slowed Cornwall to a walk. When Tristan had inherited Dare Park three years ago, the debts had been piled so high around the once-grand estate that he'd barely been able to see over them. Adding to that the rumor that the old Lord Dare's death hadn't been the accident the family made it out to be, and four younger brothers to be educated or in need of incomes, it was a miracle that Tristan Carroway hadn't immediately become the cold, liquor-pickled mirror of his father.

"Damnation," Grey muttered, and kneed Cornwall again. Apparently he was winning the race of which of them would first turn into their damned fathers.

He wasn't going to take all the blame himself,

though. Not today. After meeting those outspoken school chits, he could almost believe the headmistress had maneuvered him into making the wager in the first place. He wasn't sure whether he'd be better off trying to mold his so-called students into the sort of chits he could tolerate, or just shortening his sentence.

As he reached the manor's front entry, the doors slammed open. Charles Blumton hurtled down the chipped granite steps toward him, approaching so quickly that Cornwall shied away from his flapping coattails.

"Thank God, Wycliffe!" he panted, dodging Cornwall's prancing. "Come down from that monster and help me!"

"Help you do what?"

"Rescue Alice, of course!"

Grey jerked the reins, and the bay came to an abrupt halt. "I am not participating in one of Alice's little tantrums."

Charles grabbed onto the bridle, narrowly avoiding the gelding's snapping teeth. "No, it's not that at all. She's stuck!"

"Stuck where?" Grey asked skeptically.

Blumton hesitated. "Well, you'd better come see."

If nothing else, it would distract him from Emma. Scowling as much at that thought as in anticipation of whatever mayhem lay inside, Grey swung down from Cornwall and tossed the reins to a hovering groom.

"All right." He gestured for Charles to precede him. "Enlighten me."

Charles hopped up the steps. "I'm not really sure what happened. Your aunt, Alice, and Lady

Sylvia were chatting about that wager you made with that bluestocking chit, and then Alice decided she would get to the bottom of your ruse."

"My ruse?" he repeated coolly.

Blumton paled. "That's what she called it. I think it's a bloody fine wager."

Hobbes wasn't in the hallway as Blumton dashed through it and up the stairs, Grey following at a more dignified pace. The butler's absence concerned him more than Charles's hysterics; Hobbes had some common sense in his skull.

"Where are we going?"

Charles stumbled on the stairs. "You know, you really shouldn't leave me in charge," he said, picking himself up again. "You and Dare go riding off, and then your uncle—well, I don't know where the devil he is, and—"

"Don't you dare poke me with that! Help!"

A dozen servants and Aunt Regina were crowded around the open door of Grey's bed chamber. Considering that he'd closed and locked the door this morning, the activity didn't bode well. "What in damnation—"

"I warned her not to be such a nitwit." Lady Sylvia appeared in the doorway, and the servants scattered. She stepped back as Grey strode into the room—and stopped.

Alice Boswell stood in his window. Actually, she stood *outside* his window, on the narrow ledge just below it, and leaned into the room, one hand wrapped around the heavy curtains. With the other hand she batted at the broom Hobbes held pointed in her direction.

"Grey, save me!" she wailed as she caught sight of him.

"Step over the damned windowsill," he snapped.

"I can't! My gown is caught."

Hobbes gave him a pained look. "We've been attempting to free Miss Boswell, Your Grace, but without much success."

"They're trying to kill me!" she gasped.

"If only." Cursing, Grey stalked to the window, wrapped his arms around her trim waist, and pulled.

With a rip, the fabric of her skirt came free. Alice half stumbled into the bed chamber, clutching Grey's shoulder for balance as he yanked her forward.

"Oh, thank goodness," she sobbed, clinging to him.

"Miss Boswell," he said, his jaw clenched yet again, "do *not* enter my private chambers again without my permission."

"But Grey—"

He set her away from him, untangling her fingers from his lapels. "Is that clear?"

Tears welled in her eyes and overflowed down her ivory cheeks. Before he could applaud her theatrical skills, though, she gathered her torn skirt and fled the room. Blumton opened his mouth, apparently read the look on Grey's face, and exited on her heels. Aunt Regina followed them, an unsurprised expression on her face. Evidently she expected such behavior from the female companions of Brakenridge men.

"Hm," Sylvia murmured from the doorway. "You haven't exactly quieted anyone's curiosity, Your Grace."

He faced her, annoyed and frustrated that even

this little play hadn't taken his mind for one in-
stant away from a damned headmistress who
didn't seem to be moved at all by his kissing her.
"There is nothing to be curious about. I'm in
Hampshire at my uncle's request. The lot of you
are here so you wouldn't gab my whereabouts all
over London."

She glided up to him, all long lashes and cool
blue eyes. He hadn't quite figured out why she'd
been visiting his box at Vauxhall that night, because they were only casual social acquaintances. Knowing that she'd been hunting Tristan
explained a great deal, though it left open the
question of why she continued to remain at
Haverly.

She reached up to straighten his cravat. Perhaps she'd chosen a new target in lieu of Tristan.

"Your uncle's request explains why you jour-
neyed to Hampshire," she said in her honeyed
voice, "but it doesn't explain why you're wagering with bookish females and banning your mistress from your bed chamber."

"Because I choose to do so."

She lowered her hands and nodded. "I do like
a man who knows what he wants. Good afternoon, Your Grace."

"Lady Sylvia."

He would have closed the door after her, but
Blumton and the servants had knocked it off its
hinges during their rescue attempt. With a sigh,
Grey dropped into the chair at his dressing table.
Damnation. Alice left him with nothing but a feel-
ing of mild disgust anymore. Even the elegant
Sylvia didn't stir him, though she apparently had
further temptations in mind.

Perhaps that was it: he was used to females who pursued him. Since he'd turned eighteen, he'd been deluged with perfumed skin and dropped scarves and female callers whose carriages mysteriously broke down at his doorstep in the middle of the night. He hated it, but he expected it. Caroline had provided a small buffer until she'd decided to take the reins and run the proverbial horses off the proverbial cliff, after which the hounds had returned in force.

Emma Grenville, on the other hand, didn't seem to be interested in him at all. Given the way he'd been behaving, though, that shouldn't be surprising. He'd grown adept over the years at being arrogant and boorish just to give himself a moment to breathe while his opponents and pursuers regrouped. After today, Alice would no doubt begin trying to poison him. He would be lucky if Tristan didn't join her.

Well, he could still do something about his friend, at least. Climbing to his feet again, he went downstairs and left instructions for someone to repair his door, then headed out to find a groom and his horse. There were only three inns in Haverly's immediate vicinity; Tris was bound to be at one of them. A few glasses should put them both in better humor. At least, he hoped so.

Emma tapped her pencil against the worn surface of her desk, scowling at the pages spread out before her. It had only taken a few minutes of skimming through the duke's closely spaced figures and descriptions for her to realize that her task was going to be much more difficult than she'd envisioned, and that coming up with a better estate plan than his was going to be nearly impossible.

True, she managed the Academy and made a profit in the process. With the school, though, it was straightforward: one source of income, and the expenses for payroll, food, supplies, rent, and upkeep. An estate was infinitely more complicated, with—

"Miss Emma, another of the Haverly gentlemen is at the front gate!"

She jumped as Elizabeth Newcombe charged into her office. "Lizzy, please calm yourself."

Elizabeth glared at her. "I'm very calm, Miss Emma. I'm just wondering how many men are going to be instructing us."

"Just the one."

"Good. He's quite enough. This other one gave me a shilling, though, to come and tell you he was here." She held out the bright copper coin.

"Elizabeth, that is a bribe."

"No, it's not, because I would have told you about him, anyway."

Well, that seemed logical. "Come along, then, and we'll go see what he wants."

A crowd of girls surrounded the front gates, their giggling chatter audible from halfway across the yard. She frowned. Allowing the Duke of Wycliffe into the Academy had been an unfortunate necessity, but she had no intention of permitting the reputation of the school, or the behavior of its students, to suffer because of his presence.

"Ladies," she said sternly as she approached, "I believe this afternoon is for writing letters or for reading. We do not stare, we do not gawk, and we do not make spectacles of ourselves."

"I take all the blame on myself, Miss Emma," the tall, dark-haired viscount from Wycliffe's group drawled from the far side of the gates. "It's just my devastating charm."

Emma stopped at the gate. "The Duke of Wycliffe isn't here, Lord . . ."

"Dare. Tristan Carroway. Wycliffe was too occupied with trying to bring you to ruin to introduce us."

"Trying, perhaps, but I can assure you that he won't succeed. Is there—"

"Actually, that's why I'm here." He glanced beyond her, to the grassy park where she could still hear giggling and whispering. "Is there somewhere we could chat?" he asked.

"Men aren't allowed on Academy grounds, my lord. And unfortunately, I'm quite busy at the mo—"

"Just five minutes," the viscount interrupted, favoring her with an engaging smile. "I'll be on my best behavior."

Under normal circumstances she would have refused. Nothing about the past two days, though, had been normal. And if Lord Dare could give her some insight into Wycliffe's character, that could only be beneficial.

"Five minutes," she said, pulling the gate key from her pocket. Tobias only manned the gate when she was out in the cart or on Pimpernel, so she wouldn't have to climb down to open it. Most of the time, the gate simply remained locked against the outside world.

Emma slipped through the heavy iron and closed it again behind her. "How may I assist you then, my lord?" she asked, leading him toward the walking path which meandered in a wide circle around the Academy.

He fell into step beside her, tugging on his horse's reins to lead it along behind them. "I've come to offer you *my* assistance."

"Your assistance in what?"

"In winning the wager."

She stopped, surprised. "Why?"

Lord Dare shrugged. "General contrariness."

It was tempting to accept, but considering Wycliffe's confidence in his imminent victory, it also seemed far too convenient. "I appreciate the offer, my lord, but I'm sure you understand if I don't quite . . . trust its sincerity."

He gave a brief grin. "Zooks, you make me feel like Iago or Lady Macbeth or something. Not that I blame you, of course. You have to realize, though, that we have something in common."

"And what might that be?"

"We both want to see the Duke of Wycliffe lose."

Emma frowned. "But I thought you were his friend."

"I am. That doesn't keep me from finding him completely insufferable, sometimes. I've decided this will be good for him."

Hope touched Emma as she studied the expression in his light blue eyes, less amused than she expected. To have a landed lord assisting her would more than even the odds. "His Grace offered his own expertise to me, so I can't think how accepting yours could possibly be cheating," she said slowly.

"It wouldn't be cheating. It would be brilliant."

It would certainly serve Wycliffe right. She drew a breath. "Shall we go for a walk then, my lord? I have a few questions for you."

Lord Dare nodded. "I am at your service, my lady."

Chapter 7

Grey looked down at his guard. "Your head-mistress sent *you* to escort me?" he asked, lifting an eyebrow.

Elizabeth Newcombe shook her head, gesturing at sharp-elbowed Miss Perchase behind them. "I thought Miss Perchase might wish the company." The infant leaned closer and cupped a hand to her mouth, whispering, "She has the vapors."

"Ah." Leaving Cornwall with the troll, he fell into step beside the little chit as Tobias swung the gate closed and headed back to wherever he went when he wasn't guarding the fortress. "And where is Miss Emma?"

The Latin instructor cleared her throat. "Miss Emma is otherwise occupied."

"Otherwise occupied with what?"

"With studying estate management," Lizzy supplied.

Grey glanced toward the stairs as they entered the main building. "She's in her office, then? I did require a word with her this morning."

"Oh, no. She drove out to Haverly with that other gentleman."

A few things that had been bothering him since yesterday clicked into place. "Lord Dare, you mean?"

"Yes. He gave me a shilling."

"Elizabeth," Miss Perchase remonstrated, too late to quell the chit's tongue.

That explained why the rat hadn't been at any of the local inns or taverns yesterday afternoon. He'd told Tris to have a go at Emma, but he hadn't meant it, damn it all. And now they expected him to sit in a classroom all morning while Tristan explained how water helped crops grow and charmed the headmistress right out of his grasp.

"Are students allowed to leave the Academy grounds, Miss Perchase?"

"I . . . it's . . . it's not encouraged, Your Grace."

Lizzy looked up at him. "We are, but not without an instructor."

A slow smile touched his lips. "I'm an instructor."

"My . . . Your Gr—"

"You want to take us out? But you're supposed to be teaching us ballroom decorum."

"I cannot condone—"

"That begins well before a ball. And London has parks and gardens, you know. Dozens of them. Why don't you and Miss Perchase fetch your classmates, and I'll have the tr . . . Tobias rig out some transportation for us?"

Elizabeth looked at him dubiously. "All right, but I don't think Miss Emma would like it."

"Then she shouldn't have hired me. I'll be waiting for you out front."

With another suspicious look at him, Elizabeth grabbed the Latin instructor's hand and hurried off. Humming, Grey retraced his steps outside. The entire old monastery echoed with whispers of female voices and lavender perfume. He wondered what the monks would think of having these hallowed floors, upon which they'd knelt to worship, being trod by countless chits bent on hunting husbands.

The troll kingdom turned out to be the stable. Other than an old two-seater curricle, the only transportation the Academy possessed was the cart Emma had driven yesterday. With a sigh, Grey helped Tobias rig it out. At last count he owned three phaetons, four coaches, a barouche, and five curricles, and he could think of at least two cronies in London who would die of laughter if they ever saw him driving five little chits in a cart. Emma was going to pay for this, and he knew precisely how. The thought of her slender body spread beneath him, her auburn curls lying across the pillow while he took his delicious revenge, left him taut with impatience.

"Ye taking the young ones out for a nature study, then?" Tobias asked as they brought the rig around to the front door.

"Something like that. Did Miss Emma say where she was headed this morning?"

"Aye."

Females had no idea how to hire proper servants. "And where was she going this morning?" he asked, doubting that Tobias had any idea how patient he was being or how thankful the gatekeeper should be for that fact.

"With that other fellow from Haverly."

Grey took a deep breath. In about another two minutes he was going to thrash the man. "Tobias, have you considered what I—"

"Hold on, Your Grace," the old groom interrupted. "I've worked here for thirty years, since the day Miss Grenville opened the doors. I'm an old tomcat, and these girls—all of 'em—are my kittens. *Nobody* harms my kittens. So whatever trouble you've a mind to cause for Miss Emma, don't expect me t'make it any easier for you."

Grey looked at Tobias for a long moment, reassessing his estimation of the troll. "Interesting," he finally drawled, "but I'm here to win a wager. Your 'kittens' will receive no harm from me." If a certain cat among them wanted to play, though, he would be more than happy to oblige.

"I'll be keeping my eye on you just to be sure of that, Your Grace."

This was becoming decidedly less amusing. "I'll keep that in mind."

The front doors burst open, and his students hurried down the steps, Miss Perchase trailing behind and looking as though she was about to have an apoplexy. The girls all looked so . . . pristine as they gathered at the back of the vehicle: prim bonnets and matching pelisses and shawls, three of them carrying quaint little parasols. Grey scowled. What in damnation was he doing, instructing virginal, infant chits how to catch husbands?

"What took you so long?" he grumbled.

"Miss Emma says we must always be properly attired," the senior girl, Lady Jane something, said brightly. "We had to fetch our bonnets."

"Splendid. Let's get going then, shall we?"

They remained by the tail of the vehicle, looking at him expectantly. Finally his little guard sighed. "You're supposed to help us up," she said.

Stifling a curse beneath a smile, Grey stalked around the back of the vehicle and one by one offered them his hand as they stepped up over the low lip of the tail. The groom stood holding the dilapidated horse and grinning gap-toothed at him.

Once the chits and their chaperone were settled, he climbed onto the low seat and took the ribbons. "We'll be back in time for luncheon," he announced.

The groom stepped back from the cart. "Mind the turns," he said. "Old Joe can get a bit cantankerous."

As Grey was a member of the four-horse club, driving a cart and pony was about as challenging as sitting on a tree stump. He clucked at Old Joe and started the cart rolling toward the front gate. "Go let us out, why don't you?"

Tobias did so, and as they started up the rutted lane toward Haverly, a small hand touched Grey's shoulder. "Where are we going, Your Grace?"

"It's a surprise."

"Is it far?"

"I don't know." He glanced over his shoulder at a pair of serious brown eyes. "Why?"

"Mary doesn't travel very well. Miss Emma usually has her sit up front."

Grey returned his gaze to the road. "Do you want to sit up here with me, Miss Mawgry?"

"No, Your Grace," the quiet voice answered. "I'll be fine."

"She's fine," he said, for the little chaperone's benefit. For all the chaperoning Miss Perchase was doing, she might as well have been dead in the back of the wagon.

Elizabeth leaned up against his back, little hands on both of his shoulders. "She's going to be ill," she whispered in his ear.

This was absolutely going to kill him—and Emma Grenville knew it, no doubt. In fact, giving him an apoplexy had probably been her plan all along. He couldn't make her pay the rent if he was dead.

He pulled Old Joe to a stop. "Miss Mawgry, why don't you join me?" he asked, turning around in the seat.

Miss Perchase put a hand to her chest. "Your Gr—"

"It's the driver's seat, not Gretna Green," he said shortly. "Miss Mawgry?"

The brunette did look a little gray-cheeked as she rose. "I'm very sorry, Your Grace," she muttered. "I just need to face forward."

If Elizabeth hadn't spoken, the chit would have cast up her accounts without uttering a word of protest. "I prefer the wind in my face, myself," he said, relenting a little. He stood and helped her onto the driver's perch beside him. "Speak up, next time."

"Miss Emma says men don't like to hear complaints."

He wondered where Miss Emma had learned that bit of information. "Neither do men like persons vomiting in their carriages."

"Yes, Your Grace."

They clattered down the road again. "Better?" he asked.

"Yes, Your Grace. Thank you."

The relative silence lasted for two minutes, while Grey tried to decide where Tristan might have escorted Emma. Probably the nearest cattle pasture—Haverly had at least two dozen new calves this spring, and females adored babies of any species.

"Your Grace," the little annoyance behind him piped up again, "are you rich?"

"That's one question a lady is never supposed to ask a gentleman."

"Oh. But how is anyone supposed to find out anything, then?"

"Observation and subtle inquiry." This teaching business might not be so godawful, after all.

"May we observe, then?"

"Please do." If it kept them quiet while he scouted for Emma and Tristan, all the better.

A few moments of furious whispering erupted behind him and then stopped. The estate road appeared on their left, curving around the Academy's duck pond, and Grey coaxed Old Joe into a wide turn. The old horse responded readily enough, and he relaxed a little. That old groom was a damned trouble-making nuisance. All in all, the morning was progressing better than he'd anticipated.

"All right," a hushed voice finally said.

A blue bonnet appeared over Grey's shoulder and craned forward over the driver's perch, peering in the direction of . . .

Devil a bit. "What are you looking at?"

Miss Perchase uttered a faint squeaking sound.

"I'm trying to see your boots, Your Grace." Lady Jane, her cheeks crimson, peeked at him from around the rim of her bonnet and vanished behind him again.

"Ah." He guided the cart around yet another pothole. The last thing he wanted was for Miss Mawgry to vomit on his unseen Hessian boots. Grey scowled. Actually, the very last thing he wanted was for the young chits to report to their headmistress that he'd been encouraging some sort of lascivious behavior. "Given that our . . . relationship is that of teacher and pupils, I suppose direct questions are acceptable. So yes, I am wealthy."

"Do you spend a great deal of time in London, Your Grace?" one of the other chits, Miss Potwin, asked, while the other infants congratulated her on her choice of question.

He wondered if they would ever ask anything unexpected. "During the Season, yes. The rest of the year, I have obligations at my—"

Mary Mawgry leaned forward and vomited all over his boots. Reflexively Grey grabbed her shoulder to keep her from toppling off the seat. At that same moment, Old Joe must have decided he was thirsty: declining to follow the curve in the road, he towed them straight to the edge of the pond. The right front wheel dropped into a deep mudhole.

"Bloody—"

Before Grey could complete his curse, the cart tipped sideways into the water. And so did he.

Shrieking females splashed into the water all around him, while the ducks exploded, squawking, into the air. In addition to the water being damned cold, it was also deeper than he expected; as he tried to stand, he submerged completely again.

Mary Mawgry was closest, already paddling for the bank and ungainly in her sodden green gown, Miss Perchase right behind her. The other girls had landed further out in the water, and he swam in their direction, his boots heavy with the weight of the water.

He grabbed Julia Potwin by the elbow as she thrashed around unhelpfully. "This way, Miss Potwin," he grunted, towing her toward the bank until the water was shallow enough for her to stand.

"Help!" Lady Jane shrieked breathlessly. "Lizzy can't swim!"

Whipping around, Grey caught sight of the prim straw bonnet just as it sank beneath the murky surface. His chest tight with alarm, he launched himself out into the pond again. As he reached the spot where she'd disappeared, he dove straight down.

With his second grab he caught a handful of material, and hauled upward. As they broke the surface, he held his own breath until she gave a huge gasp for air.

"Thank God."

The little chit began flailing madly, her elbow ramming him in the cheekbone. "Don't let me drown!" she gasped, writhing in his grip.

"I won't, Lizzy. Relax. I've got you."

With a squeak she wrapped her arms around his neck, clinging to him with a death grip. Grey choked but began towing her toward the bank. They were close enough to make it before she asphyxiated him.

As he caught sight of the rest of the girls struggling onto dry land, he nearly changed his mind and headed for the opposite bank. He'd found Dare and Emma, after all. Or rather, they had found *him*. Tristan was wrapping a horse blanket around Lady Jane's shoulders, while Emma Grenville charged down the bank, looking as though she meant to—

Damnation. "Emma, *stop!*"

She splashed into the water, landing a few yards from him, and immediately began paddling madly in his direction. Lizzy freed one arm from around his neck to grip her headmistress's sleeve, and at least he could breathe again.

As they reached the bank, Tristan hauled the females up. While Grey bent over to catch his breath, he looked sideways at Emma, standing there like a mother goose with her goslings gathered around her.

The sun outlined her slender body through the wet gown, and Grey stayed crouched over longer than he needed to, taking her in.

"You've frightened the ducks," Tristan drawled, though his gaze was on the young females rather than the pond.

"Frightened myself, too."

Emma detached herself from her goslings and stomped up to him. "Your Grace, I demand to know what happened! What in the world did you think you were doing, bringing *my* stu—"

"*My* students," he interrupted. "We had an accident."

She snapped her jaw shut, glaring at him while water dripped off his nose. "This contest is over," she ground out.

"Then you lose."

"I—"

"Miss Emma," Lizzy interrupted, slogging over to the headmistress and plucking her sleeve, "it *was* just an accident." She sneezed.

"God bless," everyone uttered in near unison.

"Thank you. We don't want you to lose your wager because of us," the little one continued, then turned to look up at him from beneath her drooping bonnet. "And His Grace saved my life."

He didn't feel very heroic. "I wouldn't go *that* far."

"Oh, no," Lady Jane piped up, "it was magnificent."

Tristan cleared his throat. "Perhaps we should get everyone back to the Academy."

Emma, a blush creeping up her damp cheeks as she continued to glare at Grey, turned her back on him to face Dare. "Yes. I'm afraid, though, that the girls won't all fit in the phaeton."

"I'd like to walk," Mary Mawgry said in a dull voice, her face white.

"Me, too," Elizabeth echoed immediately, taking Mary's hand in hers.

The rest of the girls followed suit. Grey eyed them, surprised. Mary's reluctance to climb back into a carriage, he could understand. The rest of them, though, should have been clamoring for a chance to ride back to the Academy with Tristan and change out of their wet, muddy, and now decidedly unbecoming gowns. Yet they elected to trudge back with their travel-troubled friend.

"We're walking," he said. Lifting an eyebrow at Tristan's skeptical expression, Grey scrambled back down the slippery bank to where Old Joe stood chest-deep in the pond, guzzling water happily. The overturned cart wedged against his backside didn't seem to bother him in the least.

As he ducked into the water to unfasten the harness, footsteps splashed into the pond behind him. Even with the lemon scent of her hair doused by pond water, he knew who it was. The hairs on his arms prickled. "Stay out of the water, Emma," he grunted.

"It's a bit late for that," she said in the practical tone he'd already become used to hearing from her.

"You shouldn't have jumped in before, either. I had the situation well in hand."

"It didn't appear that way to me. And just how is this preparing them for a London ball?"

He hadn't quite figured that out himself, but neither did he have any intention of confessing that he'd been prowling for her. "Where did you get this damned mule?" he asked instead.

She stiffened. "Old Joe is a gift from a dear friend. The Academy took him in to save him from the slaughterhouse—and he's been a valuable asset."

Grey grunted as he pulled the last fastening free. "You shouldn't have gone to the trouble."

"*I've* never had any difficulty with him."

"Of course not. The two of you have the same temperament." Before she could respond to that, he grabbed Old Joe's halter in one hand and her elbow in the other, and hauled both of them up the bank to dry land.

"Please do not drag me about. I am not a . . . a horse."

Wycliffe only grunted, but Emma thought she had made her point. As soon as she got her feet under her, she pulled free of his grip, and without so much as an "I beg your pardon for being so rude and strong," he let her go.

The sight of her girls thrashing about in the deep water had terrified her to her bones. Knowing now that they were safe filled her with a kind of giddy relief, even though she wanted to be furious at Wycliffe.

"Ladies," she said, gathering the shivering girls around her again, "why don't we put our hats and shawls in the phaeton? If Lord Dare doesn't mind transporting them back to the Academy, that is."

Lord Dare, the only dry person among them, stood glaring at Wycliffe. "Of course I don't mind. I feel shabby, though, driving off alone."

Miss Perchase coughed. "If I might, my lord, this has been quite enough excitement for me."

"Splendid." Grey walked over, handed the instructor up into the seat, and then tethered the cart horse to the back of the phaeton. "There. Miss Perchase and Old Joe can keep you company."

"Not exactly what I had in mind," the viscount muttered, so quietly that Emma barely made out the words. With a glance in her direction he climbed back up into the high seat. "We'll alert everyone about the emergency."

The look the two men exchanged as the phaeton rolled down the road made Emma blush. They couldn't be fighting over . . . her, of all people. True, Wycliffe had kissed her once, but he had done that just to distract her from the wager.

"Shall we?" Wycliffe asked, looking elegant despite his dripping tawny hair, soggy cravat, muddy boots, and missing coat. Emma blinked. His damp lawn shirt clung to the muscles of his strong arms and chest, revealing them in clear detail. She doubted there was a spare ounce of fat on his tall frame.

As she lifted her face, he was looking straight at her. Her blush deepened, and he raised an eyebrow. "Is something wrong, Miss Emma?"

"No. Of course not. No thanks to you, though. Come along, ladies." She looked over her shoulder at him, clenching her jaw against the lure of his raw masculine beauty. "I'm sure you'll wish to return to Haverly at once and change out of those wet clothes."

He fell into step beside her as she started up the road. "Not at all. I left my horse at the Academy, anyway."

"Oh."

With their bonnets and shawls missing, and in the company of a hatless and coatless man, the lot of them looked like gypsies. Yes, Wycliffe had acted in a heroic manner, and yes, he had in all likelihood saved Lizzy from grave injury or worse, but this was certainly not what she had bargained for when she had agreed to the wager.

"I think we need to revisit the rules of this contest," she said, in her calmest and most reasonable tone.

"Don't be a coward."

"I am *not* a coward! These girls are my responsibility, Your Grace, whoever is instructing them. Aside from that, your—"

"Call me Wycliffe," he interrupted, tucking her hand around the damp arm of his shirt.

"I don't want to call you Wycliffe. And please do not interrupt me."

"Uh, oh," Henrietta said from behind them. "The last time Miss Emma told me that, I had to write a five-hundred-word grammatically correct essay on the virtues of not interrupting people."

Wycliffe lifted an eyebrow. "Is that to be my punishment, Emma?"

His amused expression made it seem an improper question. Everything he said to her, though, seemed to have some underlying scandalous meaning. "You aren't one of my students. If you were, you would be in danger of failing out of the Academy."

The girls giggled. The duke only tugged her a little closer.

"So you teach impertinence toward one's social superiors?" he asked mildly.

Emma clenched her jaw. "I teach that there are moments when a woman must stand up for herself—particularly when there is no one else to do it for her."

Wycliffe looked away, apparently engrossed by the flock of crows settling into a nearby birch tree. "Which rules do you wish to alter, Emma?"

She didn't know when he'd given himself permission to use her first name, but she liked the way he said it, and the drawl in his deep, cultured voice. Drawing a breath, she increased the distance between them, though she didn't remove her hand from his arm. That would have been rude.

"I worry that whatever wisdom you impart to these students," she began, searching for the words that would convince him without leaving her open to a counterattack, "will be less significant than the fact that you, the Duke of Wycliffe, sat in a room with them for an extended period of time."

He was silent for a moment. "We're fully chaperoned. And I'm not about to damage my reputation *or* theirs."

He was right—but she couldn't tell him her real reason for objecting to his continued presence when she didn't know it herself. "I don't think having a chaperone present will matter, Your Grace," she said doggedly.

"Ladies hire male dance masters, for God's sake," he retorted, scowling. "Men hire them for their daughters."

"And we want to learn about London Society and ballroom decorum," Julia put in.

Emma glanced over her shoulder at the five girls walking close—far too close—behind them. "Learning about Society won't do you any good if you're too ruined to join its ranks. His Grace is a . . . single gentleman."

"What do you suggest, then?"

"I suggest that you do the honorable, gentlemanly thing and concede," she said.

"No."

She frowned at him. "That's not very helpful."

"I'm not here to be helpful—except to my students."

"Considering your first outing with them ended with several near drownings, I have to express doubt about your helpfulness."

"It was my fault, really," Mary said in her quiet voice from behind them.

The duke turned, walking backward to face the girls. "Nonsense. That damned mule is entirely at fault."

A wave of tittering giggles brought Emma to an abrupt halt. "You meant to say 'that unfortunate horse,' I'm certain," she stated, glaring at him.

He looked straight back at her. "I believe I'm capable of expressing myself without your assistance."

Elizabeth tugged his damp sleeve. "We don't use profanity at the Academy," she whispered.

His expression softened as he looked down at Lizzy, and Emma's heart gave an odd flip-flop. The Duke of Wycliffe did possess compassion, even if he rarely chose to show it.

"Is 'deuced' acceptable, then?"

"I think that's a vulgarism."

"And common," Emma added. "But better than profanity, I suppose, if you can't do without one or the other."

"Am I a student or an instructor, then? It's deuced confusing." As he turned to face forward again, she caught the wink he gave the girls.

"I don't find it confusing in the least," she retorted. "You are neither."

"Then you concede?"

Emma wanted to growl at the impossible man. "All I concede is that the contest is untenable! Win or lose, I see no benefit for the Academy or its students!"

The duke was silent for a long moment. She had been insane to ever agree to such a wager. And now she couldn't seem to rid herself of it, or him.

"All right," he said finally.

She blinked. "I'm . . . glad you see it that way," she said, trying to hide her surprising disappointment.

"You have no idea how I see anything," he retorted. "And I'm not suggesting you've won anything, my dear headmistress."

"No?"

"No. Since I am a . . . single gentleman, this," and he gestured back at the girls, "shall remain *your* class. *I*, however, will be your guest lecturer. You can dawdle about Haverly counting sheep, and we shall be close beside you, conducting class."

"How does that—"

"*Your* class, in the open, with witnesses. As far as anyone else is concerned, I will merely be escorting you on my uncle's property. And *you* will be there to witness personally that nothing improper occurs." He eyed her. "Nothing wrong with that, is there?"

She could think of myriad things wrong with that, including the obvious fact that he would likely attempt to disrupt her estate studies at every possible opportunity. On the other hand, she could just as easily do the same thing to him.

And all of the other participants—Lord Dare, Lord Haverly, and the girls—were *her* allies, really.

"I think that would be acceptable," she said slowly.

The girls cheered. The Duke of Wycliffe had the poor manners to look smug, but Emma wasn't so certain he hadn't just lost himself the wager. She dearly hoped so, anyway.

Chapter 8

⁓⊙⊙⁓

The ladies abandoned Grey on the Academy's front steps. He glared at the closed door, his stiffening cravat beginning to scratch him, and his fine Hessian boots squishing and caked with mud and algae.

"Rotten luck," Tristan said from behind him.

He'd forgotten the viscount was in the vicinity. "How so?" he asked.

His damp coat smacked him in the chest as he turned around, and he caught it reflexively. Dare, dry and comfortable and not footsore from having trudged a mile and a half in wet boots, sat on the phaeton's high seat.

"Well, you know what they say about first impressions," the viscount drawled. "Starting with a swim in the duck pond and nearly killing the lot of them wouldn't be my preferred way of teaching young ladies their place in the world, but you're the expert."

Grey opened his mouth to reply, but with a flick of the ribbons Tristan sent the phaeton down the drive. Someone—the troll, probably—had left Cornwall tethered to the post at the foot of the steps. He leaned back against the animal's warm flank. Obviously no one wanted him at Miss Grenville's Academy. He didn't particularly want to be there, himself. If not for his odd attraction to the headmistress, he would have been back at Haverly, interviewing potential estate managers, dodging Alice and Sylvia, and perhaps spending the afternoon fishing.

He shook out his coat. When little Elizabeth Newcombe had slipped beneath the pond's surface, he had been terrified. It was something of a surprise, really. In that moment, Lizzy had ceased to be one of the enemy and had become a helpless, frightened little girl.

Grey pulled his pocket watch free and flipped it open. It had stopped, the hands stuck at half past eleven. By now it was well past noon, and he had accomplished nothing except to demonstrate his fallibility to both Emma and his students. She hadn't even informed him where or when they would be conducting class tomorrow.

Hm. The troll was nowhere in sight. Grey draped his coat over Cornwall's saddle and strolled up the front steps. He half expected armed guards to appear as he pushed open the door and entered the hallowed halls, but nothing so dramatic happened. In fact, if not for the faint sounds of female voices and footsteps on other floors, he might have thought himself in an empty building.

Feeling more than a little like a burglar, he climbed the stairs to the second floor. Miss Emma's office was on the near left side, the door slightly ajar. Taking a breath, he pushed open the door and leaned inside.

The small room was empty. Books, no doubt the ones borrowed from Sir John's office, surrounded the desk. Open tomes cluttered the chairs, the desktop, and even a window sill. She'd begun her research, obviously. Closing the door quietly, he made his way to her desk.

Already, she'd made remarkable progress. Several pages of questions written in her neat hand occupied the middle of the desk. Queries about acreage, yield, irrigation, the current and future price of beef—she knew which damned questions to ask, even if she didn't yet have the answers.

To his surprise, he found the profusion of notes and books . . . stimulating. He blew out his breath. This was positively insane. Women were nothing new, and he'd known many intimately. Emma Grenville was forthright and intelligent and independent, and quite unlike any other woman he'd ever met. And he found her damned arousing.

He heard a noise in the adjoining room. That door, like the one opening into the hallway had been, was slightly ajar. Glad he'd kept quiet to this point, Grey crept toward the opening.

Emma padded into sight and vanished again behind a wardrobe. Grey leaned against the door frame, watching, as she came into view again.

Her long hair hung in loose auburn waves down her back, and she wore only a shift, the damp material nearly transparent as she crossed in front of a window. He instantly went hard.

He should have realized that someone as dedicated to her work as Emma was would locate her sleeping quarters close to her office; the arrangement was practical and efficient. Placing his hand against the door, he slowly pushed it further open. The arrangement was also nicely convenient.

"Emma," he murmured, from the doorway.

She jumped, whirling around to face him. "Your Grace!"

"I told you to call me Wycliffe." He allowed his gaze to travel the length of her and back. "You look delicious."

Belatedly she looked down at herself. With a deep blush she hugged her arms across her chest. "What are you doing here? Get out!"

"That wasn't the response I was hoping for. I don't bite, for God's sake."

She scampered to the small bed and grabbed for an old robe which lay across the coverlet. "Out!"

"What is that?" he asked, gesturing at the dowdy covering. "Cotton? Wool?"

"It's wool," she snapped. "What do you care?"

"You should have a silk robe," he said softly, taking a step forward. "I could buy you a dozen."

"Mine serves quite well, thank you very much. Now, stop right there!"

He stopped, surprised. Women never refused pretty gifts when he offered them. He'd try something else, then. "It occurs to me that there might be another way you could win this wager."

He deliberately looked her up and down again, to make his intent perfectly clear. With the blasted robe shielding her, the view wasn't quite as enticing, and he was becoming mightily annoyed at himself for being so unable to help his heated reaction to her.

Emma lifted her chin. "I presume you are talking about matters of the flesh?" she asked, her voice not quite steady despite the defiant stance.

A slow smile curved his mouth. She was undeniably bright, but at the same time exceedingly naive. " 'Matters of the flesh?' " he repeated. "You sound like a schoolgirl, Emma. What I'm talking about is warm skin and hot caresses."

"Fornication."

Grey lifted an eyebrow, surprised again when she didn't give way. "To quote Shakespeare, 'making the two-backed beast.' "

She cleared her throat. "I am not interested."

"Liar. You're trembling for it." He leaned back against her chest of drawers, folding his arms across his chest. She couldn't be uninterested. As badly as he wanted her, she *had* to want him, even if she wasn't yet ready to admit it. Luckily, he was fairly patient.

"I'm not afraid of you," she continued. "I *am*, however, supposed to be setting an example for my students. I will not tolerate having a man in my private rooms."

"Men abound outside these walls, Emma. If you don't know how to deal with them, how can you expect to teach your students to do so? I would think that would be your utmost concern."

"You would be wrong. And I do not have to fall from a cliff to know it would be bad for my health." She stalked forward, planting her bare feet in front of him. "I pity you," she said.

Suddenly this little encounter wasn't so amusing. "And why is that?"

"Your self-delusions must constantly get you into embarrassing situations."

Grey lowered his brows. "Explain."

"You came to the Academy for the purpose of shutting it down, you nearly drown several of my charges, you insult women with your every breath, and yet you expect me to swoon into your arms simply because you say it must be so."

No one in Grey's long memory had ever spoken to him like that. Anger coursing through him, he gave a stiff nod. "I see. Thank you for clearing up my misconceptions. Good day."

Before she could respond with an even more insulting comment, he strode out the door. At the stairs he barged past a handful of schoolgirls. Ignoring their polite greetings and giggles, he continued down to the first floor and out the front door.

"Damned blasted female," he muttered, yanking his coat free from Cornwall's cantle and swinging up into the saddle.

He didn't need to moon after Emma Grenville. At Haverly he had two females practically panting to service him. One woman would suit as well another.

He kicked Cornwall in the ribs and set the bay off at a canter, barely slowing to let Tobias pull open the gate.

Damnation. He couldn't even believe his own

delusions any longer. One female was not the same as any other; he'd discovered one who intrigued and enticed him as no other female ever had. And she was the one, of course, who didn't want anything to do with him.

He really couldn't blame her; he *had* been rather hostile from the outset—which didn't change the fact that he wanted to bury himself in a woman who obviously considered him contemptible. *Pitiable*, she'd said. Following her earlier contention that he was unimpressive, he didn't sound very tempting.

"Your Grace?"

Grey pulled up sharply on the reins, narrowly avoiding a collision with the fashionable young man who stood squarely in the middle of the road. "What in damnation do you think you're doing?" he snapped.

Freddie Mayburne danced backward to avoid Cornwall's sidestepping. "I was waiting for you. Your friend in the phaeton," and he gestured over his shoulder toward Haverly, "said you'd be along shortly."

"Why were you lying in wait for me?"

"You're instructing Lady Jane Wydon, and I would be grateful if you would deliver a note to her. From me." He dug into his coat pocket and produced a folded piece of paper.

Grey looked at him for a moment. "I am not a letter carrier," he said stiffly. "Deliver it yourself."

"No men are allowed on Academy grounds," Mayburne said, grabbing Cornwall's bridle.

Grey was beginning to wish he wasn't an exception to that particular rule. "Then send it by post."

The lad gave a slight smile. "But Your Grace, then everyone will know about it. Surely you understand that my interest in Jane is a private matter."

"Unless it's to your advantage to impress her with your adoration in public."

"Of course."

For a moment, Grey felt as if he was talking to a younger version of himself. "If your interest is sincere, why not speak with her father about it?"

"I'm not trying to win Lord Greaves's approval. Not yet, anyway. First I have to convince Jane."

Greydon looked at him cynically. "And Jane's money."

The smile deepened. "You do understand."

With a deep breath, Grey swung out of the saddle. He knew the Marquis of Greaves, and Freddie didn't look like his idea of a son-in-law. "You do understand that Lady Jane is seventeen, and still in the schoolroom."

"And next year, everyone in London will be after her. She's lovely as an angel, and rich as Croesus."

Greedy as he seemed to be, at least Freddie wasn't after Emma. "What was your conversation with the headmistress about?"

"The iron maiden? She won't let me anywhere near Jane; she even burned one of my letters right in front of me last month. That's why I thought to take up my quest with you, Your Grace. In London, all the ladies seemed to delight in talking about you. Your advice would seem to be sound."

Wonderful. "Yes, I am frequently the subject of

gossip. Drop your trousers in public, and you could achieve the same."

Freddie chuckled. "Actually, they talked endlessly about how they felt ready to swoon when you entered a room. And—"

"Women discussed this in front of you?"

For a moment Frederick's smile became sheepish, the expression making his features look momentarily younger and more innocent. "I have five aunts."

"I see."

"And so, I humbly request your assistance in winning Lady Jane Wydon's heart."

At least he hadn't made a secret of being equally interested in Jane's—or rather, her father's—purse. It was a bit mercenary even for Grey, and Emma certainly wouldn't like it. On the other hand, Freddie's success would undoubtedly cause further trouble for Miss Grenville's Academy, and would give him another card in his deck against Emma. "Why don't you join me for luncheon at Haverly?" he asked.

The lad gave a self-assured grin. "Splendid, Wycliffe. You won't regret this."

No, but Emma Grenville probably would.

For the first time in recent memory, Emma Grenville was late coming downstairs to breakfast. It wasn't that she anticipated the meals too much to be tardy for them; rather, she was her students' primary role model in politeness and propriety. If she were late, they would place less importance on being on time.

Isabelle Santerre looked up, surprise on her oval face, as Emma skidded into the dining hall just as the most junior students rose to clear the tables. She stifled a grimace as she hurried to the front of the room.

"My apologies, ladies," she said, trying to regain her breath. "As you know, our instruction routine has been upended over the past few days. I would like to assure you that this will not continue much longer, and that the end result should be more money for the Academy and its programs."

Applause rippled through the hall, though she wasn't certain whether it was in response to her speech, or in approval of the continuing presence of the Duke of Wycliffe. And the dratted thing was, she wasn't certain which pleased *her* more, either.

"So, please proceed to your classes. My social graces students, Miss Perchase, if you will assemble on the front steps?"

Isabelle intercepted her at the door. "You are going to continue with this, even after yesterday?"

Emma took the French instructor's arm as they made their way down the hallway. "I considered the dilemma all night, Isabelle," she said in a low voice. She'd also spent a large share of time last evening contemplating silk dressing gowns and large, virile dukes. "The benefits of winning the wager are too great to pass by, whatever the inconveniences."

"The inconveniences? You all nearly drowned, and then he practically assaulted you in your own bed chamber!"

"Hush. It was nothing near an assault."

"What would you call it, then?"

"An argument. Unpleasant, to be sure, but nonthreatening."

It hadn't even been unpleasant, really. Of course, all Wycliffe wanted was to satisfy his base carnal desires, but she had never been the subject of any man's base anything, before. It was . . . titillating, in a way, to be desired by such a fine-looking specimen—even if he was arrogant and condescending and patronizing.

"I know you have good sense," Isabelle was saying. "But *s'il vous plaît*, do not let this contest hurt you."

"Don't worry, Isabelle. The well-being of my students and the Academy will always come before anything else."

She parted from her friend at the front door and went outside, where her students waited for her.

"Miss Emma, isn't Wycliffe coming?" Lizzy asked, tying the strings of her bonnet beneath her chin.

"His Grace, you mean," Emma corrected.

"He said we should call him Wycliffe."

Well, fine. When he'd encouraged her to call him by his titular name, she'd thought that might be some special privilege, reserved for friends and the females he was hunting. Obviously that wasn't the case.

"If he gave you permission," she said smoothly, "you should do as you think most appropriate. And no, I don't know whether he will be coming by today, or not. That being the case, we will walk to the near pasture at Haverly, and conduct today's lesson on the way."

"Walk? Drat," Elizabeth muttered, the rest of the girls echoing her.

"Yes, walk. We are cartless at the moment, and your lessons and my studies both need attention. This way, we may accomplish both."

Despite the confident statement, she had no idea how she would manage both the task of teaching ballroom etiquette and learning agriculture simultaneously. She couldn't abandon the girls, though, simply because their guest instructor was unreliable. Nor would she neglect her part of the wager, also for the girls' sake.

They started down the drive, and Tobias nodded as he pulled open the gate for them. "Wally Jones and me'll haul the cart out of the pond this afternoon. I'll have it looking good as new."

She patted him on the shoulder. " 'Good as new' would be a miracle. I'll happily settle for having all four wheels in working order."

As they walked north, the rumble of wheels heading toward them stopped Emma short. "To one side, ladies," she instructed, trying to pretend that she didn't have a very good idea who was coming toward them, and that her pulse hadn't begun to speed in response.

A phaeton rounded the bend and came to a stop beside them. "Miss Emma," Lord Dare said, hopping to the ground and doffing his hat in the same motion, "I am here to render assistance."

She smiled, though she couldn't help feeling disappointed. The viscount was so . . . not Wycliffe. "My thanks, Lord Dare, but as you can see, we are walking today." The phaeton had been so nice to ride in yesterday; she couldn't imagine owning such a marvelous, well-sprung contraption.

"I don't think we'd all fit up there, anyway," Elizabeth said to no one in particular.

"Perhaps you might meet us at the near pasture," Emma suggested.

Light blue eyes took in the flock of young females ranged behind her. "I thought Wycliffe was taking your class today."

Apparently Dare and Wycliffe weren't communicating very well. That was interesting. "I assume he has other business to attend to this morning."

The viscount shrugged. "Oh, well. His loss; my gain."

More clomping of hooves came on the heels of that declaration, and Emma held her breath again. A large open barouche appeared, followed by a great black coach emblazoned with the Wycliffe coat of arms. The Duke of Wycliffe sat in the barouche, legs crossed at the ankles, one arm outstretched along the plush red seatback, and a cigar stuck at a jaunty angle between his teeth.

"Oh, my goodness," Mary Mawgry whispered in an awed tone.

The sight *was* rather impressive. In fact, Emma had never gazed upon such a spectacular-looking vehicle—or man.

"Damned show-off," Lord Dare muttered under his breath. His normally affable face was set, his eyes narrowed and annoyed.

"Good morning, ladies," the duke said, standing as the barouche rolled to a stop. "Where shall we conduct our studies today?"

"Where did the barouche come from?" the viscount asked. "Your uncle doesn't own one."

"The Earl of Palgrove lent it to me yesterday evening."

Emma blinked. "Palgrove is a good eight miles north of Basingstoke."

Green eyes met hers. "Closer to ten, actually. Nice fellow, Palgrove." He held his hand down to her. "Shall we?"

She straightened her shoulders. "And the coach?"

"I didn't know how many guards and chaperones and other hangers-on you'd have accompanying you." For the first time he glanced at Dare. "This way there's room for everyone."

"I want to ride in the coach," Julia stated.

"So do I," Henrietta added, to no one's surprise.

"Perhaps your groom might take the phaeton back to Haverly, then, and I'll accompany you." Dare's hand touched Emma's shoulder, though she hadn't been aware of his approach.

Wycliffe nodded, gesturing to the liveried groom who sat beside the coach's driver. "Danielson, take the phaeton back to Haverly. At a walk, if you please."

"Yes, Your Grace."

Before she could think to protest, Dare and Wycliffe lifted her up into the barouche, one man on each arm. Elizabeth piled in after her, while Jane and Mary followed with more decorum. The other girls and Miss Perchase made for the coach.

"Elizabeth, do not bounce on the seat," she instructed.

The duke tapped on the floor with his ivory-handled walking stick, and the vehicle started off.

"And you think not bouncing will assure Lizzy's success in Society?" he drawled.

Sometime yesterday, they'd all ended up on first name terms. She felt rather left out. "I think not bouncing is the proper way to behave," Emma corrected sharply.

"I'm not going into Society, anyway," Lizzy said, taking Mary Mawgry's hand and patting it. "Let me know if you're going to be ill, and I'll make them stop," she whispered.

"I thought the barouche might be well-sprung enough to prevent any discomfort, Miss Mawgry," the duke said.

So now the Duke of Wycliffe was traveling twenty miles to secure a proper vehicle for one of her—his—students. Emma frowned.

"Oh, it's wonderful," Mary said, smiling. "Even nicer than my father's. I think I'll be fine. Thank you for your concern, Wycliffe."

Emma's scowl deepened. So Mary felt chatty today; that was unusual. She kept her gaze on the passing hedge grove. She certainly didn't want to make shy Mary self-conscious by gaping at her.

"Why aren't you going into Society, little one?" Lord Dare asked from beside her.

Lizzy wrinkled her freckled nose. "I want to be an instructor, like Miss Emma. Or a governess. I haven't decided, yet."

Wycliffe lifted an eyebrow. "Really?"

"Yes, really."

Clearing her throat to warn the outspoken girl, Emma turned to more directly face Dare. "I've been doing some research, my lord. Why did you suggest an oat crop yesterday, when barley is selling higher at market?"

"Oat's less costly to grow. You don't have to worry so much about irrigation, and even if the crop ruins, the local farmers will still buy it as hay."

"But in the near field, the duck pond could irrigate the crop for next to nothing. Profit versus cost, barley is the more sound choice."

Dare looked at her, his expression mildly surprised. "You're right, of course."

The duke's eyes seemed alight with amusement and, unless she was gravely mistaken, approval. That was odd, considering he didn't think she could add two numbers together, much less comprehend the fluctuating price of barley.

"If you'd asked me about the crop," he said, "I would have recommended barley."

The viscount shifted beside her, but remained silent. Something had definitely set the two men at odds with one another. If it was she, well, she couldn't help feeling flattered despite her practical nature. Her well-married friends would never believe a duke and a viscount were sparring over her, of all people.

"If you'd recommended barley, I still would have researched the alternatives," she said, just so he wouldn't have the last word.

"I would hope so."

"Wycliffe," Jane asked, "do all of London's assemblies allow waltzing now?"

Turning his gaze from Emma, he nodded. "Even the stodgiest have been forced into permitting it, since the alternative is that no one will attend. They all accept Almack's, though, as the watermark. Without permission to waltz there, don't expect to be allowed to do it elsewhere."

"So you recommend the waltz?"

"I recommend anything which requires a man and a woman to embrace."

"Your Grace!" Emma warned, over the giggles of the girls.

"If you'll excuse me, Emma," he said mildly, "I'm conducting a lesson."

"A lesson in lewd behavior!" she snapped.

"A lesson in ballroom decorum and on being successful in Society, actually," he amended.

His smug, arrogant expression irritated her immensely. "Just remember that I, too, will be one of the judges at the end of this contest, Your Grace."

"Since when?"

"Since now."

"Very well. But planting barley in one field won't win you any wagers. You're going to have to work harder than that, Emma."

So now he was giving her advice—as if she needed it. Well, perhaps she did, but not from him. "As that American naval fellow said, 'I have not yet begun to fight.' "

"Perhaps you should begin, then. You don't have much time." Before she could respond, he faced Jane and Mary again as though she had ceased to exist. "Men like to waltz, whether they're any good at it or not. The best female partner, therefore, is one who is not only proficient, but one who can make the fellow look better than he is."

He was trying to pull her into another argument, obviously, but this *was* his class, and they were his lessons, and if they continued in that vein, they would be fairly harmless. That would mean less work for her to unteach them later.

"Pray continue," she said, and turned to Lord Dare. "Since I am working on improving Haverly's circumstances as they currently exist, how long would it take to clear two acres and level it for construction?"

"Building another Academy?" the duke interjected.

"Teach," she said, flipping her hand at him.

Dare cleared his throat. "Perhaps you'd rather have this discussion later."

Emma took the viscount's gloved hand and squeezed his fingers. "His plans are already completed, or very nearly so, and I certainly have nothing to hide."

"Very well. Do you have an idea where you want to locate this construction?"

"Yes. Somewhere alongside the creek, preferably on the far side of Moult Hill. We don't want to spoil the view from the manor house—or from the Academy."

"Well, you—"

"We've arrived, Your Grace," the barouche driver announced. "Where do you wish me to stop?"

A small herd of cattle grazed on the far side of the meadow. "This is perfect," Emma said.

"Here, Roscoe," the duke echoed, as though the driver was incapable of interpreting her comments. The man was impossible.

They piled out of the barouche as the coach stopped behind them. Grey stifled a sigh, watching the other two girls and the fragile Miss Perchase rejoin their group. He should be grateful, he supposed, that Emma hadn't assigned twenty or thirty of the little chits to his care. With three of them in the barouche, he could just about keep track of both their conversation and the head-mistress's; with five, the task would become much more difficult, especially with damned Dare present.

The young ones jabbered around him in some obscure adolescent female language. Towering over them as he did by a good two feet, he had no trouble at least keeping Emma in sight.

Dare beside her, she walked up to Simmons and Roscoe. "Thank you, gentlemen," she said with a smile, "for not detouring us into the duck pond."

Ah, sarcasm. As if she wanted to be certain he got her point, Emma sent Grey a coy sideways glance. Having slain him with her wit, or what-ever she thought she'd accomplished, she wrapped her arm around Tristan's. After a mo-ment of low-voiced discussion, they strolled off in the direction of Uncle Dennis's cattle.

Grey watched the soft sway of her rounded hips as she headed away from him. Much as he wanted to level Dare, if she intended on dis-cussing land management, putting some dis-tance between them was probably wise. Just listening to her talking about barley in the barouche, he'd nearly had to place his hat over his trousers. There was clearly something very wrong with him.

"Wycliffe, are you certain we're allowed to call you Wycliffe?" young Lizzy asked, thankfully pulling his attention away from the head-mistress's backside.

"I said you should. And what I say is generally adhered to." He studied the cherubic upturned face with the sprinkling of freckles across the bridge of her nose. "Why?"

"Miss Emma said we shouldn't."

Oh, she had, had she? "We'll do as she says, then."

All of the faces looking at him fell with absurd expressions of disappointment. "We will?"

"Yes. You may no longer call me Wycliffe. You may call me Grey."

Lady Jane chuckled. "Miss Emma won't like that."

"Why not?"

"It's not very formal," Lizzy stated.

The others nodded. Before he could ask why Emma insisted on so much formality, Henrietta, followed by Julia, curtsied at him.

"Jane and Mary said you might instruct us about waltzing."

He'd actually meant to discover how much nonsense the Academy had stuffed into their heads, but he could do that just as easily while they attempted to dance. "I am at your disposal."

Now Emma was pointing at the cattle and saying something to Tristan. At his response, she laughed and jotted down some notes in the sheaf of papers she'd been toting. Grey narrowed his eyes. Blast it, that should have been *his* laugh, and *his* company she was enjoying.

The girls looked at him expectantly, perhaps waiting for him to pluck an orchestra out of his pocket. He glanced at Emma again. Well, if she meant to leave the class to his ministrations, then so be it.

"You do know how to waltz, I presume?"

"Yes. Miss Windicott instructs us in all the latest dances."

"That's promising. Lady Jane, will you do me the honor?"

The black-haired beauty nodded and stepped forward. "All right."

Grey held up his hand. "First mistake."

"What did I do?"

"Your response didn't flatter me in the least."

"I said yes," Jane protested, blushing.

"Yes, in the same tone as if someone had asked you to lend them a quid."

Julia and Henrietta wore identical looks of puzzlement, while Mary seemed baffled and Lizzy looked as though she wanted to hit him for chastising Jane. Of even more significance, Emma had turned her back on the cows.

"Allow me to explain. A dance, and most particularly a waltz, begins the moment a man approaches you. When he asks you to do him the honor of dancing with him, he's really asking that you make him feel honored."

"Flattered, you mean."

"Exactly."

"When do *we* feel flattered?' Lizzy asked.

"You're already flattered, because he's asked you to dance."

"That's stupid. Miss Emma says—"

"Miss Emma isn't teaching this class. I am. You are flattered." He sent another glance up the meadow; Emma seemed to have forgotten the cattle entirely. Miss Perchase had apparently lost the ability to speak. "Elizabeth, will you do me the honor of this waltz?"

The little chit looked up at him and batted her eyelashes. "Grey, you flatter me."

"Good. Now—"

"But, oh, I'm so overwhelmed," she continued. "The honor is . . . too . . . great." Gasping, she put a hand to her forehead and fainted into the grass.

It took all of Grey's control not to laugh. By God, she reminded him of Emma. He lifted an eyebrow. "That's a bit much, Elizabeth," he said dryly. "And besides, now you've shown me your legs, and I'll have to marry you."

She propped herself up on her elbows. "If getting married is that easy, why do we have to do all the waltzing? If I wanted to marry you, I could just walk over and lift up my skirt."

"Lizzy!" Jane gasped, turning bright red.

"*Enough!*" Emma bellowed, charging into the middle of their little circle like an angry lioness. "No one is lifting her skirt for any reason! No one is *discussing* lifting her skirt! Is that clear?"

"Yes, Miss Emma," the girls echoed, while Lizzy scrambled to her feet.

The headmistress whipped around to face Grey. "A word with you, Your Grace?"

He followed her as she stalked away from the others. Even the cows must have sensed her ire, for they began trotting in the opposite direction.

"These are not any of your light-skirted female acquaintances," she said in a low, fierce voice. "These are young girls who cannot afford to make a single mistake once they enter Society."

He wasn't stupid enough to argue with her. "I know."

"You are not to discuss means or opportunities for improper behavior, nor are you to condone such behavior by treating it as no more than a jest."

"I won't."

Emma opened her mouth to continue, then slowly closed it again. "You've already announced that you would be quite happy to see the Academy gone. You'll forgive me for my lack of faith in the sincerity of your efforts to help my students succeed."

She had every reason to doubt his motives. Every morning he awoke unsure of them, himself. "Whatever you may think of me, Emma, you may rest assured that I would never set out to lose a wager."

"Good."

"Nor have I ever backed down from a challenge," he continued, holding her gaze and not entirely certain why he felt the need to continue. She didn't look remotely in the mood to be seduced. "And you, my dear, are a challenge."

Emma lifted her chin. "You possess nothing I want."

Grey smiled. While he wanted to pull her into his arms and prove her wrong, he would settle for words. "I possess several things you want. You just don't know about them yet."

She started to turn away, but he reached out to run his fingers along her arm.

"And I can give you more than you ever dreamed of."

"I don't need or want your money, except what I will win with this wager."

"I'm not talking about money. I'm talking about pleasure, Emma. Deep, warm, satisfying pleasure."

She pulled her arm away, but not before he felt her shiver. He *did* affect her, whether she would admit to it or not. And eventually, he vowed, she would.

Chapter 9

∽◦◦◦◦◦∽

Emma sat on a stump and looked through her notes as the duke and his students waltzed and did a great deal of chatting and laughing across the clearing. Even with Miss Perchase there, she had no intention of letting the group out of her sight.

"That's the most pleasant I've seen him behave toward females in over a year," Dare said, as he pitched stones into the small creek.

"You mean he used to be nicer?" she asked, glancing at the tawny-haired duke for the hundredth time.

The viscount shrugged. "Not by much. To be fair, though, I suppose it's not entirely his fault. Women have been trying to waylay him into marriage since he turned eighteen."

"Which explains his attitude of superiority toward females, I suppose," she mused, "but not his dislike."

Dare skipped another stone across the water. "For that, Miss Emma, we can all thank Lady Caroline Sheffield."

Emma paused in her note-taking. "*The* Lady Caroline Sheffield? The one who attended—"

"Your Academy. Yes."

"Did she break his heart?"

With a short laugh, the viscount sank into the grass beside her. "Worse than that. She came within a whisker of trapping him into marriage."

Emma had never liked Lady Caroline. Now, she liked her even less. "He dislikes all women because one female was dishonest? That's absurd."

"You'd have to ask him about that. Now, why all the questions about cattle?"

To her annoyance, she would rather have continued discussing Wycliffe and what, exactly, constituted a whisker. Blinking, she returned to her notes. "It's just that I don't see why Lord Haverly's set on Sussex cows. They're not particularly good milk providers, and the beef is merely palatable. In addition, they require a great deal of grain for fattening."

He cleared his throat. "I'm afraid I don't know much about cattle. Dare Park is squarely in the middle of sheep country." Tristan looked over his shoulder at the group of dancers. "I hate to say it, but Grey's the expert where cattle are concerned."

"Hmm."

"Ask me about brickworks, though, and I can

make your head spin with my bounty of knowledge."

Emma laughed. "I may risk it, my lord."

"Call me Tristan. Everyone does."

She wasn't certain whether he was simply being friendly or whether he had something more on his mind, but he'd been helpful thus far, and she did like his easy manner—especially in comparison with Wycliffe's antagonistic, seductive one. "Tristan it is. And I suppose you should call me Emma."

He smiled. "With pleasure, Emma."

"Have I missed anything interesting?" Wycliffe asked, strolling over with his students trailing along behind him.

Not even glancing over his shoulder, Tristan resumed tossing rocks into the creek. They plopped rather than skipped now, but aerial acrobatics probably weren't the point.

"We've just been discussing cows," she said.

"Ah." He turned to his students. "Ten minutes' rest, ladies. I need to let my toes recover."

As Emma expected, they didn't need a second request. The girls scampered off along the creek. "Stay in sight of the carriages," she called after them.

Wycliffe put one of his booted feet on the stump beside her and leaned over her shoulder to view her notes. She resisted the urge to cover them up; as he'd said, the majority of his plans for improving Haverly were already completed, and she didn't have anything to be ashamed of. Some of her initial ideas seemed diabolically clever, if she did say so, herself.

"You don't like Sussex-bred cattle?" he asked, flicking the notes with his long fingers.

"I'm considering the suggestion of selling them and acquiring a stock of Herefords."

He leaned closer, tucking a stray strand of her hair back behind her ear. "A Hereford will cost you three times the price of a Sussex."

"But they'll fatten on grass, and fertilize a fallow field." She consulted her notes, trying to ignore the disturbing tendency to lean toward the large male presence beside her. "And they'll sell for four times what Sussex beef will bring."

"You've been studying."

Emma scowled. "That would seem to be a necessary part of winning the wager."

"Might I suggest keeping the cows and adding a Hereford-bred bull into the herd? That would cut your expense, and in the next few years increase the value of the beef."

She met his gaze. "Yes, but how much credit will I get for improvements that won't be born until next spring?"

"I'd take it into account," the viscount said, his back still to Wycliffe.

"As would I. But it's still not enough to win you the wager, Emma."

"As I recall," she said, trying not to sound haughty, "your plan calls for adding a Hereford bull. Obviously duplicating what you've suggested wouldn't help me in the slightest, either."

"And adding an entire herd of new blood will increase Haverly's debt, not its solvency."

Finally Dare climbed to his feet. "It's an idea, Grey," he said, facing them, "not a definite plan. The rest of us are allowed to have ideas. We don't all know the answers from birth."

"And I do?"

Emma looked up as the two men locked eyes. An odd, heavy disappointment touched her, and she lowered her eyes before either of them could notice it. They weren't quarreling over her, after all. It was too silly, really, to think that these two splendid males might be at odds over her.

"So," she said aloud, reminding herself that she was practical, and that logic dictated this turn of events was for the best, "this isn't about me."

They both looked at her. She stood, brushing the leaves from her skirt.

Grey lowered his boot from the stump. "What are you—"

"Excuse me," she interrupted, heading toward her students. "The girls and I will take the barouche back to the Academy for luncheon."

"I brought luncheon," Wycliffe said behind her.

She continued along the creek, trying to decide when she'd become such an idiot that she believed her own daydreams. "Vanity, thy name is woman," she muttered.

A hand gripped her elbow. "And why do you suddenly admit to that?" the duke's voice rumbled.

She felt her cheeks turn crimson. "Excuse me?" she stammered, and pulled free of his grip.

"You're probably the least vain female I've ever encountered," he said, moving up to walk beside her. "What did I miss back there?"

Emma quickened her pace, though she knew she didn't have a hope of outdistancing someone with a stride as long as Wycliffe's. "You didn't miss anything. We all simply have too much to accomplish to allow time for dilly-dallying. Ladies?"

He was silent as her students stopped gathering flowers and assembled before her, but she could feel his gaze on her face, trying to figure out why she'd suddenly begun behaving like a madwoman. Even if she managed to figure it out for herself, she had no intention of enlightening him.

"You said this wasn't about you," the duke finally stated. "To which 'this' were you referring?"

"Miss Emma, may Jane and I put the lupines in our room?" Elizabeth asked, lifting a handful of the pretty blue flowers.

"Of course you may. Are you ready to return to the Academy for luncheon?"

"Grey hasn't shown us how to gratefully decline an invitation to dance." Henrietta adopted her familiar stubborn expression. "And I'm to dance with him next."

Emma looked at her charges, all of whom had their eyes on the Duke of Wycliffe. His large, virile presence had immediately attracted her notice; she didn't know why she should be surprised that he had caught the girls' attention, as well. The realization, though, complicated the situation immensely. Enough about her own uncertain heart—she had five young ones to protect from a jaded rake. And fifty more back at the Academy, all susceptible to his charms. She didn't think their infatuations would cost her the wager, but the more serious possibility of young, broken hearts gave her pause.

"We've already discussed how to gracefully decline an invitation. Come along, back to the barouche."

"Not 'gracefully,' " Julia said. " 'Gratefully.' "

Emma stopped. " 'Gratefully?' " she repeated.

Certain she must have heard wrong, she turned to the duke. " 'Gratefully?' "

Despite the arrested look on his face as he gazed at her, he didn't appear to have heard a word of the conversation. "You meant that you thought the disagreement between Dare and myself was over you," he announced.

With effort she didn't turn tail and run. "That is not what I meant. I am quite capable of elucidating my own thought processes, thank you very much."

"Then do so. Explain."

She squared her shoulders. "Your conversation over who was born with which knowledge had nothing to do with the wager, and was therefore a waste of my—and my students'—time. Now, what do you mean, saying these young ladies should learn to 'gratefully' decline an offer to dance?"

"That's for my class to know, and for you to discover once you've lost the wager."

"I thought you had nothing to hide," she protested, putting her hands on her hips and wishing he didn't tower over her so effectively.

"No, that was you. I have hundreds of secrets."

Several of them, she very much wanted to know. "It's a shame, then, that you have no one in whom you can confide. Ladies?"

She turned on her heel, only the sound of muttered protests and skirts swishing through grass telling her that they followed.

"What time shall I come by for you in the morning?" the duke called after her.

Drat. Seeing him every day was so . . . frustrating, but there was no way to avoid it. Even more annoying, she wasn't all that sure she wanted to avoid him, anyway. "Nine sharp, if you please."

"I'll see you then."

"Yes, fine." Seeing him at nine wouldn't be the most aggravating part. Knowing that they would be spending the day together again tomorrow, she would spend the night tossing and turning while she tried not to think of him. That was even worse, because in her dreams he wasn't nearly as annoying.

"Are you going to make me walk back to Haverly?" Tristan asked.

Grey turned around as the barouche rumbled out of sight. The damned female was always escaping before he was finished with her. "No. You're the one with hornets in your hat. I'm as charming as always."

"Which isn't saying much."

"Hm. *Now* you may walk." Tristan didn't appear at all amused by that, and with a sigh Grey relented. "For God's sake, Dare, I was joking."

"You aren't very funny these days."

The viscount was right, but Grey shrugged it off and climbed into the coach. After Tristan joined him, Simmons started the vehicle through the glade and back in the direction of Haverly.

"How was your class today?" the viscount asked, after several moments of silence.

"Interesting." With a scowl, Grey leaned back against the plush black seat. "How was your conversation with Emma?"

"Inter—"

"Particularly the bit where you mentioned Caroline."

Dare's expression became defensive. "That was just in passing. Emma wanted to know why you were so despicable, and I said she would have to ask Caroline. And you should be instructing your chits, not eavesdropping."

The remaining bits of Grey's good humor faded. "She said I was despicable?"

"Not in those words, but it was hinted at fairly strongly."

"How strongly?"

"What do you care? She's a female. And a headmistress." With an exaggerated shudder of distaste, Dare pulled his pocket watch free and flipped it open. "Leave her to me, my boy."

"Ha. She'd flay you alive with that tongue of hers."

Dare frowned. "Emma? She's one of the most warm-hearted females I've ever met." The viscount's expression grew more thoughtful. "Perhaps it's just you she detests. You know, all that trying to 'rob her of her livelihood' business."

"I am not trying to rob anyone of anything," Grey snapped. "I am attempting to make her realize her place and function in the world."

It sounded pretentious even to him, but the way his motives for continuing to antagonize her changed daily, he decided not to try rephrasing. It would likely only come out sounding worse.

His uncle's cook would be less than pleased that her splendid luncheon of baked chicken and peach pies remained uneaten, but Mrs. Muldoon's good humor didn't concern him overly much. *He* was less than pleased that Emma had whisked herself and her students away, and reason and logic didn't help him justify his frustration in the slightest.

"How long will you have Palgrove's barouche?"

Grey stirred. "As long as I want it."

"I thought so."

"You thought what?"

"You bought it, didn't you?"

Damnation. "What if I did?"

"For Miss Grenville's Academy—which you'd like to see burned to the ground? You don't see anything odd in that?"

"It's for Uncle Dennis. He can do whatever he likes with it."

"I'm sure he and your aunt will have daily occasion to tour the countryside in an eight-seater barouche."

Grey eyed him. "I liked you better when we weren't speaking."

Tristan leaned forward. "Grey, I've seen you make business deals that left the losing side weeping. If you're just playing here, then so be it, but I hope you're aware of the consequences."

"So now you're my conscience? Leave off, Dare. I know what I'm doing."

"Are you certain about that? Sylvia and Blumton have already begun plying your relations for information about Emma and the Academy, and don't expect Alice to sit by and say nothing about her cold bed while you're out hunting other game."

That didn't bode well. He'd been so distracted by Emma and the wager that he hadn't even been aware of the maneuvering going on behind his back at Haverly. The fact that he was distracted at all was troubling. But Tristan was looking at him, so he shrugged. "I thought you were referring to the consequence of breaking underaged chits' hearts."

"That, too. None of them are your typical hard-bitten wagering sorts."

Grey forced a grin. "So you think I'll come out of this looking foul? It's a price I'm willing to pay. How many people even know about it, any-way? You, me, Blumton, and a few dozen spin-sters of varying ages." The thought was actually comforting. "I really don't have anything to lose."

Tristan didn't look convinced, and in truth, nei-ther was he. Obviously the fresh Hampshire air had rendered him completely insane. He'd lost the ability to separate business from pleasure, so he was making a muck of them both.

The question, then, was how to clean up the mess.

By the time they arrived back at Haverly, he'd come up with the beginnings of an answer, and he spent the next few hours mulling it over. It was as-tonishingly simple. Emma Grenville had a fine wit and a rare, lovely smile. She had a slender build and pert, beckoning breasts, and he desired her. He therefore merely had to accomplish one task: he had to make her desire him.

"What are you smiling about?"

Grey jumped. His entire annoying party sat prattling in the drawing room, and he hadn't heard a thing they were saying. In fact, he couldn't recall much about dinner, either, except that there had been boiled potatoes. Again—another product of his uncle's economizing. If he didn't get Emma out of his system soon, people were going to begin thinking him soft-headed—or worse, soft-hearted.

"I occasionally smile just because I feel like smiling," he drawled, leaning over to select a cigar from the box on the table.

Alice scowled. "It's not as if we don't all know, Grey."

His smile faded. "And what is it you know, Alice?" Deliberately he lit the cigar and took a long puff, ignoring his uncle's affronted look and Aunt Regina's delicate cough. He didn't care whether his smoking offended the ladies or not. He wasn't teaching etiquette this evening.

Hobbes entered the room. "Your Grace, my lords and ladies," he intoned, "Miss Emma Grenville."

With a silent oath Grey snuffed out his cigar, rising to his feet in the same motion. The other gentlemen in the room followed suit a heartbeat later.

Miss Emma glided into the drawing room. She'd dressed in a dark green gown with a rust-colored pelisse for the occasion; she looked well, if not quite as elegant as Alice and Sylvia. Grey wanted to devour her. Since he couldn't, he settled for running his gaze along the length of her slender, curved form and imagining.

"Emma, what brings you here at this hour?" Aunt Regina asked, her face concerned. "The Academy is well, I trust?"

The headmistress smiled, reaching out to squeeze the countess' outstretched hand. "Yes, everything is fine. Thank you for inquiring, my lady."

"You must tell us the reason for your visit," Sylvia cooed, cupping a glass of Madeira. "We haven't seen you since the evening you favored us with your . . . interesting rendition of Nurse."

"I apologize for not having you over to the Academy, but I'm afraid we're not equipped to accommodate visitors."

"Hm. Dare and Wycliffe seem to visit often enough." Sylvia sent Grey a sly sideways glance.

Grey drew a slow, annoyed breath. He might hope to lure Emma into misbehaving, but she hadn't done so yet, and he wouldn't have them insinuating that she'd done something improper.

Before he could give Sylvia a set-down, though, Tristan bent down, gazing toward Sylvia's dainty feet. "What is that, my dear?" he asked, toeing something none of them could see. "Oh, my, it seems you've coughed up a hairball, Lady Sylvia."

Grey lifted an eyebrow at Sylvia's affronted expression. "Don't look at me for sympathy," he said. "You began it."

"Actually, Your Grace," Emma said briskly, "*you* began it. As the host of the party here at Haverly, you should be attending to their entertainment and comfort. Given the amount of time you've spent instructing my students, I'm not surprised Lady Sylvia—and your other esteemed guests—should feel slighted."

She was in fine form this evening—both physically and mentally. "I appreciate your concern over the minimal time I've been able to spend with my guests," he returned smoothly, "though it behooves me to point out that you have interrupted a pleasant evening we've been spending in one another's company."

"Greydon," his uncle chastised.

Emma only nodded. "Indeed I have, Your Grace, for which I apologize. I shall be as brief as possible."

Damn. He'd wanted her to stay. Emma was far too clever for him to be fencing with her without first considering her reply.

"But you still haven't said why you're here," Alice said, her lips curved in a smile that looked closer to a snarl.

"Alice, you have all the subtlety of a dog bite," he returned. "I'm sure she'll tell us when she's ready to do so."

To his surprise, the headmistress blushed. "I'm afraid it's a personal matter. I require a word with you, Your Grace."

That was more like it. Moving forward, he gestured her toward a side door. "After you."

"Grey, what about—" Alice began in a whining voice.

"Excuse us for a moment," he said, cutting her off.

He shut the door behind him, watching Emma as she turned to face him. Her hands were clasped firmly behind her, and unless he was greatly mistaken, she was nervous.

"What can I do for you, Emma?" he asked in a low voice.

"First, open the door."

Damnation, lusting after a proper chit was frustrating. Reaching back, he cracked open the door. "There."

"More."

Swallowing an oath, he pushed it another inch. "Enough?"

"A foot at least, Your Grace."

"Fine."

When he'd complied she lifted her chin, finally meeting his gaze. "Thank you. With my students present, I haven't had an opportunity for a frank discussion with you."

If she began chatting about farming, he wouldn't be responsible for the consequences, open door or not. Her presence alone was enough to leave him aching. "Discuss, then," he said, taking a step toward her.

"Very well. I haven't seen much of the world."

He took another step closer. "I know."

"And you've seen a great deal of it, I suppose."

"I have." Three more steps and he would be close enough to touch her.

"I am aware, however, of the way the world works."

"Good." One step down, two to go.

Finally she seemed to notice how close he was getting. Shifting her hazel gaze between his feet and his face, she cleared her throat. "I know, for instance, that when compared with London, Hampshire must seem very dull."

"Not entire—"

"And that you, as a duke, do not like and are not accustomed to boredom."

With a slight smile, Grey shook his head, noting that they were at least out of the line of sight of the drawing room occupants. "I am frequently bored, and prefer to be challenged, though I believe we've had that discussion already."

"Yes—yes. That's my point, in fact. In order to keep yourself from being bored, you've convinced yourself that I'm some sort of . . . of a challenge."

He lifted an eyebrow, wondering which of them she was actually attempting to convince. "And you're here to inform me that you're not a challenge. Is that it?"

"Well, yes. I am a headmistress at a girls' school."

Her full, slightly parted lips beckoned to him. "Emma," he murmured, "you are a very great challenge."

"But—"

Grey leaned down and captured her mouth.

His warm lips teased and pulled, until Emma couldn't tell who was kissing whom. Her head kept saying that she should run away as fast as she could, but her head didn't have a chance against the molten heat of Greydon Brakenridge.

Arms of banded iron swept around her waist, pulling her to him. She could feel his arousal, his heat, pressing against her, and she groaned as warmth swept down her spine. He *did* desire her. He wasn't just teasing.

She twined her hands into his hair, and he deepened the embrace of their mouths. He was a rake, she desperately reminded herself. A very experienced rake, with two other women in this very house that he'd probably held in the same strong, warm embrace. Two women, just through the half open door from where she and the duke stood.

"Stop!" she hissed, yanking his hair.

He lifted his head, his eyes dark and his breathing as harsh as her own. "Why?"

"You go too far." His elegant hands, intimately cupping her bottom, seemed to burn through her gown to her flesh.

"Isn't this what you came here for, Emma?" he murmured.

"No!" Abruptly, though, she wondered if he wasn't correct.

"Then why didn't you write me one of your stimulating letters?" He dipped his head, running his lips across her throat.

Emma wanted to melt into him. Several of her married friends, especially the Countess of Kilcairn and the Marchioness of Althorpe, had attempted to describe what being the object of a man's desire felt like, but all of their words had been inadequate. Woefully so.

"A letter," she managed, "wouldn't have been sufficient."

"I agree. You've made your point much more clearly this way." His mouth found the base of her jaw.

"My point. Oh, good lord." *What had her point even been?* "Yes, my point." With every bit of self-control she possessed, Emma pushed her hands against his chest.

It was a pitiful effort, but he released her. She thought she'd escaped, until he stroked the back of his fingers along the low neckline of her gown. "I have a point to make, too, Emma."

She backstepped. "No doubt you do. But—"

"Kiss me again," he murmured, pursuing her. *Oh, my goodness, she wanted to.* "Let me speak," she demanded, putting her hand over his seeking mouth.

He tugged it away. "Speaking does not seem to be something you're shy about," he returned dryly.

"Humph. As I was saying, your presence in Hampshire is unusual enough that you have attracted the notice of my students."

"Your students."

"Yes." From his skeptical expression, he knew very well whose notice had been attracted, but at the moment that wasn't the point. "And even more, your presence at the Academy, and your . . . physical attractiveness . . . well, surely you understand that it's very easy for young ladies to be swayed by a kind word and a pleasing countenance."

To her relief, he nodded. She didn't think she would have been able to continue much longer.

"You're concerned that your students may develop a tendre for me."

"Yes, exactly."

"And that in doing so, they might cost you the wager."

"What?" she stammered. "The wager has nothing to do with this! I am talking about the . . . fragile hearts of young girls."

Wycliffe looked at her for a long moment. "You are, aren't you?" He sighed. "I have no intention of behaving in such an underhanded manner. I'll win the wager easily enough without resorting to that."

She nodded. "Thank you; I'm glad you understand. We have rules, and whatever your motivations for . . . pursuing me, I cannot—I will not—allow you to keep sneaking into the Academy—into my bed chamber—when a school full of young, impressionable females might see you and misinterpret your actions." He continued to gaze at her in silence, so she continued. "Is that clear?"

"Are you going to have this conversation with Dare?"

"That isn't necessary."

"And why is that?"

Now his expression was serious, even angry. Even—though her pulse fluttered again to think it—jealous. So part of the animosity between the two men *was* over her. A small thrill ran down her spine.

"Tristan has not been in my bed chamber. Nor has he kissed m—"

" 'Tristan'? You call him 'Tristan'?"

She flushed. Blast it, she should have been paying more attention to what she was saying. But she'd been too occupied with the idea that an actual—two actual—males found her desirable. "He asked me to," she offered lamely.

"Then I ask you to call me Grey. Will you do it?"

"Your Grace, I am not here to assign nomenclatures, or to participate in your little game of one-upmanship. I am here to make certain you understand both the rules of the Academy and the reason we have them. Please—"

"Will you?" he repeated, his tone and expression becoming dark.

Her pulse skittered again. "All right. If it will keep you from pummeling anyone, yes. I will call you Grey."

"Then do so."

"I just did."

"No, you didn't. You referred to me as Grey. Call me by my Christian name, Emma."

She sighed, hoping she looked more composed than she felt. "As you wish, Grey."

"That's more like it. Now, where were w—"

The door opened the rest of the way. "Greydon? Is everything all right?"

Grey closed his eyes for a moment, his expression unreadable, before he faced the doorway again. "Yes, Uncle Dennis. We've been discussing the wager."

Belatedly, Emma realized how close to one another they were standing. Swiftly she took a step back, folding her hands together. "It's just that I have a few doubts about the wisdom of some of the things His Grace is teaching my students," she said briskly.

Lord Haverly's smile wavered a little, and Emma winced. It was bad enough that she be seen in nearly private conversation with a man. For her to be discovered within touching distance of him would be enough to ruin her in London. Thank goodness none of her students was present; she was becoming an abysmal role model. And as for kissing Wycliffe, touching his hard chest and feeling his strong arms pulling her close . . . she would worry about that later.

"Well, I still believe this wager is a great deal of nonsense," Haverly said. "I don't suppose the two of you will listen to an old man's opinion, though."

"Not at the moment," the duke returned. "Excuse us, uncle, but there are a few more points we need to clarify."

Thanks to their previous embrace she knew precisely which point of his he wanted clarified, and Emma knew if she didn't escape at once, she probably wouldn't have the willpower to do so. "I believe I've stated my reservations, Your Grace. It is now up to you to satisfy them."

Grey faced her. "I believe I'm up to that task," he said in a low voice, his eyes glinting.

Damnation. She'd said the wrong thing—again. Hopefully Lord Haverly wouldn't notice her blush in the dim room. "I shall be going, now," she said, trying not to rush her words.

"You could stay for whist," the earl suggested, obviously making an effort to be his usual jovial self.

"Oh, no. Thank you for the offer, but I'm already breaking curfew, I'm afraid."

Brushing past Grey and Haverly, she entered the drawing room again. The tall blonde woman, Alice, looked at her with such hatred that it startled her. The others, Tristan and Lady Haverly included, bore speculative looks that she found nearly as disturbing.

"Did Tobias drive you?" the duke asked from behind her.

"No. I rode Pimpernel."

"You went riding alone at this hour?"

His voice was sharp, though she wasn't certain whether he was concerned for her safety, or appalled that a female had managed the ride to Haverly manor in the dark without becoming lost. "I have ridden alone frequently, Your Grace. I hardly think to find highwaymen on Haverly land." She curtsied to the room. "Good night, my lords and ladies."

"You are *not* riding back in the dark on your own."

Emma paused in the doorway. "Are you presuming to dictate to me, Your Grace? I am not one of your servants. Good evening."

She made it to the stairs before she heard his footsteps thudding behind her. Squaring her shoulders, she continued down to the first floor. Grey didn't say anything as he drew even with her in the main hallway, but she could practically feel the heat radiating from his large, strong form.

Finally she couldn't stand the silence any longer. "It's kind of you to walk me to the door, but it's quite unnecessary. I know my way."

"I'm not walking you out," he grunted. "I'm accompanying you back to the Academy."

"You are n—"

"Argue all you want," he interrupted, "but you have your rules of etiquette, and I have mine. You are not riding off alone in the dark."

She'd barely managed to escape intact from the conversation in the sitting room. She didn't dare go off alone with him again. Her lips felt swollen and bruised from his kisses, and her heart hummed with wild emotions she couldn't even put a name to. "Then send one of your grooms."

To her dismay, he smiled. "Afraid to be alone with me?"

"No! Non—nonsense. I fear your guests will begin gossiping about your odd behavior, and I don't wish to be involved in a scandal."

"My guests are my concern. You are more interesting."

Hobbes opened the front door for them, and

Emma preceded Grey down the shallow marble steps. When she heard the door close behind them, she turned around and jabbed a finger into the duke's chest. "You presume too much. Simply because you find me 'interesting,' like some three-legged goat in a carnival, does not mean that I find you interesting."

He looked at her. "You seemed to be plenty 'interested' a while ago."

With effort she held his gaze. "I will admit that you kiss well. You've had a great deal of experience, no doubt." He opened his mouth to reply, but she cut him off. "As I said, I know how the world works. I know why I 'interest' you, and I know precisely how long that 'interest' will last.

"This is where I live. I have nowhere else to go. So I would appreciate it if you would keep your 'interest' in check until such time as you lose your wager and take yourself and your coaches back to London."

Finally, he gave a slow nod. "Collins!" he bellowed in the direction of the stable. "Saddle a mount and accompany Miss Emma back to the Academy!"

"Yes, Your Grace."

"Thank you." She turned on her heel and walked toward the stable.

"Emma," he continued in a low, soft voice behind her, "you don't know everything."

She kept walking. A moment later she heard him return to the manor. Perhaps she didn't know everything, but she knew she was right about him. And the miserable thing was, she wished she were wrong.

Chapter 10

❦❦**I** really don't think that's right," Mary Mawgry said.

Grey glanced down at her, and at the rest of the girls, seated in a semi-circle at his feet. With effort he kept his back turned to the noisy chicken run behind Haverly's stable, and the three figures standing beside it. Even not looking at her, he couldn't keep his thoughts off Emma.

"Of course it's right," he returned, speaking up a little to be heard over the squawking chickens. "Men like women who are *capable* of playing an instrument. Being expected to sit through and listen to a performance, though, is considered pure torture."

"That's nonsense." Elizabeth scowled at him. "I love listening to music."

"You, my dear, are a female. I wasn't talking about you."

"You never talk about us," she returned, fearless as always. "Only about how to make men like us."

"Isn't that the point?" he asked, lifting an eyebrow.

Jane sighed. "It would be nice to be liked simply because we're likable," she said, absently plucking blades of meadow grass and letting them blow through her fingers. "Not because we know how to answer every question in a pleasing manner."

Grey stopped pacing. "Isn't that what Miss Grenville's Academy teaches? I'm just refining the process."

"Not very well." Lizzy stood, brushing leaves from her walking dress. "If some man says the sky is green, I'm not going to say, 'Oh, yes, my lord, the sky is green,' just because he's an earl, for heaven's sake." She bowed and sat again.

"He's a very stupid earl," Julia muttered, and Henrietta laughed.

This didn't make any sense at all. Rubbing his chin, Grey studied the chits arranged in the grass before him. They all seemed to have a fair share of intelligence, particularly Jane and Lizzy. Up until this moment they'd followed his instructions and listened to his lessons and explanations without complaint, though their questions and commentary had been rather amusing. He'd even been enjoying himself; or he would have been, if he hadn't been so damned frustrated by Emma.

Unable to stop himself, he turned around. The headmistress, wearing a plain yellow morning dress, chatted with Tristan and Uncle Dennis's chicken keeper. Her sheaf of notes had grown to book size, and still she continued jotting things down, making measurements, and refusing to ask him any but the most inane questions. As he watched, Tristan put a hand on her shoulder as he interjected something into the conversation. She laughed—the laugh she never had for the Duke of Wycliffe.

Grey clenched his jaw. For four days he'd kept away from the haughty miss. For four nights he hadn't slept, instead spending the time pacing and cursing and making up revenges, all of which involved the two of them being naked. In the evenings he made up lesson plans for his students, lesson plans the ungrateful chits now seemed to think were merely a poor joke.

For the first time, it occurred to him that he might lose the wager. Grey shook himself. For God's sake, he was a duke. He never lost at anything.

He turned back to his charges, who now chatted and giggled together. "Hypothetically," he said, sitting cross-legged in the grass with them, "if an earl did approach and inform you that the sky was green, how would you respond?"

"I'd tell him he was batty as a belltower," Lizzy announced.

"You would not." Jane sat forward. "Miss Emma says there are two ways of looking at any question or statement. The first is that the speaker is being sincere, and the second is that he isn't."

The young chit even sounded like the headmistress. "Continue," Grey urged.

"If he's sincere, he's soft-headed, and contradicting him won't do any good."

"So you humor him," Grey said, and the girls nodded.

"And if he's insincere, he's trying to make himself look witty or clever or intelligent, and—"

"—and he's therefore seeking an opportunity to make an impression," Mary took up.

"So you humor him." Again his charges nodded.

"Unless his intent is without a doubt malicious, in which case you say 'pardon me,' curtsy, and leave the conversation." Julia counted off the steps on her fingers.

Several things which had been troubling him began abruptly to make sense. "What's the difference, then, between my advice and Miss Emma's?" he asked, just to hear how they would word the answer.

"Because you just tell us to agree with everything a man says, no matter how ridiculous it is. Miss Emma tells us how to do it knowing his intent, and seeking the way that most benefits us."

"And," Elizabeth said stoutly, "she teaches us about everything. Not just stupid blind earls and remembering to flatter nobles when we waltz with them."

The curriculum she'd painstakingly written out for him in her letter came to mind. In his initial interpretation, it hadn't been all that impressive. "Geography" had meant learning the major capitals for parlor games. "Mathematics" had been what the chits learned so they would understand how much they spent on clothing.

None of it would have required actual learning or intelligence.

Not for the first time, he wondered whether he had underestimated Miss Emma and her Academy. She clearly considered most males only one step removed from gorillas; since she didn't spend any time around men, he had to wonder why she viewed them with such contempt.

The girls sat gazing at him, and he shook himself. "If Miss Emma's taught you so well, what do you think is left for you to learn?"

"I want to know why Miss Emma says you're a rake," Lizzy stated.

Grey narrowed his eyes. "You'd have to ask Miss Emma about that."

"Well, what is a rake?"

Mary patted Elizabeth's shoulder. "You're too young for that class. A rake is . . . a man who tries to kiss lots of women."

"Oh, good God," Grey muttered.

"What?" Mary asked, frowning.

Grey frowned back at her. Providing a definition of rakes and answering any of the questions likely to follow had little to do with the ballroom etiquette lessons he'd mapped out for the chits. On the other hand, with inaccurate information like Mary's, the lot of them were likely to end up with lifted skirts two minutes after they arrived in London. He glanced at Jane. If they made it as far as London.

"Tell us," Lizzy urged.

"Yes, please."

Jane's quiet plea affected him more strongly than Elizabeth's; she was older, and she was being pursued by a rake. One with whom he'd spent several hours last week, encouraging and coaching.

"Just a moment," he said, standing.

Emma and Tristan were stretching measuring tape along the length of one of the chicken coops as he strolled over. The chicken keeper flushed to the top of his bald pate as Grey reached them, making him wonder which sordid details of his life Tristan had been regaling Emma with now.

"Did the little chits frighten you away, Wycliffe?" the viscount asked.

"I need to speak with you for a moment," he informed the headmistress, ignoring the two men. "In private."

"All right," she said after a hesitation, handing the end of the measuring tape to the chicken keeper. "Excuse me."

She would have stopped just out of earshot of the chicken run, but Grey kept walking until he'd rounded the near corner of the stable. He heard her pause as she realized where they were headed, and only let out a breath when her footsteps continued after him.

"I hope you're not going to attempt to lecture me about chickens," she said, rocking back on her heels and acting precisely like a nervous young lady making every effort to appear calm. "I know all about chickens."

"Your students have asked me to explain what a rake is. And they didn't mean the farming tool."

Her mouth opened, then closed again. "Oh. I've already explained that—"

"Did you actually tell them a rake is a man who tries to kiss lots of women?"

Emma blushed. "Well, not in those words."

Grey snorted. "That's criminal."

Immediately her expression became defensive. "In some cases I am bound by the dictates of polite society, whatever I might wish to say. And besides, isn't kissing what you tried to do to me?" she asked, her voice indignant.

"No, I *did* kiss you, Emma." He took a step closer. "Do you really think that was all I wanted?"

She put a hand on his chest. "Stop."

"Why? I already kissed you, which is apparently all I was inter—"

"Don't make fun."

"Don't mislead those girls. There has to be a better way to explain things."

Her hand remained on his chest, and it took more willpower than he'd expected to keep from looking down at it, especially as he felt her dainty fingers curl around the top button of his waistcoat. Sweet Lucifer, she was killing him.

"Why do you even care?" she asked, avoiding his gaze.

"Why are you presuming to dispense information on a topic you obviously know nothing about?"

"I know about you."

Grey reached out and tilted her chin up with his fingers. "I don't think you do," he murmured.

Slowly, so he wouldn't frighten her off, he leaned down and touched his lips to hers. She responded with a soft sigh, tiptoeing to deepen the kiss. That was what he'd done wrong before, he realized, relishing the play of her soft mouth against his. He'd pushed, tried to guide and control their contact. Emma being Emma, she first balked, and then attacked him with her finest weapon—her wits.

So, even though he practically vibrated with tension, he let her break the kiss, and didn't pursue her when she did so. For a long moment she looked up at him, her gaze dreamy and unfocused. Then she blinked and lowered her hand from him.

"I would like your permission," he said, in the same quiet, nonthreatening voice he'd used before, "to tell your students about rakes, and to answer any other questions that might spring from that one."

"I couldn't allow such a thing. It has nothing to do with the conditions of the wager, anyway."

"Emma, if they all go into the world as naive about men as you are, it won't matter a whit if they know the capital of Prussia, or how to dance prettily."

She drew a breath, and using all of his willpower he kept his eyes off her pert, heaving bosom. "I am not as naive about men as you seem to think," she said, bitterness touching her voice.

"But—"

"However," she interrupted, "neither will I deny my students knowledge which might assist their success."

He nodded, surprised, and more than intrigued by her statement. "Good."

"You will only have these discussions when I am present. If I ask that you cease, you will do so immediately. Is that clear?"

"Clear as glass. I have no wish to overwhelm Miss Perchase with practical information."

"I still don't understand why you want to be so helpful, after that whole 'gratefully declining' nonsense."

He didn't blame her for being suspicious, because he had no explanation himself. "I'm trying to win a wager," he said.

Her expression grew more contemplative. "You still don't have a chance. This is the first time, though, that you've actually turned in the right direction."

The Duke of Wycliffe had brought luncheon, and three footmen to serve it. Considering that they all sat out on blankets in the meadow, alfresco style, having liveried servants walking among them offering chicken and cucumber sandwiches seemed absurdly overdone. The girls, though, enjoyed it. Emma did, as well, even if she would never tell the duke so.

She looked over at him again, munching on a sandwich and surrounded by females half his size. He'd been different today. She couldn't quite put her finger on it, but when he'd kissed her she hadn't felt cornered or overwhelmed. The kiss had been heavenly, and if she'd ever had a chance of another peaceful night's sleep, it was gone forever now.

"So you want to expand the coop area?" Tristan asked as he sat cross-legged beside her.

"The price of beef has been soaring since the war. The nobility might still be able to afford it, but I imagine the rest of London has already turned to fish, chicken, and pork. Haverly could supply chicken on the . . . hoof, as it were."

He nodded. "It'll bring in a few more quid, I'm sure."

"It won't be enough to win the wager. I know, I know." Emma set a peach on her thick stack of notes so they wouldn't blow away. "But every little bit helps."

When she glanced up again, Grey held her gaze for a moment, then returned to his conversation with Julia and Henrietta. Emma sighed.

A plucked daisy appeared before her. "Cheer up," the viscount said, twirling the flower in his fingers. "We'll be out of Hampshire before much longer."

Emma smiled. "Oh, it's not that. I enjoy being out-of-doors like this." In truth, the thought of Wycliffe leaving Hampshire didn't cheer her up in the least. It would make life more simple again, perhaps, but it didn't make her happy.

"Miss Emma, it's been almost an hour. Can we continue our lesson now?"

"May we continue," she corrected Lizzy.

"*May* we continue?" her youngest student repeated.

Emma's nerves fluttered. She had discussed rakes with the older girls, in terms of dangers to be avoided. Wycliffe was right, though. Her practical knowledge in that area was sadly lacking, and it was an important topic—particularly for students like Jane and Mary, who would be out in Society among all the male dangers very soon.

"Yes, you may," she answered.

Tristan climbed to his feet. "Back to the chickens?" he asked, holding his hand down to her.

She allowed him to assist her to her feet. "Actually, I'm going to sit in on this lesson."

"I thought you'd decided to chaperone from a distance today."

"I had, but I believe this particular topic requires my undivided attention."

Tristan looked at Grey. "And which words of wisdom will His Grace be imparting to the flock this afternoon, then?"

"I'm going to teach them about rakes."

The viscount froze. "Really?"

"Yes. Care to volunteer any of your own experiences for the class?"

Dare eyed the students with almost comical horror. "Actually, I think I'll go take a walk and gouge my eyes out with a stick."

"Are you a rake, too?" Lizzy asked, squinting one eye against the dappled sunlight of the meadow.

He cleared his throat. "Excuse me, ladies. Blumton said he was going fishing at the duck pond this afternoon." He began walking backward. "I think I'll join him."

As the viscount vanished into the trees, Elizabeth returned her attention to Wycliffe. "Is he a rake?"

"Not a very good one, I'm afraid."

Hm. This was *not* going to become a treatise on the heroics of rakedom if Emma had anything to say about it. "I count that as a point in Lord Dare's favor," she said.

The servants cleared the remains of luncheon and retreated to the vehicles. Emma sat opposite Wycliffe so she could see his expression and be in good position to silence him if the need arose, as per their agreement. Of course, it also meant that he could gaze at her for the entire length of the lesson and gauge exactly what effect his speech was having on her.

Emma took a deep, steadying breath. His little lesson would have no effect on her whatsoever. She wouldn't allow it to.

"Everyone settled?" At the girls' nods, Grey leaned forward, balancing his elbows on his knees. "All right. I suppose we should begin with the basics: do you all know the difference between males and females?"

"Your Grace!" Miss Perchase blurted, blushing.

He lifted an eyebrow. "Yes, Miss Perchase?"

Emma cleared her throat. Perhaps this hadn't been such a wise idea, after all.

"I was not aware that this was going to become a discussion of . . . that sort of thing," the Latin instructor stammered.

"What sort of thing?" Lizzy asked.

"Suffice it to say, Your Grace, that my students have all had *basic* anatomy," Emma offered.

"Oh." Elizabeth nodded sagely. "You mean breasts and man-parts."

Wycliffe choked. With her eyes, Emma dared him to comment on Lizzy's phraseology. She and Lizzy were definitely going to have to have a long talk about her youngest student's bold, forward manner of speaking.

He cleared his throat. "I suppose that definition will suffice," he said after a moment. "A rake, then, knows all about breasts and . . . man-parts, and how well they go together."

"Is that why he likes to try to kiss ladies?"

"Lizzy, hush," Jane said. "Let Grey explain."

Emma was rather curious to hear his explanation, herself. "Yes, continue."

"A rake . . . knows what women like. Part of what women like is being kissed. Women also like it when someone pays attention to them, and talks with them, and asks them to dance. Rakes just happen to be better at this than other men."

Emma narrowed her eyes. He hadn't asked her to dance, but he'd done everything else. And she'd liked it; all of it. Apparently, though, that was just because he was so good at it. Part of her wanted to know what else he was good at. The other part of her was afraid she would like what she found.

"So rakes like to play games with women's emotions?" she asked, folding her hands in her lap.

A muscle in his lean cheek twitched. "Some do. Others are just naturally . . . charming."

"How is it charming to fool someone into thinking you like them?" Henrietta asked.

"Are you saying," Emma put in, "that a rake is a male with the position and wealth to act as he chooses despite Society's strictures?"

Lizzy was nodding again. "It doesn't sound very nice. Are you certain you're a rake, Grey?"

Wycliffe blew out his breath. "I'm not that kind of rake."

"Well," Jane said, frowning, "what other kind of rake is there? And how do you tell if a man is a rake or not?"

Emma leaned forward. "Yes. Please tell us."

"Well, for one thing, the good sort of rake's flattery is genuine." He sounded short. "Just because someone says nice things doesn't mean he isn't sincere about it."

"Sincere or not," she said slowly, "it's more than flattery that a rake has in mind, isn't it? And what he has in mind could very well ruin a lady's reputation."

The duke glared at her. "Only if he gets caught."

"Humph. Ladies, please know that a true gentleman will never ask a woman to engage in . . . activity that might be harmful to her reputation or her well-being. If you are asked to do something that you even hesitate about, it is probably something you shouldn't be doing." Grey opened his mouth, but she continued. "I have a very good friend, for instance, who allowed a man—a marquis—to escort her into a garden to apologize for some ill behavior. This man then kissed her in front of witnesses, and they were forced to marry."

"The Vixen," he muttered, his jaw beginning to clench.

"Yes."

"You might note, though," Grey put in, less humor in his voice, "that there are females who intentionally lure men into compromising *them* for the very reason that they want to be married."

"Whoever allows that to happen, man or woman, is a fool." Frank discussion or not, Wycliffe's personal prejudice against women had no place in it.

"If you had ever actually been to London and experienced Society," he shot back at her, "you might realize that walking a path isn't nearly as straightforward, or as black and white, as you seem to think."

"I have been to London," she burst out, standing, "and I found it sadly lacking in decency. And I find anyone who can defend the immorality of rakedom to a group of young girls to be precisely the same."

Tears filled her eyes, blast it all. Through the blur she could see the girls staring at her in openmouthed amazement. The look on Wycliffe's face was much harder to read.

"Excuse me for a moment," she managed, and strode off toward the trees.

If the duke followed her, she was absolutely going to scream. Her students already thought she'd gone mad; if he ran after her, they would think her odd behavior was because of him.

Yes, she was confused by his arrogance and his splendid kisses, and yes, she did feel flattered by his occasional compliments, even if they were only meant to distract her from winning the wager. Mostly, though, she was mad at herself for beginning to look at him fondly, when he was, after all, just another man who thought he knew everything, and that she couldn't possibly be right about anything.

It was Jane who came after her. "Miss Emma?" she called. "Are you all right?"

Hurriedly Emma wiped the tears from her cheeks and emerged from behind the beech tree she'd been using for cover. "Jane? Heavens, you shouldn't be out here by yourself."

"We were worried about you. Grey said I should give you a few minutes to compose yourself, and then come find you."

"And where is Wycliffe?" she asked, her voice sounding shrill.

"He left to go fishing with his friends."

Emma froze. "He left you alone?"

"No. The barouche and Miss Perchase and the servants are still there. He said that you were angry and that he didn't want you to hit him, so he would continue our lessons tomorrow." Jane took her hand, squeezing her fingers.

"I wouldn't have hit him," she returned. "I definitely would have scolded him, though, for trying to teach you such dreadful lies."

Lady Jane smiled, though her eyes remained serious. "I thought it was helpful. For one thing, I think Freddie Mayburne might be a rake. I'm not sure, but I shall certainly pay more attention from now on."

"Jane, you know I just want you all to do well in your lives, wherever they may take you."

"I know that. You should tell Lizzy, though. You know how she gets upset when someone else is upset, especially if it's you. She forgets that you're not just Miss Emma."

Emma slowed, looking at the dark-haired beauty. "I'm not just Miss Emma?"

"No. You're also Emma Grenville, a woman who owns her own business, tries her best to make successes out of silly young girls, and cares for everyone else's happiness above her own." Jane smiled at her. "She even takes on wagers with dukes so she can afford to help even more young girls."

"My goodness." Emma squeezed Jane's hand tightly, tears pricking her eyes again. "I sometimes forget that you're not fourteen any longer.

You've become a young lady—one I would be proud to call a friend."

Jane kissed her on the cheek. "I just try to be like you."

Chapter 11

❧

"You aren't going to catch anything, fling-ing your hook into the water like that," Charles Blumton said.

Grey ignored him, launching his fishing line through the air and watching the splash as the weighted end thunked into the pond.

"Now *I'm* not going to catch anything, either."

"You weren't catching anything anyway, Blumton," Tristan said from his seat on the rocks. "All the fish suffered apoplexies and died when those schoolgirls fell into the water last week. We'd be as successful if we shot into the water with pistols."

Charles chuckled. "I have a friend, Francis Henning, who tried that once. He told me he spent all day trying to catch the titan of all trouts in a stream at his uncle's estate, but it wouldn't come out from under some boulder or other. So he got his pistol and tried to put a round into it."

Tristan was biting the inside of his lip. "What happened?"

"The ball ricocheted off the boulder, back up out of the water, and went through his Grandmother Abigail's hat. Said she walloped him in the head with her umbrella. Nearly killed him."

"Seems only fair."

Grey barely noted the conversation. Emma had run off crying, and it had been his fault. Women had certainly cried in his presence before, and it had merely annoyed him. They were all so damned *good* at it. But Emma's tears had bothered him. They continued to bother him.

What she'd said bothered him even more. She'd been to London, and someone, some *man*, had hurt her. He wanted to know who it was. At the same time, he wanted to prove to her that not all men were like the damned puff-guts who had distressed her. Grey looked up as a phaeton bearing Alice and Lady Sylvia rolled up and stopped. He took a slow breath. Good God, this was getting confusing.

"Grey, you promised to teach me how to fish," Alice said, hiking her skirts up as she trod through the grass and brush to his side.

He handed her the rod. "Here. Stick the line in the water until something tugs on it."

She looked dismayed. "And then what?"

"And then we'll all faint from surprise," Tristan said, "since there obviously aren't any fish in this pond."

Sylvia sat on a rock, twitching her skirt out into

a graceful fall around her ankles. "Why are you all standing here, then? Waiting for mermaids, I suppose? Or schoolgirls?"

Grey would have handed her a setdown to shut her up, but Sylvia rebounded much more quickly than Alice, and he wasn't in the mood to spar. Instead he abandoned Alice to the fishing pole and took a seat on the boulder beside Tristan.

"How did your lesson go?" the viscount asked. "On second thought, don't tell me. I shudder just imagining how much damage you've done to our gender."

"Do you recall Emma ever being in London?" Grey asked, keeping his voice pitched low.

"No. Why?"

"She said she'd been there. From her choice of vocabulary, I get the impression that the experience wasn't a pleasant one."

"Did she say when she was in town?"

"No."

Tristan remained silent for a moment. "I don't know, Grey. She wouldn't exactly have traveled in our circle. She's got highborn friends, but she would still have been an instructor at a girls' school."

"That's the same conclusion I came to." Grey tossed a pebble into the pond. If she'd been anywhere in the vicinity of London, though, he felt as if he should have, would have, sensed it.

"I take it she doesn't approve of rakes? I hope you didn't tell her I was one."

"I said you weren't a very good one."

"Oh. Splendid."

"What are you two conspiring about?" Sylvia cooed, lifting a perfect eyebrow.

"Probably about how they intend to leave us moldering in solitude for the rest of the summer." Alice stalked over and handed her fishing pole to Charles. "I am not impressed with fishing."

Blumton looked from the pole in his right hand to the one in his left. "It's a man's sport, Alice."

"Yes," Sylvia agreed. "Standing about waving your pole in the air and waiting for some poor creature to get tangled on it."

"Sounds as though you've been caught and thrown back in," Tristan said.

She faced the viscount, her blue eyes wide and innocent. "One can't help but notice, Dare, that you don't even have a pole."

"That's in *your* honor, my dear. I don't want to risk you getting tangled with me again."

Grey only half-listened to the argument. Frank and straightforward as she was, Emma would have been appalled at the entire exchange. It was demeaning to both sides—and a few weeks ago, it could just as easily have been he as Tristan who was speaking.

"I'm going to have my students join us for dinner at Haverly on Thursday," he announced. "We will also have dancing."

"What? You want to set a school full of little girls loose on us?" Blumton straightened so quickly, he nearly fell face-first into the pond.

"Not a school full," Grey corrected. "Five girls. Plus Miss Emma, I would imagine, and whichever other chaperones she feels are appropriate."

"Gads," Blumton said, looking horrified. "You can't mean for us to—"

Grey stood. "You and Dare will both be in attendance. I need gentlemen for my students to practice with. I'll have Freddie Mayburne over, as well." It was possible that he'd misjudged the lad and that he truly did care for Jane. If Mayburne had merely been acting the rake for his benefit, then he still deserved a chance. Blumton continued to look contentious, so Grey strolled to his side. "Look at it as your contribution to helping the correct side win the wager."

The dandy cleared his throat. "In that case, it's our duty to our gender."

"Well, I think it shall be a complete bore," Alice said, pouting.

"Oh, I don't know about that," Sylvia countered. "I for one am looking forward to a chance to chat with our dear Miss Emma."

Damnation. If there was one thing he didn't want, it was Emma being subjected to Lady Sylvia Kincaid's cat scratches. He would have to devise something to keep Sylvia occupied. Grey glanced speculatively at Tristan.

No, Dare mouthed, obviously reading his thoughts.

Hm. The idea had potential, anyway. There had to be something Tristan wanted. Anything but Emma, of course. Emma was his.

The strength of that thought startled him, and it kept him occupied for the rest of the day. Even while he sent off notes to Freddie and to a well-recommended string quartet located in Brighton, his mind was on Emma.

That certainly wasn't unusual, because thoughts of her—mostly in her damp, transparent shift—already took up a great deal of his time. This, though, was different. It wasn't just sex—a surprise of titanic proportions, considering sex was the only reason any woman had ever interested him. No, he wanted to *talk* with her. He liked the sound of her voice, and he liked trying to decipher the way her mind worked.

All evening he found himself halfway to conjuring some reason he needed to see her at once. All evening he kept himself rammed into his chair by the drawing room window, and pretended to read Byron's latest offering. The dark, sensual poetry did nothing for his mood, and twice he nearly flung the book across the room.

Even Alice seemed to sense how tightly he was drawn, for after her first attempt at thinly veiled flirtation met with only a glare, she subsided. When he finally shot to his feet and announced that he was going to bed, everyone else in the room looked relieved.

Halfway out of his coat, the answer came to him. He snatched the gray superfine out of his valet's startled fingers and shrugged it on again. "I'm going riding."

"But Your Grace, now? It's past midnight."

"I can tell time, Bundle. Don't wait up for me."

"Y—yes, Your Grace."

It was simple, really, and he couldn't believe he hadn't thought of it earlier. He needed to invite Emma and his students to the Haverly soirée.

Emma was half asleep when she heard her office door open. Frowning, she pulled the blanket over her head and pretended not to hear. The books strewn around her on the bed shifted, and either her foot was asleep or a pencil was jabbing her in one toe, but she was too tired to care. Students did come to see her at odd hours from time to time, but it had to be nearly one o'clock in the morning, for heaven's sake.

Something hit the floor in her office. "Blast," she mumbled, sitting upright. She rubbed her eyes, yawning and then stretching. Oh, well. Peaceful sleep was fairly rare these days, anyway. When she did doze off, she always dreamed about the same thing: the Duke of Wycliffe.

Staggering into her robe, she shuffled to her bed chamber door and pushed it open the rest of the way. "Is everything all right?" she asked. Midnight visits only seemed to happen when something was amiss.

"I dropped your damned *History of Farm Animals* on my foot," a low, masculine voice drawled.

Thankfully she recognized the voice even as she drew in a startled breath to scream. The sound caught in her throat, which was a good thing, or she would have roused the entire Academy with her shriek. "What—what in heaven's name are you doing here?" she gasped.

The Duke of Wycliffe bent to pick up the fallen book. "Does it tell whether the chicken or the egg came first?" he asked, setting it back on her desk.

"I don't know. I'm only . . . to goats." It occurred to Emma that she might be dreaming, after all. Surreptitiously she pinched her thigh. "Ouch."

He strode over to her. "Are you all right?"

Somehow he seemed even larger up this close and in the dark. "Yes, I'm fine. But you should go. Now."

"Don't you want to know why I'm here?" He reached out and straightened the collar of her robe, tugging her a step closer to him in the process.

"Why . . . why *are* you here, then?"

"I came to invite you to a soirée at Haverly," he said matter-of-factly. "On Thursday evening. I thought my class might benefit from an evening of dining and dancing with actual members of the *ton*."

She fleetingly wondered whether he was drunk, but quickly dismissed the thought. He didn't smell like liquor, and he spoke with his usual clarity. "Oh. You might have sent over a note to tell me that."

For a long moment the duke looked down at her, though she didn't know what he could see in the murky darkness of her office. "And I'm sorry if I upset you this afternoon," he said finally. "I didn't mean to."

"We can discuss this tomorrow, Your Grace."

"I couldn't sleep."

"Which is no reason for you to break into the Academy and frighten me half to death."

His teeth gleamed in the darkness as he smiled. "Then I owe you a second apology."

"Will you please leave? I need to put in at least an hour of research in the morning, before breakfast."

"I could help, you know. I submitted my final plans to your Sir John this afternoon."

"And how would that look, if you helped me to beat you? As if you would. No thank you. I have all the information I need right here." She gestured at her cluttered office and the stacks upon stacks of research books.

"A book, no matter how diverting, is no substitute for actual experience." His fingers, still wrapped into her collar, pulled her another step closer, until they were practically touching.

Having a logical conversation in the dark with a tall, handsome rake was extremely difficult. Her mind wanted to wander off in all sorts of tantalizing directions. But he was probably counting on the fact that he turned females' minds to mush merely by his virile presence. "I am sure you believe that, Your Grace. I find that books serve me quite well, thank you very much."

"I don't believe you."

The low murmur started a warm, tingling sensation that traveled slowly up her legs. "And why is that?" she managed.

"I see all these books around you, covering every topic known to mankind, but how much do you know about actual life, Emma?"

"Just because I have chosen to devote myself to teaching and the gathering of knowledge doesn't mean I'm some sort of hermit, closed off from the world."

"It means exactly that you're some sort of hermit, pretending you're above feeling warmth and desire."

She was feeling quite warm, at the moment. "I prefer to use my mind rather than my . . ." she gestured down the lean length of him, ". . . my *mentula*, like men do." Even saying the word in Latin, she blushed profusely, and hoped he couldn't see her discomfiture in the dark.

Grey lifted an eyebrow. " *'Nihil est in intellectu quod non feurit in sensu.'* John Locke."

She should have known he would speak

Latin—which meant he knew precisely which part of his anatomy she'd referred to. Her own Latin was quite rusty, now that she had Miss Perchase teaching the class. " 'There is nothing in the mind . . . which exists apart'—no—'separate from, the senses.' Goodness. How long have you been saving that up?"

"Probably for as long as you've had *mentula* memorized." His fingers caressed her cheek. "What's a schoolgirl doing learning words like *mentula*, anyway? You didn't learn it here—not where male anatomy is referred to as 'man parts.' "

She couldn't possibly blush more than she was doing now. "None of your business, Your Grace."

He leaned against the bookshelf behind him, tugging her up against him in the process. She had to put her hands up against his chest to keep from pressing her body along his. "I'll wager it was curiosity. You're probably the brightest woman I've ever met. Why should you stop your learning at a certain point just because the books stop teaching?"

She *was* curious, and growing more so by the moment. The play of his muscles beneath her hands fascinated her, and the low rumble of his voice shivered down her spine. She wanted to explore every inch of him, and wrapped her fingers into his waistcoat to keep them securely in place. Just being alone with him made her feel hot and light-headed and very, very wicked.

"I don't know what you're talking about," she stammered, her voice shaking.

"You mean there aren't other words you've

memorized? Other words you want to know the true meanings of? *Machaera*, perhaps? Or *follis?*"

If he continued, she was going to faint. "Stop that at once."

"Too vulgar?" he murmured. "Do you prefer *capulus*, or *temo?*"

If she hadn't been thinking about sword hilts or poles, she was now. Involuntarily her gaze strayed down past his hard chest, and then whipped back to his face again as his hands shifted, tugging her long hair forward over her shoulders. His fingers tangled into her curls, twining and gently twisting until she could barely breathe. "You're only trying to shock me," she said, swallowing.

"No, I'm not. I'm trying to show you there's a difference between knowing a word and knowing what it means. Take *interfeminium*, for example— the place between a woman's thighs. It's more than just a word, Emma."

Before he'd crashed into her life, she thought she knew the word "kiss." Until he'd kissed her, though, she hadn't known—really known—what it meant. Until tonight she'd never thought of Latin as arousing.

Even the anatomical vulgarisms she'd memorized had seemed clinical, which was the only reason she'd been able to utter them. When the Duke of Wycliffe said them, though, fire seared through her.

Grey leaned down and gently touched his lips to hers. "Let me teach you, Emma," he whispered.

Why me? If she asked aloud, he might remember that she was just a headmistress; that he already knew countless women who didn't need his lessons and could provide him infinitely more pleasure than she could. "You'll stop if I ask you to?" she breathed.

"Yes. But you won't ask."

"You're very sure—"

He captured her mouth in a deep, slow kiss. Inexperienced as she was, she felt the difference this time; his touch was more focused, and more leisurely, as though he knew they wouldn't be interrupted tonight.

The logical part of her realized that this could be the best, last, and only chance for her to discover what it was like to be in a man's embrace. Her heart and her nerves and her flesh all came to tingling, burning awareness at his touch, like time had stopped and accelerated all in the same moment.

"Emma," he murmured, as he shifted his mouth to caress her bare throat, "you're choking me."

"What? Oh, I'm sorry." Her hands were wrapped into the material at his chest so tightly she was surprised she hadn't ripped something. She opened her fingers, laying them flat against his hard chest. "I don't know what I'm supposed to do."

He lifted his head to look at her. "What do you want to do?"

"Touch you."

Grey drew a slow breath. "Then touch me."

Shaking and weak-kneed, Emma looked down, then returned her gaze to his face. "You're not going to laugh at me tomorrow, are you?"

He tilted his tawny head, his eyes searching

hers in the dark. "Where did you come from?" he whispered. "I've never known anyone like you." He caught her mouth again, more roughly this time. "No, I won't laugh at you."

Her heart hammered so hard she thought he must be able to hear it, or at least to feel the pulse at her throat beneath the caress of his lips. His hands slid down her shoulders, brushed the sides of her breasts with an intimacy that made her gasp, and parted her robe at the waist. Grey slipped his arms inside the warm wool, around her hips, and nudged her backward until her thighs came up against the desk. The whole time, his mouth sought hers, teasing and seeking and stealing what remained of her ability to think and to breathe.

When he moved his hips against hers, she felt his arousal, hot and hard through his breeches. Moaning, Emma slid her arms around his neck, kissing him open-mouthed as his tongue plundered her mouth.

To her surprise, Grey took a half step backward. Sudden panic rose in her chest. He couldn't want to stop; not now. "Did I do something wrong?" she asked shakily.

He shook his head. Lifting his hands to hers, he freed her grip on his shoulders and pulled her arms back down to his chest. "Touch me," he repeated, his voice a low, sensuous growl.

She stared at his chest, both because the view fascinated her, and because she felt so exposed and vulnerable that it would kill her to look up and see that, despite his reassuring words, he was laughing at her.

Grey tilted her chin up, making the touch another caress. "Don't think so much," he murmured, his eyes glittering and dark with desire. "Just feel."

Taking her hands again, he slid them up his chest, under his lapels. Finally she realized what he was doing, and helped him shrug out of his coat. Through the fine cambric of his shirt, his arms were warm and strong. She shivered again. Dreaming about being naked with him and actually doing it were two completely different things.

"Now it's my turn." His motions much more confident than hers, Grey slipped the robe off her shoulders and let it drop to the desk behind her. Then his mouth found her collarbone and trailed along the skin to the low neck of her nightgown.

Mouths were wonderful. She'd never imagined the touch of someone's lips against her flesh could be so . . . stimulating.

Emma fumbled with the buttons of his waistcoat, and managed to unfasten them without popping any of them off. More sure now, she pulled it from his shoulders and went to work on his cravat.

He held still, letting her fight with the intricate knots. "You're a quick study," he said, trailing his fingers along her neckline, and dipping them beneath the ruffles.

"You're a good teacher—so far."

This time he chuckled. "So far? I think it's time to advance to the second lesson." Untying the bow which hung between her breasts, he slowly slipped the garment down her shoulders.

As cool air touched her breasts, Emma drew in a ragged breath. She couldn't convince herself any longer that she was dreaming. The Duke of Wycliffe stood before her, running his fingers along her skin, caressing her in places no man had ever seen, much less touched. "This is too much," she gasped, catching his hands as they cupped her breasts.

"Why is it too much?" His fingers moved a little, brushing across her nipples.

She gasped again at the sensation, her nipples hardening in response to his light touch. "I don't know. I just feel . . . I feel as though I'm coming out of my skin."

"Is it an unpleasant sensation?" His fingers moved again, stroking her.

"No . . ." she moaned.

"Then enjoy it," he whispered. "I am." Grey dipped his head, and his tongue took the place of his fingers.

"Oh, good heavens," she panted, arching against him, tangling her fingers into his hair to yank him even closer.

She felt his muffled chuckle all the way through her. No wonder he wanted her to touch him, if his touch felt so electric to her. Trembling, she pulled the tail of his shirt free from his breeches.

His suckling deepened, pushing her backward on the cluttered surface of the desk. Her shoulders bumped a stack of books, and impatiently she pushed them to the floor. "If this is your way of distracting me from the wager, it won't work," she stated breathlessly, running her hands up his chest, beneath his shirt, feeling the play of his muscles as he lifted her up to sit on the desk.

Grey lifted his head from her breasts just long

enough for her to pull the shirt off over his head. "I'm feeling terribly distracted," he murmured, sliding her gown the rest of the way off. Standing between her legs, he kissed her hungrily, leaning forward and pushing her shoulders down.

Naked, flat on her back, with him leaning over her, Emma should have felt vulnerable, yet she felt strong and powerful. Her body ached for him, for something only he could give her. "Grey . . ."

Long, sure fingers moved in slow, lazy circles from her breasts, down her stomach, down her abdomen, down the curling dark patch of hair, and touched her. Emma bucked, grabbing onto his shoulders at the white hot pulse of lightning which shot through her. She barely recognized the low, keening, wanting sound as coming from her own throat.

"Jesus," he whispered, his voice shaking. He kissed her again, roughly, and with his free hand undid his belt and breeches.

Emma raised up on her elbows, breaking the embrace of their mouths. "I want to see you," she stated.

"And I want to feel you. I want you, Emma. I want to be inside you."

She couldn't answer. Grey bent down to yank off his boots, straightening again as his breeches followed. He was a tall, big-boned man, and as she stared at his erect manhood, the little bit of her brain which still functioned noted that he was well proportioned. *Very* well proportioned.

"Emma," he murmured, running his thumb across her lips, "are you learning anything new?"

She nodded mutely, unable to tear her gaze

from his *mentula*. "My goodness," she breathed. "May I . . ."

"Touch me? Please do."

Sitting up, her knees on either side of his muscular thighs, Emma reached down with shaking fingers. As her fingers brushed the smooth, warm skin, his muscles jumped. It startled her to realize that she affected him, maybe as much as he affected her. She wasn't the only one who trembled.

Slowly he ran his hands up her knees and her stomach to fondle her breasts again. This mutual touching was at least as pleasurable as mouths and tongues. Emboldened, she curled her fingers around his girth and stroked him.

He froze. "Don't do that," he hissed, his teeth clenched.

Instantly she released him. "Did I hurt you?"

"No. It feels . . . very good, but I'm not ready for that yet."

Swinging her legs onto the desk, he climbed up over her. Their thighs met, his arousal pressing against the innermost part of her. Grey kissed her again, hot and open-mouthed, and she wrapped her arms over his shoulders, pulling him closer. He shifted, nudging her bent knees further apart, then slowly, with a deep, satisfied groan, entered her.

The sharp pain surprised her, and she gasped. At the same time, the sensation of him filling her was the most erotic, satisfying pleasure she'd ever known.

"I'm sorry," he said, pushing himself up onto his hands and looking down at her. "I won't hurt you again."

"I'm all right," she managed. "You just surprised me."

Grey smiled. "And you surprise me. But there's still more to this lesson."

What could be more remarkable than being joined like this?

Then he moved his hips back and forward again. Emma arched her back, moaning helplessly.

With a slow, steady rhythm he continued to move in and out of her. She dug her fingers into his back. No longer did she feel like she was on fire; she *was* fire, and he was fire, and the way he moved and filled her was so . . . right.

The pulsing sensation tightened and grew inside her as his rhythm deepened and quickened. "Grey," she gasped, lifting her hips to meet his thrusts.

He kissed her again, his gaze dark and intent on hers. She tried to meet his eyes, but then she couldn't as everything inside her tightened and shattered. A deep moan of satisfaction wrenched from her chest, and she clung to him helplessly. After a deep thrust, he withdrew and came, shuddering, against her.

Grey nearly hadn't been able to do it, to leave the tight warmth of her. Breathing hard, he slowly lowered himself to her, still keeping most of his weight resting on his arms. With the riot of auburn curls haloing her face, she seemed so delicate and so fiery at the same time, he was absurdly worried that now, after all this, he would crush her. "Thus endeth the less—"

Two of the desk's spindly old legs collapsed, dumping them both to the floor. Grey managed to twist and end up on the bottom, smacking his head against another of her damned stacks of books. The resulting crash of wood, books, and bodies was tremendous in the sleeping darkness.

"Damnation! Are you all right?"

"Shh." Emma put her fingers over his lips.

Despite the blow to his head, having her lithe body straddling his hips was very pleasant indeed. Grey kissed her fingertips. "Relax, Emma. It's two o'clock in the morning. No one heard—"

Down the hallway, a door squeaked open.

"Oh, no!" she hissed, clambering off him. "Get out!"

"I'm naked," he said, sitting up, and very annoyed at whomever the nosy chit might be.

She whirled to face him, breathtaking in the moonlight. "Which is why you and your man-parts can't be here!" She snatched up her night-gown and yanked it on over her head.

Grey stood. "And where would you like me and my man-parts to go?"

Her gaze on him, Emma paused in her frantic pacing long enough to look him up and down. "My goodness, you're beautiful," she said slowly. "Hide."

"I am not crawling under your damned bed."

The knob on the office door turned. He'd latched the door, thank Lucifer, and it only opened a quarter of an inch before it stopped again.

"Emma? What's going on?" a female voice with a soft French accent whispered. "I heard a crash. Are you all right? Emma?"

With a pleading look, she gestured him toward her bed chamber. Grey bent down to toss her her robe, gathered up his own clothes, and strode into the room, pausing just behind the door. He wouldn't have fit under her damned tiny bed even if he'd wanted to.

The office door opened. "Isabelle," Emma whispered. "I was afraid I'd awakened you."

Grey edged closer, tilting his head to see through the crack between the wall and the half-open door.

The French instructor entered the room. "What in the world happened? It sounded as though your ceiling fell in."

Grey silently set down the rest of his clothes so he could pull on his breeches. The entire time, his gaze remained on Emma. She'd been so delightfully curious, and so responsive—he'd known she was *com*passionate, but given her highly developed intellect and disdain for men, he hadn't expected such passion from her.

"Oh, I couldn't sleep, so I decided to straighten up my office a little. I must have stacked too many books on the desk, because it just collapsed."

All by itself. Grey grinned, then realized he was short one boot. *Damnation*. He scanned the floor, but couldn't see it amid the clutter of books and collapsed furniture.

"I'll help you clean up. You shouldn't be moving things around in the dark, Em. You are lucky you weren't hurt."

"Don't bother, Isabelle. I'll just leave it until morning." Abruptly she shifted to one side, and he saw the toe of his missing boot disappear beneath the long skirt of her nightgown.

"Are you certain?"

"Yes. After all this, I think I may actually be able to fall asleep."

"All right." The French instructor returned to the door. "Oh, you may want to speak with Elizabeth in the morning. Jane said the *petite* got another letter from her mother, but she wouldn't let Jane see it."

Grey heard Emma's sigh. "That damned woman. No doubt she's asking for money again. I'll deal with it in the morning."

"*Oui.* Good night, again."

"Good night, Isabelle."

As soon as the office door closed, Grey emerged from the bed chamber. "What's wrong with Lizzy?" he asked.

Emma stepped off his boot and leaned down to hand it to him. "Nothing I haven't dealt with before."

He gazed at her. "So now you're the polite, professional headmistress again?"

"I always was."

After his stupid comment, he could practically see the wall of brick and mortar rebuilding itself around her. That bothered him immensely. He'd hoped for—he'd sought—a night of lovemaking that would purge the uncharacteristic lust for Emma Grenville from his system. But it hadn't worked. He still wanted her, even more, now that he'd tasted her. Before he'd held her in his arms, he hadn't been all that certain of his intentions. He still wasn't entirely certain what he wanted, except that he needed to stop being such a boor. Tonight was still too much of a surprise.

He took her hand, drawing her closer, then

leaned down and kissed her. The embrace was even more magnetic than before. He knew the feel, the touch, and the rhythm of her, now.

"Will you tell me about Lizzy tomorrow?" he asked, drawing his fingers along her soft skin, and not wanting to let her go. "I'll help if I can."

"I like this Grey," she whispered, running her hands down his bare chest. "If I see him again tomorrow, perhaps we might chat." Softly she kissed him back. "You have to go now."

He wanted to stay, yet he couldn't begin to decipher the turmoil in his mind while in her presence. "All right. But this isn't over between us, Emma."

"Mmmm. I might be able to stand a few more lessons."

Grey swept her up against him again. "Don't say that if you want me to leave," he murmured.

He felt her tremble. "I'll remember that."

Dressing quickly, before he could change his mind and ruin her beyond redemption, Grey slipped back downstairs and outside. As he trod across the foggy grounds and climbed the brick wall to one side of the gate, only one thing seemed clear: he no longer wanted Miss Grenville's Academy closed.

His stay in Hampshire had just become extremely complicated.

Lady Sylvia sat in the window of her bed chamber and sipped a cup of cool chocolate. The drink had started out hot, but that had been over two hours ago, when she'd intended to drink it quickly and go to bed.

And to think that when she'd first come to

Haverly, she'd been displeased with the bed chamber the countess had assigned her, as far from the duke's as the woman could manage. As she gazed down at the stableyard now, and considering how her initial attempt of seduction had been received, she could only be thankful for the view. Greydon Brakenridge had ridden off into the moonlight looking like the hounds of hell were on his heels. His return, though, was considerably more quiet and peaceful.

She continued to watch from her dark window while he led his big bay into the stable and then emerged some fifteen minutes later. Even in the fading moonlight, she could see his smile.

"Naughty, naughty, Greydon," she murmured, and finished off the last her cold, sweet drink. She had a letter or two to write in the morning. It was time to let the parents of the Academy students know what their overreaching headmistress was up to.

Chapter 12

~~~∽◯◯∽~~~

"I don't know how this could've happened," Tobias said, tipping the desk the rest of the way over onto its side. "I would've wagered this old crate would last forever."

Her arms crossed over her chest, Emma did her best not to blush. "It was bound to go eventually, I suppose."

"Well, Mr. Jones owes me a favor for me helping him straighten his plow. I'll get him to help me carry this mess out of here."

"Do you think you can repair it?"

"Dunno. Maybe." The handyman tugged experimentally on the two remaining legs, then straightened. "I still don't understand it." Wiping his hands on his trousers, he headed for the door. "I'd best go unlock the gate for them grand carriages."

"Thank you, Tobias."

As soon as he left, Emma sagged into her chair. She was tired, the muscles between her legs were sore, and she had the oddest desire to burst into song. Her next discussion of anatomy would be a great deal more informed, even if she didn't dare be any more explicit in her description of manparts.

She'd been wrong about one thing she'd said last night: what she and Grey had done had more than distracted her. She hadn't done anything resembling research all morning. Measuring the north meadow for a brickworks building seemed equally unappealing, but it was the task she'd set for herself today.

Footsteps pounded up to her open office door. "Miss Emma, they're here," Julia Potwin said, her eyes bright with excitement. Without waiting for a reply she vanished in the direction of the stairway.

Every bit of her wanted to rush to the window and look for Grey, and she sternly resisted the impulse. She was not some schoolgirl suffering her first crush.

Taking a deep breath to steady her jangling nerves, she pushed to her feet. Halfway down the stairs she realized that she'd forgotten her notes, and with a curse she hurried back to her office for them.

By the time she made it outside, her students and Miss Perchase were already seated in the coach and the barouche, chattering excitedly. Tristan leaned against the pot of geraniums which stood by the front steps, and for the moment she refused to let her gaze stray beyond him. The anticipation was . . . delicious.

"Good morning, Tristan," she said, smiling, and hoping the warmth she felt creeping up her cheeks was just the sunlight.

"Emma. You look splendid this morning." The viscount took her hand and brought it to his lips.

No lightning seared her, and no fire coursed through her veins, but that didn't surprise her. He wasn't Greydon Brakenridge. "Thank you. You look quite well, yourself."

The air stirred beside her, and her breath caught. She pulled her fingers from Lord Dare's grip before he could feel their sudden trembling. Now that the moment had come, though, she didn't want to look at Grey. He'd promised he wouldn't laugh—but what if he looked contemptuous, or as if he couldn't even remember where he'd been last night?

"Good morning." His low drawl rumbled through her.

Squaring her shoulders and sending up a quick, wordless prayer, she faced him. "Good . . . morning."

Grey's gaze met hers, full of heat and raw desire. His lips curved in a slight smile, and for a moment she thought he meant to take her in his arms and ravish her again, right there on the Academy's old stone steps beside the geraniums. Then he offered her his hand.

"Shall we?"

Emma took his fingers, and if his gripped hers too tightly or released hers too slowly when she'd found her seat, no one else seemed to notice. But she did. She couldn't seem to notice anything *but* the Duke of Wycliffe.

"Where are we going today?"

Emma shook herself. She needed to pay attention to what she was doing. "I need to view the north pasture again, if no one minds."

Grey seated himself opposite her. "Roscoe," he said over his shoulder, "the north pasture."

"Aye, Your Grace."

Tobias stood by the open gate as they headed for Haverly. Emma scarcely noted which girls were in which vehicle, or who sat next to her. Her entire being was focused on the man seated across from her. Their knees bumped as the barouche rolled through a rut, and she nearly jumped out of her skin.

"Miss Santerre said your desk broke." Chuckling, Jane took her hand. "I told Mary it was the weight of all the work you've been giving us."

Emma forced a smile. "No doubt."

"More likely it was all those research books," Grey suggested. "Farm animals and tax laws and Latin."

This time she knew she blushed. He wasn't even attempting to make this morning any easier on her. Pleasurable as last night had been, she hadn't expected this heated need that coursed through her veins every time she glanced at him. And since he sat two feet in front of her, it was impossible not to look at him.

"Make fun now, if you like," she said, trying to find her usual matter-of-fact tone, "because you won't be laughing after I win this wager, Your Grace."

"Well said, Emma," Tristan seconded.

"Thank you." Having the viscount to speak

with was a relief from her alternating self-derision and the silly wish to giggle, and she smiled at him warmly. "Did you bring those notes you mentioned?"

"Y—"

"Just remember that this estate plan is supposed to come from you," Grey interrupted, his expression lowering. "Not him."

"I'm only—"

"He's only providing some statistics," Emma snapped. "You don't need to remind me of the rules."

Elizabeth sighed, wrapping her arms around Emma's and leaning her head against the headmistress's shoulder. "I think the whole thing has been a grand adventure," she said with a wan smile.

Emma kissed her on the temple. "Yes, it has been."

Poor Lizzy was the only one with a real reason to cry this morning, and here she was trying to stop the quarreling and cheer them all up. Emma kissed the girl again. *She* was the Academy's headmistress. She needed to start behaving like one again.

"Are you well, Lizzy?" Grey asked in a quiet voice.

His expression was concerned, and it startled Emma to see him like that. He'd spouted so much nonsense about females and schooling that she'd somehow missed an important fact; he genuinely cared for the girls he was teaching. She wondered when that had happened, and whether he realized it or not.

The Academy's youngest student sighed again. "Yes, I'm quite well. Thank you for asking, Grey."

Spot-on perfect. Even Tristan lifted his brows at the proper little recitation. "Good God, Miss Elizabeth. You're not an Amazon. I've lost five quid."

Lizzy straightened. "Who did you wager with?"

"Ahem."

"Oops." She ducked her shoulders. "With whom did you wager, Lord Dare?"

Tristan nodded his chin in the duke's direction. "Wycliffe said you were quite civilized, but I didn't believe it." He leaned closer, a conspiratorial light in his eyes. "*I* saw you sword fighting on stage."

She chuckled. "I was splendid, wasn't I?"

Emma let the remark pass without comment. She owed Tristan her thanks for cheering up the young sprite.

"I thought you were rather terrifying, actually. I even commented on your ferocity at the time, didn't I, Grey?"

"He did. He was shivering. Tried to grab my hand, but I wouldn't have any of it."

The carriage-load of young ladies giggled, and Elizabeth patted Lord Dare on the knee. "You're nice. I thought you were an old stuff-boots at first, but you're not all that bad."

Grey gave a shout of laughter. The sound rolled out from deep in his chest, hearty and kind and genuine, and it started Emma trembling all over again. She could get very used to that sound, and to that feeling. Far too used to it.

Roscoe leaned back in the driver's perch. "The far side of the bridge, Miss, or right here?"

Oh—the brickworks plans. She'd nearly forgotten already. "Across the creek, if you please."

The driver stopped where she asked without Grey having to repeat her instructions. Well, that was a nice change, and about blasted time.

On the far side of the bridge, Grey made a show of handing the girls one by one to the grass. As her turn came, Emma stood and offered her hand, willing the silly thing not to shake. Instead of taking her fingers, though, the duke slid his hands around her waist and lifted her effortlessly to the ground.

Even after her feet found the grass, Grey kept his arms around her, his gaze as warm as his grip. "You do look very fetching this morning," he murmured.

"Please let me go, Your Grace," she said, knowing he must feel her trembling.

He shook his head. "Not yet." After another moment, he faced the girls. By now they had begun to whisper and giggle, and he had to raise his voice to be heard. "Ladies, an improper advance is being made. As you can see, I am larger and stronger than Miss Emma. What do you suggest she do?"

"Ask him to let you go," Mary suggested.

Grey looked down at her again. "Emma?"

She cleared her throat. He was devilishly clever, but she wondered what he would do if she raised up on her toes and kissed him—which was precisely what she wanted to do. "Your Grace, please let me go."

"Hm. No." He glanced at his charges. "Now what?"

"Ask him *why* he won't let you go," Julia called.

"Why won't you let me go?" Emma repeated.

He actually tugged her closer. "Because I want to ravish you."

"Grey," she hissed, her heart pounding, "stop it at once."

The duke only lifted an eyebrow. "Students?"

"That was stupid, Julia," Henrietta said, scowling. "Now you've made it worse."

"Well, *you* tell her what to do, then."

"Fine. Tell him everyone is watching, and that you'll both be ruined if he doesn't stop."

Emma sighed unsteadily. Thankfully, the girls seemed to be looking at the incident as just another lesson. "Everyone is watching, Your Grace. We'll both be ruined if you don't stop."

His grip tightened, and he pulled her up against him. Emma couldn't have stopped her squeak of surprise for anything, but decided it helped her case.

"I don't care what anyone thinks," the duke rumbled. "I must have you."

"Kick him in the man-parts!" Lizzy yelled.

"Good God, no," Tristan countered from behind her.

"Scream?" Mary suggested.

"Eeewww," Lizzy grimaced. "Too silly."

While they debated, Emma was becoming decidedly . . . warm. And even through her skirts, she could tell that she wasn't the only one. She smiled up at him mischievously. *Ha. Let him be embarrassed, too.*

"Minx," he whispered, his teeth clenching.

"You started this," she murmured back. "Now what are you going to do?"

"Ravish you, apparently."

"Oh, I know!" Jane clapped her hands together. "Slap him! It shows that you disapprove of his behavior, *and* it makes him look like a blackguard, all at the same time."

"*Brava*," the duke said. Before Emma could carry out Jane's suggestion, he released her and took a step backward.

She felt cold where they'd been touching. "Don't I get to slap you?"

His lips twitched. "No." He turned to bow to the girls, pulling his greatcoat closed as he did so, despite the warmth of the summer morning. "Well done, Jane. First ask, then reason, then slap." He pointed a finger at Lizzy. "No kicking."

"Those aren't the sole possible responses," the teacher in Emma compelled her to add. "You might also attempt asking once more, and then step away while saying, 'Oh, Jane, there you are,' or the like."

"I like slapping better," Lizzy stated.

"Let's try another one!"

"Yes, that was fun!"

"As you wish." His lips pursed, Grey approached her again.

Shaking her head and laughing helplessly, Emma backed up until she ran into Lord Dare. "Oh—I beg your pardon, my lord. You ladies will just have to practice with His Grace. I need to make some notes."

Grey didn't like that she was escaping; she could see it on his face. Too much more of this,

though, and she would make a misstep and give
them away. Or rather, give herself away. He'd
probably been caught doing such things before,
and Society only called him a rake for it. She
would be called ruined, and her Academy would
be called closed. Emma paused. Perhaps that was
what he'd had in mind all along.

Something of what she was thinking must
have shown on her face, because Grey abruptly
turned around and herded Miss Perchase and his
class toward a nice-looking patch of grass. Her
heart pounding, Emma hurried to the creek bank
and opened her notebook.

"Are you all right?" Tristan asked from behind
her. "That big idiot didn't embarrass you, I hope."

"Oh, no. I'm fine. I just have so much work to
do, and not much time left to accomplish it."

The viscount touched her shoulder. "Are you
certain?"

She forced a smile. "Yes, I'm certain. May I see
your notes?"

"Did Grey bother telling you that he'd decided
to host a soirée tomorrow evening for you and
your students?" The viscount pulled a folded
paper from his pocket and handed it over to her.

"A . . . a soirée?" Drat. She'd completely forgotten about the invitation—and considering the
circumstances under which it had been delivered,
she wasn't certain whether she should admit to
knowing about it or not. Not, she decided, as Tristan continued to look at her quizzically. "For tomorrow night? He'd mentioned something about
a formal gathering, but my goodness. So soon?"

"He's never been much for allowing other people in on his decisions," the viscount said dryly,

then indicated the paper. "It's the best I could remember without having the actual drawings in front of me."

Emma unfolded the paper. "This is splendid," she said, perusing it. "Dimensions with product yield, and you've even included the number of laborers and their wages. Thank you, Tristan."

He nodded. "I told you I knew all about bricks. And with the way Brighton's growing, you might want to target your sales there. Everyone sends bricks to London, but you're practically within a stone's throw of the coast."

A shadow loomed behind her. "That's sound advice," Grey's lower-pitched voice said. "And with the way John Nash is going through materials in designing Prinny's damned Pavilion, you might be able to arrange a contract for exclusive furnishment."

"Are you spying?" she asked, her voice sharper than she intended.

"No, I'm aiding and abetting," the duke answered.

"Don't you have a class to teach, Your Grace?"

He gazed at her for a moment, his expression unreadable. "That's why I'm here," he said finally, turning to Dare. "My students want to know how to tell if a man is a gambler. I thought you might be able to answer that better than I could."

Tristan scowled. "You want me to chat with those little chits?"

"Yes. You're my guest lecturer. And you'd best get over there before they think up something else to discuss, or begin calling you an old stuff-boots again."

With an uneasy glance at the laughing circle of students, Tristan smoothed his coat. "I'll fire a shot in the air if they overwhelm me."

As soon as the viscount had strolled out of earshot, Grey turned back to her. "What's wrong?"

"Wrong? Nothing's wrong." She went back to pacing out the area she'd designated for the brickworks.

"Bricks. I wish I'd thought of that. It's a damned fine idea, Emma."

"I know. I've been doing my research."

He was silent for a short time. "Will you stop striding about for a minute?" he finally asked. "I want to talk to you."

She wanted to stride right back to the Academy and barricade herself in her bed chamber—not that that would keep him out if he wanted in again. "You teased me about the desk," she shot back. "And about Latin."

"What was I suppose to do, confess that we were lying on it, naked, at the time it broke?"

Emma flushed. "Hush!" Plunking herself down in the grass, she opened her book of notes and began scribbling figures.

"Or that just thinking about that bloody desk made me want to pull your clothes off and run my hands all over you again?"

She continued making notes at a furious pace, though she had no idea what she was writing. "Keep your voice down."

He walked right up behind her, sank down to his knees, and grabbed her elbow. "Or that I wanted to make love to you again, and that I still do, right here and right now?"

Squaring her shoulders, she shrugged free of his grip and looked over her shoulder at him. "That would make it easier for you, wouldn't it? If everyone saw us, I mean?"

He scowled. "What are you talking about?"

"You want to close down my Academy, remember? Compromising me would do that. Was that your plan, last night?"

"No!" With a curse he stood up and stalked away, but almost immediately strode back up to her again. "I don't know precisely what last night meant," he said in a low, serious voice. "But I do know that I enjoyed it very much, and that I would like to do it again."

"Well, it's a good thing you have Miss Boswell and Lady Sylvia staying at Haverly, then, isn't it?"

"I don't want them. I want you."

She raised her chin. "Why?"

He knelt again, this time facing her. "Why did you want me, Emma?"

The question surprised her. "Because."

"That is not an answer."

She wanted to stick her tongue out at him. "I asked you first."

"Don't be juvenile."

"Don't avoid the question."

Swearing again, he threw his arms up in the air. "I wanted you because you . . . interest me. I feel . . . attracted to you. At the moment I'm not certain why, because you're obviously insane."

"You're just trying to change the subject."

"No, you are." He tilted her chin up with his fingers. "It's your turn. Why did you want to be with me?"

She drew a shallow breath, trying to read his

gaze. He was annoyed, obviously, but deeper than that she saw curiosity, and desire. "As you said," she managed, trying to sound calm and logical, "I was . . . curious."

"Just curious."

"Yes."

He scowled. "You, my dear, are a liar."

Curiosity didn't make a woman respond to his touch as she had. She'd wanted *him*, as he had wanted—still wanted—her.

She glanced over his shoulder and abruptly backed away. Reluctantly, Grey lowered his hand. He was pushing too hard, and in front of witnesses. Until she'd mentioned it, he hadn't even considered that he might use their indiscretion to bring down the Academy. On the contrary, he was beginning to consider how to prevent that from happening.

"Regardless of your opinion, Your Grace," she said, standing again, "I have work to do."

Damnation. He was mooning after her like a schoolboy, and he didn't want her to walk away, even for one morning. Catching her hand, he turned her back to face him. "Whatever I might think of the Academy or of the merits of instructing females, I would never—*never*—use last night to hurt you. I promised you, and I keep my word."

"Very well, Grey," she said finally, nodding.

"Now, one more thing. Lizzy."

With another glance past him at his al fresco classroom, she gestured him to walk with her. Not about to miss an invitation like that, he fell into step beside her.

"I am only telling you this because you are a

fellow instructor. It will *not* go any farther. Do you agree?"

"Yes."

"Very well. Elizabeth is somewhat young to be admitted to a finishing school, but her circumstances are unique. Her father abandoned her and her mother when she was quite young, leaving considerable debts to weigh down what had been a respectable name."

Grey nodded. "I'm familiar with the scenario."

Her sideways glance was skeptical. Despite his immediate instinct to question her about it, he kept silent. He didn't want to do anything that might discourage her from confiding in him.

"I could wish the scenario wasn't quite so common," she said in her most headmistress-like tone. "Anyway, Lizzy's mother seems to rely on the . . . goodwill of her male acquaintances to keep a roof over her head and food on the table. On occasion she comes up short of funds, or decides her life is too difficult, and so she writes to her twelve-year-old daughter to pour out her troubles about how miserable she is and about how having money would make everything right."

"Does Lizzy have an inheritance?"

"All Lizzy has is a very large heart." Her voice caught, and for a moment they continued along the creek in silence. "She takes in mending from the other girls and assists me with various chores to earn spending money, and she always ends up sending every cent to that blasted woman—as though five pounds would improve her life."

His lips tight, Grey nodded again. He had seen

Elizabeth Newcombe's generous spirit himself, and the idea that anyone—much less the little chit's own mother—would take advantage of her good heart left him angry. Bloody furious, actually.

"That's why she intends to be an instructor or a governess, isn't it?" he said quietly. "To earn an income to support her mother."

"She would never admit to it, but that would be my guess."

Something about the entire situation didn't quite make sense, yet he hesitated to ask Emma about it. He sensed that he wasn't going to like the answer—not for Emma or Lizzy's sake, but for himself.

"Emma," he said, reluctance making him draw out the question, "if her mother is in such dire financial straits, who, precisely, pays for Lizzy to attend Miss Grenville's Academy?"

She halted, turning to look up at him. "I do. Or more precisely, the Academy does."

"And how do you, or more precisely, the Academy, afford this?"

"With the profits we bring in from the other students' tuition."

"And?" he prompted.

Emma drew a breath. "And with the money we save by accepting donated items such as the cart and Old Joe, and . . . and Haverly's generously low rent."

Grey exploded. "*Bloody, damned—*"

"Lower your voice," she snapped, her eyes narrow with anger.

"That's why you assigned her to my class, isn't

it?" he demanded in the quietest voice he could manage, considering that he was about an inch away from murder.

She folded her arms over her chest. "Yes, it is. And it's your own fault." White-faced, she lifted her chin in her familiar gesture of defiance. "You might have asked what I used the Academy's excess funds for before you decided to take them away, but you didn't. Elizabeth is one of a dozen internally-tuitioned students. She deserves the same opportunities as anyone else."

"Ah, excuse me," Tristan said, striding up to them, "but I've been nominated by the class to discover what the devil is going on."

"Nothing is going on," Grey ground out, glaring at Emma. "Just a difference of opinion."

But she was right, of course. If, on the day they'd made the wager, she'd told him precisely what the Academy's surplus funds financed, he undoubtedly would have doubled the wager to close the place down even more swiftly. But despite his change of heart now, he still considered her tactics an ambush. And he didn't like being ambushed.

"I see." Lord Dare rocked back on his heels. "Well, if you're still busy differing, might I teach the girls a few card tricks?" He produced a deck from a coat pocket and did an agile one-handed shuffle.

"No, you may not," Emma said forcefully. "Despite what you men think, the purpose of this Academy is not to train tricksters, liars, or charlatans." Turning her back, she stomped through the grass toward the girls. "Today's lesson is over."

There she went again, classifying all men as

boors. He *was* going to discover why she kept doing that. Grey glared at her back, looking away only when he realized his gaze had lowered to her rounded, swaying bottom. "Thank you so much, Tristan," he grumbled, following the head-mistress back toward the vehicles.

"What did I do? Except prevent bloodshed, of course."

"Did you know she's been using the Academy's profits to sponsor additional students?"

"Didn't you?"

Grey scowled.

"You didn't? All you had to do was ask. I did."

"Well, hurray for you. I hadn't realized." He swore under his breath. "If I win this wager, she'll have to turn some of those girls—if not all of them—away."

"I doubt that'll be an issue," Tristan said, climbing into the coach.

Grey glanced toward Emma again. "And why is that?"

"I don't think you're going to win the wager."

Annoyed as he was at the comment, Grey was beginning to hope that Tristan was right.

Chapter 13

❦

Emma would have been happy to avoid attending the soirée at Haverly. Both Grey and Tristan had mentioned it to the girls, though, so she'd have had a better chance of stopping the sunrise.

The other students were none too happy at being excluded, so to prevent any jealous fits, she announced at breakfast that they would have a party at the Academy to celebrate winning the wager. It wasn't the wisest thing she'd ever done, but if she lost to Grey, then the Academy wouldn't have much time left, and they might as well go out dining on chocolate.

Isabelle scratched at her bed chamber door. "Are you certain you want me to come along tonight?"

"Absolutely," Emma answered, pulling a pair of pearl earrings from her drawer. One of her more wealthy schoolmates had given them to her years ago when she'd received a new set for a birthday. They were the finest thing Emma owned. "Miss Perchase, I'm afraid, is completely terrified of Wycliffe. With more nobles thrown into the mix, I begin to fear for her health."

"I'm happy to help."

The French instructor waited as Emma finished putting up her hair and fastened on the earrings. Her evening gown was three years out of style, but it had the advantage of only having been worn once or twice.

"You look lovely," Isabelle said. "You should remember more often to be a female instead of a headmistress."

"I am both," Emma answered, collecting her shawl and reticule. Perhaps something less low-cut might have been more appropriate, but she couldn't bear the thought of looking dowdy in the presence of the glittering nobles. Not tonight.

The din downstairs was deafening. Grey's students stood in the middle of the hallway in their evening finest. Three dozen other students surrounded them, laughing and gossiping and complaining about being excluded yet again from the handsome Duke of Wycliffe's presence.

"Wish us luck," she said in a carrying voice, and the cacophony quieted. "We have a great deal to prove tonight." Emma gestured toward the front door. "Ladies, if you please?"

The barouche pulled up just as they descended the front steps, and a liveried footman handed her, Isabelle, and the girls into the vehicle. A coach would have been more appropriate, but no doubt Wycliffe had been thinking of Mary Mawgry's aversion to closed vehicles. In a moment they were rolling toward Haverly, the coach lamps and the rising moon the only illumination along the road.

"I'm going to faint," Mary whispered in a woeful voice.

"You are not going to faint. You'll be fine. All of you will." She gave them a confident smile. "Just remember everything you've learned."

"Everything we've learned at the Academy, or everything we've learned from Grey?" Lizzy asked.

That was a very good question. "Well, since His Grace is hosting the soirée, I suppose you should follow his lessons. Always keep the Academy's teachings in mind, though. You represent me and your fellow students tonight."

"I'm not feeling any better." Mary slid lower on the plush seat.

As they turned up the drive, Emma began to feel a little light-headed herself. She knew precisely why she was nervous tonight, and it had little to do with worry over how her students might perform. She had every confidence in the young ladies—she'd taught them well.

No, she had a perfectly logical reason for fiddling with her earrings and tugging at the tight bosom of her burgundy gown. As Isabelle had pointed out, tonight she wasn't dressed like a headmistress. Tonight she felt feminine and vulnerable, and she wanted to know what Greydon Brakenridge would think of her.

"Oh, look!"

Burning torches lined both sides of the curving drive up to the manor house. Strains of well-played Mozart floated toward them on the evening breeze, and every window blazed with light. All it lacked was a crowd of vehicles and guests around the front steps, and she could believe they were attending a grand ball in London.

The barouche rolled to a stop, and a liveried footman hurried to flip out the step and hand them down. The girls' faces were flushed with excitement as they trailed the footman to the front door, where Hobbes waited with his usual stoic expression.

"Your names, ladies?" he requested, producing a piece of paper and a pencil.

"It's not necessary that you introduce us, Hobbes," Emma said, moving to the head of the group.

"His Grace the Duke of Wycliffe has ordered otherwise, Miss Emma. You are to be announced."

A shiver of pure nervousness ran down her spine. She couldn't recall ever having been announced, except as a matter of politeness when she came to Haverly to visit the earl or the countess. The girls would be at least as nervous, and as always, they would follow her example. So, feigning complete calm, she named off the students, Isabelle, and herself.

"At a formal party," she said, as they followed the butler upstairs, "you would have been issued personal invitations, which you would hand to the butler on your arrival so that you could be properly introduced without having to give him your names."

"Are governesses introduced?" Elizabeth asked.

"Not as a rule." In general, governesses didn't even attend fine soirées, but she had no intention of spoiling anyone's evening with that bit of information. She and Lizzy would discuss it later, in private.

The music grew louder as they reached the open drawing room door. "Greet your host and thank him for the invitation, then greet anyone he introduces to you," she whispered, "and then move out of the way."

"We remember," Jane whispered back, smiling.

One by one Hobbes introduced her students, beginning with Lady Jane, and one by one they vanished into the drawing room. Grey's low voice spoke just inside the door, and her stomach began fluttering again.

Belatedly she wondered whether he would still be angry over her revelations about Lizzy. He needed to realize, though, what his little wager could reap for her and the other internally tuitioned students, and if the idea bothered him, good. Now that she considered it, his anger about Lizzy's situation was actually heartening. If he hadn't cared, it wouldn't have made him mad.

"Miss Emma Grenville."

Belatedly Emma realized she stood alone in the hallway, and with a deep breath she entered the drawing room. Grey had arranged the soirée, so as the host he stood nearest the door. Just beyond him Lord and Lady Haverly chatted with Isabelle, while the girls had gathered around Lord Dare at one end of the room.

"Miss Emma," the duke said, taking her hand and bowing over it.

As he straightened, their eyes met, and for a moment Emma couldn't breathe. She'd thought him devilish handsome before, but tonight he looked . . . magnificent. The whiter-than-snow cravat at his throat sported one winking sapphire. Other than that, he was clothed in stark midnight black from his broad shoulders to his polished Hessian boots. What woman could resist him?

"Your Grace," she answered, curtsying.

Yesterday's annoyance was gone from his eyes, replaced by an unreadable look as glittering as his sapphire. He stepped closer, and for a moment she thought he meant to kiss her right there—and to her horror, she would have let him do it. Instead, he turned sideways, offering her his arm.

"Thank you for joining us tonight."

"Thank you for inviting us."

"Yes, we're so pleased finally to meet Grey's little protégés," Lady Sylvia said with a smile, gliding up to them. "We've heard so much about them, you know."

Lady Sylvia shimmered in a silk gown of opalescent ivory and green. It probably cost more than Emma's entire wardrobe, but as lovely as it was, Emma was more concerned with the expression in Lady Sylvia's eyes. Only one person had ever looked at her that way before, but she recognized it. Contempt was difficult to forget.

"I haven't heard much of anything," Alice said in a plaintive voice, approaching to take Grey's other arm. "All I know is that Grey and Dare abandon us every day while they ride about

Hampshire and pretend to be professors or something."

"I was only allowed to teach once," Tristan countered. "And that was only about the ills of wagering."

"That must have been quite a speech," Sylvia cooed.

The viscount turned to his young female entourage. "I know you wanted to spend the evening with the best London has to offer, but with the short notice, this is all we could manage."

"Tris," Grey rumbled, "no bloodshed before dinner."

Emma edged a little closer to him. "I really don't want them exposed to this," she murmured, most of her attention still on Lady Sylvia. She couldn't possibly know, could she?

"They need to be exposed to this," Grey returned in the same tone. "Life isn't ideal, Emma."

She freed her hand from his arm. "I know that, Your Grace. Better than you do."

People never walked away from him. Emma obviously didn't realize that, though, for she seemed to do it on a regular basis. Grey would have followed her, except that Alice had a death grip on his other arm and he didn't fancy dragging her around the drawing room.

Blumton was circling Jane, a quizzing glass held to one eye. "I say, you're the chit who played Juliet, ain't you?"

"I'm sorry, sir," she responded, "but I don't believe we've been introduced."

Grey felt like applauding, though Emma

looked as though she intended to take credit for Jane's composed answer.

"Ah. Allow me," he said, and proceeded to introduce his companions to the girls. He didn't doubt that Blumton would behave himself, or that he could intimidate Alice into doing so, but he wasn't so sure about Sylvia. Emma could handle her, but the girls were too young to possess their headmistress's composure and self-confidence. As he'd said, though, they needed to experience this. In London society, treachery lurked behind every smile. Trusting the world would only get them laughed at and ruined by it.

"May I see your quizzing glass?" Elizabeth asked Charles.

"Well—I—all right, I suppose so," he blustered.

The thing was attached to his watch fob, so he had to lean down in order for Lizzy to look through it. She squinted her other eye and blinked up at him through the curved glass.

"It makes your nose look rather large," she stated, continuing to examine him.

Blumton flushed. "You're supposed to look down at everyone else with it. Not at me."

"Oh. It's just meant to make everyone else look silly, then." She turned to Henrietta. "You look blurry."

Henrietta giggled. "Well, you're eye is *huge*."

"Is it?" With a thoughtful frown, Lizzy handed the lens back to Charles. "Thank you, but I've decided I don't want to get a quizzing glass."

"Chits don't use them, anyway," he returned, examining it and then whipping out his handkerchief to polish the glass.

"Thank goodness. It's ridiculous."

Hiding a grin, Grey freed himself from Alice's fingers and stepped forward. "I wouldn't exactly call that a flattering commentary, Lizzy."

"Well, what does it matter? I don't want to marry him."

The crowd laughed. Grey chuckled as well, until he noticed Emma's scowl, quickly disguised. "Even so," he added, "it's best not to insult someone who outranks you in Society."

"That's right," Blumton said indignantly. "My father's a marquis. And I wouldn't marry you, anyway. You're practically an infant."

"At least I know better than to use a stupid quizzing glass and show my big bulging eye to people."

"Elizabeth Newcombe," Emma snapped, her tone sharp. "We are guests, not the entertainment."

Lizzy subsided at once. With a curtsy at Blumton, she made her way to her headmistress's side. "I beg your pardon, Lord Charles," she said quietly, her eyes downcast.

"S'all right," Blumton returned. "Can't expect an infant to comprehend high fashion."

Hobbes appeared at the door. "Your Grace, ladies and gentlemen, dinner is served."

"Thank goodness," Alice said, grabbing onto Grey's arm again. "I suppose the remainder of the evening will be as intolerable?"

The only thing intolerable about the evening so far was that he'd barely exchanged two words with Emma. He'd spent the day trying to untangle his mood after her revelation about Elizabeth, and he still had some sorting out to do—sorting out which required her presence.

Angry as he wanted to be, he couldn't help but admire Emma for her convictions and for her commitment to them. It annoyed him to admit that she was a better person than he was. A female, no less—though he saw less and less resemblance between her and most of the other women he knew.

"Grey?"

He blinked. "What?"

Alice was looking at him, her perfect brow furrowed. "You're shaking."

"You're cutting off the flow of blood to my arm," he muttered, shrugging free.

"Beast."

Since the evening was a formal one, Grey offered his arm to his aunt. Uncle Dennis would escort Sylvia, Tristan lucked into Jane, and Blumton would spend dinner seated between Emma and Alice. The soirée was a bad idea—he'd concocted the whole bloody evening with the idea of being able to spend time with Emma Grenville, and the only way he would manage even a private word with her was if he kidnapped her and dragged her off somewhere. That notion sounded more appealing with every passing moment.

"So, ladies," Sylvia began, as the footmen came around with the platters of beef and ham, "you must tell me. With Wycliffe and Dare calling on you every day, they must have all of you swooning over them."

"Oh, no," Julia stated. "Grey and Lord Dare are rakes."

Lady Sylvia smiled. "And just how do you know that, pray tell?"

"They told us."

She glanced over at him. "That's interesting, wouldn't you say, Alice?"

"I don't think so at all."

"Well, I'm curious as to what, exactly, is being taught," Charles Blumton said around a mouthful of beef. "I can't imagine what the Duke of Wycliffe sees fit to teach young girls."

"I can," Sylvia countered.

"All instruction is supervised, naturally." Emma sliced a piece of ham into a dainty mouthful. "And I have to admit, despite my initial skepticism, that some of His Grace's insights into the workings of Society have been enlightening."

That was the closest thing to a compliment she'd ever sent in his direction. Grey lifted an eyebrow, but she had suddenly become occupied with her dinner. If he'd been removed from her all-encompassing category of useless males, he wanted to know about it. "Thank you, Miss Emma, though your admission doesn't bode well for your success in our wager."

Finally she lifted her gaze to his. "I said your insights were enlightening, Your Grace. I didn't say they were helpful."

"A good point, Emma," Lady Haverly said with her faint smile.

"My goodness." Alice fanned her face with her napkin. "I fear for our entire civilization when a headmistress is allowed to speak to a duke in such a tone."

Emma smiled. "I was merely clarifying my

statement, Miss Boswell. I didn't intend to offend His Grace, and I apologize if I've done so."

Damnation, he wished the rest of the guests would just vanish for five minutes so Emma could insult him in peace. "I assure you, Alice," he drawled, "I can speak for myself. And I wasn't offended."

"Will we be dancing after dinner?" Lizzy asked.

Grey nodded. "I thought it might be good practice."

"My goodness," Uncle Dennis said, chuckling. "I haven't waltzed in ages. That should be fun, eh, Regina?"

"Indeed. I have to say," the countess continued, "it's delightful to have a houseful of guests again. Haverly has stood quiet for too long."

"I'm happy we could oblige," Emma said with a warm smile that made Grey shift in his chair. "The two of you have done so much for the Academy over the years. I wish there was more we could do to repay you."

"You might try paying your rent," Blumton said, chuckling to himself as he slathered a biscuit with honey.

Grey wanted to throttle him. If there was one thing he didn't want to do this evening, it was to remind Emma that they were on different sides of the chasm. "She *is* paying the Academy's rent," he broke in. "Whether that amount will be reassessed remains to be seen."

"My goodness, Grey, that's quite a change from the bellowing you did a few weeks ago." Sylvia waved her fingers at Emma, leaning toward the headmistress as though the two of them were old, dear friends. "You should have heard him. He insisted that the Academy only taught females to lie and cheat and trick men into marriage, and that it should be burned to the ground."

He was going to have to murder half of Haverly's house guests before the evening was over. "Sylvia," he murmured, "if you want to—"

Utensils hit the table with a loud clang. "He would not say such a thing!" Lizzy stated, her face a mask of fury. "That's just mean. Why are you trying to cause so much trouble?"

Sylvia looked startled. "Well, my dear, perhaps you should ask His Grace what he *did* say about your school."

Lizzy looked at him, her round brown eyes begging him to call Sylvia a liar. He wished he could. "Elizabeth, when I came to Haverly, I didn't—"

"We all came to the Academy to learn things we didn't know," Emma interrupted in a quiet voice. "I would like to think that His Grace has been educated, as well."

This time when he met her gaze, she didn't look away. She'd spoken for Lizzy's sake, of course, but she'd also made it possible for him to continue working with the girls and to make a go of winning the wager—which at the moment he had no intention of doing. "I admit," he said slowly, "you ladies have surprised me. And I would like to think I've been able to teach all of you a little something, as well."

A blush crept up Emma's cheeks. He was glad she understood that he considered her his primary student—and he was aching to continue her education.

"Admirable speeches all the way around," Blumton acknowledged.

Throughout the meal, Sylvia and Blumton took turns trying to pry information from Emma about her part in the wager and how it was progressing. More troubling, Lady Sylvia seemed fascinated with gleaning details of Emma's past and upbringing from every sentence the head-mistress uttered. Emma turned all but the most inane questions aside with no visible effort, but the interrogation had Grey near to grinding his teeth.

"You know, Sylvia," he drawled, when he couldn't stand it any longer, "I've been wondering. When was it, precisely, that you developed a tendre for Tristan?"

Sylvia's mouth snapped shut before she managed a serene smile. "I'm afraid I don't know what you're talking about, Wycliffe, but that seems rather . . . personal."

He held her gaze. "Yes, it does, doesn't it?"

Tristan cleared his throat, his expression unreadable except for the twinkle deep in his light blue eyes. "This banter is all well and good," the viscount said, "but I think we need to keep in mind that the contest has only two weeks to go before the judging."

"Then perhaps we should begin the dancing." Relieved that no one had been killed over dinner, Grey pushed away from the table.

From the speed with which Emma and her students vacated the dining room, he'd said the right thing—for once, anyway. She crossed in front of him on the way back to the drawing room, and at the lemon scent of her hair, his mouth went dry.

"I'm sorry," he murmured, taking her arm and grateful for the dim light of the hallway. "The girls needed to experience this, but you didn't."

"It's nothing new to me, Your Grace."

He glanced over his shoulder. The girls and Miss Santerre preceded them, and the Haverly house guests had yet to emerge from the dining room. "I want to kiss you, Emma," he whispered. "I want to run my hands along your skin, feel you against m—"

"*Stop it.*"

He slowed, trying to read her expression in the lamp light. "You want me again, don't you?" he said fiercely. "I know you do."

"Half the time I don't know whether I'm angry with you or in lust with you." Emma blushed.

"In lust with me," he repeated, chuckling softly. "The feeling is mutual."

"Don't look so pleased. I wish I wasn't."

Elizabeth reappeared in the drawing room doorway and grabbed Emma's hand. "Come and look!"

He had no choice but to relinquish her to the little chit. He hadn't expected Emma to acknowledge such a base emotion as lust. The idea that women wanted him was nothing new, but having Emma Grenville admit to it left him feeling oddly . . . triumphant.

The orchestra had relocated to the grand ball-room. Though they hadn't had much time for decorating, Haverly's servants and the Basingstoke villagers had acquitted themselves well. Streamers and bows decorated the pillars and the windows. A few more balloons would have been nice, but Hampshire didn't have much of a supply.

"Isn't it splendid?" Elizabeth said, spinning.

"It's lovely." Emma motioned the girls to one side of the room and faced Grey again. "Thank you. They won't forget this."

"Neither will I," Tristan said, strolling into the room. "I would never have imagined. No wonder you've decided against marriage, Wycliffe; you're a splendid hostess all on your own."

Emma looked sharply at Dare, then returned to assembling her charges. Grey scowled. He supposed that she would hear the tale eventually, but he preferred that it not be tonight—not even while he remained in Hampshire.

"Grey, may I have the first dance?" Henrietta pranced up to him while Julia giggled behind her hand, obviously at her friend's daring.

"No, you may not, Miss Brendale," Emma said sternly. "This is an exercise in manners and propriety. You must wait to be asked onto the floor."

"But there aren't enough men," Henrietta whispered loudly.

"I'm afraid you'll find that happens more often than not, Miss Brendale." Tristan approached, bowing at the curly-haired chit. "Which is why it's always wise to have a secondary plan. May I have this dance?"

She curtsied. "Yes, you may, Lord Dare." She glanced at Grey. "I would be honored."

Thank God for Tristan. Even if he was merely trying to remain in Emma's good graces, he had freed Grey for the first dance of the evening. Deciding right then to make it a waltz, Grey headed for Emma. Her gaze, though, was on Dare, her soft mouth curved in an obvious smile of gratitude for his saving Henrietta from embarrassment. Damn Dare, anyway.

Blumton brushed past him. "You—little chit—what's your name again?"

Lizzy stood on her tiptoes. "Elizabeth Newcombe, Lord Charles, though you may call me Lizzy."

"Do you dance?"

"Exceedingly well, my lord."

"All right, come along, then."

She pursed her lips. "I think you should ask me more nicely than that."

Blumton rolled his eyes. "Gadzooks."

"Lizzy," Emma said in a low voice.

The little sprite grimaced, then held out her hand. "Very well, but I don't feel all that honored."

Someone in the direction of the orchestra choked out a laugh, and the players launched into a country dance. Determined not to be outdone by Blumton, Grey inclined his head toward Jane. "Would you do me the honor, Lady Jane?"

She dipped in a graceful curtsy, taking his fingers. "The honor is mine, Your Grace."

Uncle Dennis paired with Aunt Regina. Obviously used to the dearth of male partners, Julia grabbed Mary Mawgry by the hand and pulled her into the line of dancers. Alice took one look at Emma and turned her back to chat with Sylvia.

All the young ladies were skilled dancers, and he couldn't help feeling a measure of pride at the way they conducted themselves. They were a spirited lot, and there was something refreshing in engaging in a conversation with a female who might actually say something unexpected.

He glanced at Emma, seated on one of the chairs at the side of the room. When she wasn't lumping him with the rest of the boorish males on the island, she was by far the most refreshing, riveting female he'd ever encountered. He might have been somewhat in error in calling all females empty-headed, marriage-hungry charlatans, but at least he had a reason for his misconception. What was the reason for her negative views toward his gender?

He paused in the dance as a wide circle brought him before the orchestra. "Your next piece will be a waltz," he said, and continued back around to Jane without waiting for an answer.

"Oh, a waltz would be splendid," Jane said, smiling. They parted, circling, and then returned to join hands again. "You should ask Miss Emma to dance," she suggested. "Otherwise she won't have any fun tonight."

"That's a good idea," he said, applauding his own cleverness. "And Jane, don't say anything, but I have a little surprise for you this evening."

"For me?" She blushed prettily.

Grey chuckled. The soirée was proceeding swimmingly, and the best was yet to come. Tonight he would dance with Emma Grenville, and tonight he would get some answers or die trying.

Chapter 14

～⌒OᗉO⌒～

If Elizabeth didn't stop putting extra flourishes and turns into her dancing, poor Lord Charles was going to break his neck trying to keep up with her.

Emma hid a smile behind her hand. Lizzy was far too exuberant, but once she left the Academy for her career as a governess or a companion, she would never be permitted to fling her arms out and spin like a top. And everyone should have the opportunity at least once in her life to spin.

As the dance ended, she stood to collect her charges. Supposedly any poor behavior would be to Grey's detriment, but she knew quite well that the Duke of Wycliffe wasn't being judged tonight.

"Did you see me?" Elizabeth gave another spin.

"Yes, I did." Emma tugged on the girl's sleeve to straighten it. "Just try not to kill anyone, dear."

The air stirred behind her, and she turned, from her quickened pulse knowing who it must be. "Your Grace."

Grey looked down at her, a great tawny lion playing with the Academy's little lambs. "May I have this dance, Emma?" he asked, holding one hand out to her.

She flushed. "Oh, no. It's the girls who need the practice, Your Grace. I couldn't." But she'd been watching him almost every moment of the country dance, and her protest lacked heat.

He lifted an eyebrow. "I thought you led by example."

"I do, but—"

"Then let's show them how it's done, shall we?"

She eyed him, and then the excited faces of her students. "Oh, very well." Hopefully it would be a quadrille or another country dance, and she wouldn't have to spend a protracted time in his company. Just touching his hands was torture enough. To be in his arms . . .

The orchestra began playing a waltz. With a shiver, Emma allowed him to draw her out onto the dance floor. She closed her eyes as he slid one hand around her waist and pulled her closer to him.

"Don't do that," he whispered.

"Do what?"

"Don't close your eyes. It makes me want to kiss them."

Her eyes flew open. "Well, don't."

He swung her into the dance. "I'll attempt to

restrain myself. I think you should know, however, that—"

"Please tell me you aren't going to spend the entire waltz telling me how much you desire to touch me and kiss me."

A slight grin tugged at the corners of his lips. "We've already established that you're in lust with me; I'll save that bit of dialogue until we're somewhere more private."

Even the mention of being alone with him made her feel weak-kneed. "Did you say something to Lady Sylvia?" she asked instead. "Something about . . . what happened?"

"Are you referring to the other evening, when I stole into the Academy and made love to the headmistress?"

"Grey, please," she hissed.

A slight frown furrowed his brow. "No, I didn't say a word to her, nor would I ever. Why?"

"She's been looking at me rather oddly."

"You're not from London. Everyone who doesn't have a home in London is an oddity."

"It wasn't that kind of look."

Grey regarded her with a mix of curiosity and exasperation. She'd seen that expression on his face quite a few times over the past few weeks. "What kind of look was it, then? Or are we going to play charades so I can guess?"

"You saw it, as well, or you wouldn't have stopped her from questioning me."

"Maybe I like to be the only one questioning you."

Emma cleared her throat. "I'm attempting not to jump to conclusions," she pointed out. "She just seemed . . . to know something. About us. And not to be happy with it."

His expression became more somber. "You may be right. I'll find out."

She tightened her grip on his shoulder, digging her fingers into the iron-bound muscles there. "No!"

For a moment they waltzed in silence. "I'll tell you what," he said finally, gazing down at her from scant inches away, "I'll be subtle, if you'll tell me something."

Her heart thumped. Despite her protests, she hoped the something would have to do with his wanting to be with her again. She wanted future lessons from Grey Brakenridge. As many as they could possibly fit into the two weeks he had remaining in Hampshire. She didn't want him to know, though, that she yearned for his touch. He liked that she was strong; she liked it, too, and even more she needed to be that way. More even than she'd realized.

"What do you want me to tell you?" she asked cautiously.

"You said you'd experienced people like this before," he said, nodding at the Haverly house guests, "but it wouldn't have been at the Academy. Where, then?"

A different kind of nervousness ran through her. "London."

"When were you in London? I don't remember you being there."

She would have remembered *him* if they'd ever crossed paths. Of that she was certain. "London is a large place, Your Grace. And I hardly think you would have noticed me."

"Yes, I would have."

She drew a breath, dismayed that she was leaning again. Hopefully in the middle of the waltz no one would be able to tell. "I was only twelve, anyway."

For just a moment his expression darkened. "Twelve? What kind of bastard would hurt a twelve-year-old girl?"

His voice had taken on a low, dangerous edge, and that actually steadied her a little. "It was a long time ago. There's nothing anyone could have done about it, anyway."

"I could have," he murmured.

"Oh, really? And just what would you have done, Your Grace? I imagine I would have been far beneath your notice."

"I would have killed him."

That stopped her. Something in the quiet words told her that he meant it, and she realized she never wanted to face him when he was truly angry about something. "Well, he's been dead for six years, so thank you for the offer, but—"

"Who was he?"

"It's not impor—"

"Who was he?" he repeated, even more quietly.

The flicker inside her veins heated. "He was my cousin—my second cousin, actually—and it's not as sordid as you seem to think."

"So tell me."

"If it will make you quit prying, fine. He was my mother's cousin. When my father died, my mother and I had nowhere to go, and he agreed to take us in. My mother was already ill, and two months later she died as well. While she lived, he was kind and considerate, full of promises about how he would see that I was given a splendid debut in Society, and a dowry large enough to attract a good match."

"He lied," Grey said after a moment.

"Yes, he did. A week after my mother's funeral, I went for a walk with a maid. When I returned, he was standing at the door with a bag stuffed full of clothes. He said he was not going to give a scrawny female like me any charity, and that I was too young to offer him anything in return. He yanked the maid into the house, dumped the sack at my feet, and closed the door." Emma shut her eyes for a heartbeat, then looked up into his light green gaze again. "I'd never realized until that moment that people lied. Isn't that silly? I had no idea."

"What did you do?" he murmured.

"Within a week I was picked up by the constabulary for begging and vagrancy, and put into a workhouse. My Aunt Patricia, my father's sister, tracked me down and found me six months later. How she managed it, I'll never know, but it must have cost her a great deal to buy the information from my cousin's servants."

"Who was he?"

"The Earl of Ross." Just saying the name again made her bile rise, and she clenched her jaw.

"Ross. I knew him, though not well. If it's any consolation, the rumor is that he died of syphilis."

She nodded. "I heard the same rumor. I wouldn't be surprised if it were true."

"A workhouse," he whispered, anger touching his gaze again. "I can't even imagine—"

"Be thankful you can't," she said crisply.

"Is that why you're so concerned about Elizabeth? You don't want her to end up where you did?"

"My concern isn't only for Lizzy, though I do admit that she is special to me. I simply want these young ladies to be capable enough that they don't have to rely on anyone else's good graces to live decent lives."

The waltz ended. Grey looked as though he wanted to continue the conversation, but she'd told him more than enough.

However compassionate he felt at the moment, and however her heart raced in his presence, she'd seen his haughty, arrogant side. And if word ever got out that the headmistress of Miss Grenville's Academy had spent six months in a workhouse, she might as well go back to one.

Emma suppressed a shudder. She hadn't used to be so foolish; what was wrong with her? "I think Lizzy would like to dance with you," she said, freeing her hand from his warm grip.

"Em," he said almost soundlessly, "you have my admiration. And my word."

She swallowed. For a man, he was sometimes quite nice. "I thank you for both of them."

Hobbes rapped on the floor with his staff, the sound echoing like thunder in the loud room. No doubt he was enjoying the formality of the evening, even if it was for the benefit of a handful of little girls. "Your Grace, ladies—"

"Emma," Grey said again, taking a step toward her. He suddenly looked less confident, and dread touched her.

"—and gentlemen, may I—"

"Don't rush to conclusions here."

"—present, Mr. Frederick Mayburne."

Freddie strolled into the room. He was dressed conservatively, for him, with only the painfully intricate knot of his cravat marking him as a dandy and a rake. Otherwise, in his gray suit and Wellington boots, he looked nearly as austere, if not nearly so compelling, as Grey.

Trying to keep her jaw from dropping in angry astonishment, Emma spun on her heel to face Wycliffe. "What is he doing here?" she enunciated.

"We needed more men," he said, shrugging. "I thought he might—"

"I will *not* have him accosting Jane here or anywhere else," Emma snapped back at him. "We are not a matchmaking facility. We are a teaching Academy, with a reputation to maintain. No one would send their daughters here if they knew we had men waiting nearby to snatch them up before their debuts."

Grey stepped past her to greet Freddie. "I wouldn't wager on that," he murmured as he walked away from her.

Oh, this was too much. Emma knotted her skirt in her hands and stomped toward the intruder. "You are a bachelor, Your Grace," she said over her shoulder as she passed him by. "In this instance, I can assure you that your opinion doesn't matter in the slightest."

Freddie saw her coming and took a step backward. "Miss Emma, good evening," he said, his confident expression fading.

"Out," she said, continuing to advance.

"I was invited." Still retreating, Freddie threw a hopeful glance beyond her.

"He won't dance with Jane," the duke said from behind her, closer than she expected.

She slowed, abruptly conscious of the scene she was making. "Nor will he speak with Jane."

"I won't." Freddie stopped his retreat in the doorway, the farthest away he could get from her without exiting the room.

"Nor will he give letters to anyone else to be passed on to Jane."

Mayburne shook his head. "I won't."

Emma turned on Grey again. "I have your word."

He inclined his head. "You have my word."

"Very well."

She would rather have had Freddie Mayburne thrown out of Haverly, but with a last warning glare she returned to her charges. Despite her annoyance, she understood the reasoning behind the young man's presence. Grey had several times mentioned the threats of the outside world and how ill prepared her students might be to meet them. Freddie was definitely a threat, but having him here, outnumbered and under the watchful eyes of the duke, Isabelle, and herself, could be good practice for the girls.

The orchestra, apparently noticing the cessation of bellowing among the guests, launched into a quadrille. Lord Charles claimed Jane, though Emma suspected it had more to do with the young lady's title than any chivalrous impulses to protect her from Freddie's attentions.

Boots tapped up behind her. "Miss . . . Mawgy, may I have this dance?" Freddie asked slowly.

At Emma's nod, Mary curtsied and took his proffered hand. "I'm honored, Mr. Mayburne."

"Frederick, if you please."

"You see?" The duke brushed her elbow with his fingertips. "That wasn't so difficult, was it?"

"You should have warned me that he was coming."

"I had no idea even rakes were terrified of you, Miss Emma. I thought for a moment I might have to loan Frederick a dry pair of trousers."

"Very amusing. Please tell me that you do at least understand why I protested."

"I understand perfectly well why you protested. And I assume you understand why I wanted him here tonight."

"Yes."

Lizzy was bouncing up and down on her toes, looking as though she was about to burst. Grey lifted an eyebrow, his green eyes dancing despite his stern expression.

"Hm. I was going to ask you to dance, infant, but you appear to be having an apoplexy."

The sprite snatched his arm and tugged him onto the floor to join the other dancers. "I'm honored. Come on, Grey!"

Emma chuckled. When he allowed his arrogant shell to crack, Greydon Brakenridge could be very warm and amusing. And if he continued giving and then keeping his word, she was going to be dangerously in peril of liking him too much.

"Emma, may I—"

She leaned toward Lord Dare as he stopped beside her. "Ask Julia," she murmured almost soundlessly.

"—Interrupt to ask Miss Julia out for the quadrille?" the viscount continued smoothly.

"Oh, yes," Julia said, practically leaping to his side.

"Julia, decorum," Emma reminded her.

"Lizzy doesn't have any."

"Lizzy is twelve. You are sixteen."

"Yes, Miss Emma. Thank you, Lord Dare; I would be honored."

Lord Haverly had snagged Miss Boswell, and Emma led Henrietta to the chairs at the side of the room. "Are you enjoying yourself?" she asked.

"Yes. Very much." Henrietta glanced toward Lady Sylvia, who was gazing at them coolly over Lady Haverly's shoulder. "Except I don't think the other ladies like us."

"They probably don't." Whatever benefit of the doubt she'd been willing to give Alice and Lady Sylvia had vanished at the latter's cold reception toward the girls. Honesty was always best, she decided as she returned her attention to Henrietta. "This won't be the only time or place you'll encounter a cold shoulder from your peers. Unfortunately, in Society every unmarried female expects that every other unmarried female is looking for a husband. You will therefore be considered com—"

"Competition," Henrietta finished. "That's what Grey said."

"Really?" That was interesting. "How did he say it?"

"Just like you did. Except he also said always to be sure of your footing because you could never know when someone, man or woman, might try to put you off balance." She giggled. "Julia thought he meant people were going to try to knock us to the ground. I had to tell her that he was speaking figuratively."

Not necessarily. "Well, that's good advice."

Henrietta nodded. "We thought so, too."

During the next set Frederick claimed Henrietta for a quadrille, and under Emma's watchful eye he didn't so much as take a step toward Jane. The young lady had to be the reason he was at Haverly, though, and Emma wasn't about to forget that even with Grey's heady presence.

As the big grandfather clock downstairs struck midnight and the last dance came to a close, Emma stepped back from Charles Blumton and applauded. "That was splendid," she said, smiling as Grey and Henrietta joined her, "but I'm afraid we must call it an evening."

The duke nodded. "I'm pleased you came."

That sounded like he meant it just for her, but she was so flushed from dancing that she doubted another blush would show. "We thank you for inviting us." Smiling, she took the earl's hand as he approached. "And thank you as well, Lord Haverly. You are a very generous man."

"My pleasure, Emma. Regina and I have decided we shall have to do this more often, and for all your young ladies."

"It would be a fine tradition." The girls gathered around them, one by one thanking Wycliffe and Haverly while Emma beamed. Despite a few missteps, they'd done themselves—and her—proud. They'd also done Grey proud, but ultimately it was *their* success that mattered.

"I'll see you out." Grey offered his arm. Emma tucked her hand around his arm and they followed as the girls and Isabelle trooped downstairs. "How do you rate Freddie's performance this evening?" the duke asked in his low voice.

"He trod on my toe, but I suppose I do make him nervous."

"You make *me* nervous."

"As if I could." As if anyone could unnerve the Duke of Wycliffe.

"You would be surprised, Emma," he murmured, tilting his head toward her.

In the half dark, the gesture felt as intimate as a kiss. "Grey."

With a slight sigh, he straightened. "What about Freddie, then?"

"The rules don't change." She looked ahead at Jane, hand in hand with Elizabeth as they reached the foyer. "He didn't try to arrange any elopements tonight, though the thought probably crossed his mind."

"But you're not angry with me for inviting him?"

Emma wanted to be angry with him, but tonight had been too enjoyable to ruin with arguing. "Just tell me beforehand next time."

Grey nodded again. "Fair enough."

He was being far too mild and agreeable, and she could only come up with a few reasons why he would behave himself. One reason, actually. A flicker of heat started low in her belly. If they were caught, another midnight visit would ruin her—literally and figuratively.

As Hobbes held the door for them and they

made their way to the waiting barouche, though, he didn't say anything the least bit improper. He merely handed Isabelle and the students one by one into the vehicle, complimenting each of them on their dancing, or their decorum, or their bravery in partnering with Lord Charles.

"Do you think he'll give up his quizzing glass?" Lizzy asked.

"I doubt it. Though I would imagine he won't use it in your presence any longer."

Emma waited until the rest of the passengers were settled, then took his hand as she stepped up into the barouche. "Will you be teaching tomorrow?"

His fingers tightened almost imperceptibly around hers, then released her. "Yes. So I'll see you soon," he said, his gaze holding hers.

Oh, dear. "Good night."

The carriage rolled away from the manor, with the girls turning to wave at Grey's vanishing figure. Emma only glanced back at him once, just before they rounded the curve and drew out of sight. He was smiling.

Grey watched after them until he couldn't hear the carriage any longer. He'd warned Emma of his plans for later and she hadn't said a word; therefore, she agreed.

"Your Grace?" Hobbes said from the doorway.

"Hm?"

"It's rather chilly tonight. I thought perhaps you might wish to come inside."

"Is it chilly? I hadn't noticed."

With the way Emma had his blood running, he

could be in the middle of a Russian winter and not feel the cold. A chill of a different sort awaited him inside, however, and he felt it immediately.

"Lady Sylvia, is there something I can do for you?"

"I just don't see the attraction," she said smoothly, taking his arm as they returned upstairs.

He avoided staring at her, but just barely. "Attraction?"

"You and those little girls. It's simply . . . unfathomable why you would wish to spend time with them."

"I'm doing it to win a wager. And since part of my task is alerting my students to the perils and pitfalls awaiting them in London, I should thank you for your performance tonight."

"Ah." She looked at him from beneath her long, curling lashes. "Am I a peril, or a pitfall?"

"Both." He continued past her, up the stairs.

"When I attended finishing school in Wessex, we never had a duke dancing attendance on us," she went on, following him. "Our headmistress would have fainted if a man came anywhere near us. So would I."

He kept walking. "Luckily you seem to have overcome your aversion."

"Quite so. I find it best to keep an open mind."

She probably kept an open bed chamber door, as well. A few weeks ago he might have been intrigued, but tonight he didn't even spare her a backward glance.

Grey said his good nights to the others. Tristan, Blumton, and Uncle Dennis had settled back in the drawing room for brandy and a cigar and to trade tales of tromped-on toes, but he had other things on his mind. One thing, actually.

Stripping out of most of his evening finery, he pulled on a plain, dark pair of trousers. A waistcoat seemed a great deal of effort for the short amount of time he intended on wearing it, but if he ran across anyone they would probably note that he was improperly attired. They had standards for nobility, even in Hampshire.

Once he shrugged into his coat and pulled on his boots, he went to his bed chamber door, then stopped. Most of the servants had retired for the evening, but the three men remained in the drawing room. And while he could evade their notice, Sylvia clearly suspected something, and she was just as clearly on the prowl.

For his own sake he didn't give a damn whether she caught him slipping out or not, but her gossip and speculation would devastate Emma. Rubbing his chin, Grey reversed course and headed for the window. If Alice could clamber out on the ledge in her gown and stockings, he could damned well do it in boots and breeches.

The window was already open to invite in the cool evening air. He stuck one foot over the sill and ducked outside—and someone rapped on his door. For a moment he remained where he was, poised half in and half out of the window. If his guest entered the bed chamber to find him gone, though, he would be faced with some rather sticky questions when he returned. Cursing, Grey stepped back inside and shrugged out of his coat. If no one was paying too close attention, it would simply look like he'd been undressing for the evening. As he passed the bed he yanked the coverlet down with one hand.

"What?" he asked, pulling open the door.

Freddie Mayburne blinked at him. "I . . . I just wanted to thank you for inviting me here this evening."

He'd forgotten Freddie even existed. Grey nodded. "You're welcome. Good night." He pushed the door closed.

He'd only taken two steps back toward his coat and the window when the knocking resumed. With another curse he strode back and yanked it open again.

"Yes?"

"Ah. From our conversation last week," Mayburne continued, "I thought you might be a bit more . . . helpful in my quest."

"I invited you here tonight."

"And I didn't even get to speak with Jane."

Grey looked at him for a moment. He knew Freddie's type, even if he barely knew the man. In all but the lad's quest for wealth, the resemblance between them was rather strong. Or it had been. Tonight, though, Emma's words echoed in his mind—she hadn't realized that people lied, or that they were two-faced, or that they said they wanted a woman's heart when they really only wanted her purse.

"How does Jane feel about you?" he asked slowly.

Frederick's brow furrowed. "She's mad for me, of course."

"Of course." With effort Grey kept from glancing back at the beckoning window. "Tonight you began to establish that you are worthy of trust, a man of your word. The day after tomorrow you will send a note to the Academy, addressed to Miss Emma Grenville, inquiring as to whether the ladies who attended the soirée tonight might wish to join you for luncheon in Basingstoke."

The younger man gave a sly grin. "I begin to see why you have such a reputation, Your Grace."

Grey wasn't so sure he deserved the praise, if that was what it was. He knew how to seduce a woman; he'd done it more times than he could count. One complimented them, said what they thought they wanted to hear and bought them a few trinkets, if necessary, and then one bedded them.

But the problem here was twofold. One, he knew Jane. And having been in the position to instruct and interact with her, he felt . . . protective toward her. The second problem was Emma. She wasn't simply a female whose favors he wanted, though he did want them again. Badly. She'd become more than that. She was damned complicated, and to know her, to understand her, he needed to learn what moved her and what motivated her. If he couldn't do that, neither could he expect that she would return his interest and affection.

"Your Grace?"

Grey shook himself. If he spent all night mooning over her, he wasn't going to have enough time to actually go and see her. "Yes?"

"Good night."

"Good night." Grey shut the door again, listening as Freddie's footsteps headed for the stairs. He would puzzle out Jane and Frederick later.

Making sure his door was latched, he pulled

his coat back on and returned to the window. Thanks to the rough stonework and a drainpipe, descending took only a few moments. Once on the ground, he paused. Taking Cornwall made the most sense, but thanks to Freddie's delayed departure, the grooms still moved about the stable. "Damnation," he grunted. A two-mile hike in the dark didn't hold much appeal, particularly considering he would have to return the same way.

Going back to bed was out of the question. All night the scent of Emma's hair, the touch of her hand, the sound of her voice, had driven him half mad. The only thing that had kept him from dragging her into an unoccupied room and stripping her clothes off had been the thought that he would have her in his arms before sunrise.

Bloody hell, he was a duke. He wasn't supposed to have to sneak, or evade servants, or saddle his own damned horse, or go traipsing on foot through the woods to a rendezvous. She should be coming to find him. Grey sighed irritably. Emma wouldn't do any such thing, and he knew damned well that he wasn't going to sit on his ass and wait.

Deciding a few minutes delay would be better than four miles on foot, he stalked back and forth in the deep shadows until the last light in the stable went out. Normally he admired diligence, but tonight he would have been happy to see the entire stable staff drunk and sleeping hours ago. He slipped in through the door and collected Cornwall, grabbing the necessary tack and hauling everything outside to saddle the beast.

He glanced up toward the house as he swung

up onto the bay. The drawing room was on the opposite side of the manor, and all of the windows overlooking the stable were dark. Just to be safe, though, he kept Cornwall to a quiet walk until they reached the end of the drive. As soon as they passed out of earshot he urged the gelding into a canter.

The moon was half full and sitting almost directly overhead, its light enough to read by. Once he caught a glimpse of Freddie ahead on the road and, swearing, slowed Cornwall to a walk again before he ran the lad down.

As he approached the ivy-covered walls surrounding the Academy, he noticed that all of the lights were out there, as well. He wasn't surprised. It was well past bedtime for all proper chits. He smiled to himself. Emma wasn't nearly as proper as she liked to think.

Standing in the saddle, he pulled himself up to the top of the wall and dropped down the other side. Emma really needed to set some dogs out on night patrol to protect those girls. This was too simple. On the other hand, he didn't want a pack of hounds nipping at his heels while he sprinted across the moonlit grass to the building's deep shadows.

The main door was locked and bolted, but the third window he tried slid open easily. Grey slipped inside one of the classrooms and closed the window behind himself. No sense getting papers blown all over the place by the night breeze.

Silently, he made his way into the main hall and then upstairs to the second floor. Everything was peaceful and quiet, which was encouraging.

She had to know he was on his way, but no Amazon school instructors barred the way, and the troll seemed to be wherever he spent the night.

Her office door was closed, but not locked. Grey stepped inside, the slight scent of lemon in the air making him go hard all over again. The room looked different with the desk gone, but at the moment all that concerned him was that she wasn't in there, either.

"Emma?" he whispered, approaching her bed chamber door.

It opened. "I thought about sleeping somewhere else tonight," she said in a soft, low voice.

Her long auburn hair hung in loose waves around her shoulders. She wasn't wearing her robe, but stood in her nightgown and bare feet, one hand on the door. "What made you decide to stay?" he asked, using all of his self-control to keep from grabbing her to him.

She tilted her head, studying him, and he stopped breathing. No woman had ever affected him like this before. Slowly she stepped forward, laying her hand flat against his chest.

"I decided to stay," she murmured, sliding up along his body and curling her fingers into his hair, "because of this." She leaned up and softly touched her lips to his.

Grey slipped his arms around her hips, pulling her harder against him. With a groan he deepened the kiss, relishing the soft, supple warmth of her.

"I don't have a desk at the moment," she said, tilting her head back and exposing the soft curve of her throat to his kisses.

He caressed her skin with his lips and his

tongue, drawing a harsh breath as she trembled. "The bed will do."

She knew what to do, this time. He shrugged out of his coat while she unfastened his waistcoat and loosened his cravat.

"You didn't even choke me." He kissed her again, allowing her to taste and explore him as he had done to her.

"I'm a good student," she replied, running her warm hands up his chest, under his shirt.

"I can see that." Her hands slid lower, to the fastening of his breeches. "Up for another lesson?"

She chuckled, her hands straying lower. "*You* are."

His lips curving in a smile, he took her hand and spun her around, facing away from him, then pulled her up against him again. "There are still a few things you don't know," he murmured into her hair, sliding the gown off her shoulders.

"Teach me," she said breathlessly, leaning back against him as he slipped the gown down to her waist and lifted his hands to cover her breasts.

Grey closed his eyes, letting the feel of her moving against him, of her straining nipples against his fingers, soak into him. He wanted to satisfy her and teach her and make her want only him. He wanted to be the only man ever to touch her like this, the only man to make her moan with pleasure as she was now.

He swept her up into his arms and carried her to her tiny bed, barely large enough for one. He laid her down, sliding down beside her to kiss and caress her smooth skin. When she pushed at his shoulder, he allowed her to turn him onto his back. Emma yanked his shirt off over his head, then sank down to run her tongue across his nipples, as he had done with her.

"Does it feel good to you, too?" she asked, her hair curtaining them.

"Yes. I like the feel of your hands, your mouth, on me," he said, moving his hand between them, down to where she was hot and damp and ready for him.

Arching her back, Emma pressed herself against his fingers. "Wait," she gasped. "I want to make you feel this way, too."

He chuckled. "I already do."

She moved down his body, yanking his boots off, and then freeing him from his breeches. Breathing hard, she dropped his trousers off the side of the bed and resumed her exploration. As her hands tentatively, gently, stroked his manhood, Grey clenched his jaw, striving to maintain control.

Her tongue touched his tip. With a hiss he rose up on his elbows. "Emma," he managed in an unsteady growl.

She looked at him from beneath her lashes, the proper headmistress on fire. "I like you this way," she whispered, her soft breath on his hot skin near to driving him mad, "not so arrogant."

"Come here," he demanded, pulling her up along the length of his body, "before you kill me."

With his guidance she straddled his hips, then slowly sank down onto him with a shuddering groan.

The welcoming tight heat of her nearly pushed him beyond the edge of control. He stayed up on his elbows, kissing her, until she pushed him down flat and leaned over him.

"Show me," she breathed.

His hands on her hips, he showed her how to move on him. "Like this."

She complied, moaning again as he matched her rhythm. "You're right about my books; they could never describe this."

With a soft laugh he reached up to run his palms along her warm skin. Neither books nor his own substantial experience could describe Emma, either. She was unique. She took all of his focus, all of his attention, and left him breathless. "Emma," he whispered.

"Oh, Grey." She began to move faster on him, then tightened and pulsed, collapsing on his chest.

Straining for another few seconds of control while dots swam in front of his eyes, he took her hips to push her off of himself. Emma raised up again, covering his hands with hers, her eyes glinting as she held his gaze.

"No."

With a growl Grey threw his head back, pushing up toward her as he came, deep inside her. "Emma," he said when he could speak again, angry and out of breath and entirely befuddled, "why—"

She covered his mouth with hers. "Because," she murmured, stretching out alongside him.

"Because" hardly seemed the answer of an educated headmistress. If she had half the confusion of roiled emotions boiling through her as he did, though, he would accept it as good enough. For now.

Chapter 15

Stretching, Emma opened one eye—to see a pair of light green eyes looking back at her. It was the most peculiar thing; she wasn't startled, or even faintly surprised. Instead, she felt as if, for the first time ever, everything in the world was exactly the way it was supposed to be.

"Good morning."

Perfection crashed down around her ears. *"Morning?"* she gasped, flinging off the covers and sitting upright. "What are you still doing here? Oh, no!"

Looking amused and far too calm, Grey sat up as well, catching her around the waist and pulling her back against his hip. "It's barely morning. Our secret is still safe, Em."

She took a ragged breath. The little clock on her

nightstand was nearly impossible to make out in the dimness, which in itself was a good sign. "Four thirteen," she finally read. "Did I fall asleep?"

"Mm hm."

"Did you?"

"No." Slowly he ran his hand from her shoulders down her spine, warm and familiar and possessive.

Emma swung her legs back onto the narrow bed so she could see him. "Aren't you tired?"

"Yes." He bent his head and kissed her shoulder. Meeting her gaze again, he lifted an eyebrow. "Are you trying to tell me to leave?"

"The house staff rises before six." She wished she hadn't fallen asleep and that he had, so that she could look at him without his curious, knowing gaze on her, always figuring out exactly what she was thinking and feeling.

He stuffed the bed's single pillow against the headboard and leaned back, the thin blanket sliding to his hips. "You need a bigger bed," he said thoughtfully, folding one arm behind his head.

"I like my bed." She wanted to pull the blanket down farther and renew her investigation of his man-parts, but then he certainly wouldn't leave before anyone discovered him.

"I hang off at both ends," he said, wriggling his toes to demonstrate.

"You're gigantic."

"Thank you." His soft, wicked chuckle sent a rush of blood through her veins. It must have done the same thing to him, because the blanket stirred. "Come here."

"Grey, I need to sleep. I have an early class."

He sat up again, slipping his arms around her and pulling her down to rest against his broad, strong chest. "I have an early class, too," he murmured, twining his fingers lazily through her hair. "Sleep. I'll leave in time."

Oh, this was so nice. No wonder even her friends who'd once sworn off marriage claimed to enjoy it. Emma frowned. She wasn't married. One couldn't be much farther from being married than she was at this moment.

"Em? I've been thinking."

Her heart stopped, and then resumed beating again at a furious pace. As good as he was guessing what she might be thinking, he couldn't read minds. "Wh . . . what were you thinking?"

"I'm going to concede."

She blinked, freeing herself from the faerie realm where dukes married headmistresses and they all lived happily ever after in quaint old monasteries. "Concede?"

"The wager."

Emma lifted her head to gaze at his serious, thoughtful expression. "Why?"

"Because I don't want to force Miss Grenville's Academy to close."

Part of her was moved and elated, but the other part was somewhat . . . annoyed. "That's good," she said. "You've become a little enlightened, anyway."

A furrow appeared between his brows. "I thought you'd be happy to hear it."

"Oh, I am." She sat up.

He sat up. "No, you're not."

"I am. Really. It's just . . ." *Shut up, Emma,* she told herself. *Don't press your luck.* "It's very nice of you to say that. Thank you."

His frown deepened. "What?"

Blast it all. "Your instruction to your students to this point has been remarkably candid and helpful, given your position in Society."

"Given my position," he repeated, the low, dark edge touching his voice.

"You have a unique perspective, I'll admit. But do you really think that being male makes you better able to prepare those girls to deal with Society than I?"

He looked at her for a long, silent moment. "You think I'm going to lose the wager?" he asked incredulously.

She held his gaze. "You already have. You just conceded."

"I changed my mind."

It was her turn to frown. "You can't!"

He smiled, sensuous as sin. "And just who are you going to tell otherwise?" Grey kissed the base of her throat. "And when would you say it happened? You might, just on occasion, try being grateful."

"I think you should leave," she said, wishing proper ladies, just on occasion, were allowed to punch people. "Now. As far as I'm concerned, if you never conceded, the rest of tonight never happened either."

Still looking unperturbed, he stood, tall and beautiful in the dim pre-dawn light. "You say that now, but you may have more difficulty convincing yourself of it later." He dumped his clothes on the bed and shrugged into his breeches. "I know you, Emma. You wanted me. You still do."

He might be right, but she certainly wasn't going to agree with him. "I told you, Grey, I was curious. And thanks to you, I have nothing to be missish about, now." She grabbed up her nightgown and yanked it on over her head, wishing he would stop acting so damned smug. So the loss of her virginity had been as much her idea as his—he didn't need to brag about it. "You certainly aren't the only man in Hampshire," she continued with a haughty sniff. "You're not even the only man at Haverly."

Grey was over the bed and grabbing her shoulders so fast she didn't even have time to gasp. "That is a different sort of game entirely, Emma," he growled, "and one you don't want to play with me."

"Is it a game only you get to play then, Grey?" she asked, lifting her chin despite her very thin control.

His gaze searched hers for a long moment. "I haven't played with anyone else since I met you." He released her, picked up his coat and boots, and made for the door. One hand on the knob, he stopped. "By the way, Mayburne is going to invite you and the girls to luncheon in the next day or so. Turn him down."

Without waiting for a response, he left the room. A few moments later her office door opened and closed. Emma listened for another minute, then sank down onto the edge of her bed. Did his comments mean that he was jealous, or that he was ending whatever lay between them? Had he made her some sort of promise?

But what sort of promise could he possibly make to her?

"Damnation," she muttered.

Since she obviously wasn't going to get any more sleep, she dressed and lit the lamps in her office. A little table sat where her desk used to be, her Haverly report stacked neatly in the middle.

With a sigh she seated herself and read through what she'd written. Even in its rough form, the plan seemed a good one. Some initial cost was involved in renovations and start-up expenses, which worried her, as did some of the similarities to Grey's plans.

A tear ran down her cheek. She should have just let him concede, for the sake of the Academy. It didn't matter that she enjoyed the contest and didn't want him to leave Hampshire, or that he was still arrogant enough to believe that he alone could determine the outcome of the wager.

Another tear plopped onto her report, and with an impatient sigh she wiped it away. With his cryptic murmurings, all he'd done was prove that she couldn't trust him, that he cared more for his own pride and comfort than he did for anything else. More than he cared for her, certainly.

She was quiet and glum all through breakfast and the distribution of the day's mail, despite her efforts to forget the silly, stupid man even existed. The Duke of Wycliffe was neither silly nor stupid, though, which was why she could think of nothing else.

"Emma?"

Isabelle sat down opposite her, an opened letter in her hand. Henrietta stood at her shoulder, the girl's face pale.

"What is it?" Emma asked, straightening and actually thankful for any problem that might take her mind off Grey Brakenridge.

The French instructor handed her the letter. "We have a disaster."

Tobias paced at the front gate as Grey and the barouche approached. Tristan sat opposite him, though the viscount had wisely foregone any attempt at conversation this morning.

"Your Grace," the troll said, his expression even more dour than usual, "you're expected."

"I should hope so, by now," Tristan muttered.

Expected or not, only Lizzy stood on the front steps as Simmons stopped the barouche. The sprite hurried forward and grabbed Grey by the hand before his feet even touched the ground. "We have trouble," she said, tugging him toward the doorway.

His chest tightened as he followed her inside, Dare trailing them. "Is Emma well?" Damnation, he shouldn't have offered to concede and then pulled it away like that, especially when he knew damned well that he would never take the Academy from her.

"Shh," Elizabeth said, making for the stairs at her fastest walk. "I can't tell you here. But it's bad."

Was she pregnant? He'd been such a fool last night. Grey shook himself, trying to clear his head. Even if she were carrying his child, she couldn't possibly know it yet. And it wouldn't be such a catastrophe, anyway, because he would simply marry her.

He nearly missed a step, and grabbed onto the rail to keep from falling. *Marriage?* Where in God's name had that come from? Yes, he enjoyed her company—when he didn't want to strangle her. Yes, he'd barely been able to breathe at the thought of her in another man's embrace. When and how that had translated into the thought of marrying her, he had no idea. Dukes didn't marry headmistresses. And besides, he wasn't falling into that trap ag—

"Hurry up," Lizzy said, grasping his hand again and pulling him into Emma's office.

As he stepped inside his gaze immediately found Emma. She was pacing, hands clasped behind her back, her expression tired and somber. He'd done that to her. Grey made up his mind right then: the damned wager was over. He would have ended it last night, if her haughty independence and lack of gratitude hadn't antagonized him so much.

"What's happened?" he asked.

Emma jumped, looking up at him with her expressive hazel eyes. "Lizzy, thank you. Will you please give us a moment of privacy?"

"Should I flee, as well?" Tristan asked, as Elizabeth curtsied and backed out of the office, closing the door behind her.

"I . . . actually, I do need a private word with His Grace."

The viscount nodded and pulled open the door. "I'll be in the hallway."

As soon as the two of them were alone, Grey crossed the room to her. "Tell me."

Emma folded her hands together and took a

deep breath. "Henrietta received a letter from her father." She pulled a folded missive from her pocket. "In the letter he . . . informs Henrietta that he has heard some disturbing rumors that . . ." she cleared her throat, "that 'your headmistress has been engaging in highly improper conduct.' " A tear ran down her cheek. "He also says that Henrietta is to pack her things, and that he will be here on Friday to collect her."

Grey wanted to curse and smash his fist into something, but he restrained himself. Emma was upset enough. "Why," he asked slowly, "would Henrietta tell her family anything about this? And why would she say you've done anything improp—"

"She said she never mentioned anything about you or the wager."

"Well, she must have! How else would Brendale know—"

"I don't care *how* he knew anything!"

"I—"

"Don't you understand? The Academy is ruined! Lizzy—the other internally tuitioned students—what will happen to them?"

A sob wrenched from her throat. Without even thinking, Grey pulled her into his arms. She collapsed against him, sobs wracking her slender body.

For once, Grey had no idea what to say. "He's just one stupid man, Em," he murmured into her hair. "Whatever he thinks he knows, he can't be sure, or he would have come in person instead of sending a damned letter." Her crying and shaking terrified him, and he abruptly realized he would be willing to do anything—*anything*—to make things right for her. "We can fix it. Don't worry, Em."

She hammered a fist against his chest. "Henrietta's mother is the biggest gossip in London. Half the *ton* is probably chatting about how that idiotic headmistress in Hampshire is . . . is 'engaged in highly improper conduct.' And I am! I have no business running this Academy!"

"You have done nothing wrong as far as those girls are concerned. Nothing."

She lifted her face, looking up at him. "I think Mr. Brendale has already made up his mind."

"Nothing's happened except for some dim-witted correspondence," he murmured, brushing at her tears with his thumb. "All we need to do is have Henrietta write her father back that he's completely mistaken."

"No. I will not ask any of those girls to lie."

"Of course you wouldn't," Grey responded, stifling a scowl. That would have been the easiest course of action, but he obviously couldn't expect Emma to go against all of the principles she'd taught her students; she actually believed in them. "But you can't give up without a fight."

"I don't see how I can fight without . . . hurting my students even further."

Grey looked at her for a moment, an idea tickling at the back of his mind. "Only Brendale has written, right?"

"For now, yes. I'm sure there will be m—"

"And only to say that he's heard rumors that you've been misbehaving."

"Yes."

"Then that's it."

"What are you talking about?"

"He doesn't know about the wager."

Emma frowned at him. "And you think his knowing that I've been wagering with the Duke of Wycliffe will *improve* matters?"

"As far as your students know, the wager is the only reason I've been calling on you and the Academy. We'll have Henrietta explain that to her father, and invite him here for the judging."

Her gaze became even more skeptical. "How will that solve anything?"

"I made a wager with you. And I *never* lose. *Never.*"

For a moment he thought she would kick him in his nether regions, but then her expression sharpened. "Go on."

"I obviously forced you into this, because what female could stand up to me?"

"Grey—"

"Wait." He strode to the window and back. It was brilliant. Well, perhaps not brilliant, but it was better than Emma's broken-hearted sobbing. "What sort of upstanding gentleman would want to cause the Duke of Wycliffe to lose a wager?" he continued. "And to a female, yet. Besides practically being a crime, it would be decidedly . . . unhealthy for anyone to interfere."

The door opened. "It's gotten quiet in here. You haven't killed one another, have you?" Tristan drawled, leaning into the office.

The viscount's smooth tone didn't fool Grey for a bloody minute. He was genuinely worried for Emma. Feeling his hackles rise, Grey stepped between them. "Henrietta's parents think Emma's turned the Academy into some sort of bawdy house."

Her face turning white, Emma abruptly took a seat. "Everything's ruined," she muttered, lowering her face into her hands.

"No, it isn't, because we came up with a plan."

"No, we didn't," Emma said, looking up again.

That stopped him in his tracks. "Yes, we did."

"No, *we* didn't. *You* spouted off some half-witted drivel about using the wager to keep the Academy open. It won't work."

He folded his arms. "And why won't it work?"

"Do you," she said, slowly and distinctly, as though asking her students an essay question, "intend on winning or losing this wager?"

"I—"

"Because once everyone knows about it, ending the wager will prove the gossips right and ruin this Academy. Your winning the wager will cost the Acad—"

"I'll lose it," he said, daring her to argue with that.

"You'll lose," she repeated, her tone dripping with skepticism.

"Yes."

"Intentionally."

"Yes."

"Well. Even if I were to swallow my pride and the notion that you might lose whether you plan to or not, I don't understand how my winning will serve any positive purpose whatsoever."

"I will make it so."

"You're very arrogant."

"I'm never wrong."

She nodded. "You'll have to change that little

declaration to 'seldom wrong' after your intentional loss. And everyone in London will know that you lost, but not that you did it on purpose."

Grey narrowed his eyes. "As I have suggested before, you might just say you're grateful and shut up."

Emma stepped toward him. "I just want to make certain you understand that people . . . other men, especially, might very well laugh at you."

"At the risk of getting my jaw broken, she's right, you know," Tristan said in the abrupt silence.

"I know." To his surprise, the notion really didn't bother him. "More important, Emma can't have been doing anything improper if she's spent all her time chaperoning the class and devising a brilliant estate plan."

"That's a flimsy argument, at best," Emma countered.

"First things first. Have Henrietta write her letter. Have all my students invite their parents. We have nothing to hide here. And it'll give us ten days to come up with something better, anyway."

Strangely enough, Emma felt better as Grey and Tristan left the Academy. Something in his eyes had been very . . . reassuring.

"Em, are you all right?" Isabelle pushed open the office door.

"Not yet. Oh, Isabelle, how could I have been so very, very stupid?"

"It is Henrietta's father who is stupid even to think of accusing you of such things."

Tears burned at the back of Emma's eyes again. If they only knew how guilty she was. "I can hardly blame anyone but myself. *I* am the Academy's headmistress, and *I* am responsible for any disaster that befalls it."

"As His Grace was leaving, he said he would take care of everything," the French instructor countered. "Perhaps you should just let him. The wager was his idea, after all."

"Oh, yes, that would be wonderful, wouldn't it? The Duke of Wycliffe, famous for his enlightened benevolence toward all female kind, charging in to the rescue."

Isabelle turned her palms upward. "Why not?"

"Because neither his benevolence, nor his enlightenment, is likely to last past the point where the Academy becomes a public embarrassment. We will rely on those we can trust *always* to have the Academy's best interests at heart. And I'm afraid that just leaves us."

"So you have some plan in mind, yes?"

Emma sagged into her lonely desk chair. "Not yet. But I will."

As Grey had said, announcing the wager to the parents would hopefully give them ten days to come up with a plan. For once she wished the London mail wasn't quite so prompt and reliable. They might claim never to have received Mr. Brendale's letter, but he wasn't likely to believe it. And if they didn't believe it was the wager alone which had concerned Wycliffe and her, the parents would take the five girls home with them. And then by twos and dozens, the rest of the parents would follow to take their daughters away from the Academy.

As for Grey, she was simply not going to rest all her hopes on his promises, noble and generous though they might be. She knew enough of men to understand that concern over his position and his pride would take precedence over any temporary feelings he might have toward Lizzy—or her. They were lovers, yes; but he'd had lovers before, and from what Vixen had said, he never kept them for long.

She shook herself. "I'm going for a walk." A long stroll would clear her head of thoughts of Grey for a few moments, anyway. Heaven knew she had more dire things to worry about.

Nodding at a worried-looking Tobias, she passed through the gates and started up the road toward Basingstoke. Of course she could write Mr. Brendale back and inform him that nothing untoward was going on, but no one would believe her protests of innocence. Therefore, she needed to accept that London would know that the Duke of Wycliffe had entered the halls of Miss Grenville's Academy, and with her permission. All right. That was a given fact.

The logical part of her brain, the part she hadn't been using nearly enough lately, slowly began to churn into motion. Increasing her pace, she continued working at the next step of the problem. Any backlash for her idiocy would come from the families of her students. She couldn't stop it, so therefore she needed to counteract it.

With what? Well, obviously it would take a noble's support to counteract a noble's wrath. Wycliffe immediately came to mind, but she brushed the thought away. He was too entangled with her and the Academy for his protests of blamelessness to have much credence.

When the idea finally occurred to her, she couldn't believe it had taken her so long. Two of her dearest friends, fellow graduates of the Academy, had recently made very notable marriages. The Countess of Kilcairn Abbey and the Marchioness of Althorpe were definitely forces to be reckoned with.

As she reached town, she headed for Sir John's offices, and more specifically, for his writing desk. Emma allowed herself a slight, hopeful smile. Let the girls write their letters, and let Wycliffe conjure his plans. She was going to call in her own reinforcements.

Chapter 16

~~~

Uncle Dennis's skill at chess had improved over the years. Grey stood alone in the earl's office, looking down at the pieces arranged beneath the window. In one move, or a maximum of three if he attempted a delay and counterattack, he was going to lose his queen. Grey reflected that if Dennis only managed his estate with the same degree of cleverness, none of them would be in this mess.

"Did they send the letters?" Dare asked, strolling into the room without bothering to knock first.

With a slight frown, Grey shifted his remaining bishop. Better to delay the inevitable and hope for a miracle than to concede defeat. "Yes. By special messenger this morning."

"So you really intend to go through with the wager?"

"It's the only way I can see to save the Academy. If you have a better idea, please enlighten me."

Tristan sat behind the desk. "You've already become surprisingly enlightened over the past few weeks. When we arrived here, you'd have been happy to set a torch to Miss Grenville's Academy—and Miss Emma Grenville—yourself."

He felt more enamored then enlightened. Not just of Emma, but of the whole blasted school. "I may have rushed in without knowing all the facts," he admitted, glancing through the window as Alice and Sylvia, accompanied by Blumton, climbed into Haverly's phaeton for their afternoon tour of the countryside.

"Just out of curiosity," Tristan said, playing with the brass duck paperweight, "what will you do if you can't contain the damage to Emma's reputation?"

Grey faced him, leaning back against the edge of the gaming table. "That won't happen."

"Because you've already decreed a victory? Even if Brendale and the other parents wait for the end of the wager before they storm the school, it's only because they expect Emma to lose. Nasty rumors are better than facts, and they may well have both."

"I'm not an idiot, Tris. At least the ruse will give us a few more days to come up with a solution."

"And what about Emma?"

The duke met Dare's gaze, warm anger touching him at the viscount's proprietary tone. "What about her?"

"I couldn't help noticing yesterday that a certain item of your clothing was in the doorway of her bed chamber. Unless she's being visited by someone else wearing fine silk cravats with sapphire pins stuck through them, that is."

Grey clenched his fist, fighting to keep himself from hurtling across the room and pounding Dare while he explained that no man touched Emma but him. "I suggest you not repeat that observation to anyone," he growled.

Tristan looked offended. "I wouldn't. But the fact is, the rumors are true, aren't they?"

"Mind your own affairs, Dare, and I'll mind mine."

"That's all well and good, but who told Brendale? Emma swears it wasn't Henrietta."

Grey shook his head. "Emma got another letter this morning, from Jane's father. He'd heard the rumors, too."

"He wrote directly to Emma?"

"Yes. And he was even less polite in his phraseology than Brendale was." Emma hadn't cried this time, but her quiet acceptance of all blame in the fiasco had upset him even more than her tears.

The viscount cleared his throat. "I do want you to know that, your own likely heroic performance aside, I am available to assist your rescue of the Academy should the need arise."

Grey wanted to do it himself, to prove to Emma that she could trust him. Even so, the offer was something of a relief. "My thanks, Tris. I may take you up on . . ."

The phaeton rattled back up the drive. With a

frown, Grey looked through the window as his traveling companions returned. He had enough to sort through without the prying lot of them about all afternoon. Then a coach trundled up behind the phaeton, a second vehicle following it. Grey's scowl deepened.

"What the devil?" he muttered, shifting as Tristan came up beside him.

"Brendale?" the viscount suggested.

"He would have gone straight to the Academy, and he's not due till Friday at the earliest."

A footman pulled open the door of the lead coach. A dainty pearled slipper peeked into the doorway, followed by a second shoe and a pearl and blue muslin gown. A white gloved hand fluttered out, and the footman gripped her fingers as she stepped to the ground. The conservative blue bonnet tipped upward, exposing the woman's face to their view.

"Good God," Tristan murmured.

His jaw clenched, Grey muttered a quiet curse and stalked to the front door. He stopped on the top step. "What the devil are you doing here?"

"I'm pleased to see you again, too, son."

For a moment Grey felt as though he was five years old and had just pushed his cousin Georgiana into Wycliffe Park's pond. Frowning, he came down the steps to take the tall woman's hand. "Mother," he said, leaning down to kiss her pale cheek.

"Much better, Grey."

"I thought you still in London."

She returned the kiss. "Obviously. You've gotten sneaky as you've matured. I would never have expected to find you in Hampshire."

He inclined his head, offering his arm to escort her into the house. "That was the very reason I chose to come here."

"So I thought." Her pale gray eyes found Tristan, lurking behind one of the towering porticos which lined the entryway. "Dare, escort my companion."

"Good afternoon, Your Grace," he said, bowing. "Which companion would that be?"

"Whom do you think, Lord Dare?" a second female voice drawled.

Grey stifled a grin as Tristan stiffened. His mother apparently intended on torturing both him and his main accomplice. "Cousin Georgiana," he said.

The tall young woman, her curling blonde hair in a fetching knot at the top of her head, curtsied, graceful as ever in a soft green gown that matched her eyes. "Grey. How delightful that you've chosen to disrupt the Season so thoroughly."

"I'm surprised you allowed yourself to be dragged into this."

Light green eyes slid over to Tristan and back. "It wasn't by choice."

The viscount cleared his throat. "Well, if you'll excuse me, I think I'll go down myself in the duck pond."

Georgiana bent down and picked up a rock. "Here," she said, handing it to Dare. "This should help."

While Tristan made his escape, Grey returned his attention to the entourage. "Mother," he murmured, his gaze following his cousin as Sylvia and Alice came forward to greet her, "what are you doing here?"

The duchess leaned against his arm. "I was under the impression that you were going to offer for Caroline. Imagine my surprise when instead you vanish without a word to anyone, while at the same time Caroline claims ill and flees to her father's estate in York."

She didn't know the half of it. "Where did you hear I was going to offer for Caroline?"

"From Caroline, of course. You never tell me anything."

"Especially when there's nothing to tell. I never had any intention of becoming leg-shackled to that devious b—"

"So it's true."

"What's true?"

"Where are Dennis and Regina?" the duchess asked, allowing her son to lead her up the front steps and ignoring his question.

Grey shook himself. "They went into Basingstoke after luncheon," he said, guiding his mother inside and instructing Hobbes to have two additional bed chambers prepared for the new guests. If she didn't wish to answer, he could wait.

His mother kept her light grip on his arm throughout their tour of the manor and all the group's bantering small talk, and didn't set him free even after he led her to her guest room.

"Georgiana," she said to her companion, "will you please see if anyone at Haverly knows how to brew peppermint tea?"

"I'll see to it myself, Aunt Frederica." With a sideways glance at Grey, she disappeared back down the hallway.

The duchess glided into her small private rooms. "Grey, come open the window for me."

He complied, unsurprised when she took the opportunity to close the door behind them. Servants had stacked a half dozen trunks against the room's far wall. Obviously Her Grace intended on staying for awhile.

"All right, I'm listening," he said, leaning back against the window frame.

The Duchess carefully removed her bonnet. "Georgiana heard that you stripped Caroline naked in the middle of Almack's coatroom, found her wanting, and sent her away."

"The stripping was her idea, but otherwise the tale's fairly accurate."

"So you fled to Hampshire? That's not like you."

"I left London because I was tired of all the damned females who find it necessary to trap, trick, and lie in order to drag me to the altar." He scowled. "I had intended on returning already, to inform cousin William that as far as I'm concerned, he can have the title and all the accompanying headaches when I die, because I'm not going anywhere near an altar for the rest of my life."

Her gaze sharpened. "Then why didn't you return and tell him?"

"Because I made a wager," he said. "One which I intend to win."

"A wager? That's not what I heard."

"What did you hear, then?"

"That you've been conducting some sort of affair with the headmistress of that girls' school. You and Dare both, actually. You've been sharing her."

Grey swore long and loudly. "That is *not* even remotely . . ." he growled, belatedly slamming the window shut when he caught sight of one of the gardeners staring up at him in surprise. *"Damnation!"*

"You already used that one, dear."

He needed to tell Emma. The gossip was even worse than he'd realized, and the situation infinitely more serious. It wasn't just a few parents whose concerns needed to be allayed; it was London, destroying the reputation of a fine school and a finer woman.

"Grey? You're muttering."

He shook himself. He needed to make this right. If he had to tell Emma the worst of the rumors, he also wanted to be able to tell her that he'd found their source and stopped them, and that everything would be all right. "Where did you hear this?" he asked.

His mother sat on the edge of her bed. "It's everywhere."

He strode up to her. "It started somewhere," he snapped. "Who told you?"

"Grey—"

"Who?"

"Georgiana told me."

The duchess looked startled, and he couldn't blame her; he'd had messy affairs before, and he'd never been upset about the ensuing gossip and exaggerations.

"Excuse me then, Mother. I need to speak with Georgiana."

He headed downstairs, looking for his cousin. Georgie was one of the few females he could tolerate, but in the mood he was in, she'd best have used her famous insight to figure out where the damned rumors had originated.

"Your Grace," Hobbes said, intercepting him at the bottom of the stairs. "I was just coming to inform you that you have callers."

Grey stopped. "Callers?"

"Yes, Your Grace. I showed them into the library while I inquired whether you were available."

Wonderful. Probably Mr. Brendale and half the fathers of the Academy had arrived. "Are they armed?" he asked, turning for the library.

"Armed? N . . . no, Your Grace. Not that I'm aware of."

Grey pulled open the library door and stepped inside. And stopped.

His students—all five of them—stood ranged in a loose semi-circle facing the doorway. They may not have been armed, but they looked bloody determined about something.

"Where's your chaperone?"

"We escaped." Lizzy stepped forward while the others closed ranks behind her, precise as a military battalion. "Why is everyone trying to hurt Miss Emma?"

For a moment Grey had a vision of what Haverly would look like if every female he'd ever insulted or wronged appeared on the doorstep. It was getting crowded already. "I'm in something of a hurry at the moment. I'll explain things later."

Jane shook her head. "No. We want to know now. If you don't tell us, we won't help you win the wager."

For God's sake, the little midgets were trying to blackmail him. "It's complicated."

Her fists coiled and her eyes floating with tears, Lizzy glared up at him. "My mother wrote me a letter and said Miss Emma was a . . . a wanton strumpet who should have known better than to allow a rake like you anywhere near her. You said you were the good kind of rake, Grey."

Looking into Elizabeth Newcombe's innocent brown eyes, he wanted to confess everything— and he didn't even know what he would be confessing to. "Lizzy, I can't tell you right now. I want to, but I can't."

"Then we don't want to talk to you anymore. We don't like you anymore."

"And please don't come to the Academy again," Jane added. At her gesture, the girls lined up to leave.

"As you wish." With a stiff nod he opened the door for them. "Did you walk here?"

"Yes."

"I'll have the barouche hitched up."

This time it was Mary Mawgry who faced him. "No, thank you, Your Grace. We prefer to walk."

"Very well. I understand."

Georgiana leaned into the doorway as the girls trooped down the hall to the front entry. "What was that all about?"

"Those were my students," he said, moving to the window. He couldn't see the drive from there, and stifled a scowl at the realization that he would miss the little chits. It would work out. They wouldn't hate him forever.

" 'Were?' " his cousin repeated.

"I think they just dismissed me."

"Ah."

Grey glanced at her, seeing the amusement in her eyes. "That's just between us."

She nodded. "Certainly. Your mother said you were looking for me."

He gestured her inside and closed the door again. "I need to know where you think the rumors about Emma Grenville and myself originated."

"And Dare. Don't forget that he's a part of your *menage à trois.*"

"Georgie, I know you don't like Tristan, but this really isn't about him. Please."

Georgiana studied his face for a moment, her green eyes thoughtful. "I heard it from a half dozen people. Since we're related, everyone thought I should be able to confirm your involvement."

"Georgi—"

"I'm getting to it, Grey. The most interesting conversation I had was with some woman I barely know—a Mrs. Hugh Brendale, I believe. She said she'd received a horrid letter about her own daughter's headmistress. I asked to see it, and she actually showed it to me, the ninny. It was anonymous, of course, but it was franked in Hampshire."

He narrowed his eyes. "Only a member of Parliament can frank . . ." Abruptly it made sense. "It came from here. From Haverly."

"That would be my guess."

"Thank you, Georgiana."

She drifted forward and went up on tiptoe to brush her lips against his cheek. "You always provide so much entertainment, Cousin."

"Ha. I haven't started yet."

He hadn't franked any correspondence but his own, and he doubted Tristan had. Since neither Dennis nor Regina would send out any correspondence condemning Emma, that left his uncle franking letters for either Blumton, Alice, or Sylvia. And he had a very good idea which of them it was.

"Do you think we were too mean to him?" Julia asked, nearly falling down as she looked over her shoulder for the hundredth time.

Elizabeth scowled. She felt the same way, but it was his own fault. "We all agreed to make certain he knew we were mad at him."

"But he said he would explain it. We didn't give him a chance."

"You're only saying that because you're in love with him." Lizzy jammed her hands into the pockets of her pelisse and kept walking.

"I am not in love with him! You take that back, Lizzy!"

"No."

"Hush, now," Mary said, putting her arm across Elizabeth's shoulders. "I'm almost in love with him, and I'm still mad. You know what everyone's saying. And it's all because of Grey being at the Academy and what everyone says he's been . . . doing with Miss Emma."

"This is so awful," Jane said mournfully. "There must be something we can do for Miss Emma."

They rounded the bend, and stopped. Lord Dare lay stretched out on his back across the road, his arms behind his head and his eyes closed.

"Do you think he's dead?" Julia asked.

Elizabeth rolled her eyes. "Why would he be dead?" Just in case, though, she grabbed a long stick and jabbed him in the ribs.

He yelped, lunging to his feet with a speed that surprised her. "Good God!"

Trying to stifle her own shriek, Lizzy kept the stick raised between them. "We thought you might be dead!"

"Well, I wasn't," he snapped, rubbing his ribs.

"What in the world were you doing in the middle of the road?"

He looked back toward Haverly as he brushed dust from his coat. "If you must know, I was hoping a coach would come by and take me to a decent inn so I might get indecently drunk."

"No coaches ever come by here, unless they're going to Haverly."

Lord Dare sighed. "What are you doing here, anyway? Where's Emma?"

Abruptly remembering that he was Grey's friend, Elizabeth put her hand across Jane's mouth before the older girl could answer. "Just a moment. Whose side are you on?"

"That depends," he said slowly. "Which side is going to win?"

"Our side."

"Then I'm on your side. What are we disputing?"

"We're not disputing. We told His Grace that if he won't tell us why everyone's trying to hurt Miss Emma, we don't want to be his students anymore."

The viscount was silent for a moment. "Ah. And how did His Grace respond to that?"

"We don't care."

He gave a nod. "Miss Emma knows you've given Wycliffe this ultimatum?"

Lizzy thought Jane should answer that, and she took a step backward.

"Miss Emma has been worried enough."

His brow furrowed, Lord Dare gestured for them to continue back to the Academy, and he fell into step between Jane and Elizabeth. Elizabeth didn't quite trust him, though she did like the way he'd tried to explain the sins of wagering to them and hadn't succeeded at all.

"Hm," he finally murmured. "Although I want to assure you that I remain firmly on your side, I don't think you've been apprised of the entire situation." Again he glanced over his shoulder. "At the risk of my life and limbs, I'm going to tell you the horrifying but true tale of a very cynical nobleman whose eyes and mind have been opened by love, and of the evil gossip that now threatens to bollux the entire affair."

Relieved that someone was finally going to explain things, Lizzy took his hand. "Does it have a good ending?"

Lord Dare chuckled. "Damned if I know. Maybe we can help."

Emma hated waiting. Pacing and wringing her hands seemed supremely useless, but at the moment she couldn't think of anything useful. Barring the gates and setting cannons in the yard seemed an over-reaction to the parents' imminent arrival, though at least getting off a shot or two would have been enormously satisfying.

Her worry wasn't for herself, or even for most

of her well-born students; they would have homes to return to, and she could likely find work as a governess somewhere. No, it was Elizabeth Newcombe, and the other handful of students whose lives she had promised to improve, who haunted her.

Miss Perchase clattered up the stairs. "Miss Emma, they're back."

"Thank heavens!" Following Miss Perchase down to the main hallway, Emma found her five missing students cornered in the foyer, surrounded by half the Academy's residents and being pelted with questions. She had a few to ask, herself. "Where have you been?"

"We went to Haverly," Jane said, lifting her chin.

"To Haverly. Why?"

"We prefer not to say."

Lizzy was eyeing her closely, but she had no idea what the little girl might be looking for. With a glance at the curious crowd, she gestured the five girls into one of the private sitting rooms off the main hallway. "Do you know how many rules you've broken?" she asked, shutting the door behind them. "You might have been hurt, or lost! And then what would I have done?"

"Lord Dare escorted us back to the Academy," Mary said in her quiet voice, "but Tobias wouldn't let him through the gate."

"We were safe," Julia echoed. "Lizzy had a stick."

"We didn't want to make more trouble," Jane added. "We needed to take care of something."

"And you won't tell me what it was?"

"No."

She hated this part of being a headmistress. "Very well. I think you all need to contemplate what you've done, and what your parents and this school expect of our students. Go to your rooms. You will be served dinner there. I don't wish to see you again until breakfast."

"Yes, Miss Emma." Heads bowed, they filed out of the room and up the stairs to their bed chambers.

So—they wouldn't tell her what they'd been up to. She couldn't blame them for their unwillingness to confide in her, considering the blunders she'd been making, but she *was* their headmistress. She needed to find out what was going on. And besides, she really hated sitting about and waiting. Hurrying upstairs to grab her shawl and her bonnet, Emma returned to the foyer.

"Miss Perchase, I shall return shortly," she said, not waiting for an answer as she strode down the steps and onto the drive.

Her hurry had nothing to do with the fact that she hadn't seen Grey in over a day, of course. As headmistress of the Academy, she needed to be apprised of any recent developments. If her heart was pounding, it was only because of her worry, not because she was contemplating being kissed.

Hurrying as she was, she didn't take the time to look over her shoulder at the Academy and see five young faces peering out an upstairs window and giggling.

Chapter 17

Emma hurried along the road. Whatever the girls thought they had needed to say to Wycliffe, they couldn't afford any more trouble. Her own alleged misdeeds were bad enough, so now any wrong the girls did would be magnified tenfold.

As the house came into sight, she slowed. Two additional coaches stood behind the stable. Emma suppressed a nervous shudder. More people, and undoubtedly more rumors. She'd imagined a discussion with a few irate parents—not a confrontation with an entire brigade.

Hobbes pulled open the door before she could knock, and she managed a smile for him. "Good afternoon. I . . . require a word with His Grace, if he's available."

The butler nodded. "If you don't mind, I'll tuck you into Lord Haverly's office while I inquire."

She wanted to inquire about who Haverly's guests might be, but now, more than ever, she needed to act as the Academy's ambassador. Uncertain as she felt about being there with all of the awful gossip flying everywhere, she still had a role to fulfill. Keeping her hands clasped in front of her, she followed the butler into the office to wait for Grey.

Out of habit she strolled over to the gaming table. Lord Haverly, obviously sensing his imminent defeat, had moved his last bishop into the fray as a distraction. She was in the mood for a victory, though, and this one seemed more sure than anything else in her life at the moment. Ignoring the ruse, she took a white pawn with her rook, moving into position for the *coup de grace*.

"I was wondering where Uncle Dennis had acquired his sudden ability to think more than three moved ahead."

Grey shut the door behind himself and crossed the room to her. Emma tilted her face up, her pulse fluttering. Slowly he tugged the bow beneath her chin loose, then lifted the bonnet from her hair. She drew a breath, trembling at his gentle touch.

The hat dangling from his fingers, he leaned down and touched his mouth to hers. She felt it all the way down to her toes, but at the same moment she noticed something peculiar. Backing off, she wrinkled her nose. "You taste like brandy."

"Whiskey."

"Are you drunk?"

"Not yet. You interrupted me."

She couldn't read his expression. "Do you want me to leave?"

"No."

He kissed her again, soft and slow, as though for the first time. She wanted to melt into him. Something was different this time, deep and quiet and centered. As the embrace of their mouths deepened and heat wound down her spine, Emma wondered whether he had locked the door. After all, ambassadors weren't supposed to be caught bare-bottomed in the embrace of dukes.

"You have guests," she said, pulling away again.

Grey kept his free hand clasped around her elbow, not letting her get too far away. That excited her, though his mere presence was enough to do that.

"Just my mother and my cousin."

"I thought you were in hiding."

"I've been discovered." He leaned down again to rest his forehead against hers. "This is rotten business. Next time I'll keep my mouth shut and my eyes open, Emma. I promise you that."

She swallowed. Why was he promising her things? He'd never done that before. "My share of blame is at least as large as yours," she said, thankful her voice remained steady. "But I'm not here to assess degrees of guilt. Your students told me they came to Haverly this morning, but they wouldn't tell me why."

"Yes. They informed me that they consider me to be at fault for any and all rumors, and said unless I told them exactly what was going on, they didn't wish my services any longer."

Emma looked down for a moment, stifling a surprised smile. My goodness, she loved those girls. "What did you tell them?" she asked, lifting her head again.

"Nothing. The less they know, the better." He sighed. "We'll have to think up something to tell them, though, because I can't lose the wager without them."

"Win or lose, I still can't see any way out of this."

His eyes searched hers. "I think I may have a solution."

She grabbed his sleeve. "Really? What is it?"

For a long moment he was silent, his gaze steady on her face. Whatever his answer to this disaster was, he seemed very serious about it. Emma wrapped fingers around his lapels and shook him lightly.

"*Tell* me. What's your solution?"

"Mar—"

The door opened, and a dignified-looking woman with long black hair piled high on her head strolled into the room. Grey's fingers tightened on Emma's elbow, then with a twitch released her.

"Mother," he said smoothly.

She stopped halfway across the room, her inquisitive gaze on Emma. "So you're the headmistress who's been servicing Dare and my son all Season," she said.

The duke said something low and brief in reply, but Emma couldn't hear it. All of London—Grey's *mother*, even—thought her a whore. The Academy was lost. White spots suddenly began floating in front of her eyes. The rushing pulse of her blood roared in her ears, and then everything went black.

Grey heard Emma's uneven intake of breath, and whipped around just in time to catch her as she collapsed. His heart pounding, he swept her into his arms and made for the doorway, scarcely noting his mother as she moved out of his way.

"Hobbes!" he bellowed, reaching the stairs and taking them two at a time, "get me smelling salts! And send for a physician!"

Dimly he heard the household roar into action behind him, but his attention was on the limp figure in his arms. Damnation, he'd done this to her—with his own abject stupidity and selfishness. He should have broken the news to her before a stranger could hurt her with it.

With a curse he kicked open his bed chamber door, knocking it off its hinges yet again, and carried her inside. Shaking, he gently laid her down on the bed.

"Em?" he whispered, brushing a strand of her auburn hair from her pale forehead. "Emma?"

"Move," his mother said, taking a jar of smelling salts from the panting butler as the two of them nearly collided in the doorway.

While Grey numbly shifted sideways, she leaned over Emma, loosening the fastenings of her pelisse. Frederica held the bottle beneath the headmistress's nose. After what seemed like hours but must have been only seconds, Emma's eyes fluttered open. A moment later she gasped a breath and then batted the bottle of smelling salts away from her face.

"My goodness," she rasped, coughing, and sat up.

"Lie down," Grey commanded, beginning to breathe again.

Her eyes found him and then slid away again. "Nonsense. I merely became overly warm, walking over here. I'm fine."

More footsteps skidded into the room, and without looking Grey knew damned Tristan had arrived.

"Emma?" the viscount said, pushing through the growing crowd of servants and guests.

"Lord Dare," she said, paling again. Shooting Grey's mother a look of abject humiliation, she sat up quickly, scooting to the edge of the bed. "Your Grace, could you arrange for someone to take me back to the Academy? It seems I've overexerted myself. I should have ridden Pimpernel, but the day was so nice, and . . ."

"Of course." Grey started to cup her elbow, but she jerked away from him.

"Perhaps Hobbes might assist me," she managed, her voice shaking.

"You should stay here," Grey insisted, alarmed all over again, "until you're certain you're feeling better." Or at least until he had time to explain that he did have a way to make everything right, so that no one would be able to insult her with impunity again.

"I will feel better back at the Academy," she returned stiffly, still avoiding his gaze. "I wish to leave now, if you please."

With a swift glance at Grey, Hobbes helped her to her feet. As they reached the hallway, Grey noted that the crowd of servants had perceptibly thinned—with such speed that he knew his mother had to have been involved. He would thank her later, after he expressed his anger at her loose tongue.

Dare had hurried downstairs ahead of them, and the phaeton was at the foot of the steps as the viscount held open the front door. Emma held onto the butler until the groom put his hands around her waist to help her onto the vehicle's high seat.

Unable to stand it any longer, Grey strode forward as the groom circled the back of the phaeton to climb onto the seat on the far side.

"Emma," he said in a low voice, "for God's sake, don't leave it like this."

Still she wouldn't look at him, but instead made a show of taking her bonnet from a footman and tying it under her chin.

"Please," he continued. "I promise that everything—"

"Don't make promises you can't possibly keep," she murmured in a flat, bleak tone. "I have never expected a great deal of my fellow man. Good day."

It was most certainly *not* a good day, and it was growing worse by the moment. He'd caused the woman he cared for to faint and then allowed her to ride off, *unchaperoned*, with another man.

"Her Grace requires a word with you, Your Grace," Hobbes said, out of breath and red-faced. "She is in the earl's office."

The butler had probably never seen so much chaos in his entire term of employment as he had witnessed today. "Thank you, Hobbes. And help yourself to a brandy."

"Thank you, Your Grace."

His mother sat behind the office desk, reading a letter, as he entered the room and closed the door firmly behind him. "That was inexcusable," he said tightly.

"You might have mentioned that to me before she arrived at Haverly," she said, her gaze trailing along the missive.

"I didn't think you required *me*, of all people, to caution you against repeating gossip and injuring someone's feelings."

She looked up. "Pardon me, dear, but did you just say that a female has feelings?"

He leaned back against the door. "That's a hell of a way to make your point."

The duchess sighed. "I know. I owe Miss Emma a considerable apology. She isn't at all what I expected."

Grey scowled. Whatever she meant by that, he didn't like it. And he bloody well wasn't going to feed her suspicions by saying anything. "You summoned me," he reminded her instead. "If you merely want a companion while you read your correspondence, I'll fetch Georgiana."

She went back to the letter. "I'm not reading my correspondence; I'm reading yours."

"*What?*" All Grey could do for a moment was look at her. He knew which correspondence it was, of course; the duchess wouldn't have bothered spying on his business correspondence. She must have seen it on his bed stand while he was distracted with Emma. "Don't think," he said slowly, his eyes narrowing, "that just because I allow you to meddle in my life, I am not quite capable of keeping you out of it."

Her gaze on him, she refolded the letter. "For heaven's sake, Greydon, how was I supposed to know that you actually liked her? You've never particularly cared about any of your mistresses before. You practically left Caroline naked in the middle of a ballroom. Of course I had to read your letter—you never *tell* me anything." She sat forward. "Unless you wish to do so now?"

"Only that things have become somewhat . . . complicated," he hedged. "I will ask you one last time to stay out of them."

The duchess stood. "While I might be inclined to do as you ask, I doubt the rest of your peers will be as patient." She strolled to the door and handed the letter to him. "She'll have a mob after her in a few days; she's actually invited them to the Academy, from what I hear. And they'll be even less diplomatic than I was, I'm afraid."

"I know." Grey pulled open the door, then hesitated. "I may need a female to . . . speak on her behalf."

"I won't make any promises until I have more conversation with her than we managed today."

"Fair enough."

Now he needed to make sure Emma would even speak to one of them, after the mess he'd made. He'd been about to suggest that Emma marry him in order to quiet the gossips, but now she probably wouldn't believe him.

At least he had the beginnings of a battle plan, though. And the first order of business was to sort out the enemies from the allies. Only then could he approach the fair maiden and see whether she would allow him to perform a rescue.

With that in mind, Grey went looking for Sylvia. He found her just as she was stepping out for a walk in the garden. She disliked the country air, as far as he knew; obviously she'd gotten word that he was tracking her down.

"Allow me to join you," he said, offering his arm as she stepped onto the stone path.

With a smooth smile, Lady Sylvia nodded. "You are gallant today."

"I wouldn't wager on that." Guiding them past the fork which led to the wildflower garden, Grey kept them headed toward the park and the distant pond. Pushing her into it was beginning to seem like the best idea he'd had all day—short of marrying Emma, of course.

"Ah. Perhaps you might answer a question, then."

He lifted an eyebrow. "And which question would that be?"

"Why are we having this pleasantly brisk walk?"

They *were* charging toward the pond at a rather swift pace. Taking a breath, he slowed their approach. "That depends on how you answer three questions of mine."

"Ask your questions then, Grey."

"First, to whom did you send those two letters last week? The ones you charmed my uncle into franking for you."

Sylvia sent a quick glance back toward the house, as if to see whether anyone else might be strolling this afternoon. "My goodness, you ask such personal questions—first about my relationship with Lord Dare, and now about my private correspondence. I might almost think you jealous, Grey."

Not bloody likely. Her evasiveness, though, confirmed his suspicions. "Secondly," he drawled coolly, continuing them on the curving path down the sloping hill, "why would you send *any* correspondence when—if you'll recall—you promised me before we left London not to disclose our location to anyone?" He deliberately kept the questions turned in his direction and away from Emma; he'd made enough trouble for her without adding Lady Sylvia Kincaid to the list.

Her alabaster cheeks paled beneath their carefully applied rouge. "Oh, dear, has someone given us away?" She put a hand to her heart, much better at feigning innocence than Alice was. "I hope you don't think it was I who wrote Her Grace or Lady Georgiana, because I assure you that I didn't."

Grey stopped, facing her. He kept silent, watching her as she looked from him to the pond almost at their feet and back again, her expression of innocence warring with one of horrified realization.

"Grey . . ."

"Hm?"

"What are you thinking?"

"I'm deciding what my third question should be." He folded his arms across his chest. "The one that first comes to mind is, 'can you swim?' "

Sylvia took a step backward. "You can't be serious."

"What leads you to believe that I'm not?"

"This is preposterous. Anyone would have done the same thing. I just happened to think of it first—not that Alice has the wits of a hedgehog. A woman has to stand up for her own best interests."

Emma had told him the same thing, but for a completely different set of reasons. And satisfying as tossing Sylvia into the pond would be, he would have a hard time justifying it to the headmistress or himself. "Lady Sylvia, pack your bags. One of my coaches will take you back to London within the hour. If I set eyes on you again, I won't bother asking first whether you can swim. Get out of my sight."

She opened her mouth, looked at the water again, and quickly turned back up toward the manor house. Grey watched her go inside, then he returned to the house. One other guest at Haverly needed to return to London before he attempted to talk to Emma again.

Alice sat at the pianoforte playing something glum by Bach. Subtlety had never been her strong suit, though initially he had found that refreshing. "Alice?"

She looked up, the last notes trailing into discord. "Sylvia was just here. You're sending me away as well, I suppose?"

A few short weeks ago, he would simply have said "yes" and showed her the door. Now he hesitated, looking for a diplomatic way to word his response. After all, she had fulfilled her part of their relationship. She was what she was; any dissatisfaction on his part was his fault. Emma Grenville was a better teacher than he'd expected, if she could make him consider Alice Boswell's feelings.

He shrugged. "We both know you'd be happier in London. And I have no doubt you'll easily find a more pleasant . . . friend than I've been to you."

"Don't be nice now," she sniffed, gathering her skirts and standing. "I wouldn't stay even if you asked me to."

"Then why did you come to Hampshire with me in the first place?"

"I like your money. And I expect a nice gift when you return to London. Something sparkly."

"Something sparkly it is."

"Good."

As Alice went upstairs to summon her maid and pack, Grey headed for the stable. Emma would still be angry and hurt, but he needed to do some explaining.

Emma watched as the phaeton left the Academy grounds and Tobias pushed the gates closed. As it vanished, she plunked herself down on the top step, sinking her head into her folded arms.

"Emma, what's happened?" Isabelle hurried down out the front door.

"Oh, Isabelle, what a morning you've missed."

The French instructor sat beside her. "Tell me."

"Wycliffe's students escaped, and they wouldn't tell me why they'd gone to see His Grace, so I went to Haverly to ask him myself."

"But of course."

"When I arrived there, though, the Duchess of

Wycliffe and her entourage had already arrived, straight from London."

"*Mon dieu!* The . . . rumors?"

"Apparently," Emma said, her spirits sinking even further at the memory. "Anyway, I decided, as the ambassador of the Academy, to take the opportunity to make a good showing." She fell silent, her mind and heart not quite ready to face exactly what had transpired in Lord Haverly's office. She really couldn't blame herself for fainting. To hear the duchess say such things . . . It had been nearly as bad as being turned out into the streets of London more than twelve years ago.

"Go on," Isabelle prompted in the silence. "You are the Academy's ambassador to Haverly."

Emma lifted her head, saw the curiosity and concern on her friend's face, and bent down again. "The ambassador fainted."

Silence. "Fainted, you said?"

"Yes. When I opened my eyes I was in the duke's bed chamber, with the duchess holding smelling salts under my nose. Could anything be worse than it already is?" Emma wailed, her voice muffled in her folded arms. "Could I possibly destroy the Academy any more efficiently?"

"That remains to be seen," Isabelle said cryptically.

Emma straightened, to see her friend's gaze aimed toward the front gates. She looked, as well, and her heart jolted. Grey sat on his big bay, Cornwall, arguing with Tobias. The gatekeeper obviously didn't want to let him in, and the duke just as clearly wasn't going to take no for an answer.

She wanted him to come in, so she could yell at him for not telling her how awful the rumors had become, when he obviously knew. What had his damned plan been, to humiliate her even farther?

Tobias looked over his shoulder at her, his expression pleading, and with a small sigh she nodded. The poor handyman shouldn't have to bear the burden of her stupid naivete. With an impatient flick of the reins, Grey sent Cornwall forward as soon as the gates opened.

"Isabelle," Emma said, rising, "I require a private word with His Grace."

"Are you cert—"

"Yes, I'm certain."

Grey reached her just as Isabelle closed the Academy's heavy double doors behind her. Emma liked being on the steps, because as Wycliffe dismounted and strode up to her, they were practically the same height.

"Emma, you can't think I meant to—"

"Just a moment, Your Grace," she said, the cool steadiness of her voice surprising her. "I don't expect you to think of me or look upon me any differently than any other woman you've known. It would have been nice, though, if you had bothered to tell me that even your mother—"

"I was going to tell you," he interrupted, scowling. "And I have no intention of allowing you to be hurt like that by anyone else. Ever."

"And how do you propose to stop it?"

Her choice of words made him swallow nervously. She didn't look receptive to *any* proposal he might offer—and in light of her arguments, it almost seemed the coward's way out. It shortcutted actually setting things right by blanketing her with the protection of his name. He owed her more than that.

"Emma, we still have time to fix this."

"*You* still have time," she countered. "No one cares if you've been misbehaving." She straightened her skirt. "None of this is helpful, and to be honest, your being here isn't helping anything, either. Please go."

For a long moment he looked at her, eye to eye. Then with a slight nod he turned and mounted Cornwall. "Very well, Emma." The horse sidestepped, and with a wrench he brought the bay back under control. "But whether you've given up or not, I haven't."

She didn't answer, and he turned toward the gate. At the same moment the door flew open, and Elizabeth Newcombe came hurtling down the steps.

"Gr— Your Grace!"

He stopped, looking over his shoulder. "Miss Elizabeth?"

Emma watched as the Academy's youngest student marched up to the big bay horse and presented Grey with a folded piece of paper. "We wanted to clarify our position," she said, so perfectly that she must have memorized the statement.

Grey took the paper and stuffed it into his pocket. Before he could say anything, Lizzy returned to the steps and grabbed Emma's hand.

Touching his hat, the duke kicked Cornwall into a canter. Tobias shut the gate behind him with a loud clank that rang like the clap of doom.

"We should have some tea," Lizzy said, looking up at her, "except that I can't leave my room."

Emma wiped a tear from her cheek. "We'll have tea tomorrow," she said. If her heart didn't give up beating and stop by then. At the moment, she wasn't willing to wager on her chances of survival.

Chapter 18

Females.

Grey liked it better when he'd been able to dismiss them all as dim, cloying, perfumed mantraps of a foreign species. He'd obviously made a grave mistake, and now he was paying for it.

In the space of one morning he'd informed the family matriarch that he had absolutely no intention of ever marrying. Then the woman he was beginning to think he'd like to spend the rest of his life with had turned him down before he could even propose. To top it all off, his students dismissed him, taking away any chance he might have had to lose the wager with any sort of dignity.

He'd figured that being the Duke of Wycliffe would ensure that the mess with the Academy would work itself out. A few choice words from him, and like magic the problems would vanish. The loose ends of his arrogance had slapped him right in the face. Even worse, he'd made things worse for Emma with his blundering. She was the most compassionate, kind-hearted, forgiving female he'd ever known, and at the moment she could barely stand to look at him.

Grey swore. Getting what he wanted had always been so easy that half the time it hadn't seemed worth the effort. Now, though, he couldn't even breathe when he thought of never seeing Emma again. Now that getting what he wanted wasn't a question of pride or comfort, but of his continued ability to live, he had no idea what to do.

He nearly rode right past the black gelding grazing in the shade near the duck pond. Tristan leaned against a beech tree, his arms crossed over his chest and a cheroot clamped between his teeth.

Grey wasn't in the mood to chat, and with a stiff nod he urged Cornwall forward. Before he rounded the turn out of sight, Tristan bent down and lifted a bottle resting at his feet.

"I have whiskey," he said, amidst a puff of cigar smoke.

A minute later, seated on one of the boulders bordering the pond and a cigar in hand, Grey tilted a long swallow of whiskey down his throat. "Thank God for you, Tris."

"I grabbed the bottle the moment I set eyes on your cousin," the viscount muttered around his cigar. "Your family absolutely loathes me, don't they?"

"When Georgiana discovered you were with me, she probably volunteered to come along."

"I doubt that." Accepting the bottle back, Tristan took a swallow. "All jesting aside, what in damnation is wrong with you?"

Being criticized was also a new experience, and one he only found tolerable when Emma was doing it. "Why?"

Tristan shrugged. "If I had what you have, I wouldn't be sitting here drinking with the likes of me."

Grey eyed him as he took the bottle back. "What is it that I have, exactly? We all know I've been a complete ass, and now I'm paying for it."

"Glad to hear you admitting to it, anyway. You didn't happen to receive any correspondence over the past few hours, did you?"

With a frown, Grey dug into his coat pocket and pulled out Lizzy's note. Half his attention and all his suspicions on Dare, he unfolded it.

"Anything interesting?"

Grey read the brief message once, and then a second time. In Jane's neat, rounded hand, it said only, "We want to help you lose." He lifted his head. "You had something to do with this, I presume?"

"I might have clarified a few things." Finishing off the whiskey, Tristan stood. "You did this to her, Grey. Make it right."

"I'm attempting to," he growled. "And I don't need you to tell me what I've done."

"Well, if you decide you do need me for anything, I'm available." The viscount swung up into the saddle. "Consider me your able second."

The cigar and the whiskey seemed to help clarify his thoughts. His main task was obviously to save the Academy. The wager had become a secondary concern; Emma's winning or losing it wouldn't make any difference since she had already been judged and condemned by half of London.

A proposal from him—and her acceptance of it—would protect her. And he *would* marry Emma Grenville; the how and the when would come later. But he had no idea how the Academy parents would view their union. He didn't see any possible way the Academy would survive this. He'd set out to close it, and now that he'd changed his mind, he looked likely to succeed.

He returned to his uncle's office to write a quick reply to his students, thanking them for their generosity and cooperation and suggesting a meeting first thing in the morning. Including them would be tricky, since he couldn't risk exposing them to further scandal, but he didn't want them angry at him, either—and he could use the help. Besides, he didn't have much time left.

"No! Absolutely not!" Emma's tiny office was bursting at the seams with arguing students.

"Miss Emma, we *promised*," Lizzy said, her expression earnest.

"He told me that you dismissed him. You don't need to see him again. Enough damage has already been done."

"Too much," Jane said. "And now we're going to fix it."

"The problem isn't yours to fix. It's mine."

Much as she appreciated the gesture, she was responsible for their futures.

Elizabeth stepped around the newly-repaired desk. "I have nowhere else to go," she said quietly. "I want to stay here. You have to let us help."

A tear ran down Emma's cheek. Oh, she'd ruined everything—especially for young Lizzy. "Elizabeth, you can't fix every—"

"A promise is a promise," a calm voice said from the doorway.

Emma jumped. "Alexandra," she breathed, pure relief filling her at the sight of the tall, blonde-haired woman standing in the doorway. "Ladies, please excuse us for a moment."

"But we're supposed to meet him *this morning*," Lizzy insisted.

"A five-minute delay isn't considered rude," she said, shooing them toward the door.

"Could you please have someone tell Tobias to allow Lucien onto the grounds?" Alexandra asked, nodding as the girls passed her, curtsying.

"Lizzy, Jane, have Tobias let Lord Kilcairn in, and show him to my office."

"Yes, Miss Emma."

As soon as Henrietta pulled the door closed behind her, Emma rushed forward and threw her arms around the countess. "You look so well, Lex," she managed, tears overflowing her eyes.

"I feel very ungainly," Alexandra replied, rubbing her rounded stomach when Emma could finally bear to relinquish her tight hug.

Now that support had arrived, Emma wasn't quite certain how to go about explaining everything—probably because she had no logical reason for anything she'd done since Wycliffe's arrival. "You made good time."

"We'd already packed, as soon as I heard the rumors. We nearly crossed your letter on the way out of London. Vix and Sin should be here by noon." Lady Kilcairn pulled off her shawl, folding it over the back of one of the chairs. "Emma, I don't know how much you've heard, but—"

"I've heard enough," she answered, her gloom returning.

"How could this have happened?" Alexandra seated herself cautiously in one of the stiff office chairs. "No one who knows you could possibly think—"

"Please don't, Lex. I just . . . I don't know what to do."

Alexandra looked at her. "I've never heard you say that before."

"I've been saying it a great deal over the past few days. I don't know what's come over me, and I have no explanation."

Someone knocked at the door, and she stepped over to open it. Lizzy and Jane, their eyes wide, stood on either side of a tall, lean man dressed all in black. His lips twitching, he nodded at her. "Your guards are practically Amazonian."

"My lord." Emma stepped aside to allow the Earl of Kilcairn Abbey into her office. "Thank you, ladies. Do not leave the grounds without me."

"Oh, faddle," Elizabeth grumbled, backing out and shutting the door.

Kilcairn strolled past his wife to look out the office window. "After all the rumors and your damned Charis the gatekeeper, I expected more of a boudoir-like interior here."

"Lucien," Alexandra said, lifting an eyebrow. "Be helpful."

"I might be, if someone tells me exactly what's been going on." He sank down in the deep window sill. "And you might want to have someone tell Charis to expect Althorpe. I doubt he'll be in as good a mood as I am when they arrive."

"I will." Emma opened the door again to find half the student body lurking in the hallway, if fifty curious young ladies could be said to lurk. She gave instructions to Henrietta and Julia to alert Tobias, ordered the girls to disperse, and ducked back into the office. Then she looked from Alexandra to Lucien. "Would you be more comfortable in one of the sitting rooms?"

"Actually, since we left the inn this morning I've been obsessed with those old chairs your aunt used to keep in the downstairs sitting room. Are they still there?"

"Of course they are. I never should have had you come all the way up here." Another tear ran down Emma's cheek. Aunt Patricia would never have allowed this mess to happen.

"Hm," Lucien mused with a dark glance in the direction of Haverly. "It appears I'll be shooting Wycliffe, after all."

"Not until we've heard everything Emma has to say, Lucien." Alexandra patted him on the shoulder.

The Academy came first, Emma reminded herself; the students and the Academy. Her own embarrassment didn't matter. Her own happiness didn't matter. Sometimes, though, since she'd met Grey, she wished that it did matter.

They headed downstairs to the nearest sitting

room. With a sigh, Alexandra sank into the softest, oldest chair in the room. Chuckling, Lucien fetched her an extra pillow and sat on the arm of the chair beside her, twining his fingers with hers. Knowing his reputation as a dark and dangerous man, Emma found the change in him surprising. Love seemed able to work miracles for everyone but her, she noted glumly.

"All right, I am as comfortable as I will be for the next month," Alexandra announced. "Tell us what's happened."

Sighing, Emma told them, starting with Wycliffe's damaged coach and ending with the note he'd sent the girls. She left out only the bits which involved kissing and naked bodies. Those things mattered only to her, and for her it was too late. She'd asked for help in saving the Academy—not her tattered dreams of self-respect and of Greydon Brakenridge.

"And from that the gossips decided you were Delilah and Jezebel, all in one? Something's missing," the earl said when she finished.

"What do you mean?" she asked, trying not to blush and knowing she was failing miserably.

The sitting room door opened, admitting a black-haired swirl of violet that engulfed Emma in a tight hug. "Where is that damned Wycliffe? I'll shoot him myself."

The duke was in more trouble than he realized. A dark-haired man two or three years younger than Kilcairn, and of much the same build, strolled into the room next. "Emma, that gatekeeper of yours is even more rabid than I remember," he said, shifting the bundle of blankets he carried in his arms.

"Lord Althorpe," she returned, curtsying as well as she could with Vixen still attached to her. "And that would be Thomas, I presume?"

The marquis grinned, instantly altering his demeanor from dangerous to affable. "It would be."

He held out the bundle, and Lady Althorpe released Emma to take it into her own arms. "Thomas," she said, smiling, "meet your other godmother."

Emma peeked into the bundle to see large brown eyes blinking at her sleepily. Young Thomas Grafton, the infant Viscount Dartingham, yawned and stretched his tiny fists into the air. "My goodness, Victoria," she whispered. "He's perfect."

"Until he gets hungry, anyway," the marquis returned with an indulgent smile. "His caterwauling can rattle windows."

Vixen chuckled. "It's indescribable." Then her violet gaze grew serious. "I suppose we've missed all the details of your story, but a wager with Wycliffe began all this mess?"

Emma sighed. For two minutes she'd been able to forget everything but how good it was to see her friends again. Even while she gazed at baby Thomas, though, in the back of her mind she'd wondered what a child of hers and Grey's would look like. "The wager, and someone's . . . interpretation of our subsequent dealings together," she admitted, shaking herself free of such ridiculous daydreams.

"Would you care to summarize the major points?" Victoria handed her son back to Sinclair so she could hug Emma again. "I can't bear to see you look so forlorn."

"I want to hear it again, too," the earl said, standing. "Over luncheon, perhaps?"

"Luncheon?" Emma blinked. "Is it so late?"

"I'm famished," Alexandra said, "though I nearly always am, these d—"

"Oh, no." She'd told the girls she would give them an answer in five minutes. That had been long ago. "I'll be right back."

"Emma?"

"Just a moment."

She dashed into the abandoned hallway and checked the classroom where they held their London social graces lessons in Wycliffe's absence, but the girls weren't there. Her panic growing, she raced to the front door. Blast it all, if they'd ventured again, unescorted, to Haverly, no one would believe the school was anything but a refuge for hoydens and lightskirts, and she the worst of them all.

Outside, she stopped.

A cluster of students stood at the gate talking with someone on its far side. Tobias stood close by, scowling.

"Ladies," she said sharply, approaching at a fast walk, "what are you doing out here?"

"We're having our meeting," Lizzy stated. "We haven't done anything you said we shouldn't."

She needed to start being more specific in her instructions, obviously. "When I said you weren't to leave the Academy grounds, I thought that would have implied that I didn't want you conversing with anyone outside them, either."

"Emma, they're trying to help," a low, masculine voice said from beyond the gate.

Attempting to ignore the tingle of awareness curling down her spine, Emma frowned. "The last we spoke, Your Grace, your intention was to lose this wager."

"It still is." Grey leaned against the gate, his light green eyes following her every move as she paced.

"I've been thinking about that. With the rumors concerning my . . . propriety, I cannot allow my students to perform poorly or to look ridiculous, and I certainly won't allow them to lie. The disservice to them would far outweigh any benefit to the Academy."

"That's what we're working on," Jane said, her expression serious. "We aren't completely daft, Miss Emma."

"I know you're not. I'm just . . . very frazzled."

"That's why we're helping." Elizabeth, the one with perhaps the least and the most to lose, gave Emma an encouraging smile. "Everything will work itself out."

She forced a return smile, hoping it looked more genuine than it felt. "I hope so." With a glance in Grey's direction, though she didn't have the willpower to meet his gaze, she rubbed her hands together. "Ten more minutes, and then you will return inside for luncheon."

"Emma," Grey said, before she could escape, "I'm told you've recruited assistance."

She stopped. "Yes, I thought bringing in a few Academy supporters might help the outcome."

"Who?"

"You'll have to wait until Saturday, Your Grace."

The duke wrapped his hands around two of the gate posts. "Who is staying here with you?" he asked again, his voice harder.

It was far too late for him to be acting jealous, but the part of Emma that knew all of this awfulness was because she cared for him, leapt at the chance to get even. "Men aren't allowed to stay here," she said curtly, "as you know. The Marquis of Althorpe and the Earl of Kilcairn Abbey will be lodging at the Red Lion."

His eyes narrowed. "Althorpe and Kilcairn. Their reputations won't do much for the Academy's good name. Reconsider."

"They've already promised their help." She paused, debating whether to continue, but hurt goaded her on. "I really don't think you're qualified to assist where my . . . honor is concerned."

His mouth tight, he looked at her for a long moment. "Ladies, please give us a minute of privacy," he murmured, his gaze keeping Emma rooted in place.

"All right, as long as it doesn't count as one of our minutes." Lizzy led the group, and an equally reluctant Tobias, out of earshot.

"Come here," Grey said.

Emma put her hands behind her back, not feeling all that safe even with a closed gate between them. Her pulse hummed in reaction to his nearness, even when she was furious and hurt. "I'll stay here, thank you, not that things could get much worse."

"I don't want to shout. You can take two steps for the sake of the Academy, can't you?"

So now he was exploiting her concern for the school. With a frown Emma edged closer. One step, then a second. "For your sake, this had better be about the Academy."

"I've turned you into a cynic now, have I?" His eyes searched hers again, though she had no idea what he hoped to see.

"I told you before that I don't blame you for this. I blame myself for behaving in a manner I knew to be improper."

That wasn't quite true, because she *did* blame him—but not for what he expected. He'd made her yearn for things she'd never dreamed even existed prior to his arrival in her life.

He leaned closer against the iron bars, his hands still gripping two of them. "I wish you *would* blame me, Emma."

Her breath stopped. "And why is that?"

"Because if you did, I would at least have a chance of redeeming myself. If you leave me out entirely, I don't know how to get back in."

"You can't get back in." She paused, but something in the almost vulnerable, almost worried look on his face made her want to continue. "I don't like games, Grey. I don't know if you were playing one when we were . . . together, but I know what the results have been. And I know what the cost is likely to be. I will speak with the girls' parents on Saturday. *I* will resolve this, because the responsibility is mine."

"I haven't been playing with you, Em. At first, perhaps, but not for a long time now." He reached out one hand, catching her by the front of the dress before she could even gasp. With the same speed he yanked her up to the gate. "Give me some chance to help you. Please, Emma."

"No, Grey," she said, her voice breaking.

"Please," he repeated, his voice a husky, barely audible whisper.

"If you want to keep that hand, Wycliffe, I suggest you let her go."

She hadn't heard their approach, but Althorpe stood a few feet behind her, Kilcairn slightly to his left. In a one-on-one fight, Grey outreached and outweighed either of them. Together, she wouldn't wager much for his chances.

Alarmed, she nodded. "All right," she whispered quickly. "One chance. Now, let me go."

He held on for the space of a dozen heartbeats, then released her. "I'll only need one." With a smile that touched deep inside his eyes, he backed away from the gate. Only then did he look at the two noblemen. "I'm available anytime either of you want to come outside and play."

Althorpe shrugged out of his coat, dropping it to the ground. "Now sounds good."

"No!" Emma put out her hand to stop the marquis.

At the same moment, Lucien caught his shoulder from behind. "Not in front of the children," he murmured, his icy gray gaze on Wycliffe. "But soon."

Shaking herself, Emma turned her back on Grey and gestured for the two dark-haired peers to accompany her back to the main building. She was somewhat surprised when they did so. "I promised him ten minutes with his students," she explained when Kilcairn lifted an eyebrow at her.

Vixen and Alexandra stood together at the top of the steps, watching Emma return with Lucien and Sinclair flanking her. As she approached, she looked back over her shoulder toward the gate.

"What do you think?" Alexandra asked quietly.

"The same thing you do," Vixen returned, shifting Thomas higher up on her shoulder. "Our Emma's in love."

"Mm hm." Alexandra smiled as they returned to the foyer. "And it's about damned time."

Chapter 19

Hobbes, at his station by the front door, looked as if he was considering retirement. "Your Grace, Lady Sylvia Kincaid and Miss Boswell departed for London some thirty minutes ago, and Lord Dare is counseling Frederick Mayburne in the billiards room."

"Why does he need counseling?"

"He did not confide in me, Your Grace." The butler looked glad of that fact.

Grey sighed. He had a damned lot of work to do, and only two days to do it. Impatient as he was to move forward with his plans, he didn't want to leave a wild card like Freddie Mayburne loose and unaccounted for.

In the billiards room, Tristan lounged in one corner while Freddie leaned over the table and set a hard shot against the cushion, scratching the smooth velvet surface in the process.

"What's happened?" Grey asked.

"He's ruining the billiards table, for one thing." Tristan leaned on his cue stick. "I didn't know what else to do with him."

Freddie lifted his head. "Ah, Wycliffe. You've been busy, I hear."

Grey narrowed his eyes. "What precisely have you heard?" If there was one thing he didn't need, it was this idiot spreading still more rumors about Emma.

"Just that you've been gadding about the school lifting skirts while the rest of us aren't even allowed through the gates. I had no idea that while you were advising me about Jane, you were practicing on the headmis—"

Yanking the cue stick out of Tristan's hands, Grey slammed it against the billiards table. "*Enough!*" he roared.

Jumping at the sound, Freddie belatedly began backing toward the door. "Enough for now, but I doubt you'll be in Hampshire much longer. The iron maiden looks to be gone even sooner." He leaned his cue stick against the wall. "Which leaves me, still in Hampshire, with Jane."

"Get out of this house," Grey growled, striding forward. "If I see you anywhere near that Academy, I will personally see to it that you become a castrato." Yanking the door open, he shoved Freddie into the hallway, narrowly missing Georgiana in the process.

Freddie scrambled for the stairs. "That's my point, Wycliffe. You won't be here," he said defiantly.

As he passed Georgiana, she kicked him in the leg with one slippered foot. "And I'll have everyone thinking you already are a castrato," she added.

Grey didn't unclench his hand from around the billiards cue until the front door slammed downstairs. "Damn it," he muttered.

"Do you really think that's the best way to get rid of him?" Tristan asked, joining him in the doorway.

It wasn't, but Grey could only hope the lad was intimidated enough that he would stay clear of Jane until he had a chance to warn her about the blackguard. "It'll do for now."

"Hm," Georgiana said smoothly. "Castratos. You're one, aren't you, Lord Dare?"

"Not yet," Tristan drawled, and returned to the billiards room.

Grey had never quite figured out what had caused the animosity between Tristan and Georgiana, but he thought it might've had something to do with the infamous "Kiss Georgie" wager of several years ago, which Dare had won. It was simply better not to allow them in one another's company for any extended period.

"Georgie?" He lifted an eyebrow.

She smiled and strolled toward the music room, where he could hear Aunt Regina playing the pianoforte. "Just two friends, jesting," she said lightly.

Georgiana and Dare were closer to blood-crazed enemies than friends, but he liked the word. That was what he and Emma had become; friends. He liked chatting with her and learning her mind as much as he enjoyed learning her body. When this was over with, he could envision nothing more pleasurable than to go strolling through the gardens at Wycliffe Park with Emma and talk about crop yield or something. Grey gave a small, grim smile. Good God, he was yearning for domesticity—and even more, for Emma Grenville.

"Hobbes," he said, descending the stairs, "I'm going into Basingstoke. I'll be back shortly."

"Yes, Your Grace."

Halfway out the door, he paused. Emma was right about one thing; he'd already caused enough trouble, and while he didn't give a hang what anyone thought of his comings and goings, he *did* care if they caused more hurt for Emma. "Don't tell anyone where I've gone," he said.

The butler nodded again. "Yes, Your Grace."

"Ah, unless Miss Emma comes by and asks."

"Yes, Your Grace."

Hobbes probably thought he'd lost his mind, but the butler would have been wrong: he'd lost his heart. And whatever the outcome of this mess, he needed to be sure that he didn't lose Miss Emma Grenville, and that her Academy didn't have to close.

Sir John Blakely seemed surprised to see him as he strolled into the solicitor's small office. "Good afternoon," Grey said, sitting in one of the chairs facing the desk.

"Your Grace. This is unexpected, to say the least."

Pulling off his riding gloves and dropping them into his hat, Grey nodded. "A bit irregular, perhaps, but I require your assistance. My solicitors are all in London, and as you've pointed out, you are the only one in this part of Hampshire."

"How may I assist you, then?"

So far, so good. Given Sir John's friendship with Emma, he hadn't been certain how cooperative the solicitor would be. "Two things. Or three, depending on your recommendation."

"I'm listening."

"First, in your estimation, how much does it cost to put a student through one year of schooling at the Academy? Books, meals, tuition, clothes, et cetera."

Again the solicitor looked surprised, and delayed a moment before answering. "Well, I have done such calculations before, for . . . select students. The information certainly isn't secret, so I suppose relaying the numbers to you wouldn't be stepping into private Academy concerns. The cost for a one-year term is approximately two hundred pounds."

"And a recommended course of study is three years, is it not?"

"Yes, though it varies from one to four years."

And students like Lizzy Newcombe would no doubt find educational opportunities available to them until their eighteenth year. "The fees are paid in advance yearly, I presume?"

"Generally, though a monthly payment schedule may also be arranged. Is there someone you wish to send to the Academy?" The solicitor's brow furrowed. "Though given your . . . wager, I can't imagine you would do such a thing."

Grey nodded. "I would appreciate if you would draft a paper to transfer two thousand pounds from one of my London bank accounts to

Miss Grenville's Academy, for sponsorship of up to ten young ladies chosen at the discretion of the faculty board. Said fund is to be transferred on a yearly basis for the next ten years."

The solicitor stared at him. "I—that is . . . this is exceptionally generous of you, Your Grace. I was under the impression that you genuinely disliked the Academy."

"I used to. Now I don't."

Sir John had the intelligence not to question him further on that subject. "So I see. You, ah, had a second topic you wished to discuss?"

"Yes. I would like a second account set up, in the amount of twenty-five thousand pounds. This—"

"Excuse me," Sir John interrupted, his pencil jumping, "but you did say twenty-five *thousand* pounds?"

"Mm hm." Grey knew the amount of money and power he could wield shocked and impressed a great many people, but he'd grown up with it, and having money had only provided a means to an end. He wanted to charge in on a white horse and rescue Emma and her beloved Academy, but at the moment he was still marshaling his forces.

"Very good, then. Twenty-five thousand pounds. For, ah, what purpose?"

"To be held in trust for the Academy, with the interest to be used as needed for upgrades, repairs, and supplies."

Something thunked to the floor behind him. "Why?" Emma's gasp came from the doorway.

Grey cursed as he came to his feet. "What are you doing here?"

"Returning some of Sir John's research books," she stammered. "What in the world do you think you're doing?"

"This is a private business transaction," he growled, striding up to her, "and none of your damned affair."

"If it concerns the Academy, it *is* my damned affair." Putting her hands on her hips, Emma glared up at him. "And I demand to know what sort of game you're playing now."

"I'm not playing anything. I've come to realize my opinions about the Academy were based on erroneous information, and now I'm attempting to make amends."

She didn't look impressed. "Isn't that a little like shutting the barn door after the horse has escaped, been captured, killed, its hide made into shoes, and the barn burned down?"

"You've been saving that one just for me, haven't you?" he asked, lifting an eyebrow.

"Don't you dare think this is funny. If I haven't said it plainly enough already, allow me to repeat myself: stay out of my affairs."

"So you would refuse aid to the Academy, just because it comes from me?"

"There *is* no Academy. Or there won't be, after Saturday."

He opened his mouth to reply, then snapped it shut again as he remembered Sir John's presence. "Outside."

"I am not going to create a spectacle and be the object of further gossip and scandal by being seen with you in the street."

Leaning closer, Grey took her chin in his fin-

gers. Even angry, she blushed, and his body re-
acted as it always did. "I need to talk to you," he
said in a low voice. "In private, with no yelling."

For a moment she held his gaze before she
backed out of his grip. "Sir John, I apologize for
even asking, but would you mind—"

The solicitor stood. "I'll be in the bakery, if you
should need me," he said, walking past them to
collect his hat and exit.

Emma folded her arms across her breasts. "All
right, Grey, I'm listening."

At least she hadn't reverted to calling him "His
Grace." "Any more letters?" he asked conversa-
tionally, trying to blunt the sharp edge of her
anger.

"Only ones answering the invitation. Lizzy's
mother has declined, but the other four sets of
parents will arrive Saturday morning. Apparently
they will be traveling together."

Grey winced. A mob, to lynch Emma. "I'm
sorry."

"It's not necessary for you to apologize."

"Yes, it is."

"N . . ." She trailed off. "Is your throwing
money at my Academy part of your apology?"

"No. It's part of my enlightenment." He took a
step closer. The timing for a proposal was
abysmal, but neither was it fair to leave her thinking she was out of options, when she had another
way to save herself. "I began to tell you part of
my plan the other day. Might I do so now?"

Emma shrugged. "If you wish."

In truth, it upset her immensely that he was
there, and that he'd apparently been doing some-

thing nice for the Academy. She hoped that whatever he was about to say would make her angry, so she could at least face him without crying.

"Very well." Grey moved past her to the door and locked it, then faced her again. "My plan."

She scowled. "Yes, your plan. What is it? Though I don't believe in miracles. I'm much too old for th—"

"Marry me."

Emma stopped breathing. *"What?"*

He smiled. "It does tie everything off rather nicely, you have to admit."

She couldn't believe it. He hadn't said what he'd just said. Not the man who'd sworn to all and sundry that he would never step near an altar. "That—that makes no sense," she stammered, the blood pounding in her ears. She hoped she wasn't going to faint again.

"It makes perfect sense."

He leaned down to kiss her, but before he could connect, Emma put her hand against his chest and pushed. It was hardly enough to move him if he'd chosen to press the issue, but he stopped.

"I'm—no!"

Grey frowned. "And why not?"

"I told you I would take care of this. Your offer is . . . very generous, but I made my own choices, Grey, and they didn't have conditions attached to them. You don't need to . . . sacrifice yourself for my sake." She was speaking too fast, piling excuses one upon the other, but if she stopped talking she would have to realize that Grey Brakenridge had offered to *marry* her—the kindest, most generous thing anyone had ever done for her.

"You're turning me down?" he asked incredulously.

"Of course I am. Grey, I'm a girls' school headmistress, for goodness' sake. You are—"

He covered her mouth with his fingers. "Please don't remind me that I'm a duke again. I know that."

"But it's the truth!" she retorted, grabbing his fingers away from her mouth. "You *are* a duke, and besides that, a man with no respect for females. How could I—"

"You don't believe that any longer," he said, his voice softer.

"You presume too much," she managed.

"I never do." Softly he stroked her cheek with his knuckles, and she trembled. "I am aware, however, that we are pressed for time, and so I leave you the choice: discuss our impending marriage, or the plans to save the Academy."

Was he deliberately attempting to befuddle her? It was working. "The . . . the Academy."

Grey nodded. "I thought so."

Everything was racing by too quickly for her to make any coherent sense of it. She wanted to talk about why Grey seemed determined to marry her, and she wanted him to hold her in his strong arms and make all of her problems and worries vanish. But she'd chosen the Academy, and he'd accepted that, too.

Concentrate, blast it all. "You can't lose the wager," she forced herself to say. "If the girls look bad, it's the Academy that's failed. Not you."

"I've been thinking about that. I'm going to distance myself from the teaching process."

"How?"

Leaning down, he kissed her softly on the lips. "We'll make it clear in a roundabout way that your Miss Perchase was keeping up the actual instruction while I was making shockingly bad pronouncements and in general promoting fiddle faddle."

"So the girls can still look good, and you will lose the wager." Raising on her tiptoes to touch his lips again seemed such a fine idea that she couldn't resist. He really hadn't asked her to marry him, had he? "And then what?"

"And then I'll concede that after I forced you into the wager, I realized that I had absolutely no chance of instructing the students half as well as you did. When the completely unfounded rumors began, we were both shocked and offended—which was when we decided to have the parents come and view their daughters' progress. And just to prove that we're all honorable folk, I will marry you."

"To prove . . ." Emma drew a shallow, disappointed breath. "I think that may work for the girls, but offering to wed a headmistress to deflect any scandal? Aren't you afraid you'll look foolish?"

He gave a soft smile. "There's only one person whose opinion I care for—and if she is happy, then I am happy."

She swallowed, hope soaring. "That's very nice, even if you don't mean it."

"Allow me to convince you, then."

He captured her mouth in a deep, hungry kiss.

Before she knew it, Emma was sitting in Grey's lap as he dropped into Sir John's chair. "This is nice, too," she said, as he kissed her throat.

"God, Emma, I can't keep my hands off you," he murmured, trailing his mouth along the base of her jaw.

"I like your hands."

At that, one of his hands slipped under the front of her gown to cup her breast. As his fingers caressed her sensitive nipple she gasped, arching her back. In response, he stirred beneath her thighs.

"Does this feel like honor and guilt, Emma?"

His whisper, warm and soft in her ear, made her shiver again. While one hand continued touching and caressing her breast, the other crept down her thighs to begin gathering her skirt.

"Grey!" she gasped.

"Shh. You don't want anyone outside to hear, do you?"

No, she didn't want to be interrupted. She longed for this, and had missed him every second that he wasn't in her presence. After Saturday, after the wager was over, he would have no more reason—and no more excuses—to extend his stay in Hampshire.

Whatever he said about marrying her, it was probably just guilt and lust. He slipped an arm around her waist, lifting her so he could pull the gown up over her hips. In a moment her bare bottom settled back down on him.

And she was grateful for *his* lust, because she loved being the focus of his attention and his desire. Angry as his arrogance made her sometimes, she loved him, and these few delicious encoun-

ters made it all right. Once reality returned he
would realize they could never marry, but at least
she would have this.

His hands curved up the insides of her bare
thighs, his hands so warm and knowing they
practically left her panting with want. "Grey," she
whispered.

"Lean forward."

Grasping the edge of the desk, she bent forward, and he freed himself from his breeches.
With his hands guiding her hips, she sank back
down again, feeling him sliding hard and hot inside her. He moaned, their joining clearly giving
him as much pleasure as it did her. Grey lifted his
hips against her as she rocked against him, gasping as fire flooded her veins.

They came together, and Emma couldn't help
her deep, satisfied sigh, as he slid his hands
slowly around her waist and pulled her back
against him again. "Perhaps when this mess is
finished, and I find a position . . . somewhere,
you could come and visit me every so often," she
said, turning to kiss him. "And we could renew
our acquaintance."

He froze mid-kiss. "What?"

"It wouldn't be hurting anything, you know.
The damage has been done. I like being with you,
and it's not as though I have any prospects."

Grey took her shoulders and held her away
from him. "You have one very willing prospect,
damn it!"

"It doesn't make any sense," she insisted.

"Emma," he said, his low voice resonating
deep inside her, "I have recently discovered that
sometimes not making sense is the only thing that

makes sense." He set her upright, tugging her skirt back down for her. "You're the Academy's mistress. I want you for my wife."

"But—"

"Just think about it." He scowled as he shoved his rumpled shirt back into his trousers. "No, don't think about it. You think too much as it is." While she stared at him, trying to follow his half sentences and mutterings, he leaned down and kissed her slowly and possessively.

"I'll see you Saturday, at ten in the morning," he continued, returning the desk and the chair to their former condition. "Be ready for anything."

He opened the door and exited, pulling it closed behind him. Blinking, Emma sat in the chair again. "My goodness," she murmured, trying to straighten her hair, which seemed to have become rather disheveled.

What her heart wanted and what her mind knew was possible were becoming further and further apart. He claimed he wanted her not just for an evening, not just for pleasure, but for the rest of their lives.

But did he truly love her—and enough to be laughed at and scoffed at by his peers? What of his mother, who thought her a common strumpet?

Standing, Emma headed for the rear of Sir John's office. A small tray with a few bottles sat on a cluttered table. She searched for a moment, found a glass and then the brandy, and poured herself a stiff drink. She had the feeling that by the end of the week she would be needing quite a few of these.

Chapter 20

The coaches arrived early. Emma, tying the ribbon at the waist of her plainest, most conservative gown, peered down through her bed chamber curtains. Four coaches, and four sets of parents, stepped onto the Academy's long, gravel-covered drive. The morning's drizzle had deepened into a steady rain, as though the heavens had sympathy for her plight.

As she watched, two more coaches and then a third rolled onto the grounds. Emma frowned. "Who could that be?" More trouble, undoubtedly; she couldn't imagine more assistance arriving at this late date.

Her office door opened. "Emma?"

"In here," she called, sitting at her dressing table to pull her hair up into a conservative bun.

Her hands shook so much she could barely hold her brush, but she was determined to have a professional appearance.

Isabelle slipped through the half-open door. "We have a problem."

"Another one?"

"I'm afraid so. More parents arriving; even the ones whose daughters haven't been involved with the wager."

Emma nodded. "I'm not surprised. The wager isn't the problem; I am."

"Nonsense. You are not to blame for any of this."

She was, but her first priority was to make sure the reputation of her students remained unblemished. Whatever Grey's plan, she couldn't leave the Academy's future to the fates.

Even the parents not attending today's events had sent her letters maligning her judgment and questioning the soundness of her mind, and she knew, if all else failed, what it would take to save her aunt's school: she would resign. It left her sick with guilt and worry to even contemplate it, but if that was what the parents required, she would do it.

Emma took a deep breath. "Well, my dear, let's gather our students and show their parents how much they've accomplished."

Lifting the heavy binder which held her part of the wager, Emma led the way to the morning room where Grey's students had gathered. The girls wanted to conclude the wager, to prove the Academy's schooling better than Grey's. They naturally didn't realize that the wager was important only in that it gave her and Grey a legitimate reason to be seen in one another's presence—just as her estate plan, hard though she'd worked on it and proud of it as she was, was pertinent only because it illustrated that she'd been occupied with things other than the Duke of Wycliffe.

The most awful part of all this was that all her protests of innocence would be lies. She *was* carrying on an affair with Grey, and even with this disaster she didn't want to give him up. Since her cousin's betrayal when she'd been twelve she'd hated lying, and had made every effort to instill that same sentiment in her students. It would be so hypocritical to lie to save the Academy.

"Miss Emma, I wore my most professional gown," Lizzy announced.

Emma followed the French instructor into the morning room as Lizzy twirled up to her. "You look lovely," she said, forcing a smile. "All of you do."

"We'll do our best, Miss Emma," Jane said, taking her hand. "We promise."

"I know you will. You are all fine students, and even finer young ladies."

She'd tried to make it clear that they would be defending their own reputations, and that of the Academy; whatever was said about her was a completely separate issue. It wasn't really, and even with the financial situation of the school resolved thanks to Grey, if no students were allowed to attend, Miss Grenville's Academy would be ruined. She'd tried not to put too much of a burden on the girls' shoulders, tried to hide her own anxieties from them, but even so it seemed such a large task for such young ladies.

"Is Grey here yet?" Lizzy asked. "We can't pretend he's silly if he's not here."

Her nerves shrieking, Emma glanced at the nearest clock. "The meeting isn't to begin for another few minutes," she said in her calmest voice.

The morning room door squeaked open, and she jumped, whipping around with her hand to her chest. Her leaping heart hoped it would be Grey, but it was Miss Perchase's pale face that leaned into the room.

"Your friends are here, Miss Emma," she said in a shrill, nervous voice. "I did as you said, and put them in the dining hall with the parents."

"Thank you, Miss Perchase. We'll be down in a minute."

The Latin instructor bobbed her head like a frightened quail. "They . . . it's a bit . . . tense in there," she squeaked.

Emma's pulse accelerated again. "Thank you," she repeated, her own voice shaking.

Pacing back and forth while the girls chattered nervously, Emma resisted looking at the clock until the larger one out in the hallway began to strike ten. Grey had said he would be there, yet there was no sign of him. She swallowed. Perhaps he'd changed his mind about lending his assistance. She'd warned him about the scandal this might cause, and perhaps he'd finally listened.

Emma squared her shoulders and made for the door. So he had abandoned her. It wasn't the first time someone had done so. A tear squeezed from one eye, and she impatiently brushed it away. So he hadn't meant it when he'd suggested they marry—she had heard that men would say almost anything when in the throes of passion. Obviously now better sense had prevailed.

"Miss Emma, are you all right?" Lizzy asked, taking her hand.

"Yes. I'm just fine." Her heart was broken and she was about to lose the Academy, but she could still help the girls—she hoped. She faced her students. "Well. With or without His Grace, we must proceed. Follow me, ladies."

"I don't know." Grey scowled at his reflection in the dressing mirror. "Are you certain I don't have anything more respectable-looking than this?"

Bundle's left eye twitched. "Not in Hampshire, Your Grace."

Grey glanced over at the clock on his mantel. Nine-fifteen. He should have been at the Academy already, but if he arrived too early, he wasn't certain he would be able to keep his hands off Emma.

He wanted to grab the headmistress, sweep her off her feet, carry her into his coach, join her inside, and instruct the driver to take them to Gretna Green. If he didn't allow any stops except to change horses, they might make it to Scotland and the closest church therein before she managed to escape him.

He strode to the rain-streaked window which overlooked the garden. "You told Hobbes to have my coach hitched up, didn't you?"

"I did, Your Grace."

His door rattled and opened. "Sweet Lucifer, Grey, even Beau Brummel would be dressed by now." Tristan slipped inside and shut the door behind him.

"I *am* dressed. This is a strategic delay."

"The parents will probably be there by now. Are you certain you don't want us mingling to soften them up?" Tris asked.

Grey didn't particularly feel like being friendly or conciliatory; these people had insulted his Emma, and they all deserved a good thrashing. On the other hand, they were the parents of his students, chits he had come to look upon with a great deal of fondness.

"I don't think we're the appropriate parties to soften anyone up, considering," he muttered. Grey paused, looking at Dare with his dark blue jacket and polished Hessian boots. "In fact, Tris, I don't think you should go, at all."

The viscount frowned. "Why in damnation not?"

"Because the rumors—" Grey stopped, pinning his valet with another glare. "Out."

"Yes, Your Grace."

Once Bundle was gone and the door closed again, Grey folded his arms. "Because the rumors concern Emma's improper conduct with you."

"And with you," Tristan snapped. "At least my rumors are unfounded."

"But the wager gives me a legitimate connection to Emma and to the Academy. Your being there might cast more suspicion on the entire aff—"

"All right, all right," Dare grumbled, throwing his hands up. "You'd damned well better tell me what happens."

"I will." *Probably, anyway.*

The patter of water against the window caught his attention again as he took a last look at himself in the dressing mirror. He supposed he looked as unobtrusive as a man four inches above six feet tall could look.

"The rain's getting harder," Tristan said unnecessarily, following him into the hallway and down the stairs. "The road'll be a mess."

"It's only two miles. I think I'll manage."

"Are you certain you don't want m—"

"Stay here, Dare," Grey interrupted.

"I will. But I won't like it."

Grey nodded at Hobbes as they entered the foyer. "If my mother inquires, I'm not certain when I'll be back."

The butler remained where he was, one hand on the front door handle. "Ah, Your Grace?"

Dread touched Grey's heart. Emma hadn't fled, had she? He'd never even told her he loved her, for God's sake. "What? What is it?"

"The, um, the coach, Your Gr—"

"I told you to have it hitched up," he interrupted, scowling. Grey pulled out his pocket watch. He needed to be at the Academy. Emma would be wondering where he was.

"I did, Your Grace. It's just that—"

"*What*, damn it?"

"Her Grace and Lady Georgiana took the coach, Your Grace."

Grey stopped. "Took it where?" he enunciated, his jaw clenched.

"They didn't say." Hobbes pulled at his neckcloth. "I would assume they went to the Academy, Your Grace."

"So would I." Grey cursed.

"I'm having one of Her Grace's coaches prepared, if you care to wait a mo—"

"Saddle Cornwall. I don't have time to wait."

"Yes, Your Grace."

Yanking open the door, Hobbes hurried out into the rain, Grey on his heels. Damn the duchess, anyway. Was she trying to delay him, to take away any chance he would have to defend Emma? If that was her plan, it was going to fail. He had a few plans of his own.

The girls, Isabelle, and Miss Perchase trailing behind her, Emma reached the bottom of the stairs and turned up the corridor toward the dining hall. A different kind of dread had settled in her heart; one that had nothing to do with the loss of her reputation and her Academy, and everything to do with the thought of never seeing Grey Brakenridge again. Never hearing his voice, never seeing his face, never feeling his touch, ever again. She might as well be dead. She'd wanted independence; well she had it now.

The sitting room door opposite her opened. "Miss Emma." A tall, willow-thin woman with silvering dark hair stood in the doorway, her dark-eyed gaze on Emma.

Starting, Emma faced her. Her mind scattering in a hundred different directions, she curtsied. "Your Grace."

"I wasn't sure you would remember me, considering that you were unconscious for the majority of our first meeting." The elegant duchess looked her slowly up and down, while the girls began whispering behind her.

"Yes, I remember. I . . . thank you for your assistance."

The duchess's mouth tightened. "Considering that my remarks were what caused you to faint, I find your thanks to be overly generous."

Lizzy stepped forward. "You made Miss Emma faint?" she demanded.

"Hush, Elizabeth. It was a misunderstanding."

Frederica Brakenridge lifted an eyebrow, the expression reminding Emma painfully of Grey. "A misunderstanding," the duchess repeated. "That remains to be seen."

"Your Grace, I would appreciate if we might continue this discussion at a later time," Emma suggested. For heaven's sake, she had too many other things to worry about right now. Interpreting insults—and the duchess's presence at the Academy—would have to wait until she had more time. "If you'll excuse us, I'm afraid we have a very full schedule to—"

"Yes, you do. This, however, will only take a moment." Frederica stepped aside, motioning Emma into the sitting room behind her.

"I—"

"If you please, Miss Emma."

All she needed was for Grey's mother to call her a whore in front of the girls. "Very well. Ladies, please wait for me in the hall."

The Duchess of Wycliffe followed her inside the room and closed the door behind her. "You've created quite a stir, my dear."

"I have participated in a wager which has unfortunately garnered more attention than I had anticipated," Emma corrected, trying to keep from hunching her shoulders. "A great deal of the blame for which falls on my shoulders."

"But not all the blame." Frederica Brakenridge crossed the room to sit in one of the overstuffed chairs beneath the window. She didn't invite Emma to join her.

Emma preferred being close by the door, anyway. She wasn't quite certain what the conversation was about, or why the duchess had taken over the sitting room as though she owned it, but for goodness' sake, the woman might have had a little compassion. She was nervous enough, already. "No, not all of the blame is mine. At the moment, though, all I can do is lament my poor judgment and attempt to salvage what I can of the Academy's reputation."

"And what of your own reputation?"

"I have no illusions where my reputation is concerned. I simply don't want what I may—or may not—have done to reflect upon my students or upon this school."

"And which is it? May? Or may not?"

She tried to stop her sudden scowl, and thought she'd managed to hold back everything but a twitch in her left eye. "As I said, that doesn't signify today, Your Grace." The personal questions began to annoy her. "And if I may be so bold, Your Grace, why does my folly interest you so much?"

The duchess sat back, stretching her hands along the chair's arms. "*You* interest me, Emma Grenville. Something about you has intrigued my son enough to keep him in Hampshire for a month."

"Are you certain it was me?" Emma asked, trying to keep from blushing.

"Reasonably so. He has been known to tire of Society and disappear for a week or ten days with his friends and his . . . entertainment, until they bore him as well and he returns. Obviously, though, this time my son has not returned to London. The question becomes why. Or rather, why not."

For all Emma knew, he might be on his way back to London at this very moment. She swallowed. This had been easier when they'd been discussing her reputation. Poor as the day looked to end up for her, she didn't want to begin lying; not now, and not to Grey's mother. Misdirection, though, was another matter entirely. "His Grace did make a wager. I gathered that he dislikes the idea of losing."

The duchess nodded, a brief smile softening her expression. "So he does."

Down the hallway, the dull murmur of voices in the ballroom abruptly became more audible. Emma jumped. She didn't want the girls confronted by their parents without her present to serve as a buffer. "Excuse me, Your Grace, but as you know, I have several things to take care of today."

"Of course." The Duchess of Wycliffe stood. "Despite what my son might say, I am not nearly as obtuse as he thinks. Nor am I as hard-hearted as he likes to tell himself. You inspire trust, Emma. It is a pleasant surprise."

Emma blinked. "I'm afraid I still don't understand the reason for this conversation, Your Grace."

"Well, you only have a short time to figure things out. Allow me to point you in the right direction. You are well born, are you not?"

She hated this line of questioning, but she'd been asked it often enough by parents of prospective students that at least she knew how to answer it without hesitating. "I am, Your Grace. My parents died when I was young, though, and I was raised by my aunt."

"At Miss Grenville's Academy."

"Yes, Your Grace."

"An educated woman," Frederica murmured, so quietly that Emma wasn't certain whether she was meant to overhear. "Another pleasant surprise."

Emma's head was swimming. Clearing her throat, she gestured at the door. "I beg your pardon, Your Grace, but—"

"Yes, I know. The wager." Frederica pulled open the door, looking over her shoulder at Emma as she did so. "Thank you for speaking with me, Miss Emma. I think you've been misjudged."

"I . . . thank you."

The duchess smiled. "Don't thank me yet." With a last look she vanished down the hallway in the direction of the dining hall.

What in the world had that been about? If the duchess was looking for a clue as to her son's uncharacteristic behavior, Emma didn't have any insights to offer. She'd expected—and needed—Grey to be at the Academy today, so at least she would know that she wasn't completely alone.

Obviously, though, she was alone, and even the presence of her students and of Alexandra and Vixen couldn't change that. Everything was up to her, and it was time to stop putting it off.

Shaking from head to toe, Emma rejoined the girls to lead the parade into the dining hall. "Good morning," she said as they entered the room, and the roar of accusing voices began.

Grey bent his head against the heavy rain. Even with his greatcoat on he was likely to be soaked to the bone by the time he reached the Academy. But that didn't matter, so long as he got there in time to step between Emma and the wolves.

He would have looked more respectable if he'd been dry and in his coach, but he was willing to settle for merely being intimidating. The plan he and the girls had come up with was a good one, provided Emma would play along, and he ran through his part again as he rode.

Something in the glade to his left caught his attention. He looked in that direction just as a heavy tree branch swung around with the force of a catapult and slammed him in the face. Stunned, he lost his balance and tumbled backward off Cornwall, landing hard enough to wrench his shoulder and knock him out cold.

It must have been less than a minute before he blinked his eyes open in the driving rain. Dazed, Gray lay where he was for a moment, trying to pull air into his lungs. When he finally managed to sit up and put a hand to his head, it came away bloody. The rope that had held back the branch hung a few feet behind him.

"Bloody hell," he muttered.

This had been a deliberate ambush, but no

highwaymen or assassins emerged from the trees. Nothing but himself and the rain.

And no horse, either. Shaking his head to try to clear it, he caught sight of a horse and rider vanishing far ahead along the curving road, Cornwall's backside retreating beside them. He couldn't make out anything of the rider but a dark lump, but he recognized the horse.

"Freddie damned Mayburne," he murmured, wiping blood and rain from his eyes.

The lad had an even more nasty, devious streak than he'd realized. And he was quite a bit more intelligent, too. With Emma ruined and Grey not there to defend her, Freddie could swoop in, imply that the girls' reputations were destroyed as well, and generously offer for Jane's hand despite that—because he so deeply loved and admired her.

Her father wouldn't like it, but the Marquis of Greaves was a supremely practical man. Who would want an unmarriageable daughter cluttering up the house when an offer had been made?

Eyeing the muddy, rutted road grimly, Grey staggered to his feet, shook as much mud from his greatcoat as he could, and started on toward the Academy at a head-jarring lope. They'd all just run out of time.

"I would like an explanation as to why you allowed the Duke of Wycliffe onto Academy grounds at all, much less permitted him access to our daughters."

The Marquis of Greaves stood in front of Emma, hands folded over his chest and his eyes glinting with fury. He'd obviously been appointed spokesman for the parents, though that didn't keep the rest of them from muttering and glaring at her.

Emma kept her chin high. For the sake of the girls, she could face anything. "The Duke of Wycliffe proposed a wager, the conditions of which were completely proper. He was constantly supervised, and the students never left alone without a chapero—"

"And why, Miss Emma, did you agree to participate in a wager in the first place?"

Alexandra and Vixen were standing to one side with their husbands, but Emma kept her gaze steadily on the marquis. "It was quite simple, Lord Greaves. The winning of this wager would have afforded the Academy the opportunity to sponsor a number of less fortunate young ladies, giving them the means to better their futures."

Hugh Brendale, Henrietta's father, joined Greaves at the front of the mob. "Less fortunate young ladies don't belong at this Academy. I didn't send my daughter here so she could associate with orange girls and milk maids. And that doesn't even begin to explain your own conduct."

Emma felt her cheeks burning. "Whatever has been alleged about me is insignificant, so long as you understand that your daughters and their reputations have not been injured in any way."

"Of course it's significant. You're the headmistress." Greaves stepped forward, taking Jane by the arm. "My daughter debuts in London next year. And what will everyone be saying? That she was instructed by that Jezebel in Hampshire who ran a bawdy house disguised as a girls' school."

"That is completely untrue! I have never—"

"Don't say that!" Elizabeth shouted.

"Lizzy," Emma hissed.

"Miss Emma taught us never to be rude to one another," the youngest student continued. "And you are being very rude."

"This is how you teach females their place in Society? I am a marquis, girl, and you are an ... infant. You do not speak to me unless it is to answer a question directly."

"Seems to me the infant makes a valid point," Lucien Balfour drawled, his expression cold as icicles. "Let's keep this civilized, shall we?"

Greaves scowled. "I think we passed civilized the moment I opened that letter detailing eyewitness accounts of Miss Emma Grenville engaging in fornication with the Duke of Wycliffe and Viscount Dare."

"Oh, *mon dieu*," Isabelle said softly. Miss Perchase gasped and fainted.

"The problem is even more serious than that, ladies and gentlemen."

Emma whipped around as Freddie Mayburne strode into the dining hall, Tobias on his heels and looking angry enough to chew nails. The boy looked somewhat windblown and disheveled, but if he'd gotten past Tobias, it hadn't been without some sort of confrontation.

"Freddie!" Jane gasped, paling.

"Frederick Mayburne," he acknowledged, sketching a bow to the marquis. "You must be Lord Greaves. It is an honor to meet you, my lord."

"I tried to stop him, Miss Emm—"

"It's all right, Tobias," she whispered back at him. "Please return to your post."

"Aye, Miss. Blasted whelp." Muttering under his breath, the handyman retreated to the front gates.

Freddie stuck out his hand, and after a moment Greaves, looking even more angry, shook it. "This is how you protect your students, Miss Emma? By allowing strange men on Academy grounds at their whim?"

"I did not allow—"

"If you'll excuse me, my lord," Freddie interrupted, "I do not make a habit of calling on the students here. The circumstances today, however, are unique."

"I would say so," Hugh Brendale agreed.

"I have long been a supporter of this Academy," Freddie continued, casting a contemptuous eye in Emma's direction. "In light of the rumors—which were a complete shock to me, I assure you—I contacted several sources in London looking for some sort of confirmation."

"You're a big liar, Freddie," Lizzy spat.

"Be quiet, Elizabeth," Emma warned her. Not many schools offered tuition-free positions; if this Academy closed, Lizzy's education—and her hopes of becoming a governess—would be dashed beyond recall.

"To my surprise," Freddie continued, undaunted, "I discovered that even before her most recent lapse, Miss Emma has been less than a model citizen."

"Explain, Mr. Mayburne."

"With pleasure. Miss Emma Grenville, it seems, spent several months in a work house."

Alexandra covered her eyes, while Vixen gasped and had to be restrained by her husband.

Emma wanted to do nothing more than join Miss Perchase in a dead faint. Only the thought of the girls kept her on her feet. She could run away and become a hermit when this was over; she had nothing to look forward to, anyway.

"My youth was not the most fortunate, no," she said quietly. "I don't see how that has any bearing on my teaching abilities. Up until now, my term as headmistress of Miss Grenville's Academy has met with approval and success."

"Not so," Greaves spat. "You have been headmistress for two years. In that time, none of the graduates you instructed has made an advantageous marriage. Even the Duke of Wycliffe can't be bothered to be present and defend you as anything more than a high-reaching lightskirt. Whatever prompted this . . . wager, he obviously felt even he could do a better job of instructing them than you could."

And she had thought she couldn't possibly feel any more guilty and less significant. The smug, offended faces of the parents, and the shocked and angry looks from her friends hurt, but it was nothing compared with the expressions on Jane's and Mary's faces.

The younger girls looked angry and confused, but Jane and Mary knew. The exchanges between Grey and her, the looks, the arguing—they knew. Today was a farce, because all of the rumors and accusations were true.

"I'm so . . ." A tear ran down her cheek. "I'm sorry," she whispered.

"Miss Emma?" Lizzy said, tears welling in her own eyes. "Please don't let them talk to you like that."

Freddie cleared his throat, his gaze dismissive. "I would like you to know, Lord Greaves, that despite this despicable happenstance, I find Lady Jane to be a model of perfect female behavior. In fact—"

"How dare you?" Emma shrieked, white fury and the knowledge that she had absolutely nothing left to lose, making her put her stupid propriety aside. "You . . . fortune hunter! You've been hounding Jane for a year, and now you think this entire . . . disaster means nothing except an opportunity for you to—"

"Miss Emma," Lord Greaves interrupted, "you're not helping anything."

Tears blurring her vision, Emma jabbed a finger in Mayburne's direction. "Whatever you think of me, please do not believe that this man has anything but the most base reasons for pursuing Jane."

"You have no right to pronounce judgment on anyone else's actions, Miss Emma. You are nothing if not a poor examp—"

"Perhaps you'll listen to me, then." To Emma's surprise, Grey's cousin Georgiana stepped forward. "I was present when Wycliffe confronted Mr. Mayburne, warning him to stay away from this institution."

"He did?" Emma stared at Lady Georgiana.

"Another female," Brendale growled.

The dining hall door slammed open again. *"Mayburne!"*

If not for his size and the sound of his roar, Emma wouldn't have recognized the Duke of Wycliffe. Soaking wet, his greatcoat covered with mud and leaves, and blood trickling from a deep cut on his forehead, Grey charged into the room, making straight for Freddie.

Mayburne only had time to utter a faint gasp before Grey hit him. They went down in a muddy, thrashing heap. Grey got to his feet first, and yanked Freddie up by the collar.

"You damned ape!" he snarled, and slammed his fist into Freddie's jaw.

Soundlessly, Mayburne collapsed. Grey leaned over to grab him again, then stopped. Breathing hard, he toed the blackguard. It figured Freddie would have a glass jaw just when Grey was in the mood to give him a good thrashing. As he faced Emma, though, every ounce of anger, the pain in his head and shoulder, everything ceased to matter except her.

Her face was drawn and white, her hands shaking, and her cheeks wet with tears. "Em?" he murmured.

"Where . . . where were you?" she breathed, her voice breaking.

"I—"

"Wycliffe! What the devil is the meaning of this? You, of all people, have no right to be at this Academ—"

Grey whipped around to face Lord Greaves. "Donald," he snapped, "what have you been saying to this woman?"

"We have been expressing our indignation at her conduct," the marquis replied, taking a small step backward.

The intimidation was certainly working. "And which conduct would that be?" he demanded.

"You know very well, Wycliffe." Mr. Brendale, a large, swarthy man who didn't look at all like

Henrietta, pointed at Emma. "Conduct she has been unable to deny. Emma Grenville belongs in prison, not at the head of a finishing school."

Obviously this had gone far beyond the bounds of the wager—Emma was right; it was about her, and not the conduct of their precious, ignored daughters. "Prison," he repeated blackly. "And so Henrietta belongs in prison, as well, I suppose?"

"Hen—you go too far, Wycliffe!"

"No, Brendale, *you* go too far. Any accusations you make of Emma, you make of your own daughters. She has been their teacher, their advisor, and their friend." He gestured at his students, all teary-eyed and clinging to one another. "Have you found any fault with them? Have you seen any evidence of lascivious behavior? Each and every one of them has exhibited nothing but bravery, intelligence, and loyalty throughout this debacle—which is more than I can say for you, their parents."

Greaves was shaking his head. "This isn't about our daughters, Wycliffe. It's about the conduct of their headmistress. That is the beginning and the end of this matter."

"I don't think it is, Gr—"

"Excuse me, Your Grace," Emma said in an unsteady voice.

When he looked at her, her face was gray. "Emma?" he murmured, alarmed.

"I thank you for clarifying the objective of this . . . investigation," she continued. "And I am glad to hear from Lord Greaves that the Academy isn't being blamed or its integrity questioned. I am the only one whose conduct is being questioned, and so I must of course remove myself from the students and the school."

"No," he said, striding toward her.

"Lord Greaves, Mr. Brendale, allow me to tender my resignation as headmistress of Miss Grenville's Academy. However strong my personal attachment to the school, even more I wish for it to continue teaching young girls to be successful in the world. If that can only take place in my absence, then so be it."

"You see?" Freddie said, rolling into a sitting position, "I told you it was she who was unfit to be here."

"Oh, shut up, Freddie," Jane said, thwacking him on the head with Emma's notebook. With a grunt Mayburne collapsed again.

Grey grabbed Emma's arm, half afraid she would bolt and he would never see her again. "This is ridiculous. None of this is your fault. It's mine. You love this school."

"It *is* my fault. I allowed all of this to happen. Please let me go, Grey."

He heard the murmur of voices in response to her use of his Christian name. For a moment he searched Emma's tormented hazel eyes. "All right, then," he said softly, "resign. But in my opinion, you've done the impossible. You've convinced *me*, Emma. Me. I pushed you into this wager because of my half-witted prejudices about educating females. In the weeks since then, I have come to admire the teachings and the mission of this Academy, and to realize that you embody all of a woman's best qualities."

"Grey, stop," she whispered, another tear running down her face.

He shook his head, brushing her damp cheek with his thumb. "No. If they won't have you here, then I would like you with me. You are the finest teacher, the finest woman—the finest person—I've ever known. I love you, Emma. Please, will you m—"

Lizzy stepped forward, tugging on his muddy sleeve. "You're supposed to kneel," she whispered.

With a slight grin, Grey nodded. "Thank you, my dear."

He sank down on one knee and pulled the signet ring from his finger. Taking Emma's shaking hand in his own, he slid the huge garnet onto her finger. "I love you, Emma," he murmured, gazing up into her eyes, "with all my heart. Please, for God's sake, will you marry me?"

She searched his face for so long that he began to fear she would turn him down. Finally she collapsed into his arms, wrapping her arms tightly around him. "Yes," she whispered. "Yes, I will marry you."

Grey tilted her chin up and kissed her. "Thank God," he said fervently, brushing the rest of the tears from her face. "Thank God."

"I thought you'd left," she sobbed, her voice muffled against his neck.

She was getting filthy, but he didn't want to let her go. Ever again. "Freddie ambushed me and stole my horse. I'm afraid I may have been a bit . . . stern with Tobias on my way in here. I was in something of a hurry."

Emma lifted her head to kiss his cheek. "I love you, very much," she said.

"I thought you were going to get away from me, for a moment."

She smiled through her tears. "And I thought you wouldn't ask me again. I've been so stupid."

"Never."

"Again? You've asked her before?"

Grey stood, one hand still gripping Emma's, as the Marquis of Greaves reached them. "I've been in pursuit for some time," he said brusquely. "And will assume any and all remarks made here today against my duchess were simply said in the heat of the moment."

"Yes. Yes. Of course."

He'd half hoped Greaves would utter another insult so he could set the man on his backside, but the marquis apparently had more sense than that. "I assume, then, that we can adjourn this little meeting?"

His mother came forward. "I would like to invite everyone to Haverly for luncheon. I think a celebration is in order."

Chuckling, Grey kissed Emma again. "A celebration, indeed."

Chapter 21

Emma could tell that Grey wanted to talk with her, and she still had several questions for him. On the ride back to Haverly, though, his mother and cousin had joined them in the coach, apparently deciding to minimize the possibility of any further improprieties before the wedding.

The wedding. Marriage with Grey Brakenridge. She could scarcely believe it, after the nightmare of the morning. He had said it in front of witnesses and repeated it several times, however, so it had to be true. She wanted it to be true, with all her heart.

"You might have arrived earlier and spared Emma some of that nastiness," the duchess commented, as they turned up the drive.

Grey scowled, though he squeezed Emma's

fingers; he hadn't let her go since the dining hall, as if he was afraid she might vanish. "I would have been there earlier, if you and Georgiana hadn't absconded with my coach."

"Yes, well, I needed to speak with Emma."

"And I want a report of everything that was said before I arrived." Anger touched Grey's face again.

Emma shook her head. "No, you don't. They are parents; they're supposed to be concerned about their children."

"Humph." Frederica flicked a piece of mud from Grey's greatcoat. "It seemed to me, Emma, that they were more concerned with throwing about disparaging remarks and insults."

It was odd, suddenly being on a first-name basis with the Duchess of Wycliffe—soon to be the dowager duchess. Emma swallowed. A duchess; she never would have imagined such a thing.

Grey lifted an eyebrow, then winced and touched his free hand to his forehead. "So you're on our side now, Mother?"

"I've always been on your side. It merely took some observation to determine which side that was."

Lady Georgiana, a slight smile on her face, leaned forward to touch Emma on the knee. "When will you hold the wedding?"

"As soon as I return from Canterbury with a special license," Grey answered. "I'm not taking any chances." He lifted Emma's hand, kissing her fingers. "And I thought we might wed at Haverly, so your students will be able to attend."

"My *former* students," she corrected, sadness

touching her heart. Her Aunt Patricia had devoted her life to that Academy, and Emma had lasted only three years. What would happen to it now?

"I have some ideas about your former school," Grey murmured, as though he could read her mind. She'd been half convinced that he could, anyway.

"What?"

"Later," he replied, as the coach rolled to a stop.

Hobbes pulled open the door, Dare on his heels. "Well?" the viscount demanded, taking a quick step backward as Georgiana emerged from the coach.

"We're getting married," Grey informed him, smiling at Emma as he lifted her to the ground.

"It's about damned time. And what happened to you, Wycliffe? You look as though someone pitched you into the mud."

"Someone did."

The guests trailed into the manor and upstairs to the drawing room. Everyone seemed chatty and friendly, as though they'd merely been out for a morning drive. Emma knew better, and though for the girls' sake she would never bring it up again, neither would she forget.

"Em?" Grey tugged on her hand. "I need to speak with you for a moment."

"The guests—"

"Forget them. My mother invited them, anyway; she can entertain them for five minutes."

He led her into Lord Haverly's office and shut the door. "That was still rude," she informed him.

Grey leaned down and kissed her. "They deserve it. And I deserve a moment of privacy with my bride."

She kissed him back, revelling in the warm strength of him. "Thank you," she said quietly.

"For what? Other than being late and making a muck of everything, of course."

Emma smiled. "The last time someone tried to get rid of me, I ended up on my own for six months, until Aunt Patricia rescued me. You didn't let me go at all."

"Jesus, Em," he whispered, taking both her hands.

The tender, passionate look in his eyes was nearly enough to make her cry again. "So," she said, clearing her throat, "tell me your ideas about my former students."

He hesitated. "I know how much the Academy means to you," he said, his expression growing even more serious. "If you want to remain head-mistress, no one can stop you, now. I'll move Miss Grenville's Academy brick by brick to Wycliffe Park, if you wish it."

"No. If I stay on, the scandal won't be forgotten. And the Academy belongs here."

"Then might I suggest that with the increased funding the school will be receiving, it could use a good administrator?"

Emma put her hands to her mouth, overwhelmed. "Funding? You would—"

"Of course I would. How else will girls like Lizzy be able to obtain the education they deserve?"

"My goodness, I love you," she whispered.

"The feeling is mutual. And I want you to

know, my next conversation with Sir John will be about Lizzy. She'll have adequate funds to do whatever she chooses with her life."

Sweeping her arms around his neck, Emma kissed him again. "You've turned out to be an excellent student," she managed, tears overflowing.

"I had an excellent teacher," he murmured. "Oh, and one more thing. Uncle Dennis loved your brickwork idea so much he's already sent to London for an engineer. I, for one, want to read that estate plan of yours in its entirety."

"You don't have to keep trying to make amends," she said, cupping the sides of his face with her hands. "I really don't blame you for any of this."

"I assure you, I'm being entirely selfish," he returned, touching his lips to hers. "I find discussing barley crops and rainfall with you to be very engrossing."

She smiled. "Really?"

"Definitely. I want to continue learning."

"You have a great deal of potential," Emma replied, chuckling. "And with a little more instruction, you'll make a very good husband."

"A little more instruction?" he murmured, leaning down to sweep her into his arms as she laughed breathlessly. "How about beginning another lesson right now, Miss Emma?"

Dear Reader,

Now that you've come to the end of your book I'm sure you're like me—eager to discover something new to read and longing for a fresh, exciting, sensuous romance to entertain you.

Remember, each month there are four delicious Avon romances to choose from, so even if you've just finished one, there are three more awaiting you where romances are sold. And *next* month you'll be able to choose from these four unforgettable titles.

A Notorious Love by **Sabrina Jeffries:** She's a proper young lady, compelled to join forces with a dashing rogue to rescue her runaway sister. He's a man no proper young lady should be seen with—but he's devastatingly attractive . . . and oh, so irresistible. Sabrina Jeffries is a rising star, whose work sparkles with wit and sizzles with passion—this book is truly unmissable!

Next Stop, Paradise by **Sue Civil-Brown:** If you love contemporary romance that is high-spirited, delightful, and truly unique, then don't miss this one! When a small town lady cop matches wits with a handsome, smooth-talking TV journalist, well, you know something special is going to happen! With a touch of magic and a whole lot of charm *Next Stop, Paradise* should be on your book-buying list.

Secret Vows by **Mary Reed McCall:** It's always exciting to bring you a book by a brand-new author . . . one who has a spectacular career ahead of her. In *Secret Vows* you'll find a soul-stirring love story between Catherine of Somerset and Baron Grayson de Camville. And though severe punishment faces Catherine if she fails in her mission, she can't help but fall in love with this man she's been forced to marry—and ordered to destroy.

An Innocent Mistress by **Rebecca Wade:** He's a rugged bachelor sworn to avenge his imprisoned brother; she's the fiery woman known as the mistress of a fabled bounty hunter—but is she concealing a secret identity? Passion flares . . . and no one is quite who they seem to be in this surefire blockbuster of romance.

There you have it—four brand-new romances from the premiere publisher of romance . . . Avon Books.

Enjoy,

Lucia Macro

Lucia Macro
Executive Editor

REL 0801